MYTHOLOGY OF BRAHMA

Hindu Tradition Series

It aims to bring together books of academic standard critically interrogating the series. The focus is on cultural, religious and social developments.

- The Mahabharta and Greek Mythology : *Fernando Wulf Alonso*/ TR. ANDREW MORROW
- Viraha Bhakti : *The Early History of Krsna Devotion in South India*/ FRIEDHELM HARDY
- Classical Hindu Mythology : *A Reader in the Sanskrit Puranas*/ ED. AND TR. BY CORNELLIA DIMMITT AND J.A.B. VAN BUITENEN
- India and the Hellenistic World: KLAUS KARTTUNEN
- Engaged Emancipation: *Mind, Morals and Make Believe in the Moksopaya (Yogavasistha)*/ EDS. CHRISTOPHER KEY CHAPPLE & ARINDAM CHAKARABARTI
- The Patiyagramanirnaya: *A Puranic History of some Brahman Communities)*/STEPHAN HILYER LEVITT
- Mythology of Brahma : GREGORY BAILEY

Mythology of Brahma

Gregory Bailey

MYTHOLOGY OF BRAHMA / GREGORY BAILEY

Second Revised Edition: Delhi, 2021

ISBN : 978 81 9481 58 9 1

Published by
Motilal Banarsidass Publications
93, Shyam Lal Marg, Darya Ganj,
New Delhi-110002 (India)
mlbd@mlbd.com

MLBD Cataloging-in-Publication Data
Mythology of Brahma / GREGORY BAILEY
(Hindu Tradition Series 6)
ISBN : 978 81 9481 58 9 1
Acknowledgement, Abbreviations,
Introduction, Conclusion,
Bibliography, Index.

Printed by : Repro India Limited

Contents

Acknowledgements

This is the second edition of a book first published in 1983. Whilst I have corrected the many errors and misprints that appeared in the first edition, I have made many changes and hopefully improved the book in order to produce what is not just a reprint but a substantially new edition.

During the intervening thirty-six years I have received much help from too many colleagues to mention. Alf Hiltebeitel, Jim Fitzgerald and Adam Bowles have improved my knowledge of the Mahābhārata over many years of conversations. I have also learnt much from the group of scholars associated with the Dubrovnik International Conference on the Sanskrit Epics and Purāṇas, especially Mislav Jézic, Peter Schreiner, Renate Söhnen-Thieme, John and Mary Brockington. The translation and analysis of the Rāmāyaṇa completed by Robert Goldman and Sally Sutherland-Goldman has been an inspiration in understanding Sanskrit epic literature, as has been the work of Angelika Malinar on her readings of the Bhagavadgītā. McComas Taylor's work on Purāṇic recitation has also caused me to rethink how the Mahābhārata might have been recited and what implication this had for the reception of its myths. I have also accomplished much whilst working at the Institut Française d'Indologie in Pondicherry and thank especially François Grimal for his on-going hospitality.

Finally, I thank my partner Kerri Schoof and my children for their patience whilst this book was being produced.

Abbreviations

AB	Aitareya Brāhmaṇa
ABORI	Annals of the Bhandarkar Oriental Research Institute
AP	Agni Purāṇa
AS	Asiatische Studien
AV	Atharva Veda
BDCRI	Bulletin of the Deccan College Research Institute
BḍP	Brahmāṇḍa Purāṇa
Bhg	Bhagavadgītā
BhU	Bhṛhadāraṇyaka Upaniṣad
BhP	Bhāgavata Purāṇa
BSOAS	Bulletin of the School of Oriental and African Studies
BVP	Brahmavaivarta Purāṇa
ChU	Chaṇḍogya Upaniṣad
CIS	Contributions to Indian Sociology
Cr.Ed	Critical Edition
DN	Dīgha Nikāya
EI	Epigraphica Indica
ERE	Encyclopedia of Religion and Ethics
GDhS	Gautamīya Dharmasūtra
GP	Garuḍa Purāṇa
H	Harivaṃśa
HDS	History of Dharmaśāstra
HR	History of Religions

IIJ	Indo-Iranian Journal
It	Itivuttaka
J	Jātaka
JA	Journal Asiatique
JAOS	Journal of the American Oriental Society
JB	Jaiminīya Brāhmaṇa
JIP	Journal of Indian Philosophy
KauṣU	Kauṣītaki Upaniṣad
KB	Kauṣītaki Brāhmaṇa
KP	Kūrma Purāṇa
LP	Liṅga Purāṇa
MaitrīU	Maitrī Upaniṣad
MBh	Mahābhārata
Mhv	Mahāvastu
MkP	Mārkaṇḍeya Purāṇa
MN	Majjhima Nikāya
MP	Matsya Purāṇa
Ms	Manu Smṛti
MS	Maitrāyaṇī Saṃhitā
MU	Muṇḍaka Upaniṣad
PaP	Padma Purāṇa
PU	Praśna Upaniṣad
Rām	Rāmāyaṇa
ṚV	Ṛig Veda
ŚB	Śatapatha Brāhmaṇa
SBE	Sacred Books of the East
SK	Sāṃkhyā Kārikā
SN	Saṃyutta Nikāya
ŚP	Śiva Purāṇa
ŚvetU	Śvetāśvatara Upaniṣad
TB	Taittirīya Brāhmaṇa

TS	Taittirīya Saṃhitā
VāmP	Vāmana Purāṇa
VāP	Vāyu Purāṇa
Vin	Vinaya
ViP	Viṣṇu Purāṇa
Vr	variant reading
WZKSA	Wiener Zeitschrift für die Kunde Süd und Ostasiens und Archiv für Indische Philosophie
ZDMG	Zeitschrift der Deutschen Morgenländischen Gesellschaft

Introduction

The purpose of this book is to examine Brahmā's distinctive position, and the meaning of his roles, within the broad ensemble of Indian mythology. In general his mythology has only been studied in relation to that of Viṣṇu or Śiva and not as a subject with an intrinsic value of its own. Although there have been several brief studies devoted exclusively to Brahmā, all have tended to lay stress on quite specific aspects of his mythology at the expense of a comprehensive view. Some monographs which have attempted a cross-sectional view over the whole field of Hindu mythology have provided a moderately comprehensive picture of this god's mythology, yet because of their breadth they have only elicited a superficial understanding of it.[1] The net result of both kinds of studies is a multiplicity of interpretations of the god's mythology. No general accord has been reached on the question of his distinctive place in Indian mythology or on the meaning of his mythology. This in itself is sufficient reason for a new study of the god.

In Indological scholarship over the past two hundred years the god Brahmā has been focused upon because of his pre-eminent role as the creator god in the *trimūrti* comprising himself, Viṣṇu and Śiva, and because, unlike the latter two gods, he never seems to have acquired much of a devotional following. That situation may be expressed as a paradox: Brahmā plays a major role in mythology, whilst seemingly not being worshipped as an object of devotion. Nor does he appear to be a prominent god in Vedic literature, becoming important in the *Mahābhārata*, certain Pāli

1 Bhattacharji, 1970, pp.317-48; Daniélou, 1964, pp.232-53.

texts, and continuing to be prominent in Purāṇic mythology to the extent it develops beyond what is found in the *MBh*, and the *Rām*. to a much lesser extent. As creator of everything in the creation of the universe his role becomes fundamental given the attempt to systematize cosmogony in terms of creation, preservation and finish (destruction), a systematizing process reaching its fullest development in the Purāṇas. This systematization may well have been a theoretical development designed to impose a kind of order onto a conception of the universe in terms of a very long-term historical origin, transformation and completion, a conception requiring a theological/mythological justification to sustain it, given the premier importance of mythology in South Asia as a mode of communication of cultural and religious truths.

The continuation of Hindu mythology over two thousand years guaranteed that Brahmā retained a prominent position in the awareness of most Hindus. This has been so even where he was not worshipped along the lines of the important devotional gods and goddesses, whose popularity partially rests on a belief in their capacity to provide immediate benefits to their worshippers. In this sense he is like Indra, who continues to play a role in mythology, but rarely receives worship in a devotional context.

Yet Brahmā is not simply important because of his role in the cosmogony. In several ways he is associated with foundational forms of knowledge, the sacrifice and the status of the brahmin as defining the correct workings of the orthoprax society. What this means is that he is powerfully associated with correct forms of knowledge and its dissemination, just as Viṣṇu is associated with kingship as the preeminent mode of maintaining social and cosmic order, and Śiva with destruction-epitomized in his destruction of Dakṣa's sacrifice–and disdain for society reflected in his asceticism. As such this complicates any kind of simplistic view as to how his role in mythology might be understood.

Both aspects–his role as creator and his connection with the brahmin class in all of its aspects–are significant not just because of their expression in Hindu myths, but also because it is these two themes that are so strongly connected with him in early Buddhist literature, mainly in Pāli, but also occasionally in Sanskrit. In almost all cases where he appears in Pāli literature he is an object of satire, as if the authors of these texts somehow saw him as a competitor of the Buddha, and arguably believed his role as creator necessarily conferred a very high status upon him as a god emerging out of the decline of the pantheon associated with the Vedic thirty-three gods. He is much less of an object of satire in Buddhist Sanskrit literature, probably because it was composed at a time when Buddhism had become firmly established across South Asia in a very conspicuous and institutionalized manner. But the importance in Pāli literature of his recognition as creator and disseminator of knowledge is significant in providing us with at least one 'external' interpretative frame by which to understand his mythological roles as they are found in Hindu literature where he is usually not treated as an object of satire.

What I have learnt during the thirty-six years since this book was first published is that the period–let us say 300BCE-200CE–where Brahmā is given widespread exposure in both the *MBh.* and the earliest Purāṇas as well as early Buddhist literature, was one of considerable transition in most aspects of South Asian culture and society: Buddhism was becoming very firmly consolidated in terms of following and financial wealth; the class system was becoming institutionalized as a means of providing some kind of theoretical structure for a society becoming increasingly complex; small scale societies were being replaced by large-scale societies; the brahmins were under increasing pressure to define their role as the class of educators and ritual specialists in the face of an expanding range of religious options; theories of kingship involving maintenance of the normative society were being developed; and the extensive mythology inherited from Vedic tradition was being both vernacularized and systematized in order to take account of the *avatāra* theory and the theology of the *trimūrti*, both given a sense of immediacy to the broad population by the inclusion of devotional material.

What each of these factors suggest is that the presentation of the mythology in which Brahmā plays an important role was being developed at a time of considerable change in a totalistic sense, plus–and this is of demonstrable importance–an awareness of this change and a realization that something must be done to harness it for the benefit of cultural elites. That is, the mythology, perhaps the principal means of communicating a normative brahminical culture–whether through literary recitation, art or performance–was being reworked for particular social and religious reasons. In addition, certain deities, plus the mother goddess, were being elevated beyond the status they may have had in the earlier Vedic mythology preserved in the first three strata of Vedic literature.

Attempts to present these perceived changes in a systematic way that allowed them to be anchored in the traditional antiquity of Vedic culture–still not a vestige in the Early Historic Period, though overwhelmed by other religio-cultural streams–meant the development and application of several different interpretative frames. Some of these explicit frames would include the *caturvarga*, and *pravṛttidharma* and *nivṛttidharma*, both having a very strong social component to them in the sense that they rest upon a clear view of society/polity and what the opposite of this might be. Withiṇ this might be added the *varṇāśrama* theory, which really overlaps with *pravṛtti*, whilst developing its socio-religious implications in terms of a specific life plan. From an entirely devotional perspective we are presented with *karmayoga*, *jñānayoga* and *bhaktiyoga*, mainly restricted to the *Bhg*, but each providing a catch phrase for how individuals can orientate their behaviour in the socio-religious world.

Each of these–what might be called hermeneutical devices for both shaping and interpreting data–are explored in didactic texts in the *MBh*, the Purāṇas and the Dharma literature, but their appearance as catch phrases suggests their meanings were well known in elite circles without needing to be spelled out extensively. As such they provide a distinctive hermeneutical device by which the mythological roles of the principal gods and the themes dominating the myths might be understood. Of course, this does not mean some kind of one to one transparent connection as an ideational means of understanding the motives determining how the gods act and how these might be understood in regard to the larger concerns of the elite members of society.

In the Dharma literature and those sections of the *MBh.* and the Purāṇas that include this kind of material the overwhelming impression given is that they are defining normative forms of behaviour. This is what is suggested by the almost constant use of the verb in the optative when recommendations are made about correct behaviour. Where the myths become interesting is that the characters within them violate constantly this model of normative behaviour. In this sense, they are an accurate reflection of real world behaviour where contradictions of the normative are the norms themselves. As such the behaviour of gods both reflects the normative and the breaking of the normative. This is especially so in Śiva's mythology, as exposited so well by O'Flaherty[2], but Brahmā too breaks the normative rule for a restrained brahmin when he lusts after Śiva's wife, Pārvatī, at their marriage.

Between them the three gods of the *trimūrti* create, oversee and participate in a functional world that brings together a whole variety of living beings–many having supernatural powers–in a set of living arrangements conducive to some of these groups having opposing aims as what might constitute the best form of behaviour guaranteeing felicity in the present and long term survival for their own place within the system. The most obvious opposition here is between the various groups of demons and the gods who are always fighting each other over who should have the highest status in the triple world. A further kind of opposition is between those individuals who refuse to remain within the group into which they were born and leave it in order to amass a degree of personal power they can use to elevate their own status amongst those around them without rejoining the appropriate group. Brahmā and Viṣṇu are required to deal with the problems arising from these oppositional positions because such positions threaten the normative systems of social and cosmic organization predicated on the idea of *dharma* they spend so much of their own

2 O'Flaherty, 1973

effort in attempting to establish and maintain. What I think the mythic roles of the gods of the *trimūrti* are attempting to tell us is that the ordered world (or triple world) is a fragile place, that the order imposed upon all groups in society by the elites, whilst wholly desirable, is constantly open to violation, possibly leading to outright collapse.

It is likely these elites were brahmins, though the economic and political elite would also have to be brought onside as well. Olivelle's[3] work on the *āśrama* system is very relevant here, providing an explanation as to how the brahmins were attempting to take some control–if only theoretical–over a social and cultural situation that had been evolving and becoming complex over several centuries as the brahmin elite moving out of the northwest were confronted with people of different cultures, languages, economies and societies. Many of these would certainly be resistant to change, but would somehow have to be accommodated in a more expansive view of the world–than Vedic ritualism–where the power, economic, religious and political, lay in the large urban conurbations. In order to ensconce themselves in this power relationship the brahmins had to prove themselves indispensable to the groups who held economic and military/political power, and to demonstrate this to groups beyond the power centres. Finally, they had somehow to fit these other groups in, especially where the devotional practices could do away with the intermediation of the brahmins.

The *MBh* is a fundamental transitional text because it developed at least three ideological positions–*pravṛtti* and *nivṛtti*, the *caturvarga*, and the *āśramas* and mythological expressions of these in the form of the *trimūrti*. Whether all these are compatible or can be reinterpreted in relation to each other does not seem to have happened much in the texts where they occur often. At an ideological level they all overlap and each encompasses in their own way the fundamental contrast between life in the social environment of class and caste and economic obligations, and

3 Olivelle, 1993.

abandonment of social obligations for life outside of society, paradoxically a lifestyle which was also institutionalized. Whilst the lifestyles described normatively in a range of texts are strongly idealized, the actual situation on the ground must have been much more fluid, at least this is how both Hindu and Buddhist texts treat what must have been an extremely variable situation.

Whilst there may have been tensions between these life-styles–a principle one being the contrast between the householder and the ascetic–in practice, I can only agree with Olivelle, when writing of the development of the classical *āśrama* system, he says, "A close reading of these early texts leads us to the conclusion that the āśrama system was created not by the conservative mainstream in order to encompass in a stifling embrace new ideas and institutions that it had failed to suppress but by Brahmins who shared these ideas and ideals and who sought exegetical loopholes to introduce them into the Brāhmaṇical mainstream."[4] This also applies to the development of *pravṛttidharma* and *nivṛttidharma*, but not so much to the *caturvarga* which sits securely within both the latter and the *varṇāśramdharma*. In any case, the kinds of classificatory systems–defining forms of behaviour, goals and hierarchy of goals–substantially overlap and definitely attempt to bring together the different socio-cultural and religious expectations defining the different roles of the householder and the ascetic.

When one reads the Dharmasūtras and Gṛḥyasūtras that deal in a formal way with expositing these systems, one finds very little reference to myth and the treatment of deities is usually in terms of listing of names in contexts where they must be evoked. There is little interest in the kind of presentation of mythic narrative occurring in post-Vedic narrative literature. It is likely the Dharma literature was only transmitted within small groups of brahmin

4 Olivelle, 1993 p.96. See also p.100, "Its purpose was rather to create a scheme within which the pivotal category of *dharma* could be extended to include religious modes of life different from that of the Brāhmaṇical householder."

ritualists and intellectuals, whereas the mythic material received a much broader audience, in part because it was likely recited in vernacular forms. Where the two differ is that the Dharma literature develops its systems of classification in scholastic manner, whereas the narrative literature illustrates and explores the life-styles associated with these classificatory systems.

This is where the roles of the gods, demi-gods and other semi-divine figures–who appear frequently in this mythology-come into play. Though they have capacities transcending human limitations, they do function in ways that correspond with the modes of behaviour normatively described in the Dharma literature and the twelfth and thirteenth books of the *MBh*. One would not classify the individual gods in terms of any of the individual parts of the classificatory systems exclusively, except perhaps in the case of Brahmā who stands firmly within the *pravṛtti* framework, which encompasses the first three components of the *āśrama* system, and the first three components of the *trivarga*.

Brahmā comes across as a restrained figure who establishes the normative conditions under which the inhabitants of the triple-world will live. These conditions fall under the rubric of *dharma*, the comprehensive development of which–and debate about–is arguably the most important theme in the *MBh*. both didactically and narratively. Brahmā is intimately associated with *dharma* in its formulation and dissemination, but also works consistently to preserve its implications for the hierarchical organization of beings in the triple world and the extent to which they observe this hierarchy and function within their own *dharmas*. Brahmā intervenes only when there is a very real threat to the workings of the triple world.

Since the publication of *The Mythology of Brahmā* in 1983 there has been little new research directly on this god. Four exceptions can be named. One is Nathan McGovern's article, "Brahmā: An Early and Ultimately Doomed Attempt at a Brahmanical Synthesis,"[5] the second is the edition and translation

5 McGovern 2012.

of the *Puṣkaramāhātmya* by Aditya Malik,[6] and the third is found in Bruce Sullivan's 1990 book[7] on Vyāsa. To this can be added J. Gonda's book, *Prajāpati's Rise* To *Higher Rank*,[8] which deals with the most important precursor to Brahmā. Beyond these there is precious little else. I deal with each of these contributions in the relevant chapters (1, 3 and 8) to which they apply. Yet Brahmā remains a god of importance in both epics and then subsequently in Purāṇic mythology, not to forget his iconographical presence in both Buddhist and Hindu sculpture. Finally, there is the increasing awareness of Brahmā as a deity in contemporary Thailand, where he arguably performs a similar role to Gaṇeśa in India.

Finally, I would add that an important consequence of the primacy of *pravṛtti* values as a formative factor in Brahmā's mythology has been that a study of the god's mythology is simultaneously a study of such values. In view of this the aims of the book are threefold. Firstly, to given an exposition of Brahma's mythology, taking into account all the roles he plays and all the major myths in which he appears. Secondly, to demonstrate the unity to be found in the mythology of this god, a unity reflecting the centrality of *pravṛtti* in his mythology, thus providing the key for a coherent interpretation of his disparate roles. Thirdly, to show the importance of underlying 'ideologies' and value systems as interpretative keys in the study of South Asian mythology.

---

6 Malik 1993

7 Sullivan 1990.

8 Gonda, 1986.

PART ONE

Brahmā's Position in Indian Religious History

Chapter 1

The Worship and Status of Brahmā in Ancient India

Of the three gods of the Hindu *trimūrti* it has almost become an orthodoxy that Brahmā never attained a large following of devotees or was worshipped as a *bhakti* deity in the same way as Viṣṇu and Śiva.[1] Certainly, the two latter gods gained ever-increasing popularity from the beginning of the Common Era onwards, a popularity reflecting their success as deities who very early had been placed in the forefront of devotional movements, which so transformed all Indian religions. However, considering Brahmā's widespread appearance in the epics, Purāṇas, the Pāli Canon and some early Buddhist Sanskrit texts, such as the *Lalitavistara* and the *Saddharmapuṇḍarīkasūtra*, it might be expected that this reflected a broad popularity, especially in north India. In fact, there is some evidence Brahmā was widely venerated in north India in the few centuries preceding the beginning of the Common Era.[2] This evidence is examined in this chapter in an attempt to place Brahmā within the general context of Indian religious history during the period six hundred BCE to five hundred CE. Only a general overview is intended for a monograph would be required to account for every detail.

---

1 This orthodoxy may have begun with Roth, 1847, p.84. More recently it has been replicated by Gonda, 1960, Vol. 1, p.264; S. Bhattacharji, 1971, p.347; Banerjea, 1974, p.513.

2 See Bailey, 1979, pp.149-70.

Brahmā in Vedic Literature

The name Brahmā when referring to the god, and not to the specialist priest of the *śrauta* sacrifice, occurs only a few times in late Vedic literature. In one passage of the *ŚB*. he is listed with a number of other gods and called a *deva*,[3] and he is also named several times in the early and middle Upaniṣads[4] In each passage little is said about the god that is not found in much greater detail in post-Vedic narrative literature. This may be significant because his absence in early and middle Vedic literature in contrast to his widespread occurrence in post-Vedic and early Buddhist literature signals an expansion and transformation of the religious and cultural world far beyond Vedic ritualism.

The frequency of his appearance and the central position he is accorded in many of the myths occurring in the epic and Purāṇas, and the early biographies of the Buddha, indicates Brahmā was a deity of considerable importance. It seems inconceivable that his importance in this body of literature would be the result of a sudden development, so it is likely that there were a few centuries before these texts appeared during which he may have been worshipped beyond priestly circles. An earliest limit for recognition of him as a god is 800 BCE if we accept that as the date of the composition of the *ŚB*. If the Suttapiṭaka accurately represents religious conditions in the fourth and third centuries BCE, then this gives about two hundred years for Brahmā to become a popular god as reflected in the two Sanskrit epics and Buddhist Sanskrit literature. It is possible he was more popular in the late Vedic period than literary tradition suggests, in circles

---

3 *ŚB*. 10, 1, 3, 8. Cf. 5, 2, 2, 8 and see also *GB*. 1, 4, 10 *atha yad abhiplavam upayanti brahmāṇam eva taddevaṃ devatāṃ yajante brahmā devo devatā bhavati*. See further *GB*. 1, 1, 16; 1, 1, 23; 1, 4, 10; *Sāmavidhāna Brāhmana*. 1, 1-3; *Śaṅkhāyana Āraṇyaka*. 15; and *AV*. 19, 9, 2 and 19, 43, 8. But in the latter there is some doubt as to whether it is referring to the god or the specialist priest.

4 *ChU*. 8, 15; 3, 11, 4; *KauśU*. 1, 5; *MU*. 1, 1, 1; *ŚvetU*. 5, 6; 6, 18; *MaitrīU*. 4, 5; 5, 1; 6, 5.

whose religious views were scarcely reflected in the literature. However, against this view is the likelihood that in the epics and Purāṇas Brahmā embodies the values of a developing orthoprax Hinduism dominated by *varṇāśramadharma*, values prefigured in the the Brāḥmaṇas. As such he was probably widely known amongst the ritual specialists who are the foundation of the brahmin class in post-Vedic literature.

If Brahmā the god does not appear much in Vedic literature, words derivative of the root *bṛh*, which has given rise to his name, appear frequently. It has been a truism amongst some scholars that Brahmā is the masculine personification of the *brahma* which has appeared extensively in texts from the *ṚV*. onwards.[5] Yet other derivatives of *bṛh*, such as *brāhmaṇa* and *brahmā*, should also be considered when tracing the development of Brahmā from early Vedic literature. The word *brāhmaṇa*–'the one who possesses the *brahma*'–referred to the member of the *varṇa* of that name. Originally *brahmā* as a masculine word was a name designating the supervisory priest in the *śrauta* sacrifice, whereas the word *brahma* in the neuter gender has accumulated several meanings over time. In the *ṚV*. it meant 'hymn', 'formula', 'something that one speaks or chants in the prayer' and 'a kind of energy expressed through speech'.[6] It also designated the three Vedas in their totality and as individual texts.[7] In addition it names the philosophical absolute of the Upaniṣads and is the quality possessed by the member of the brahmin class, analogous to the *kṣatra* of the kṣatriya and the *viś* of the vaiśya, hence it is polyvalent.[8]

With this range of meanings attributed to the word *brahma*, it must be asked which of them or which number of them Brahmā

---

5 Roth, 1847, p.85; Radhakrishnan, 1962, Vol.1, p.250; Hopkins, 1974, p.189; Masson, 1942, p.81; Ruben, 1947, p.228; Thieme, 1960, p.135, n.1.

6 Renou and Silburn, 1949, pp.1, 9, 15, 17.

7 Oldenberg, 1916, p.728.

8 Renou and Silburn, 1949, p.15; Oldenberg, 1916, p.735; Biardeau, 1969, p.77.

personifies, and what such personification might mean. Even to ask this question implies some questionable assumptions. In the first place, to hold this view about Brahmā's beginnings is, in Gonda's words, to 'implicitly admit the chronological priority of the "impersonal brahmnan".'[9] There is insufficient evidence in the earliest Vedic literature to be certain that the neuter word *brahma* is necessarily earlier than the masculine word *brahmā*, as also applies to the concepts associated with them.

Secondly, the ancient Indians never really drew a definite line between personal and impersonal.[10] Many passages could be cited where little distinction is drawn between these two aspects of Brahmā, of which the following is representative:

> In the beginning Brahma was this universe. Then it emitted the gods, and having emitted them it made them ascend into these worlds–Agni into this world, Vāyu into the atmosphere and Sūrya into the sky.
>
> Now, there are higher worlds and there are higher divinities. He (*sa*) made these divinities ascend into these higher worlds. Just as these three worlds and these three divinities are manifest, so are these higher worlds and these higher divinities manifest. He made these higher divinities ascend into these higher worlds.
>
> Then Brahma (*atha brahmaiva*)[11] went to the remote sphere. After it had gone up to the remote sphere, it thought, "How can I descend into these worlds." Then he descended with these two, with name and form… .[12]

Accordingly, it is safer to say that in some 'idealistic' circles

---

9 Gonda, 1950, p.62.

10 Gonda, 1950, pp.62ff.

11 The number of times *eva* follows brahma/brahmā in Vedic texts is significant, because the correct *sandhi* used seemingly prevents a decision being made about which gender applies to the word, especially in the absence of a qualifying masculine or neuter pronoun.

12 *ŚB*. 11, 2, 3, 1-3. See also *JB*. 2, 369-70, trans Caland, 1919, pp.205-7.

brahma was completely divested of any personal attributes; whereas in other circles (represented in many passages of the oldest Upaniṣads) personal and impersonal were interwoven in respect of brahma.

There are compelling reasons to view Brahmā's early development as a process of apotheosization of the *brahmā* priest. In the *śrauta* sacrifice he is the official who oversees the whole sequence of rituals constitutive of the complete sacrifice. His task is to direct the other officiants and he only intervenes actively in order to conduct expiatory rituals whenever they make mistakes. His position is well summarized by Silburn:

> Amongst the officiants, it is on the *brahmā* that falls the risk of watching over the perfect continuity of the sacrificial forms. Seated to the south of the sacrifice he presides over the correct general arrangements silently and without moving. It is he who embraces in the unity of a mere glance the unanimity of the parts of the rite. Attentive, he is the guardian who protects the sacrifice and is always ready to repair any error which could creep into the ritual order. Like a chief of the orchestra he directs the entire ceremony. He gives the signal for setting it in motion, he scans the important moments of the rite. The officials ask him for permission to commence the ritual, to begin the chant, etc… .[13]

This could serve as a description of the principal functions of Brahmā. As the creator he is the instigator of creation, sets it

---

13 Silburn, 1955, p.90. More recently Brereton (2004) has offered a more refined view when he writes about the role of the brahmán being substantially redefined following the image given in the ṚV, "But also, I believe, he inherited the sacrificer's role as the embodiment of knowledge and expertise that gave the sacrificer the right and ability to perform the sacrifice. While in the early Ṛgveda the priests were representatives of the sacrifice, in the classical Vedic rite, it is the *brahmán*, who becomes the knowledge that the other priests express in their actions and the silence that is the matrix of their speech. Because he assumes the role that once belonged to the sacrificer as sage and ritual expert, he takes his seat next to the sacrificer and acts on his behalf." (pp.341-42)

in motion and he is there when it ends in the *pralaya*. Just as the *brahmā* priest must maintain continuity of the rite, so too must Brahmā ensure continuity of creation until the right time has come for it to end. There are many occasions in the mythology where Brahmā has to advise gods and others on ways of dealing with crises threatening to destroy the triple-world before the appropriate time. Such advice and the action he sometimes takes to avert the worsening of these crises could be analogous to the rites of expiation the *brahmā* priest is obliged to perform if continuity of the sacrifice is not to be prevented by 'evil forces' unleashed by mistakes in execution of the ritual.

Other more specific parallels between the two are cited later on.[14] However, the outline just given should be sufficient to show how misleading it is to trace Brahmā's beginnings back to just one of the derivatives of the root *bṛh*. Except for the Brahman understood as the ontological absolute, all the meanings of the words *brahmā* and *brahma* are reflected in, and have shaped, the figure of Brahmā. Rather than specify his exact conceptual beginnings (if this possible of any god), it is more important to be aware that the various meanings of these words derivative of *bṛh* strongly reflect a ritualistic milieu. The roles Brahmā plays in epic and Purāṇic mythology express a worldview directly continuing–albeit more systematized–the ritualistic worldview of the Brāḥmaṇas, yet translated into a much broader ideational and behavioural framework.

Brahmā's Position in the Epic and Purāṇic Pantheons

Although it is supremely difficult, and likely simplistic given the way most Hindus worship a variety of gods, to define an epic and Purāṇic (or pantheons) in a strict sense, it is obvious even from a cursory reading of some of these texts that certain gods seem to have a more central role than others. This is most noticeable in the Purāṇas where the Sanskritic representation of devotional mythology and worship focusses on Viṣṇu, Śiva, Devī

14 See below pp. 100-109.

and subsequently Gaṇeśa, though perhaps less so in the *MBh.* where Viṣṇu and Śiva assume priority. Both are clearly regarded as very important gods in all this literature, whereas others like Indra, though still important, are often depicted in the mythology in a position subordinate to the first two gods, in large measure because they never attracted devotional cults around them.

Several scholars using a text-critical methodology first developed by W. Kirfel have developed schemes of textual history having considerable implications for establishing Brahmā's relative position in the pantheon, especially in relation to Viṣṇu and Śiva.[15] In a series of articles, P. Hacker attempted a reconstruction of early Indian religious history by constructing a history of texts.[16] Adhering to a rigorous philological methodology in an attempt to determine the relative ages of texts and portions of texts which correspond almost literally, he isolated putative later interpolations and reworked passages, leaving what may be an 'Ur-text'. Utilizing Text Groups 2A and 2B of Kirfel's four-fold division of the Purāṇic cosmogonic passages, he hypothesized the presence in these passages of three different textual layers, each expressing its own religious idiosyncrasy.[17] Hacker concludes, "The oldest layer is a Brahmāism (or Svayambhuism) associated with ideas of the original waters and the World Egg. In the second layer, an attempt is made to harmonize these beliefs with Sāṃkhyā philosophy, which at that time was intellectually attractive; … in it the theism remains Brahmāism. Finally, in the third layer, Śiva or Viṣṇu is the highest god."[18]

Using a similar methodology Chatterjee has shown the *Sṛṣṭi Khaṇḍa* of the *Padmapurāṇa* to be a work strongly influenced

---

15 Though more recently there has been considerable questioning of this methodology. See Bailey, 1987. The problem with this method is that it does not take seriously the complexities surrounding oral transmission of literature.

16 Hacker, 1960, pp.341-50; 1964, pp.232-35.

17 See Kirfel, 1927, pp.7-136.

18 Hacker, 1960, p.349.

by those who held Brahmā to be the highest god.[19] He points out that "The Sṛṣṭi or Puṣkara khaṇḍa was originally compiled by the Brahmā worshippers as is evidenced from the name Puṣkara which is to be an abode of that deity… . The evidence of the Tamil lexicon Pingalaṅdai and the preface to the extant Skanda-p. point to the fact that Brahmā was the predominating deity of the Padma-p."[20] He goes on to show that in parallel passages of the *Matsya* and *Padma Purāṇas* the text of the latter was altered in such a way that Brahmā instead of Viṣṇu appeared as the highest god.[21] Re-editing of this type–that is, if it is mechanical re-editing–may be a clear indication of a certain group of people holding Brahmā in very high esteem and likely worshipping him.

Similar conclusions can be drawn from a study of the cosmogonies found in *Ms.* 1, 5-11; *MBh.* 12, 160, 11-21; 13, 138, 14-19; *MkP*. 47 and *PaP.* 5, 2, 83ff. Illustrative is *MBh.* 13, 138, 14-19ab, a passage dealing with the power of the brahmins:

> Is not the best of brāhmaṇas a protector of living beings and the maker of these living worlds? Knowing that, why are you confused? Similarly Prajāpati, who is Brahmā, is the unmanifest and the origin and end (*prabhavāpyaya*) of everything, by whom the entire moving and unmoving universe was produced. But some unlearned people[22] prefer to think Brahmā was born from an egg, and that from the egg when it was split came the mountains and regions, waters, the earth and the heaven. But this could not have been witnessed. How? Since there was utter darkness then. However, the egg is traditionally called the sky and the Grandfather was born from that.
>
> You might say, "How could he stand, because there would be nothing there then? But it is also said that the Lord exists

---

19 Chatterjee, 1967, pp.24ff. Cf. Hazra, 1940, pp.121-2.

20 Chatterjee, 1967, p.27.

21 Chatterjee, 1967, pp.27-31.

22 It would be interesting to know who these 'unlearned people are, but they are never identified, except with the word *apaṇḍitāḥ*, almost a formulaic expression in the *MBh.* and some Buddhist texts.

in a state completely of fiery energy, that is, as the I-maker (*ahaṃkāra*). King, there is no egg. However, Brahmā is the creator of the world...".

The arguments presented here attempt to justify the high status of brahmiṇs in relation to the other *varṇas*. It asserts that Brahmā is the best of brahmins and his importance rests on his role as supreme creator, not merely a secondary demiurge subordinate to an egg. Accordingly, his importance is tied in with the status of brahmiṇs in relation to the other *varṇas*. The specific assertion that he is the supreme creator is also noteworthy since the majority of cosmogonies attribute the egg's origin to an infusion of the virility (*vīryam*) of Viṣṇu or Brahmā into the primeval waters.[23] Hence the creation, or at least the impetus of creation, is ultimately sheeted back to them.

Two epithets found in this passage are used in the Purāṇas of the supreme god, who for the performance of creation, preservation and destruction, manifests himself through the three gods of the *trimūrti*. Depending on whether the particular Purāṇa is Vaiṣṇava or Śaiva,[24] Viṣṇu or Śiva is presented as the one god who is equated with *pradhāna* and *prakṛti*, whose nature is *avyakta* and who is both *puruṣa* and *prabhavāpyaya*.[25] In the Purāṇic cosmogony these epithets are only used collectively of the god who is the highest god in that particular Purāṇa or that specific version of the cosmogony. They are occasionally used individually of the lesser gods in the same Purāṇa, and collectively of Brahmā in the *MkP*, where he is regarded as the supreme deity:

When *pradhāna* is being agitated the god called Brahmā is born,

---

23 *H*. 1, 23-25, where Viṣṇu fertilizes the primeval waters with his *vīryam*. Cf. *Ms*. 1, 8-11, where Svayambhū (Brahmā) is the fertilizing agent.

24 In the *Gaṇeśa Purāṇa* (1, 13, 24-46) Gaṇeśa himself does not operate in a manner standing beyond the *trimūrti*, but removes obstacles to Brahmā's capacity to create. Śākta Purāṇas are also similar in giving the ultimate power to the goddess.

25 *KP*. 1, 4, 9; *BḍP*. 1, 3, 11; *MkP*. 45, 34; *ViP*. 1, 2, 21.

situated in the interior of the egg, just as I have told you. At first he is the agitator, and then he, the husband of nature (*prakṛti*), is that which should be agitated. He also exists in the form of *pradhāna* with its contraction and manifestation. Though born he is the source of the universe.

Although he is without characteristics he takes possession of the characteristic of impetuosity (*rajoguṇa*) and becomes Brahmā when engaging in creation. As Brahmā he emits creatures; then, having an excess of goodness (*sattva*) he becomes Viṣṇu and performs the task of protection in accord with the law. Thereafter, having an excess of the darkness characteristic (*tamoguṇa*) he becomes Rudra. The three worlds sleep after he has compressed them. Though having the three characteristics he is devoid of them.[26]

This is a typical illustration of the *trimūrti*[27] doctrine, the development of which maintained Brahmā's status in mythology where it otherwise may have declined.

Similar qualities, designated in epithetical names, are used of the highest god when he (or occasionally she) is attributed as the creator. Within the epics and Purāṇas at least two distinct kinds of epithets are used of most gods. The first type refers to specific functions performed by, or particular episodes in the mythology of a particular god. In this category stand epithets of Viṣṇu such as Mādhava, 'Killer of Madhu' and Hayaśiras, 'Horse-Head', or of Brahmā such as Svayaṃbhū, 'Self-born', and Caturmukha, 'he who has four faces'. Epithets of the second type are used indiscriminately of most gods, and even of the Buddha. They are represented by Bhagavan, Prabhu, Vibhu and a host of others taking the form of compounds ending with the words Īśa, Īśvara or deva. Since these have the generic sense of Lordship over a group of gods or the universe, it is probable they are only used regularly of a god who is simultaneously accorded a high status

---

26 *MkP*. 46, 11-15; *PaP*. 5, 2, 105ff.

27 An early reference to the *trimūrti* can perhaps be seen in *GB*. 1, 1, 25.

in the pantheon, but typically also by devotees of these gods in *stotras*.

Many examples of this second type of epithet can be found in relation to Brahmā. Some are included in the following list:

Īśa	*MBh.* 1, 58, 43; 12, 250, 4; 289, 58;
Īśāna	*MBh.* 1, 36, 22.
Īśvara	*H.* 1, 17; *MBh.* 3, 32, 39; 33, 1; 33, 19; 12, 59, 25; 249, 11; 250, 3; *Rām.* 1, 41, 13; *ŚP.* 5, 29, 7.
Īśvareśvara	*MBh.* 12, 250, 12.
Jagatprabhu	*MBh.* 3, 259, 20; 12, 249, 2.
Jagannātha	*MBh.* 13, 151, 4; *MkP.* 45, 19; 50, 42.
Tridaśeśa	*MBh.* 3, App. 1, 16 line 105.
Tridaśeśvara	*MBh.* 12, 249, 6.
Tribhuvaneśvara	*MBh.* 12, 59, 25; *BḍP.* 1, 19, 141.
Devadeva	*MBh.* 3, 80, 41; 12, 250, 12; 13, 6, 4; *ViP.* 1, 14, 10; *KP.*1, 2, 86; *Rām.* (C) 7, 10, 39; 7, 94, 17
Devedeveśa	*Rām.* (C) 7, 61, 22.
Deveśa	*VāmP.* 35, 49; *Rām.* (C) 1, 43, 16; 1, 62, 3; *KP.* 2, 34, 43.
Deveśvareśāna	*KP.* 1, 44, 3.
Parameṣṭhin	*MBh.* 1, 1, 30; 1, 7, 23; 3, 98, 6; 98, 19; 186, 2; 5, 126, 40; 126, 44; 126, 45;
Parameśvara	*MBh.* 1, 36. 22; 13, 73, 15; *MkP.* 46, 9; *Rām.* (C) 1, 56, 6.
Prabhu	*MBh.* 3, 31, 33; 31, 36; 12, 249, 1; 13, 83, 57; *H.* 4, 7; *MkP.* 48, 17; *Rām.* (C) 1, 15, 5.
Vibhu	*MBh.* 1, 58, 43; *KP.* 1, 2, 34; *MkP.* 48, 35.
Sarvalokaprabhu	*Rām.* (C) 2, 22, 11.

This list is not exhaustive, and it should not be thought from the number of references in the *MBh.* that the epithets are necessarily used more of Brahmā there than in the Purāṇas.

Where there is a concentration of such epithets for the same god in any particular passage, it may be assumed that passage reflects a time when the god was accorded a high position in the pantheon and correlates with the role he played in mythology. Or more specifically, they may simply reflect a form of flattery in situations where it was known he would provide boons for those who performed the appropriate austerities. Such a passage containing several epithets is *MBh.* 12, 248, 13-250, 36. It narrates how Brahmā became angry with the people on the Earth, who, being immortal, were oppressing Earth with their combined weight. Brahmā threatened to burn the worlds–to introduce death. But a very servile Śiva came and begged him not to do so and to let human beings remain immortal. After some time Brahmā became pleased and created Death (Mṛtyu), who very reluctantly agreed to perform the task of killing creatures, thereby creating a balance between mortality and immortality. Epithets of the second type are used of Brahmā in this narrative about a dozen times. Also, the position of Śiva, here subordinate to Brahmā and contrary to Śiva's position elsewhere in the twelth and thirteenth books of the *MBh*, possibly indicates a period when his status was lower than Brahmā's.[28] In contrast, it may simply be saying that if Brahmā is the creator, he must also create death.

Another passage suggestive of Brahmā's high position in the pantheon is that telling of the events leading up to and the

---

28 Holtzmann, 1884, pp.197-8, cites other passages he believes subordinate Śiva to Brahmā, but in none is the difference as striking as in the passage cited above. Moreover in the Purāṇic passages where this conflict between death and immortality is played out, any status difference between the two gods is never clearcut and changes continually. The concern in the Purāṇas is the subordination of death to immortality rather than of one god to another. For references see O'Flaherty, 1975, p.135.

description of Janamejaya's snake sacrifice.[29] Kadrū has cursed all her offspring, the snakes, to be sacrificed by King Janamejaya in his snake sacrifice, a curse Brahmā condoned because of the excessive number of poisonous snakes on the Earth (*MBh.* 1, 18, 7-10). Vāsuki, king of the snakes, overheard the gods speaking to Brahmā about the sacrifice. They said,

> Who indeed, other than Kadrū, would curse in this way the beloved sons to whom she had given birth, Grandfather, and in front of you, God of gods?[30]

Now that the snakes had heard the gods' speech, Vāsuki himself accompanied the gods to see Brahmā and again they said:

> Lord, Vāsuki fears for the curse and worries greatly. Pray pull out the thorn that sticks in his mind because of his mother's curse, for he wished his kinsmen well, God. For this King of the Snakes has our welfare at heart and does us favours. Show him your grace, Lord of the Gods (*kuru prasādaṃ deveśa*), and appease the fear in his mind.[31]

Brahmā predicted an ascetic named Jaratkāru would stop Janamejaya's sacrifice and so be the saviour of the snakes. Then follow some legends about this ascetic and his son Śṛṅgin, a worshipper of Brahmā in the devotional manner. He refers to Brahmā as a supreme god (*devaṃ param*) and the Lord devoted to the good of all creatures' (*īśānaṃ sarvabhūtahite ratam*), and performs *pūjā* to him.[32] At length, events go as Brahmā predicted and the snake sacrifice was performed on schedule until interrupted by Jaratkāru.

Only a few of the epithets cited above have been used here. Yet they occur in contexts, and in conjunction with language, usually associated with *bhakti*, consistent with the manner Brahmā is portrayed here where he bestows *prasāda* onto his devotees who

---

29 *MBh.* 1, 13-58.

30 *MBh.* 1, 34, 7-8.

31 *MBh.* 1, 35, 5cd-7, following Van Buitenen, 1973, p.96. I have added the Sanskrit.

32 *MBh.* 1, 36, 22; 1, 46, 3. See below pp. 37-39

worship him with *pūjā*. Being seen in this way implies that at least in some circles he was seen as the highest god, this being one of the theological attributes of a god worshipped in this manner.

Brahmā's Status in the Pāli Canon

The widespread appearance of Brahmā in the Pāli Canon is evidence of his importance during whatever period–perhaps 300BCE onwards–it is a product.[33] He is seen in certain Buddhist texts as representing visible aspects of brahmin pretentiousness, part and parcel of which is his assumption of his own important role as creator, and dispenser of knowledge. This is so even where the Buddhist texts show an awareness of an emerging Hindu pantheon, complete with a Pajāpati who is different from Brahmā. Leaving aside the question of dating the early Pāli texts–that is, the extent to which, if at all, they interpret critically the teachings of the earliest Upaniṣads–there is the problem of what Brahmā really represents there. He appears often in conjunction with Indra as an acolyte of the Buddha, or at least as flanking the Buddha in subordinate positions. This is especially prominent in sculptures from Gandhāran art up until Pāla sculpture and even later. Does this mode of depiction mean Brahmā and Indra were the most important deities in whatever the Brāhmaṇical pantheon might have meant in the fifth century BCE and later?[34] Or does

33 Cf, Hacker, 1964, p.234, who writes, 'The texts of the Pāli Canon which speak of Brahmā as the great and powerful god correspond to the oldest layer of the Purāṇic cosmogony where Brahmā is attested as the highest god.' He also rightly asserts (p.235) that Brahmā's decline in the emerging Hindu pantheon is mirrored in some of the later Mahāyana texts where Brahmā is subordinated to both Viṣṇu and Śiva. This seems to contradict the evidence of the *Lalitavistara* where those two gods rarely appear.

34 What does it even mean to talk about a Brāhmaṇical pantheon at that time? Would this just include the full list of gods included in the later Brāhmaṇas, Āraṇyakas and the Upaniṣads, only a few of whom such as Prajāpati, Indra, Varuna and Rudra play important roles in mythology? In what ways would these deities have been

it reflect the Buddha's own recognition of the complementarity between brahmin and kṣatriya which was becoming such an important element of brahmin social and political theory in the early Upaniṣads?

But if the oldest texts of the *Suttapiṭaka* can be dated to a period equivalent to the middle Upaniṣads (300BCE-100BCE), it is true that Brahmā has a much higher profile in these texts than in the Upaniṣads. What can be made of that? That Brahmā was a popular god regarded as too worldly to be associated with the more abstruse religious environment of the Upaniṣads; that he was known in some oral or textual traditions now lost to us, but possibly represented in the *MBh*. and some Pāli texts? At the least we can say that he recognizes himself as a creator in the Pāli Canon, and the Buddha seems to know of no other creator gods. Additionally, he is known as a figure who somehow represents and consolidates Vedic knowledge, the privileged possessors of which is how the Buddha regards the brahmins to be representing themselves as a group.[35] If, as the Buddha constantly argues, the brahmins are arrogant and conceited, then so too is Brahmā himself when he appears in those narratives asserting himself to be creator of the universe. Of course, there is humour in this, as there is meant to be, and there is so much in the Buddha's parody of brahmins that is intended to be self-deprecating.[36]

In a recent article about Brahmā standing at the centre of a

---

venerated? I note here the much more extensive pantheon listed in the *Lalitavistara* dating from the first or second century CE. See Ch. 17 (Vaidya, p.183) Various groups bow to Brahmā, Indra, Rudra, Viṣṇu, Devī, Kumāra, the Mother, Kātyāyanī, the Moon, the Sun, Vaiśravaṇa, Varuṇa, Vāsava, the Nāgas, Yakṣas, Gandharvas, Asuras, Garuḍa, Kiṃnaras, great snakes, Rākṣasas, the deceased ancestors, ghosts, Kumbhāṇḍas, and deva, rāja and Brahmā sages. Perhaps comparable as an early equivalent is *GB*. 1, 4, 8ff.

35 See Visigalli, 2016, pp.809-832.

36 See Gombrich, 2001, pp.95-108.

brāhmaṇical synthesis, McGovern[37] rightly alludes to the clichéd description of Brahmā–really a list of epithets–that could easily give the impression he is being treated as a supreme deity in some circles. This description occurs seven times and in three different contexts. Whilst it could easily be read as a critique of the idea of an eternal creator god, it is also, or primarily, a critique of the belief in the existence of any permanent entity. It is not a coincidence that the episodes in the Pāli Canon where Brahmā is described with these is told each time within the context of a story. Even where the critique of the same doctrine is told each time, nonetheless it is always embedded as a distinctive part of a particular story, which surely would have made it more acceptable to a listening audience.

Of the seven places[38] where Brahmā is described with the listed epithets, I will focus on the version found in DN 1, 17-19, whilst alluding to some of the others. This begins with the proposition that: "There are, monks, some ascetics and Brahmins who are partly Eternalists and partly Non-Eternalists, who proclaim the partial eternity and the partial non-eternity of the self and the world in four ways. On what grounds?"[39] Then it illustrates this with a narrative. Due to shortening of his life or because of loss of good karma one being (*satto*, the language expressed with deliberate vagueness) falls away from the Ābhassara heaven and appears in Brahmā's empty palace. "Alone for a long time, he experiences unease, he finds no enjoyment, and is quite anxious, thinking, "Oh,

37 See McGovern, 2012 and below.

38 *SN*. 1, 142 *DN*. 1, 18 (occurs twice), *DN*. 1, 221, *DN*. 3. 29-30 (occurs twice); *MN*. 1. 327; *AN*. 4. 89; *Iti*. p.15. It may be significant that this narrative never occurs, to my knowledge, in Buddhist Sanskrit literature.

39 Trans. Walshe, 1987, p.75. DN 1. 17. *Santi bhikkhave eke samaṇabrāhmaṇā ekaccasassatikā ekacca-asassatikā ekaccaṃ sassataṃ ekaccaṃ asassataṃ attānañ ca lokañ ca paññāpenti catūhi vatthūhi.*

if only other beings would come here."[40] This statement implies he experiences emotion, though how he would know of the existence of other beings is not explained, unless he knows his other prior rebirths. What he does then is to try and think them into existence. And for the same reason as he fell other creatures fall after he has made this request, and enter into companionship with him. Following this: "Then, monks, that being who first arose there thinks, "I am Brahmā, Great Brahmā, Conqueror, Unconquered,[41] Seeing the goals of others, Controller, Lord, Maker, Creator, Best, Assigner, Master of Himself, Father of beings past and future."[42] Whilst there may be some doubt about the exact meaning[43] of several of these epithets, the overall intended impression is not in doubt at all.

And the idea of presenting himself as creator and controller is further confirmed by him when he goes on to say, "These beings were created by me. What was the cause of that? Because I had previously thought, 'Oh, if only other beings would come here. This was in my mind, and these beings came here.' And those

---

40 *Tassa tattha ekakassa dīgharattaṃ nibbusitattā anabhirati paritassanā uppajjati: 'aho vata aññe'pi sattā itthattaṃ āgaccheyyun ti.* (DN.1. 17)

41 'Unconquered': *anabhibhūto*. Cf. *MaitrīU*, 2, 7 where the *ātman* "wanders here on earth from body to body, not overcome (*anabhibhūto*), as it seems by the bright or dark fruits of action."(HMU. p.417 modified) He stands in contrast to the *bhūtātman* which is "being overcome (*abhibhūyamānaḥ*) by the bright or the dark fruits of action…" (3, 1 HMU, p.417-18) And 3, 2 where we find *eṣo 'bhibhūtaḥ prākṛtair guṇair iti…*

42 *aham asmi brahmā mahābrahmā abhibhū anabhibhūto aññadatthudaso vasavattī issaro kattā nimmātā seṭṭho sañjitā vasī pitā bhūtabhavyānaṃ.* [*DN*.1, 18]

43 MN. 1, p. 327 trans. Ñāṇamoli and Bodhi, 1995, p.425, "for this Brahmā is the Great Brahmā, the Overlord, the Untranscended, of Infallible Vision, Wielder of Mastery, Lord Maker and Creator, Most High Providence, Master and Father of those that are and ever can be."

beings who had arrived after him think, 'This honourable one is Brahmā… We were created by this Brahmā. Why? Because we saw him here as the first who had arisen. We appeared after him.'" Note the distinction between pronouns, when he says *aham* and they say *ayam kho bhavaṃ*. And note the contrast: *mayā ime sattā nimmitā…* with *iminā mayaṃ bhotā brahmuṇā nimmitā…* And the reason for attributing creator status to him: "We saw him as the first who had arisen."

But this is not the end of the description and of the attempted elevation of Brahmā's status. The text goes on to say, "And this being that arose first is longer-lived, more beautiful and more powerful than they are."[44] Following this some being is said to fall into this world and becomes an ascetic wanderer (*samāno*), undertakes the appropriate meditation, and then "he thereby recalls his last existence, but recalls none before that. And he thinks: "That illustrious Brahmā…he made us, and he is permanent, stable, eternal, not subject to change, the same for ever and ever.[45] But we who were created by that Brahmā, we are impermanent, unstable, short-lived, fated to fall away, and we have come to this world."

That is, he is a masculine figure, quite at variance with the neuter *idam*, found in other versions of the narrative where these epithets are used. In truth two different concepts are being presented here, though we might ask whether Brahmā is being treated as the masculization of the neuter Brahman, often called *idam* in the Upaniṣads. I regard this interpretation as a long shot, however, as Brahman seems not to be mentioned in Pāli texts in the same manner as he is in the Upaniṣads. On each of the occasions

---

44 Walshe, 1995, p.76. *tatra, bhikkhave, yo so satto paṭhamaṃ upapanno so dīghāyukataro ca hoti vaṇṇavantataro ca mahesakkhataro ca.*

45 *yena mayaṃ bhotā Brahmunā nimmitā, so nicco dhuvo sassato avipariṇāma-dhammo sassatisamaṃ tath'; eva ṭhassati.* A different version is given at *MN*. 1.326, but there the subject is *idam*, not the masculine Brahmā.

where Brahmā is described with the usual twelve epithets there is a reference to false beliefs being held by some ascetic who holds that: *idaṃ niccaṃ idaṃ dhuvaṃ idaṃ sassataṃ idaṃ kevalaṃ idaṃ acavanadhammaṃ. Idaṃ hi na jāyati na jīyati na cavati na uppajjati. Ito ca panaññaṃ uttariṃ nissaraṇaṃ natthīti.*[46] And in Bodhi's translation: "This is permanent, this is everlasting, this is eternal, this is total, this is not subject to pass away; for this neither is born nor ages nor dies nor passes away nor reappears, and beyond this there is no escape."[47] It would seem unambiguous that this is referring to some entity who is beyond time and does not undergo birth, death and rebirth, in direct contradiction of the Buddha's second noble truth. The exposure of the false views associated with Brahmā's appearance and presumption of being a creator is then used to refute the eternality of what is designated by the neuter *idam*. But the question that must be asked is this: does Brahmā regard himself as being eternal in these creation satires? Does the word *pathamaṃ* give a sense of constancy along the lines of the clichéd expressions for what is permanent? Surely not. It just seems to indicate temporality and gives him a claim to preeminence and priority, both of which are accepted by those who are born after him.

So Brahmā is both creator and beyond the impermanent. For my purposes this rejected assertion and the six other similar passages are important because of the list of epithets they give of Brahmā, and the possibility they are conflating Brahman and Brahmā in the critique of permanency applied here, one pertinent to Brahman and/or the *ātman.* As for the first, does it suggest they are focusing on Brahmā as a popular deity amongst the brahmins (who were the main early converts to the *saṅgha*), as the emerging creator god, or Brahman?[48] But the Buddha might conceivably have used this list of epithets as an argument for suggesting Brahmā's

46 *Bhg*. 2, 20 and *MBh*. 6, 60, 32 have direct echoes of this.

47 Bhikkhu Ñāṇamoli and Bhikkhu Bodhi, 1995, p.424.

48 See McGovern, 2012, p.10.

high status during his own lifetime, and therefore amongst the brahmins at that time.[49]

But is it really this? At the least we can be confident in assessing the list as providing recognition that Brahmā was regarded as a creator when the texts of the *Sutta Piṭaka* were composed, but we are unable to extrapolate this back into brāhmaṇical texts, except perhaps for one passage in the *MaitrīU*. Certainly some of the epithets such as *kattā* and *nimmitā*, *sañjitā*, *pitā bhūtabhavyānaṃ* would fit this category, even if not much found in the *MBh*. or the Purāṇas, except for *kartā* and *pitā bhūtabhavyānam* which may be a throw back to Prajāpati. On pp.13-14 of Ch.1 of this book I point out that most of these words or their equivalents can be found somewhere in the epics and some in the Upaniṣads, but not always in connection with Brahmā. They are never used of him as a group like this, and whilst this combination makes it easier for the Buddha easily to undermine him, I also suggest that this kind of listing could be taken as a reflection of Upaniṣadic style where lists of epithets are commonly given for a number of concepts.

Instead of trying to find exact parallels to this list in late Vedic literature and the epics, where none exist, it is better to assume the Buddhists were creating a list of epithets and qualities parallel to the *ātman* and Brahman of a type occurring often in the Upaniṣads. Anyone educated in these texts would understand exactly what is being spoken about. An example is BhU. 2, 5, 15, dealing with the *ātman: sa vā ayam ātmā sarveṣāṃ bhūtānām adhipatiḥ sarveṣāṃ bhūtānāṃ rājā | tad yathā rathanābhau ca rathanemau cārāḥ sarve samarpitāḥ | evam evāsminn ātmani sarvāṇi bhūtāni sarve devāḥ sarve lokāḥ sarve prāṇāḥ sarva eta ātmānaḥ samarpitāḥ* // and there are many others.[50] The Buddha may simply have

49 See also Masson, 1942, pp.57-8 for similar epithets in the Brāhmaṇas and Upaniṣads.

50 "This very self (*ātman*) is the lord and king of all beings. As all the spokes are fastened to the hub and the rim of a wheel, so to one's self (*ātman*) are fastened all beings, all the gods, all the worlds, all the breaths, and all these bodies (*ātman*)." Trans.

collected as many epithets that he could find relating to what he considered Brahmā's role to be in the mythology of his time and added them together into one group, to give a much more exalted image of Brahmā than if he was just accorded one or a few of these epithets. But it is also a mimicry of Upaniṣadic style and therefore of some of the fundamental axioms associated with Upaniṣadic thought.

This strategy fits in well with the broader context of this part of the *sutta*–the debate between eternality and its opposite–and its polemical aim is clear, but does it allow us to read through what is being said in order to determine Brahmā's status as a popular deity at the time this collection of epithets was being used? In the contrast between Brahmā as eternal and everyone else as not, should this be taken both as a critique of the *ātman* theory and also of the special status to be attributed to the god who is considered responsible for the creation? This might well support McGovern's theory that Brahman and Brahmā are being conflated in Buddhist literature, yet it still remains difficult to account for this god being described with all of these epithets, even in what will subsequently become Hindu texts such as the *MBh*.

Beyond the epithets and the idea that Brahmā is both a fount of knowledge and its disseminator, what else is there of Brahmā? Where else in the Pāli texts is an image of Brahmā given of a kind implied by the epithets found in the seven texts containing this list? There is no other passage, though each of these individually is given wide coverage in the *MBh*. and beyond. In part this is because the latter represents a substantial shift in religious sensitivities and practices and the intrusion of devotional beliefs and practices everywhere. The pedagogical intention of the Upaniṣads and the Pāli Canon is quite different from the *MBh*. where mythology communicates more than it does in the two former. Of course, the Buddha must have got these epithets from somewhere, and his

---

Olivelle, 1998, p.73. See also *BhU*. 3, 5, 1; 4, 4, 25; *ChU*. 8, 7, 1 and 3, *KU*. 2, 18; 3, 15 (both relating to the *ātman*); *MU*. 1, 1, 6; 2, 1, 2 *MaitrīU*. 6, 28.

portrayal of Brahmā as a pompous purveyor of wisdom must also be related to some image of the god that was being communicated elsewhere. Answers to these questions would be invaluable for definitively explaining how a masculine god Brahmā developed and how he was subsequently integrated into the emerging Hindu pantheon.

Of the epithets used in the list discussed above, some parallel epithets can be found in the epics and Purāṇas. It is likely that Issaro, Seṭṭho and possibly Vasavattī and Vasī combine together into a single group signifying lordship. This may imply a high position in the pantheon, though to be certain of this it would be necessary to determine if it is used of only a few or many gods. Īśvara is frequently used of Brahmā in the *MBh*, and epithets such as Suraśreṣṭha are occasionally found in connection with him.[51] I have found no trace of Vaśin or Vaśavartin used of him in any text. Of the others, Kattā, Nimmitā and Pitā form a distinct group and definitely refer to his role as creator. Nimmatā is the only one not attested in the epics and Purāṇas but the verb *nir/mā* is often used to designate his act of creating the world.[52] Aññadatthadaso signifies omniscience and corresponds to Sarvajña, used of Brahmā several times.[53] If Sañjita can be translated as 'Disposer' or 'Assigner of functions', it can be regarded as a simile of Dhātṛ, a name applied to the god who arranges the organization of the cosmos at the time of creation. Both function and name were taken over by Brahmā in the *MBh*.[54] Abhibhū and Anabhibhūta stand on their own and appear to have no parallels in epic and Purāṇic literature.[55]

A possible further argument for refining his status at the time the early parts of the Pāli Canon was composed is to acknowledge the two opposed ways in which he was treated, as an index of how

51 *MBh*. 7, 69, 51; *Rāṃ*. (NW) 7, 69, 27.

52 *Rām*. (C) 2, 102, 2; *ŚP*, 5, 29, 15.

53 *H*. App. 1, No. 29B, Line 24. Cf. *MBh*. 12, 175, 34; *BḍP*. 1, 1, 13; *LiP*. 1, 106, 12.

54 For details see below pp.192-93.

55 But see n.41 above.

seriously he was taken by the early Buddhists. Either he is bitterly attacked, or he is portrayed as a zealous devotee of the Buddha.[56] The aim of many of these attacks is to make Brahmā look stupid, undermining the brahmins' monopoly claim to spiritual knowledge. A good example comes from the *Kevaddhasutta* where the Buddha tells the story of a monk who wanted to know what happened to the four great elements (earth, water, fire and wind) once they had passed away without trace.[57] Firstly, he asked the four great kings, but they did not know and sent him on to four more great kings. He is sent from god to god thirteen times, being told each time that the god is more glorious than the one to whom he is speaking and so should be able to answer the question. Finally, he is directed to Brahmā, whom one might think would know the answer because he is the creator. But to build up the greatness and mystery of this god the gods of the Brahmā worlds say they do not know where Brahmā is or even why he exists; moreover, the monk is required to enter *samādhi* before Brahmā will appear. As soon as the god appeared, and the monk questioned him, instead of giving an answer he vaunted his own greatness, reeling off the stock of epithets listed earlier. Three times the monk asked the question and the third time Brahmā pulled him aside explaining that he did not want to speak in the presence of the Brahmā gods, implying that they considered him to be omniscient. He then revealed to the monk that he did not know the answer, and recommended he ask the Buddha. Such an attack humorously brings out the excessive pride of the god and specifically contradicts his own claim of omniscience (*aññadatthadaso*).

The most vicious attack of all occurs in the *Bhūridatta Jātaka*.[58] It is strongly anti-brāhmaṇical in character, directly relating Brahmā to the brahmins as a *varṇa*. Significantly, the final verse section includes several biting attacks directed against

---

56 By the time a highly devotional text like the *Lalitavistara* is composed, he is only ever portrayed as a zealous devotee.

57 *DN*. 1, pp.215-222.

58 *J.* No.543. See Alsdorf, 1977.

the lax conduct of brahmins, especially emphasizing their laxity in observance of *svadharma*, a critique not found in earlier texts of the Pāli Canon. Some of these verses specifically condemn Brahmā:

> On account of their livelihood on earth these brahmins say, "This Brahmā, Lord of all (*sabbābhibhū*) is a servant of fire." Why should the all-powerful (*sabbānubhavī*), master of himself (*vasī*), the uncreated (*animmito*), worship the fire he created?...
>
> The noble men engage in study, the princes rule over the earth, the *vaiśyas* engage in agriculture and the *śūdras* serve the others. "These were created by the Lord (*vasinā*), each to its own place," so it is said.
>
> And if this statement were to be true as the brahmins have announced it, no person who is not a *kṣatriya* would gain a kingdom. No one but a brahmin would learn mantra verses and no one else than a *vaiśya* would engage in agriculture. No one but a *śūdra* would be free for serving others.
>
> Therefore, because this statement is untrue, these gluttonous people speak falsely. Those of little wisdom believe that statement, but the wise know the truth inherently. *Kṣatriyas* and *vaiśyas* offer the sacrifice, brahmins practise weapon making. Why doesn't Brahmā put this world into order, as it is thoroughly agitated and scattered about in such a way as described?
>
> If indeed Brahmā is Lord (*issaro*) over the entire world, the mighty Lord (*pāhu*) of creatures, Lord of beings (*bhūtapati*), then why has he created (*vidahī*) misfortune in all the world? Why didn't he create all the world as happiness?
>
> If indeed Brahmā is Lord over the entire world, the mighty Lord of creatures, Lord of beings, then why did he create a world characterized by unlawfulness (*adhammena*), as well as sensual excess, falsehood and deceit?
>
> If indeed Brahmā is Lord over the entire world, the mighty Lord of creatures, Lord of beings, then, Ariṭṭha, the Lord of beings is unlawful (*adhammiyo*). Although the law exists, he has created what is not the law (*adhammam*).[59]

---

59 Translation following the edition of Alsdorf, 1977, pp.43-4, 51-2.

These highly rhetorical verses from the *Bhūridatta Jātaka* are as important for the detail they include about Brahmā as for the strident attack upon the god and what he represents. The image given of him as a creator god who undertakes (*vi/dhā*) organization of the cosmos, the social order and establishes correct conduct in terms of *dharma* and *adharma*, closely resembles what is given in the *MBh.* and the Purāṇas. It shows a very detailed and accurate knowledge of Brahmā's role in epic mythology, reflecting developments in Brahmā's role beyond those found in earlier Pāli texts. Similar to the other passage cited above from the *Kevaddhasutta*, he is attacked through epithets, where all the examples given in the verse reveal his incapacity to exercise the powers they imply, even where he is called Lord and master of himself. Even worse, he is shown to be wrought with contradictions. He may be a god of *dharma*, but he is incapable of creating a world that is other than a mixture of *dharma* and *adharma*. For the Buddhists such an imperfect world could not be the product of a god possessing the great power implied in the epithets used of Brahmā. As such, the god himself, though not the belief in such a god, is ridiculed, as is the *varṇa* to which he is closely related.

Passages where Brahmā is portrayed as the Buddha's devotee are as common as those where he is attacked and ridiculed.[60] Possibly the best example of this is the story of the Buddha's entreaty to the Buddha to roll the wheel of *dhamma*.[61] In short, this tells how having attained enlightenment, the Buddha did not want to preach the *dhamma* because he feared people would not understand it. Brahmā became aware of the Buddha's misgivings, manifested himself to him and after three attempts managed to

---

Vs.148; 150-156.

60 Though not as demonstrably as Indra's exercise of devotion to the Buddha described in the *Sakkapañhasutta*. See Bailey, 2016.

61 See *DN*. 2, 36-40; *Vin*. 1, 5ff; *MN*. 1, 168ff. Bareau, 1963, Vol. 1. pp.135-43. Some of these versions are discussed below. See pp.235-52.

persuade him to teach the *dhamma*. All versions of the story depict Brahmā as holding great esteem for the Buddha and the *dhamma*. A late Pāli text–the *Milinda Pañho*–contains some reflections on this episode that suggest Brahmā's apparent devotion to the Buddha may have been orchestrated by the Buddhists themselves. Nāgasena, the interlocutor, has been asked why the Buddha, after having become enlightened, had need of Brahmā's encouragement before he would toll the wheel of *dhamma*. Nāgasena answers:

> Moreover, great king, this is an essential rightness in all Tathāgatas, that they should teach dhamma at the request of Brahmā. But what is the reason for this? At that time all these people–ascetics and wanderers, recluses and brahmans–had Brahmā as their deity (*brahmadevatā*), respected Brahmā (*brahmagarukā*) and they were devoted to Brahmā (*brahmaparāyanā*). Therefore at the thought that the world with the devas will bow down (to *dhamma*), they feel confidence and faith in it because that one who is so powerful, famed, well known, renowned, high and lofty bows down to it–it is for this reason, great king, that Tathāgatas teach dhamma at the request of Brahmās.[62]

This passage seems a strong endorsement of Brahmā's apparent status as a deity amongst different groups of people, especially those who inhabit the Buddhist world at that time, but equally brings out his close connection to *dharma*. Language such as 'powerful, famed, well known, renowned, high and lofty' is rarely if ever used of him in Hindu texts.

The opposed attitudes taken towards Brahmā in the Pāli Canon are two sides of the same coin. They strongly endorse the view that he was considered by Buddhists, especially those who were living when the *saṅgha* had become well established, to be a rival.[63] Both attitudes are indicative of this stance. The Buddha criticized Brahmā, though usually in a muted and humorous way,

---

62 *MiP*, p.234 (PTS) trans. following Horner, 1969, Vol.2 pp.36-7.

63 Though whether this was a rival for financial patronage seems unclear. Real concerns about patronage amongst brahmins and monks only really becomes apparent about the beginning of the Common Era.

to warn against the danger of beliefs contingent upon belief in a god like him.[64] Belief in an omniscient god, one who creates, thereby implying a fixed point from which creation takes place, and the belief in the existence of a god who is a priori not subject to the conditioning factors of phenomenal existence, factors influencing every being except the enlightened, were anathema to many fundamental Buddhist doctrines. As such not only was Brahmā seen as the focal point of 'religious competition' affecting the Buddha, but important beliefs associated with him contradicted many of the Buddha's own metaphysical claims. The tactic of portraying Brahmā as a devotee, is an excellent one if Brahmā was an important god in the sense of being widely worshipped in the area where the Buddha taught. What better way to subdue a rival than to make him a convert to one's own religion!

In an article referred to earlier Nathan McGovern has argued that an initial Brahmanical synthesis was developed around the god Brahmā, a synthesis substantially reflected, and criticized, in the Pāli Canon. This was a synthesis not presented explicitly in the early Upaniṣads he argues, but is strongly implied by the prominence accorded to Brahmā in Pāli literature and the combination of qualities with which he is attributed there. It has largely been abandoned in the *MBh.* and subsequent Hindu literature, where it is fragmented and replaced by cults developed around Viṣṇu and Śiva as a Hindu reaction–a second synthesis–to the criticism undertaken by the Buddhists and others of the first synthesis. Here is his basic thesis summarized: "Indeed, in an era when Brahmanical culture was expanding into new areas and encountering new ideas and religious systems—some of which, like Jainism and Buddhism, would pose a formidable challenge to Brahmanical claims to supremacy—Brahmā would have provided a powerful synthesis of ritual values, caste ideology, and the latest philosophical speculations on ultimate reality into

64 We might ask in which circles these criticisms were launched? Mainly amongst monks, I would suggest, as they do not really address concerns the laity would have had.

one, all-powerful deity. Brahmā, I would argue, was the first major attempt at a "Brahmanical synthesis"—a synthesis of the major values and ideologies being espoused by *brāhmaṇas* in the face of competing ideological systems—but one, as we will see below, that was ultimately destined to fail. Indeed, if it were not for the early Buddhist texts, we might not know with any certainty that Brahmā was ever regarded as supreme deity, for in the *Mahābhārata*, the signs of the breakdown of the Brahmanical synthesis Brahmā represented are already quite apparent."[65]

This conclusion rests on the assumption that Brahmā did embody "ritual values, caste ideology, and the latest philosophical speculations on ultimate reality," an assumption open to question. Certainly, Brahmā in the epics and Purāṇas does represent ritualistic values as evidenced strongly by his role as preserver and disseminator of *dharma* and Vedic knowledge. As for the second component–caste, there is no certainty caste ideology developed before the beginning of the Common Era, though *varṇa* divisions were certainly tightening in what had become a highly pluralistic society, which was continuing to develop in this manner. I would rather see the portrayal of Brahmā in the *Dīgha*- and *Majjhima Nikāyas*, in particular, as representing the Buddha's impression of the arrogant self-confidence of the brahmins, developed in the process of their emergence as a corporate group expressing a now well defined set of social and religious views, at least in the manner of how the Buddha saw them.[66] As for the third component, Brahmā has never represented ultimate reality, that status being associated with Brahman in the Upaniṣads and beyond. Moreover, I would ask which Upaniṣadic text presents this kind of synthesis, if such ever existed.

If Brahmā was the centre of this synthesis, why would the brahmins choose him and not Viṣṇu or Rudra? Arguably it would have been because of his close connection with the emerging brahmin class at a time when they were seeking to consolidate their

65 McGovern, 2012, p.7.

66 See Bailey and Mabbett, 2003, Ch.6.

position. And Brahmā would have been an appropriate choice for the clichéd representation of a brahmanical world-view because he was associated with the different meanings of the word *brahman*. The synthesis McGovern suggests is a highly theoretical one that would make sense to the brahmins alone, as they were becoming increasingly aware of their status the more they moved away from the Vedic heartland located in the Punjab and Haryana. It is safe to assume, as reflected in middle Vedic literature, that the brahmins were developing an image of themselves as a group, as they probably felt the pressure of encountering many new ethnic and linguistic groups, and wanted to differentiate themselves from the source of political power, the kṣatriyas. But if such a synthesis, as McGovern proposes, was being developed in the Upaniṣads, then it was done in a very fragmented manner, and was not formalized explicitly, unless it was there by implication.

McGovern sees Brahmā being portrayed in a manner where he attempts "to straddle *pravṛtti* and *nivṛtti* as two radically separate realms," but failing, with the Buddhist critique of him an expression of this failure.[67] Yet if the ideologies and life-styles associated with these two terms could be taken as the foundation of a new synthesis, it is a synthesis only really reaching definition in systematic terms in the *MBh*,[68] where a real accommodation between an ascetic world view and a ritualistic one is strenuously attempted. Certainly, the brahmins were attempting to develop and transmit a very distinctive view of ritual and social practice in the Dharma- and Gṛhyasūtras, developed in a more popular and accessible form in the *MBh*. It is in the latter text where the synthesis–of ascetic, ritualistic and devotional lies–rather than in earlier texts and then reflected in the Pāli Canon.

---

67 McGovern, 2012, pps.18 and 21.

68 I am also now inclined to think that the first chapter of the *MU*. is developing a *pravṛtti/nivṛtti* distinction even if these words do not occur there and derivatives of *vṛt* only occur a few times. See also Bailey, 2005 and my forthcoming piece, "Preliminary Notes on Pāli *Vatt*/*Vaṭṭ* and Sanskrit *Vṛt* in the *Mahābhārata*."

In short McGovern's article asks us to interrogate the difference between Brahmā as a symbol of brahmin claims to possess *brahman*–a diffused power existing in persons, the sacrifice and the universe–and Brahmā as a deity in a particular Hindu pantheon. If it is accepted that Brahmā was considered in the Upaniṣads to represent the neuter Brahman and some kind of personification of this, and the *brāhmaṇa* as a representative of a social class, then there may be some justification of attributing him as combining the values of what come to be conceptualized as *pravṛtti* and *nivṛtti*. Certainly in the epics Brahmā is definitely associated with *pravṛtti*, an association continuing into the Purāṇas, though, as we shall see later, Malik argues that in the *Puṣkaramāhātmya* he is associated with the forest in such a way that may suggest a connection with *nivṛtti*. At the least Brahmā seems to embody a transitional shift between Vedic ritualism and the more expansive belief systems associated with *pravṛtti* and *nivṛtti*–with their easily recognizable social manifestations–, and the systematizing mythology of the *trimūrti*.

Evidence for the Worship of Brahmā

Any evidence supportive of Brahmā's worship in literary, epigraphical and archeological sources must be used with considerable caution. Isolated references in literature to his worship often refer to nothing other than that he was honoured–rather than worshipped–for his wisdom by the gods or that he was honoured as an elderly grandfather (*pitāmaha*) by members of his divine family.

In order to make conclusive statements about Brahmā worship it is necessary to seek evidence from sources which can be fairly easily dated and their locations identified, and which in some way correspond roughly to the literary sources. But we must also nuance what is meant by 'worship', because in ancient India a god could have been worshipped in the context of the sacrifice, as the singular object of devotion, or merely by his name being mentioned in passing by someone as a charm before beginning a journey or a transaction.

There are many references to the worship of Brahmā in the epics and later literature which do not fall into any of the above categories. Typical is a passage from the *MBh*, the subject of which is Yudhiṣṭhira:

> Dhaumya and the other brahmins surrounded and worshipped (*upatasthire*) him, just as the chief Immortals, equal of Bṛhaspati, worship Prajāpati [Brahmā].[69]

Here the verb *upa/sthā* could just as easily have been rendered 'respectfully attend upon, reverence' as 'worship', because the brahmins are paying reverence to Yudhiṣṭhira as King Dharma, the ruler who has ruled completely in accord with *dharma*. As such his situation is analogous to that of Brahmā who is honoured and revered by the gods as an embodiment of *dharma*. Other verbal roots such as *upa/ās*, *pary/upa/ās* and *pūj*, all capable of being rendered as 'worship', are sometimes used of Brahmā in the same way as *upa/sthā* and cannot always be considered evidence of Brahmā worship.[70]

Some of the passages where Brahmā is said to be worshipped do have to be considered as indications of a possible Brahmā cult or, more likely, the existence of a formal method of worshipping the god. In the stories leading up to Janamejaya's snake sacrifice a certain ascetic's son named Śṛṅgin is mentioned twice as a worshipper of Brahmā:

> From time to time he diligently worshipped the Supreme God, Lord Brahmā, who benefits all creatures; and when he was given leave by Brahmā he went home.[71]

---

69 *MBh*. 1, 214, 8. Trans van Buitenen, 1971, p.414.

70 See respectively *MBh*. 3, 82, 88; 5, 13, 3; 5, 48, 2; 9, 33, 14; 12, 161, 13; 12, 166, 6; 12, 273, 19 and 40; *BḍP*. 1, 19, 141; 2, 15, 36; *AP*. 84, 35; 114, 14-15; 176, 3; *MP*. 70, 42; 134, 6; *KP*. 1, 47, 6. And used with the *trimūrti* see *BḍP*. 2, 19, 27, *Brahma Purāṇa*. 216, 62.

71 *MBh*. 1, 36, 22. Trans van Buitenen, 1973, p.97.

sa devaṃ param īśānaṃ sarvabhūtahite ratam /
brahmāṇam upatasthe vai kāle kāle susaṃyataḥ //

> ...This hermit had gone up to Brahmā and made *pūjā* to him; and when he had been given leave to go... .[72]

The kind of worship being practiced here is definitely that of a devotee (*bhakta*) to his god. Devotional terminology such as *devam*, *param īśānam* and *pūjām cakāra* is present. Similarly the descriptor of Brahmā as *sarvabhūtahite ratam* is very often given as the motivation for certain actions performed by other important gods such as Viṣṇu and Śiva standing within the devotional tradition.[73] Even the necessity for Śṛṅgin to receive Brahmā's permission before he can depart is a sign that the relationship between god and man is a personal one, according perfectly with *bhakti* doctrine.

Brahmā worship of this kind also occurs in Pāli literature. In the *Mātaṅgajātaka* the Buddha is born in Benares as a *caṇḍāla* named Mātaṅga.[74] He takes a wife and offers to make her more glorious than before she had met him. In order to achieve this she is told to say to people that she is married to Great Brahmā and that this god will fly over Benares in seven days. Mātaṅga assumes the shape of Great Brahmā by virtue of the power derived from *tapas* and flies around Benares:

> ...having roamed about Benares three times, being worshipped (*pūjyamāno*) with perfumed garlands and so forth, he turned towards the *caṇḍāla's* village. The devotees of Brahmā (*brahmabhatta*) assembled there and went to the *caṇḍāla's* village...[75]

At the village they perform *pūjā* to Great Brahmā and his wife, using flowers and incense. Though it is Mātaṅga (subsequently the Buddha) disguised here as Great Brahmā, the passage seemingly

---

sa tena samanujñāto brahmaṇā gṛham eyivān /

72 *MBh*. 1, 46, 3 Trans van Buitenen, 1973, p.110.

73 For Viṣṇu see *MBh*. 3, 194, 22; *Rām*. (C) 1, 14, 17; *KP*. 1, 1, 28; 1, 1, 84. For Śiva see *MBh*. 12, 149, 110; *KP*. 1, 11, 12; 1, 13, 42; 1, 29, 20. It is also frequently used of kings and sages.

74 *J*. No. 497, Vol. 4 pp.375-90.

75 *J*. No. 497, Vol. 4 pp.377-78.

testifies to the popularity of the god and a mode of worship like that performed in devotion to *bhakti* deities in the Purāṇas.

Another passage from the *Saṃyutta Nikāya* speaks of a brāhmaṇī, mother of a monk named Brahmadeva, who was "continually offering an oblation to Brahmā."[76] Brahmā Sahaṃpati came up to her and told her to stop making such offerings as the Brahmā world was far away and Brahmā did not eat that kind of food. This is apparently an attack on Brahmā worship, implying he is too distant for the offering of oblations to influence him to act in a particular way. In addition, there may be *śleṣa* in the name Brahmadeva, meaning that the god (*deva*) Brahmā has himself become a monk, thereby casting negative aspersions on the value of devotees worshipping him.

Yet another reference to Brahmā worship comes from the *Milinda Pañho* where a certain Jotipāla has criticized the Buddha, and Nāgasena feels obliged to explain the reason for this criticism:

> For Jotipāla, King, was descended from a family of unbelievers, men void of faith. His mother and father, his sisters and brothers, the bondswomen and bondsmen, the hired servants and dependents in the house, who had Brahmā as their god (*brahmadevatā*), they revered Brahmā (*brahmagurukā*)...[77]

Their criticism of the Buddha was based on their regard for the brahmins as the most honourable amongst men, and their revulsion for renouncers.

These are not the only places in Buddhist and Hindu literature providing evidence that Brahmā was once worshipped, even as the recipient of devotional acts from *bhaktas*. However, this evidence is difficult to interpret. By itself it pales into insignificance when compared with the very detailed instructions pertaining to the worship of Viṣṇu and Śiva found in the Purāṇas and other more specific texts containing *stotras* and *pūjā* descriptions. I will consider this problem after an examination of some other

---

76 *SN*. 1, 141. *brahmuno āhutiṃ niccaṃ paggaṇhāti.*

77 *MiP*. p.222.

evidence of Brahmā worship, less tenuous than what has just been discussed.

One of the most fruitful early sources of the worship of gods, making up the emerging Hindu pantheon, and the place of their worship is provided by the numerous *tīrtha* listings found in the *MBh.* and the Purāṇas. A *tīrtha* is a sacred place, generally located near water, to which Indians have gone on pilgrimage for centuries. They are held to be sacred because they are places where gods once lived or still live, or places they created, or because gods killed marauding asuras at them, and, finally, where great sages located their hermitages.[78] However, these lists are only the first stage in determining that a god was worshipped in a particular location. Any information they yield must be supplemented by more concrete evidence–concentration of icons, temples and inscriptions. In Brahmā's case, evidence from the *tīrtha* lists locates his main centres of popularity in western India and north-eastern India around the town of Gayā.

Western India

The best known place of worship of Brahmā is at the small town of Pushkar, both now and in the past, in north-eastern Rajasthan. The temple dedicated to Brahmā stands at the edge of a large lake which skirts the town of Pushkar. There is an image of Brahmā with three visible heads in the temple's *garbhagṛha*. It is daubed entirely in red paint and tinsel, like many other images and along roadsides in India today. The temple continues to be frequented by many pilgrims who have inscribed countless benedictions in Hindi and English on its floor.

Pushkar has a long history. The *tīrtha* list found in the *Āraṇyakaparvan* of the *MBh.* is a tour of *tīrthas*, going from east to west, beginning and ending with Puṣkara.[79] Brahmā's association with it is illustrated in the following verses:

---

78 Bhardwaj, 1973, pp.97ff. discusses the reasons for the various rankings of *tīrthas*.

79 Bhardwaj, 1973, p.41 argues this indicates it "was perhaps the

When one with folded hands calls Puṣkara to mind in the morning and the evening, it is the equivalent of bathing at all fords; and in the seat of Brahmā he earns worlds without end... Just as Madhusūdana is the first of all gods, so is Puṣkara said to be the first of fords.[80] A sojourn of twelve years in Puṣkara makes a controlled and pure man achieve all the sacrifices and reach the world of Brahmā.[81]

Elsewhere in the *MBh.* Puṣkara is called the 'Grandfather's Pond' (*pitāmahasaras*), and is also mentioned as a site where he performed a sacrifice.[82] Several texts acknowledge Brahmā to be king of Puṣkaradvīpa, a possible reflection of his status at Puṣkara.[83]

Of course the *PaP.* exalts Puṣkara as the highest of *tīrthas* and relates a myth explaining its origin. Brahmā wished to perform a sacrifice and went in search of a suitable location. Whilst travelling over some forest covered mountains he dropped a lotus (*puṣkara*) he was carrying in his hand. The spot where it landed was named Puṣkara.[84] It should be noted that the *Sṛṣṭikhaṇḍa*, in which this

---

most important place of pilgrimage in the entire list of places supplied by the Epic." From this he argues that Puṣkara's past and contemporary association with Brahmā worship suggests that Brahmā was a much more important deity during the 'epic period' than today.

80 *MBh.* 3, 80, 55

yathā surāṇāṃ sarveṣām ādis tu madhusūdanaḥ /
tathaiva puṣkaraṃ rājaṃs tīrthānām ādir ucyate //

The corresponding verse in the *PaP.* reads *pitāṃahaḥ* for *madhusūdanaḥ* and *pravaraḥ* for a *ādis*. See 5, 19, 22.

81 *MBh.* 3, 80, 53, 55-56. Trans. van Buitenen, 1975, p.374.

82 *MBh.* 3, 87, 13; 9, 37, 11.

83 *MBh.* 6, 13, 24 and 30; *BḍP.* 1, 19, 140-7. Cf. *ViP.* 2, 4, 86, "On Puṣkaradvīpa there is a Nyāgrodha tree which is Brahmā's highest abode. In that Brahmā dwells, worshipped (*pūjyamānaḥ*) by gods and demons." See also Hazra, 1958, p.41.

84 *PaP.* 5, 15, 82.

myth is found, is a product of Brahmā worshippers, hence the praise of Puṣkara. It spells out at length Brahmā's association with this spot and lists the results to be obtained from visiting it.[85]

Many Purāṇas include Puṣkara in their *tīrtha* listings, but few accord it the importance it receives in the *MBh.* or the *PaP.* nor do they bring out its association with Brahmā. An exception is what the *KP.* says of this *tīrtha*:

> Puṣkara is a *tīrtha* of Brahmā Parameṣṭhin which is famous in the three worlds. It destroys all evils and gives the dead access to the three worlds… There, gods, gandharvas, yakṣas, uragas, rākṣasas and the groups of siddhas attend upon (*upāsate*) Brahmā who was born from a lotus. When a pure man has bathed there and worshipped (*pūjayitvā*) Brahmā and the rest of the twice-born, he sees Brahmā quite clearly.[86]

The *KP.* probably received its present form some time between 550 and 750 CE, and the *tīrtha* chapters may have been incorporated as late as 1250 CE.[87] This means Puṣkara was known as a centre of Brahmā worship at least as late as the beginning of the eighth century CE and perhaps as late as the twelfth century.

Besides the information about Puṣkara there is other textual evidence of Brahmā worship in this part of western India. The *Virāṭaparvan* of the *MBh.* describes the thirteen months spent by the Pāṇḍavas and Draupadī at the court of King Virāṭa. During this period a festival dedicated to Brahmā took place:

> In the fourth month there took place in Matsya a very grand festival (*sumahotsava*) of Brahmā, richly celebrated, which the people held in great esteem. Wrestlers gathered there by the thousands from all countries, O King, gigantic and powerful men like Kālakhañja Asuras.[88]

Niīlakaṇṭha comments on this in the seventeenth century:

---

85 See the entire *Puṣkaramāhātmya*, *PaP.* 5, 19; especially verses 1-56.

86 *KP.* 2, 34, 39-42.

87 Hazra, 1940, pp.70-5.

88 *MBh.* 4, 12, 12-14. Trans van Buitenen, 1978, p.43.

Brahmā's festival is celebrated by all, and is held in autumn when the corn has begun to grow. It is famous in that particular area.[89]

Other than this nothing else is said about the festival. The Matsyas are frequently mentioned in the *MBh.* as the Pāṇḍavas' allies and were amongst those utterly annihilated in the final battle.[90] According to *Ms.* 2, 19, the plain of the Kurus and the country of the Matsyas, Pañcālas and Śūrasenakas form the country of the *brahmarṣis* and rank immediately after Brahmāvarta. It seems the author of this passage regarded all these areas, located in a three hundred mile circle around present-day Delhi or further south, as places infused with brāhmaṇical culture. As if supporting their orthodoxy, one *MBh.* passage contrasts the correct religious passages of the Matsyas with the incorrect and impure practices of the Bāhlikas.[91]

Kosambi raises the possibility that the Matsyas were one of the Ṛg-Vedic ten-kings confederacy, claiming that in historic times (?) people of this tribe were settled near modern-day Bharatpur.[92] Present knowledge of the Matsyas is meager, and apart from

---

89 Nīlakaṇṭha on *MBh.* (Vulgate) 4, 13, 14-16ab. His comment and the very reference to the festival itself give rise to the question of whether placing Brahmā's festival at harvest time means he was worshipped as a kind of fertility god. Meyer, 1936, Vol.3, pp.69-70, claims Brahmā was a fertility god, but the Purāṇic evidence he cites is not convincing (see Bailey, 1979, p.161, n.44). It is quite possible that this event could have been inspired by a passage in the *ŚB.* equating the various sacrificial officiants with the seasons. Of the *brahmā* it is said, "The *brahmā* is the autumn. Therefore, when the corn is ripe, the creatures are rich in *brahman* (*brahmaṇavatyaḥ*?), so they say." (11, 2, 7, 37) The attribution of this quality to the *brahmā* priest probably relates back to his central position in the sacrifice, itself an important source of fertility.

90 References to them are frequent in the *MBh.* but reveal little. See 1, 144, 2; 2, 13, 27; 2, 27, 8; 2, 48, 25; 8, 30, 60-2.

91 *MBh.* 8, 30, 60-2.

92 Kosambi, 1965, pp.81, 131. An early reference is *KauśU.* 4, 1,

the Brahmā festival and their reputed orthodoxy, nothing else is known about their religious attitudes. Yet, Puṣkara itself is located just slightly to the west of the area the Matsyas were traditionally believed to inhabit.

What of archeological evidence? To a large extent this is lacking. The Brahmā temple in the present day town was built at the beginning of the nineteenth century by a certain Gopal Parakh from Gwalior.[93] It was built on the site of former temples which may have been connected with Brahmā worship. Only excavations would confirm the antiquity of Brahmā worship here.

There is evidence that Pushkar may have merely been one centre of a Brahmā cult once extant over many parts of western India. In addition to Pushkar, Rajasthan has temples dedicated to Brahmā at Vasantgaḍh in Sirohi state and Sevadi near Jodhpur.[94] These date from the seventh century CE. In addition to these a colonial officer, visiting the remains of Chandrāvati near Abu in 1824, discovered the ruins of a Brahmā temple.[95] At Bhinmal, located fifty miles west of Abu, there is a Brahmakuṇḍa.[96] Further south, in Gujarat, there is a temple of Brahmā at Khed Brahmā (which was still in use in 1906); and there may once have been a shrine at Nagarā in Cambay.[97] Also in Gujarat there are ruins of a Brahmā temple at Mahisa in Kheda district and a shrine at Kamrej near Surat.[98]

In addition to this, epigraphic evidence yields more

---

where Gārgya Bālaki is said to have lived amongst several tribes including the Matsyas. See also Law, 1973, pp.357-62.

93 Tod, 1914, Vol.1 p.606. Other traditions about Pushkar can be found in the *Bombay Gazetteer*, 1901, Vol. 9. Pt. 1, pp.449-52.

94 On Vasantgaḍh see *Rajputana Gazetteer*, 1879-80, Vol. 3, p.303. On Sevadi see Sankalia, 1941, p.315.

95 *Rajputana Gazetteer*, 1879-80, Vol. 3, pp.298-9.

96 *Bombay Gazetteer*, 1901, Vol. 1, Pt. 1, pp.449-52.

97 On Khed Brahmā see Cousens, 1906-7, pp.173-8. On Nagarā see Mehta, 1968, p.174.

98 Sompura, 1968, p.174.

information. An inscription of 225 CE found at Nandsā in Udaipur state mentions that a Mālava king, Soma, had allotted space for temples sacred to Brahmā, Indra, Prajāpati, the great sages and Viṣṇu.[99] Another relevant inscription dates from 1289-90 CE found on an image of Brahmā from Cambay.[100] It states that a nobleman belonging to the Gauḍa caste had an image made for the peace of his parents. Other inscriptions make significant mention of Brahmā without making him a recipient of worship. One such is an inscription found on a gate in the town of Somnath-Pattan, saying that it is inhabited by sacrificers comparable to Brahmā, and that Brahmā smiled because of the uniqueness of the town in the whole of creation.[101] Seals bearing images of Brahmā along with inscriptions identifying their owners as brahmins skilled in the three (or four) Vedas have been found at Nalanda in Bihar and in the Kutch area of Gujarat.[102] These are generally assigned to the Gupta period. It may also be significant that on many inscriptions the Caulukya dynasty of Gujarat traces its lineage back to Brahmā.

All the evidence so far adduced indicates that at certain times between the third and thirteenth centuries CE Brahmā was worshipped in a particular part of western India. Evidence from the *MBh.* relating to Puṣkara and the Matsyas takes the earlier date back to the second century BCE, if this is a tentative beginning for dating the early parts of the *MBh.* At a much later date, after the fifteenth century CE, many miniature paintings depict Brahmā in a prominent position in relation to other gods in the same picture, and occasionally he is shown receiving *pūjā*.[103]

There is one more piece of evidence relevant to Brahmā worship in western India. The significance of the cosmogonic

---

99 *EI.* No. 27, p.265.

100 Mankad, 1949-50, pp.49-50.

101 Burgess, 1976, App. Insc., No.39.

102 Thapylal, 1972, p.259.

103 See Coomaraswamy, 1923, pl. lxx. This depicts a Rajasthani miniature of the early seventeenth century showing a princess performing *pūjā* to Brahmā in a palace.

section of the *MkP*. as indicating Brahmā's high position in the pantheon during a certain period has already been noted. It is often said there that he is the highest god, and in Chs. 45-50 epithets designating 'lordship' are used of him about one dozen times–a higher concentration than in any other Purāṇa I have examined, except perhaps for the *PaP*. In introducing his translation of the *MkP*, Pargiter divides its contents into five sections.[104] Of these, the third (Chs.45-81) containing the cosmogony, and the fifth (Chs.93-106), comprise the original form of the Purāṇa according to him. He places its origin in western India near the mouths of the Tapti and Narmadā rivers and dates the third and fifth sections to about the third century CE, the other sections being composed between this date and the sixth century CE.[105] It seems hardly coincidental that this Purāṇa, one of the few where Brahmā is treated as the highest god, should originate from western India, an area where there are so many other signs of Brahmā worship.

Finally mention should be made of the *Puṣkaramāhātmya*, which was probably composed in the medieval period, likely after the 10th century and before the 17th century, though Puṣkara is given some detailed coverage in the *PP*, composed at a much earlier period.[106] Notwithstanding this uncertainty Malik rightly points out that the number of locations in Rajasthan and Gujarat sacred to Brahmā may be indicative of his high status in these areas of India, in contrast to his relative absence in other areas. This may also be related to the fact that: "Perhaps the continuance of Puṣkara as a pilgrimage place of Brahmā, similar to the example of the Hāṭakeśvara-Māhātmya, represents an attempt–in the face of the confrontation with Islam since the middle ages–to preserve the status and identity of Brāhmaṇical-Hindu culture, which Brahmā embodies in a certain manner."[107] This definitely gives direction to further research on Brahmā in Gujarat and Rajasthan,

104 Pargiter, 1904, p.iv.

105 Pargiter, 1904, p.xiii-xx.

106 The arguments are given in Malik, 1993, pp.106-07.

107 Malik, 1993, p.20.

and may be usefully linked to sources for the worship of a *bhūta* named Bomma in Kerala.

Gayā and Environs

In the *tīṛthayātrāparvan* Gayā and surroundings are listed as the site of many *tīrthas*. The name Gayā itself is listed twice, but on neither occasion is Brahmā brought into connection with it.[108] However, there are at least three *tīrthas* in its immediate vicinity deriving their sacred character from him. The first is Brahmasaras, 'Lake of Brahmā', a place said to be ornamented with the forest of *dharma*.[109] Here Brahmā erected a sacrificial pole in the lake. The second and most famous is Brahmayoni hill, where Brahmā is said to have performed the creation and bathed with the other gods.[110] The third one is simply called Brahmatīrtha.[111] Because of the generality of its name it is difficult to give it a precise location. Jacques thinks it may be the same as Brahmakuṇḍa, located west of Gayā near the Pretasilā hill.[112]

Although Gayā in the Purāṇas seems primarily to be known as a centre of Vaiṣṇavism and Śaivism, its association with Brahmā is still discernible. In the *VāmP*. Gayāśiras (Brahmayoni) is the eastern altar (*vedī*) of Brahmā,[113] and in the *MP*. Gayā is the principle *tīrtha* of the *pitṛs* and the place where Brahmā himself

---

108 *MBh*. 3, 82, 74-5; 3, 85, 6.

109 *MBh*. 3, 82, 74-5; 13, 26, 55; 13, 151, 24; *BḍP*. 2, 13, 104; *AP*. 115, 34ff. For its exact location in modern-day Gayā see Jacques, 1962, p.xxxii. A comparison of *MBh*. 3, 82, 74ab with *PaP*. 1, 38, 5ab shows how the latter may have been reworked by Brahmā worshippers. The former reads *tato brahmasaro gacched dharmāraṇyopaśobhitam*, with the corresponding verse in the *PaP*. replacing *dharma* with *brahmā*. *Dharmāraṇya* could be a descriptor rather than a proper name.

110 *MBh*. 9, 46, 20-21; *VāmP. Saromāhātmya*. 18, 21-4.

111 *MBh*. 3, 82, 88.

112 Jacques, 1962, p.xxxiv. Cf. *AP*. 115, 36.

113 *VāmP*. 23, 21 and 24.

resides.[114] In the late sixteenth century CE a non-Hindu text–the *Āin-i-Akbari*–mentions Gayā: "Geya, the place of Hindoo worship, is in this sircar (of Behar); they call it Birhm Geya, being consecrated to Brahmā…"[115] Epigraphical evidence also connects Brahmā with Gayā. In an inscription of Nayapāla Deva taken from the Kṛṣṇadvārika temple at Gayā, dated from 1044-47 CE, it is said that Brahmā (*prajānāṃ pati*) resided at Gayā which was the unbarred door to *mokṣa*.[116] Other inscriptions of the same king tell of Gayā being created by Brahmā (Vedhas) as a city of brahmins.[117] There is no doubt that traces of Brahmā's importance still lingered on there at this time and he possibly still received worship.[118]

Gayā was also revered as a sacred place in Buddhist literature. It is certainly regarded as such in the Pāli Canon, though more important for it was Buddha Gayā, located five miles south of Gayā proper.[119] For it was here that the Buddha was tempted by Māra, gained enlightenment, and was entreated by Brahmā to preach the *dhamma*. The Chinese pilgrim Hsüan Tsang, travelling through India in the seventh century CE, accounted for some of the structures he saw around the Mahābodhi temple as being creations of Brahmā erected to commemorate the Buddha's enlightenment. In Watter's paraphrase of the Chinese original:

---

114 *MP*. 22, 4-5.

115 Gladwin, 1897, p.398. Cited by Jacques, 1962, p.lvi.

116 Chakravarti, 1900, pp.191ff.

117 EI. Vol. 36, pp.86-8.

118 In summing up the religious situation of Gayā in the medieval period, Jacques, 1962, p.lix, writes, "Brahmā himself had a high position, but already must have been partly supplanted by Śiva. In fact the references to Pitāmaha are ambiguous, and today we do not know if they concern Brahmā or Śiva. What is certain is that Pitāmaha, as Prapitāmaha, is represented under the form of a *liṅga*."

119 See Jacques, 1962, pp.xxi-v, for references to Gayā (not Buddha Gayā) in the Pāli Canon.

> ... near the Bodhi tree on the west side, was a large temple containing a bronze standing image of the Buddha adorned with precious stones... The temples represented the Hall of the seven substances made by Brahmā for Buddha on his attainment of Bodhi... .[120]

Writing of a *stūpa* and a temple located at the south-east corner of the Bodhi tree, he says: "The latter contained a sitting image of the Buddha, and was on the spot where Brahmā besought Buddha, on his attainment of Bodhi, to begin the preaching of his religion."[121] These traditions related by Hsüan Tsang reaffirm earlier biographical traditions represented in the *Lalitavistara* and the *Sutta-* and *Vinaya Piṭakas*. What needs to be noted is that Brahmā and Indra are the two Hindu gods most closely associated with the crucial events surrounding the Buddha's enlightenment at Buddha Gayā. Viṣṇu and Śiva are never mentioned. But this may not necessarily mean that only Brahmā and perhaps also Indra were worshipped at Gayā.

As for archeological evidence, the situation at Gayā is considerably better than at Puṣkara. The *tīrtha* at Brahmayoni is actually a spring issuing from a hill a mile and a half south-west of present day Gayā. On the summit of Brahmayoni hill there is a small temple about two hundred years old. In the *garbhagṛha* of this temple are found images of Sarasvatī, Gāyatrī, Sāvitrī and Pārvatī, the first three being consorts of Brahmā. At the hill's base there is a *kuṇḍa* dedicated to Sāvitrī. In another part of Gayā, at the foot of Pretasilā hill, there is a Brahmakuṇḍa which likely corresponds to the Brahmatīrtha of the *MBh.* and the Purāṇas. When Francis Buchanan visited this spot in the early nineteenth century the only object of worship he found there was the Brahmapad, Brahmā's feet depicted as impressions of two feet cut in a square stone.[122] He also writes of a modern temple there: "The other object of worship in the temple is a mark on a rock supposed to have been made by

120 Watters, 1904-5, Vol. 2, p.121.

121 Watters, 1904-5, p.125.

122 See Jackson, 1925, p.33.

Brahmā."[123] Buchanan believed that the mark was probably of a very late origin, yet it does show that even in the early nineteenth century there was a tradition of Brahmā being in Gayā.

The two small towns of Rajgir and Nalanda, located about fifty miles north of Gayā, also appear to be places where Brahmā once was and still is worshipped. Rajgir (as Rājagaha) is frequently mentioned in Pāli texts as a place the Buddha often visited, and where he sometimes had conversations with Brahmā Sanatkumāra.[124] It appears in the *tīrtha* list of the *MBh*, though it is not specified as being sacred to any particular god.[125] At the southern end of the present town there is a large complex of shrines and temples centred around a Brahmakuṇḍa. The latter is a rectangular pit about ten feet below ground level, into which a hot spring flows. Along the side of its walls there are twelve identical images of Brahmā, each having one head and seated in *padmāsana*. They do not appear to be very old. When I visited it in December 1975 many people were performing *pūjā* there with flowers and money strewn in front of the images. There are several other *kuṇḍas* in this temple complex, some containing images of Brahmā. Slightly to the north of the actual Brahmakuṇḍa is to be found a large Viṣṇu temple. It appears to be related to Brahmā in some way, judging from the images of the god located in the roof near the centre of each wall. Although the images and the shrines are of recent age, there is a possibility temples and shrines have existed on this site since the Gupta period.[126]

123 Jackson, 1925, p.34. Cf. pp.48-9, for other reputed activities of Brahmā in Gayā. On p.54 he writes about a Brahmā temple he discovered in an area slightly east of Buddha Gayā: "In an area of several temples, the last temple is that of Brahmā but I am persuaded that all figures are that of Nastik." The existence of such a temple has not been mentioned in later surveys of Buddha Gayā undertaken by Mitra, Cunningham and others.

124 Eg. *SN*. 1, 151-3.

125 *MBh*. 3, 82, 89.

126 Information received from the Director-General of Archeology,

Evidence of Brahmā worship at Nalanda comes from the thousands of seals found at the site of the old Buddhist university there, most carrying figures of bodhisattvas or of a *dharmacakra* flanked by gazelles.[127] Only a few seals have been recovered that carry figures of Hindu deities. They are generally dated at about the seventh or eighth century CE.[128] Brahmā figures appear on some seals and are usually accompanied by an inscription stating that the seal's owner is a brahmin proficient in the three vedas (*traividya*).[129] It is to be expected that Brahmā would be 'patron' of those people devoted to Vedic study, because this is the background of orthodoxy from which he came and which is so strongly reflected in the roles he plays in mythology.

Admittedly, the evidence from Nalanda is sparse, but when placed together with what has come from Gayā and Rajgir does lend support to the view that Brahmā was widely worshipped in this part of Bihar. From a very early period Gayā has been a place of great sanctity for Hindus and so it is probable that it was the original centre for Brahmā worship in these parts of India.

Evidence of Brahmā Worship in Other Parts of India

There is also considerable evidence of sporadic worship of Brahmā in other parts of India. In addition to the Brahmā temple at Pushkar, Banerjea lists three 'early medieval and late' Brahmā shrines located at Dudahai and Khajuraho in Madhya Pradesh and at Unkal near Hubli in Mysore.[130] Oppert lists four Brahmā temples located in South India.[131] One of these at Cebrolu (in the Krishna District, Tamil Nadu) was built near a Brahmakuṇḍa and dates from the eighteenth century CE. The other three are located at Kalahasti (North Arcot), Kutanar (near Mayavaram) and

---

Bihar State in December 1975.

127 Sastri, 1942, p.26.

128 Thapylal, 1972, pp.258-9.

129 Thapylal, 1972, pp.193-4, 258.

130 Banerjea, 1956, pp.514-15. See also Deva, 1969, pp.51-2.

131 Oppert, 1893, pp.292-6.

Tiruvannamalai. He also mentions a Brahmā temple at Varanasi and I have personally seen Brahmā ghats built along the bank of the Ganges in Varanasi. The Bombay Gazetteer mentions a Brahmā temple at Kolhapur in Maharashtra.[132]

In his section on Brahmā Oppert devotes a few pages to the belief in the Brahmabhūta. He writes:

> Among the population of the west coast, especially among the Tulus, where the devil-worship prevails, Brahman is not only revered as a god, but also as a spirit or Bhūta. In fact all castes worship him, and he is universally adored; he has in reality his special place of worship in nearly every big landed estate. At Sirva, Brahman is represented with four heads, his image is about two feet high and is made of *Pancaloha* or the five metals, gold, silver, copper, tin and lead. He rides on the goose or hamsa in the usual position, one of his hands holding a water jar, while the other has a rosary or *japamālā*, and the two remaining are folded on the chest and contain the Sālagrāma. The officiating Brahman or *bhaṭṭa* enters the temple daily after his bath with a water jar and pours the water over the image. He then fills, while muttering the usual mantras, the holy sankha (conch-shell) with water and sprinkles the latter over the image. This done, he puts sandal and a garland on the head of the idol and offers some cooked rice to the god. These ceremonies occupy about three hours. The evening service is the same but only shorter, it lasts about two hours. The neighbouring Brahmans and Sūdras celebrate every year a great festival, during which the image of Brahman is carried about within the precincts of the temple and a special *pūjā* is performed.[133]

This god is portrayed in sculpture in human form riding on a horse and holding a sword in his right hand, As such he corresponds to the god Brahmadeva, belief in whom is widespread even today amongst some of the tribal societies on the Karnataka coast.[134]

---

132 *Bombay Gazetteer*, 1901, Vol. 9, pt.1, p.502, n.4.

133 Oppert, 1893, pp.296-7. Cf. *Bombay Gazetteer*, 1901, Vol. 9, pt. 1, p.502, n.4.

134 Settar, 1971, pp.34-7.

These observations raise a number of questions. To what extent does the figure who is called Brahmabhūta, Brahmadeva, Bomma and Bharma among other names, represent a continuation of the Brahmā of the epics and Purāṇas? And if there is continuity, does it mean that the worship of Brahmadeva under these names is a continuity of Brahmā worship under a form different from what might be expected from a reading of the classical texts? Until more research is undertaken on the cult of Brahmadeva/Brahmabhūta and the development of Brahmā worship in western and southern India, only tentative answers can be given to these questions.

There are some features of the Brahmabhūta described by Oppert that definitely appear to have resemblances in Brahmā's mythology. The Tulus have a myth about Brahmā's fifth head being cut off by Śiva:

> A legend asserts that the fifth head of Brahman, after being cut off, prayed to Paramesvara, who advised it to descend to the earth and to associate with the bhūtas. According to a Tulu tradition the present Brahman (Bermere, Berume, Baruma, Bermā or Bomma) is only a portion of Brahman united with the serpent god (nāga dēvaru). Śiva is said to have been jealous because Brahman had four faces and eight eyes, while he had only three. He therefore cut off one of these four heads, and when this head asked him what he should do, Śiva told him to unite itself with the serpent (nāga), torment mankind and to extort the offerings for himself.[135]

This is just a version of the famous Purāṇic myth which recounts how Śiva cuts off Brahmā's fifth head and as a consequence is pursued by the personified *brahmahatyā*, 'the act of killing a *brāhmaṇa*'.[136] None of the Purāṇic versions of the myth seem to include the motif of the severed head uniting itself with a *nāga* and tormenting human beings. However, the evil nature of the severed head is implied in the Tulu myth and also in many Purāṇic versions

---

135 Oppert, 1893, pp.300-1. For another version see p.299, n.17. See also Brückner, 1995, p.186-97; 482-85; 500-504, for some more myths involving Bemmeru.

136 See *ŚP*. 3, 8, 36-9, 1-57; *KP*. 2, 31, 1-111; *VāmP*. 2, 18-3, 51.

where it is depicted as saying evil things, manifesting excessive pride and even gazing at women forbidden to Brahmā. This kind of example certainly suggests continuity between the Brahmā of the epics and Purāṇas and the contemporary Brahmadeva/ Brahmabhūta. An analysis of all the myths about the latter deity would probably reveal a large dependence on the epics and Purāṇas for motifs and imagery.

Chronology of Brahmā Worship

It is well known that very few Indian texts can be dated with any degree of certainty. Therefore, since much of the evidence for Brahmā worship is textual, any attempt to date the main period of his popularity and worship will necessarily be speculative. The *tirthayātrāparvan* lists about twenty *tīrthas* sacred to Brahmā. Apart from those already discussed the remainder are located in central India around the Ganges-Jumna Doab and further along the Ganges to Prayāga. It is probable that by the time of most of the Purāṇas the number of *tīrthas* listed as sacred to Brahmā have considerably diminished, whereas those sacred to Viṣṇu and Śiva have increased. Due to sectarian reworking of the majority of Purāṇas it is difficult to know for certain if this diminution does actually mirror the pattern of worship in northern India during the period(s) reflected in the Purāṇas. If Brahmā was ever widely worshipped over North-central India–the evidence from the *Mbh*, some Purāṇas and the Pāli Canon suggests this–then it must have been during the period reflected in the *Mbh*, the original form of the *Rām*. and the older Pāli texts.

Van Buitenen speculates that the origin of the main plot of the *Mbh*. falls somewhere in the eighth or ninth century BCE.[137] Its scene of action is the Ganges-Jumna Doab and it reflects an earlier period than the *Rām*. whose main scene of action is further east in Kosala. He goes on to assign a rough dating of composition of the text included in the Cr. Ed. as lying between four hundred BCE

---

137 Van Buitenen, 1973, p.xxix.

and four hundred CE.[138] This gives an eight hundred year period during which Brahmā could have been a popular god, widely worshipped in the area already suggested.

Holtzmann believed that Brahmā was a product of the older sections of the *Mbh.*, though he does not explain what these old sections are, or to what period they are to be dated.[139] There is little doubt that in the twelfth and thirteenth books of the *Mbh.* Viṣṇu and Śiva are much more important than in the other books. But Brahmā too has an important position in these supposedly late books–in part because they map the filling out of the *trimūrti* doctrine as a theological organizational scheme–and Kṛṣṇa seems to be the dominant deity in the first ten books.

Brahmā's earliest appearances in Sanskrit literature are in the late Brāhmaṇas and the early Upaniṣads. Both series of texts belong to a milieu in which sacrifice was the basis of religious thought and praxis, though the Upaniṣads do introduce important speculations about the nexus between the *ātman* and Brahman. The Brāhmaṇas contain a distinct mythology centred on the theory of sacrifice as an organizing principle, however Brahmā himself never appears in this mythology even though the world-view it inculcates is expressed in his roles in the epics and Purāṇas. So the late Vedic texts furnish no information about Brahmā other than that he was known in India at that time, perhaps from eight hundred to six hundred BCE.

If the Hindu texts are difficult to date, so too are the early canonical Pāli texts which contain so much material about Brahmā, and probably reflect a period when he was an important god widely worshipped in north India or represented

---

138 Van Buitenen, 1973, p.xxv.

139 Holtzmann, 1884, pp.167-9. Cf. von Schroeder, 1887, p.461, "The time when the personified Brahmā was worshipped as the foremost, undisputed and supreme God, lies perhaps between the seventh and fourth century BC. And because of that, in my opinion the first composition of the Mahābhārata as a great heroic poem must have taken place in the same period."

the emerging brahmin *varṇa*. What however is the period this body of texts reflects? It is reasonably certain that the division of the Canon into the *tripiṭaka* must have been complete before the second century BCE, because *brahmī* inscriptions of this period contain the words *trepiṭaka*, 'versed in the *tripiṭakas*' and *peṭika*, 'versed in a *piṭika*'.[140] Presumably the individual *piṭakas* or individual *suttas* existed for a few centuries before being grouped together, so individual *suttas* could conceivably date back to four hundred BCE. At the least many *suttas* must date back to the third century BCE, a date corresponding well to the earlier period of the *Mbh*. Hence, it is probable Brahmā was a very popular and widely worshipped god in north-central and north-east India (and perhaps western India) from the beginning of the fourth century BCE or slightly earlier.

It is more difficult to date the decline in his popularity and when he ceased to be worshipped on a large scale. He continues to be worshipped in various parts of India as the object of devotional practices and this probably holds good for the whole period beginning about the fourth century CE. It is probable he was still worshipped over a large area of western India when the cosmogonic sections of the *MkP*. and the *Sṛṣṭi-khaṇḍa* of the *PaP*. were first composed. Certainly he must have been popular in the specific areas where these texts received their particular 'brahmāising' imprint. Pargiter thought the date of the cosmogonic sections of the *MkP*. was about the third century CE.[141] The *Sṛṣṭi-khaṇḍa* probably reached its final form by the tenth century CE but the first nineteen chapters, definitely showing the imprint of Brahmā worshippers, were most likely composed in the middle of the fifth century CE.[142] A Brahmā sect may have existed in the sixth century CE since the astronomer Varāhamihira states that only those well versed in the Vedas could install

140 Lamotte, 1958, pp.164-5.

141 Pargiter, 1904, p.iv.

142 Chatterjee, 1967, pp.35-6.

Brahmā images, just as only Bhāgavatas and Pāśupatas could install images of Viṣṇu and Śiva.[143] In addition, the chapters on image-making in the *MP*, composed between 550 and 650CE, contain instructions about the construction and consecration of Brahmā images.[144] However, rather than being definite evidence for the existence of a Brahmā cult, both the latter examples may merely represent a desire for completeness by their respective author(s).

In short, on the basis of available evidence it seems likely Brahmā was worshipped over certain parts of northern India from about 400 BCE to 400 CE.[145] If the older parts of the Pāli Canon accurately mirror the state of brāhmaṇical culture during the Buddha's time, the earlier date can be pushed back to at least 400BCE.

Was Brahmā ever worshipped as a Bhakti god?

Gonda has defined the notion of a personal god in Indian religion in the following way:

> The Supreme Being as the Creator, the ruler and sustainer of the Universe as primal and eternal, benevolent and the Father of men, as invisible, omniscient and the guardian of morality. Finally, to be the truly supreme Being, the personal God (with a capital) must be unique.[146]

I would add that for this god to be personal there would also have to exist the possibility of an unmediated relationship between god and devotee. All of these features are found in what I would term a *bhakti* god,[147] one who is regarded as supreme by his or

143 *Bṛhatsaṃhitā*, 60, 19. Cited in Chatterjee, 1967, p.10.

144 See Chatterjee, 1967, p.10.

145 Cf. the dates given by Hacker, 1961, p.112. On the basis of a text-critical analysis of certain passages of the *MBh.* he argues for the existence of a Brahmā sect beginning at a time between the first centuries BCE and CE and lasting until the fifth century CE.

146 Gonda, 1975, Vol. 4, p.1.

147 See further Bailey, 1998.

her worshippers, who is worshipped with *pūjā* and who extends favour (*prasāda*) to devotees.

Much of the evidence so far cited from the literature, both Hindu and Buddhist, suggests Brahmā was worshipped in ways characteristic of a *bhakti* god. In some passages a cluster of epithets ending with the words *deva* and *īśa* are used of him. Such epithets are consistently used in Indian literature of the supreme personal god, and, of course, very frequently of Viṣṇu and Śiva. Brahmā too is portrayed as the recipient of *pūjā*, and as being worshipped with flowers and incense, all characteristic *bhakti* modes of worship. Finally, in some contexts he is asked by certain individuals to extend his favour to them. In making such a request they are functionally his *bhaktas*.

Contemporary evidence of Brahmā worship also leads to the conclusion that he was worshipped as a *bhakti* god. Modes of worship practised at Rājgir have already been cited in this context. An earlier view of Brahmā worship is given by Cousens in his description of the Brahmā temple at Khed Brahmā, which was still operative in 1906:

> The temple worship is carried out by Kheḍāvala Brāhmaṇas (i.e. resident Brāhmaṇas of Kheḍ Brahmā) who are Audīcha Brāhmaṇas and followers of the Śukla Yajurveda. Worship is performed twice daily, in the morning before 10 o'clock, and in the evening at about seven. It is conducted without reciting the Vedic mantras, the Purāṇic mantras only being used. The things used in daily worship are water, sandal, rice and sugar. The image is bathed on both occasions. On the fifteenth of Srāvana Suddha the annual mahā worship is performed, when, in addition to the things used in daily worship, other things are added, viz. the ablution with milk, curds, ghi, honey and sugar, and then the naivedya consists of cooked food. Mahā pūjās are also performed on Dīvāli days… .[148]

---

148 Cousens, 1906-7, p.177.

No doubt a similar kind of worship is carried out in the Brahmā temple at Pushkar.[149]

Despite this evidence, the view that Brahmā was (and is) widely worshipped as a *bhakti* god can only be made with the greatest reserve. At best the evidence cited is sporadic. What is lacking are the detailed handbooks of theology and ritual worship found in respect of Viṣṇu and Śiva, either in the Purāṇas or in specific kinds of texts such as the *Pañcarātrasaṃhitas*. Nor does Brahmā's role in mythology suggest he was conceived of as a *bhakti* god. Unlike Viṣṇu and Śiva he does not transcend the Law (*dharma*) or reflect the notion of *mokṣa* as his ultimate value. On the occasions when he is asked to confer immortality (which is technically the same as *mokṣa*) by demons whose ultimate aim is to violate the Law (*adharma*), he refuses it.[150] His refusal is based on a strict adherence to the Law: that immortality is restricted to those who have it by virtue of their birth into a particular class of beings, such as gods.

Viṣṇu and Śiva, on the contrary, paradoxically transcend the Law at times and often grant *mokṣa* as a reward for single-minded devotion to them, even to those beings who have violated the Law.

---

149 For some details see *https://en.wikipedia.org/wiki/Brahmā_Temple,_Pushkar*. Sighted 2/4/2019.

150 See below pp. 290-93.

PART TWO
Preliminaries

Chapter 2

Value Systems in Hindu Mythology

The Hindu epics and Purāṇas are a vast repository of mythology. Within this body of literature there are thousands of tellings of myths, the majority being mere variants of each other, utilizing a common stock of motifs and imagery. In the literature of all periods the same myth is commonly found recurring in dozens of versions. These myths are constructed from motifs such as the conflict between gods and demons, Agni's withdrawal of his flame, the incest of the creator with his daughter, the diminution of the Law on the earth and its resurgence, creation and destruction of the cosmos, Śiva's marriage to Pārvatī, and many others. However, the myths themselves are not subordinate to the motifs. They derive their content from the finite stock of motifs and their particular form from the way the motifs interact.

To grasp the meaning (or meanings) of these myths it is essential not only to have a thorough knowledge of the motifs, but also to penetrate beneath them to the value systems[1] expressed through the myths and which also have a shaping influence on them. The underlying presence of such value systems becomes clear after a reading of the myths and the expository śāstric literary

---

1 Throughout this book I have used the term 'value system' in a sense similar to 'ideology' as denoting an abstract system of ideas embodying a distinct view of the world and of the behaviour of people within it, and which is represented in all kinds of media in most cultures. Usually these value systems are both implicit and explicit, and are occasionally elaborated in formal language.

material scattered throughout the same texts in which the myths appear. The *Mbh.* and the Purāṇas are full of so-called expository material, covering topics such as kingship, the conduct of people in the various classes and stages of life (*varṇāśramadharma*), cosmogony, worship, and a multitude of others. Both myths and expository material are concerned with similar subjects, but because they belong to different genres their treatment of these subjects is different. Yet, though the connection is sometimes difficult, the same sets of values can be glimpsed beneath both myth and expository material.

Dumézil and Wikander have interpreted the mythology of the *Mbh.* from the perspective of the tri-functional ideology, so prominent in many branches of Indo-European mythology.[2]Their studies have largely been restricted to the first level of epic mythology, that is, to the conflict between the Pāṇḍavas and the Kauravas. Yet these studies definitely have important implications for the second level of epic mythology, that which concerns the gods and demons, insofar as the combatants in the Bhārata war are portions of these gods and demons reborn on earth.

The tri-functional ideology is reflected in the figures of Brahmā, Viṣṇu and Śiva, the most important gods in the epics and Purāṇas. As such it can be used as one key to unlock the meaning of the roles they perform in mythology. A striking illustration of tri-functionalisrn in the characters of these gods occurs in a passage of the *Kathāsaritsāgara*, a medieval text whose contents rework and comment upon those those of the epics and Purāṇas. In a list of the gods who come to witness a particular battle, each of the three gods is described in the following way:

> And Śaṅkara, the Lord of the universe, came there, accompanied by Pārvatī and followed by the gods, the hosts (*gaṇas*), the spirits and the mothers. And the illustratious Brahmā came, along with Sāvitrī and the rest, the personified Vedas, the appendices, the

---

2 Dumézil, 1968, pp. 1-257. The analysis of epic in terms of the tri-functional ideology has also been successfully applied to the *Rām*. See Dubuisson, 1979, pp. 464--89.

> *śāstras* and the great sages. And Hari, a warrior armed with a discus, whose chariot is the king of birds, came, together with his wives led by Lakṣmī, Kirtī and Jayā.[3]

The companions of each god are a broad reflection of that god's role in mythology, and they also correspond neatly to one of the three functions. Brahmā and his companions are strongly representative of the first function–priesthood, religion and the sovereign aspect of kingship. The Vedas and the Śāstras are sources of religious knowledge and Brahmā's wife Sāvitrī, carries the name given to the verse (*RV*. 3, 62, 10) taught immediately after the *upanayana* to every male member of the three twice-born *varṇas*. It is a symbol of the knowledge he will acquire. Finally, the great sages, symbolic of religious learning and wisdom, are definitely characteristic of the third function. Viṣṇu's companions indicate that he represents the second function–the dynamic aspect of kingship and martial force. The discus and chariot are signs of his warlike nature just as his three consorts are personifications of characteristics kings were believed to possess. Śiva conforms least of the three gods to any one function, but it is clearly to the third, if any. Not much can be said about the *gaṇas*, *bhūtas* and *devatās*, each of whom are classes of divine beings. The first two might represent Śiva in his ferocious aspect. It is the mothers, however, who directly relate Śiva to the third function, because they probably represent fertility, an important third function characteristic. This passage is only one of several where the individual gods of the *trimūrti* can be shown to conform to the tri-functional ideology.[4]

Yet it would be incorrect to assume the roles they perform should be only, or even primarily, understood in terms of this ideology. Whilst it has had a discernible influence on their roles and on Hindu mythology generally, it is certainly not the only or the most important influence. In the first place, the activities of each god range right across the three functions. A second and

---

3 *Kathāsaritsāgara*, 8, 4, 46-8.

4 For further examples see Bailey, 1981, pp.152-63.

more significant point is that each god in his own way relates to asceticism understood as a set of values and associated practices. Asceticism only fits with difficulty into Dumézil's third function. Each god's relatedness to asceticism and themes associated with it, reflects the importance in the epics and Purāṇas of a distinct set of values based on asceticism and the institutionalized practice of the abandonment of the world of social hierarchy.

Biardeau and O Flaherty have taken account of this set of values in their studies of epic and Purāṇic mythology,[5] underlying much of which they see two distinct and opposed sets of values. On the one hand there are the values of society-renouncing ascetics; on the other hand there are those of orthoprax caste society. The renouncer seeks to attain ultimate release from *saṃsāra* by consciously abandoning the values of the orthoprax Hindu society with its emphasis on reciprocal obligations between interdependent groups, an emphasis consistent only with a life of action (*karma*) in conformity with *varṇāśramadharma*. The renouncer abandons society in order to live alone in the forest. In this way he becomes an 'individual' in the sense that he no longer derives his identity, his occupation and his wife through birth into one specific caste (*jāti*), membership of which determines and sanctions all these. In brief, he becomes his own man–and it was usually men–, determining his own fate.

In the mythology and the expository portions of the epics and Purāṇas, the tension between two sets of opposed values comes to the fore. The possibility of living in conformity with either one or both life styles implied by these value systems is explored to the full. This is done with great clarity in the contrasting portrayals of Śiva as an orthoprax householder at one time and at another as a very austere ascetic, a renouncer. The same possibility is also presented in the roles of some of the other major gods. Similarly, the fundamental incompatibility of both life styles is continually brought out in the myths, as is the theoretical and practical reconciliation offered by *bhakti*. This reconciliation reflects the

5 See Biardeau, 1968, 1969 and 1971; O'Flaherty, 1973.

influence of what might be called devotional values, in part an amalgam of the other two because of encompassing both. Each of these three sets of values–with their accompanying life-styles–can be shown to have greatly influenced and shaped Hindu mythology. Thus an understanding of each is invaluable for determining the meaning of this mythology and the roles of the gods who give life to it.

Pravṛttidharma

The sets of values associated with life in orthoprax caste society and conscious abandonment of society are referred to in the Hindu texts as *pravṛttidharma* and *nivṛttidharma* respectively.[6] One passage also refers to a *yoga* of *pravṛtti* and *nivṛtti*, whilst another uses the word *pravṛttimārga*, a term close enough in meaning to *pravrttidharma* to be regarded as a synonym.[7] The existence of such compounds as these immediately implies a distinct body of underlying values governing a life style conforming to what the two base words mean. The literal meaning of *pravṛtti* is 'rolling onwards' or 'act of turning around', and this implies movement and activity. Contrary to this, *nivṛtti* means 'act of turning back' or 'act of returning', thus implying abandonment of activity. Hence the fundamental polarity in life style symbolized by these two words is already discernible in their literal meaning.

In the following definition taken from the *Mbh*, ontological and behavioural differences between the two life styles are stressed:

> The sage Nārāyaṇa said there is a *dharma* characterized by *pravṛtti*, and on it alone are based the entire three worlds, moving and non-moving. The *dharma* characterized by *nivṛtti* is the unmanifest eternal Brahman.
>
> Prajāpati then said there is a *dharma* characterized by *pravṛtti*. *Pravṛtti* is repeated returning. *Nivṛtti* is the highest refuge. *The*

---

6 *MBh*. 12, 210, 2-5; 12, 327; 12, 335, 68; *Gayāmāhātmya*. 3, 6. *MkP*. 24-42; *GP*. 3, 1, 38.

7 See respectively *MBh*. 14, 43, 24; *ViP*. 1, 6, 31.

> *sage* who is intent upon true knowledge and always perceives both good and evil [equally] is completely occupied with *nivṛtti*. He comes to the highest refuge.[8]

Although nothing is said here about action, the commentator Vidyāsagara sees *pravṛtti* as characterized by obligatory action (*kārya*) and deriving from *saṃsāra*.[9]

Signs of a division of orthoprax Brāhmaṇism into two main streams, each stressing fundamentally different social and religious views, are evident in the oldest Upaniṣads. Certain passages in the *BhU.* are critical of people who desire worldly acquisitions such as sons and wealth, whilst exalting those who become ascetics with a final aim of realizing Brahman.[10] A further sign of this divergence is the distinction made in this same Upaniṣad between the 'path leading to the fathers' (*pitṛyāna*) and the 'path leading to the gods' (*devayāna*).[11] Those following the former path are destined to be reborn in this world after death. They are said to live in villages and to worship with sacrifices, gratification (*iṣṭapūrta*) and giving. However, those who are on the latter path live in the forest, have confidence in austerity (*tapas*), and will eventually realise Brahman. This division between forest and village is symbolic of the different locational centres of the ascetic and the so-called 'man-in-the-world' who lives in society. The ascetic lives in solitude beyond areas of habitation, that is, outside the village, whereas the life of the 'man-in-the-world' is centred in the village, amongst people. It is significant in this regard that *grāma*, the Sanskrit word for village, designates a concentration of men rather than a specific spatial area.[12]

---

8 *MBh.* 12, 210, 2cd-5. Cf. *Ms.* 12, 89-90; *KP.* 1, 2, 61ff. For other discussions of these two important words see Held, 1935, pp.145-46; Gonda, 1960, Vol. 1, pp.279-83; Biardeau, 1969, pp.81-7; Bailey, 1985; 2004; 2005.

9 See critical notes on *MBh.* 12, 210, 2.

10 *BhU.* 3, 5, 1; 4, 4, 22.

11 *BhU.* 6, 2, 2; 6, 2, 14-16; *ChU.* 5, 10, 1-7.

12 See Malamoud, 1976, pp.4-5.

Other Upaniṣadic passages assert with considerable force that the efficacy of the sacrifice and reliance on ritual knowledge based on the Vedas is much inferior to austerity as a means of realizing Brahman. The *MU.* distinguishes higher (*para*) knowledge which is about Brahman from lower (*apara*) knowledge, comprising the contents of the Vedas and Vedāṅgas dealing with ritual.[13] The danger in placing reliance on the lower knowledge as a means of avoiding rebirth is stressed in several passages of this text, but not so strongly as in the following:

> Unsafe ships are these which have the form of the sacrifice. The eighteen in which the inferior work is expressed. Deluded people praise that as the best. They certainly go to old age and death, again and again.[14]

This same passage goes on to say that those who perform actions (or sacrifices-*karma*) cannot understand the truth because they are affected by impetuous desire (*rāga*). For these people, sacrifice and acquisition of merit are the most important goals to be achieved. Yet by those who follow the other stream, which leads to Brahman, they are considered to be deluded. They are themselves said to be without impetuous desire (*viraja*).[15] It is noteworthy that in the *Mbh.* and the Purāṇas the word *rajas*, which in its psychological sense is the direct opposite of *viraja*, is virtually synonymous with *pravṛtti*.

Just as the Upaniṣads illustrate the presence of a conflict between socio-religious values embodied in the notions of *pravṛtti* and *nivṛtti*, so do they reveal that attempts were made to resolve it. Two passages in the *ChU.* suggest a resolution along the lines of the classical *āśrama* system. In one of these passages it is proposed that a person who wishes to realize Brahman and not experience rebirth in the world should at first live as a *brahmacārin*, then as a householder, and in the final stage of his life he should concentrate his senses upon the *ātman* and

---

13 *MU.* 1, 1, 4-5.

14 *MU.* 1, 2, 7.

15 *MU.* 1, 2, 9-11.

only perform animal sacrifices at holy places.[16] The first three stages of the classical *āśrama* system are present here, the final stage being the equivalent of *vānaprastha*. In this stage of life a compromise is made between householder and renouncer, village and forest. *Saṃnyāsa*, the fourth stage of the classical system, is conspicuously absent from the *ChU.* passage. This could mean the line between the *vānaprastha* and *saṃnyāsa* stages did not exist at that time or that certain ascetics were in a category of their own completely beyond the confines of the three tier system. There is textual evidence in support of the latter view. In the *ŚvetU.* it is said that Śvetāśvatara declared the knowledge of Brahman to ascetics who were 'beyond the stages of life' (*atyāśramin*).[17] Another later Upaniṣad, one reflecting the renouncers' values, also refers to sages (*yati*) who are 'situated beyond the stages of life' (*atyāśramastha*).[18] They are described as having successively honoured their *guru*, thoroughly suppressed the influence of their sense organs and contemplated on the lotus-like heart which is pure, shining, free from sorrow and unsoiled by impetuous desire (*viraja*). Thus in spite of this attempt at a theoretical resolution between renunciation and 'life-in-the-world', the existing gap was by no means successfully bridged.

The *Mbh.* and the Purāṇas develop the differences between *pravṛttidharma* and *nivṛttidharma* much further than the Upanisads. These differences are presented at considerable length in a dialogue between Janamejaya and Vaiśaṃpāyana:

> [Janamejaya speaking] "The illustrious god, the Lord, takes the first offering in the sacrifices, constantly upholds the sacrifices and knows the Vedas and their auxiliaries, and yet has affirmed that teaching pertaining to the attitude of turning away from the world (*nivṛtti*). How can the god who is loved by the

16 *ChU.* 8, 15. Cf. 2, 23, 1.

17 *ŚvetU.* 6, 21. Cf. Weinrich, 1929-30, p.83, n.2, who suggests that *atyāśramin* might mean 'one who has put work behind himself.' See also Olivelle, 1993, pp.222-232.

18 *KaivalyaU.* 5.

Bhāgavatas, who is secure and still, the illustrious Lord, ordain the teachings pertaining to the attitude of activity in the world (*pravṛtti*)? How are the gods made worthy of their portions in the teachings pertaining to the attitude of activity in the world? And how are those whose minds have been turned back inculcated in the attitude of turning away from the world?...

... These worlds with their gods, demons and humans, accompanied by Brahmā, seem in every respect to be attached to rituals said to pertain to growth. But, brahmin, you have spoken of that liberation which is repose and supreme happiness. And those who are liberated on Earth, are without good merit and evil, and enter the god of a thousand rays, so we have heard. But look here! This is the eternal teaching pertaining to *mokṣa* which is so difficult to accomplish, having abandoned which all the gods have become eaters of oblations offered to the gods and ancestors.

Furthermore, how is it that Brahmā, Rudra, Śakra, mighty killer of Vala, Sūrya, the Moon, Vāyu, Agni, and also Varuṇa, the atmosphere, the two worlds, and all the remaining heaven dwellers, do not recognize their own destruction as being circumscribed, because of which they do not adopt the path which is permanent, undecaying, imperishable?

Therefore they do not reside on the eternal, stable and indestructible path. Having conceived of time as their measure they are engaged in *pravṛtti*. Focussing on time as the measure, these have adopted the attitude of on-going activity. For those who perform rituals there is a major fault in using time as a measure...."

[Vaiśaṃpāyana then narrates a creation myth beginning with the *puruṣa* and ending with Brahmā's sons creating the universe. The gods ask Viṣṇu what functions they should perform.]

[Viṣṇu speaking] "Gods, I am pleased with you. I will now point out to you the result of action characterized by return. Gods, this is your characteristic which has originated from my favour (*prasāda*). You are being sacrificed to in excellent sacrifices where honorariums (*dakṣinā*) are obtained. In *yuga* after *yuga* you will be those who enjoy the fruits of activity. Moreover, Gods, in all worlds men will sacrifice in sacrifices and distribute to you sacrificial portions prepared in accordance with the Vedas. In conformity with the Vedic *sūtras*, whoever should offer me a portion in a great sacrifice, will be made worthy by me of receiving a sacrificial portion. You are augmented by the results gained from the sacrifice and so you must sustain the worlds. You contemplate on all things and so have been created with spheres of responsibility in the world.

You are honoured with the results accruing from ritual activity and so you will perform these rituals. Your strength has increased through them and you will sustain the worlds. For you will be sustained in all sacrifices in the world of men. Then you will have to promote my welfare. Your welfare is mine. For this reason the Vedas and the sacrifices were created in conjunction with plants, because with these applied correctly on Earth the deities are pleased. This is your creation and it has been arranged according to the quality of ongoing activity, which I made, best of the gods, until the end of the *kalpa*. Lords, contemplate on the welfare of the worlds as this pertains to your spheres of responsibility."

Marīci, Aṅgiras, Atri, Pulastya, Pulaha, Kratu and Vaṣiṣṭha were the seven created by the mind. They were instituted to be the principal knowers of the Vedas and as teachers of the Vedas, and instituted as those who embody the regulations pertaining to the attitude of activity in the world in view of their role as Lords of men. This is manifested as the perpetual path of the performance of actions.

The Lord who is said to be the maker of the creation of living beings is called Aniruddha. And Sana, Sanatsujāta, Sanaka, Sanandana, Sanatkumāra, Kapila and the seventh, Sanātana, are the seven ages who are called the 'mind-born' sons of Brahmā. To them knowledge has come spontaneously and they have taken up the teaching pertaining to withdrawal. They are the principal knowers of *yoga* and also know the *sāṃkhya* teachings, as well as being teachers in the teachings pertaining to liberation in the Treatise on Liberation… ."

...In this manner, this very fortunate, eternal Padmanābha [Viṣṇu], is said to be the one who receives the first part in the sacrifice and continually sustains the sacrifice. He has made the diversity of the world and ordained the rules of ongoing

> activity, yet he resides in the practice of withdrawal, the way of those who will not die again.[19]

This passage demonstrates that the spatial dimension of *pravṛttidharma* is the triple world (*triloka*) and the temporal dimension is the *kalpa*. According to the cosmology of the epics and Purāṇas the triple world is constituted of heaven, the abode of gods; of earth, the abode of humans; and of hell, which is the abode of various types of demons. The network of relationships which ideally should exist between these groups is determined by a set of injunctions (*vidhi*) collectively called *dharma*. The term *dharma* cannot be translated by any one word in a European language, but Biardeau does manage to catch its range of meanings when she writes that it is

> the socio-cosmic order, which is good simply in so far as it is necessary to maintain a happy existence for everything constituted by the 'three worlds' … it is itself the good simply because it assures the continuity of the empirical world.[20]

The consequence of total adherence to *dharma* is the holding together (*lokasaṃgraha*) of the worlds, wherein stability prevails.[21]

The relationship between gods and men enunciated in the passage above is sanctioned by *dharma* and is chiefly characterized by its symbiotic nature.[22] Men perform sacrifices in which they

---

19 Summary translation of *MBh.* 12, 327, 1-3, 5-10; 52cd-66; 87-8.

20 Biardeau, 1972, p.58. Throughout this book the word *dharma* has either been not translated or translated by two different words. Where it refers to a specific system of behaviour such as *pravṛttidharma*, it has been translated as 'teaching'. Where it refers to the system of injunctions governing the total conduct of various groups of beings in the triple world and prescribes certain behaviour as normative, if not obligatory, it has been translated as 'Law'.

21 *MBh.* 12, 251, 25; *Bhg.* 3, 20; 3, 25.

22 This relationship is summarized very concisely in *Bhg.* 3, 10-14; *MBh.* 3, 101, 1-2; *ŚB.* 2, 6, 3, 7. See also Bailey, 1985, pp.46-50, and the important discussion in Malinar, 1996, pp.161-176.

offer shares (*bhāga*) or portions of the victim to the gods. Usually the offerings are cooked animal meat, although under the influence of the doctrine of *ahiṃsā*, vegetable offerings became the norm. These offerings are the food of the gods. In return the gods cause rain to fall and this fertilizes the earth. The interest of both groups is served when the earth is prospering (*lokasiddhi*), since ultimately both derive their subsistence from it. Men grow plants and raise animals on the earth's surface. They gain their subsistence from them and offer the remainder to the gods and other groups of beings in the triple world. Both worlds–heaven and earth–are necessarily interdependent. Animals should also be considered participants in this symbiotic relationship, albeit as passive participants. They have the role of sacrificial victim, hence they serve as messengers between men and gods. Finally, even the inhabitants of hell, the various kinds of demons have a part to play. Their conflict with the gods keeps the triple world moving. Acceptance of their role as essential to the operation of the triple world is apparent from the stipulation that in the sacrifice, a portion of the victim's blood must be set aside for their consumption.

The inhabitants of the triple world exist on the pivot of the sacrifice. A view of the world that countenances such dependence might be called 'ritualistic', because its main characteristic–the interdependence of all beings in the cosmos–is an interdependence based on the ritual. The functionaries in the ritual are assigned with very clear tasks and the flow of communication between the various participants, offerers of food and recipients is also clear cut. This ritualistic interdependence also underlies the classical division of Hindu society into four *varṇas*. Each of the three 'twice born' *varṇas* relates functionally to the sacrifice. Biardeau's words are apposite here:

> ... In the orthodox society the social function is above all defined in specific relation to the rite. The Brahman is the priest, the kṣatriya is the sacrificer as well as being at the same time the holder of the force which protects the Brahmans and the remainder of the community. The vaiśya, besides his function of being the sacrificer, is the producer of wealth that is necessary to

> maintain the ritual activity, without which there is no prosperity on earth ...[23]

Group activity is emphasized here; each group plays a role in relation to the sacrifice, just as each group in the cosmos is related to the sacrifice either as recipient or performer. *Pravṛttidharma* enshrines the values of the group, the part that goes to make the whole. *Nivṛttidharma* enshrines the value of the 'individual' who has placed the five fires, that is, the sacrifice, within himself.

In the Brāhmaṇas the entire responsibility for the technical execution of the *śrauta* sacrifice fell on the members of the brahmin class. They were accorded the highest status in the social hierarchy, partly because of their reputed high level of ritual purity and also because of their knowledge of the intricacies of the sacrificial ritual. It was possession of this knowledge that led to the belief that they could control the power produced by the sacrifice, since it was they who performed the ritual. After about five hundred BCE *śrauta* sacrifices (apart from those connected with kingship) were less regularly performed. When this happened the responsibility for performance of the sacrifice shifted from the brahmin as officiant to the brahmin as householder. This at least is the prevailing view in the epics, Purāṇas and Dharmaśāstras.

In this literature the householder (*gṛhastha*) is accorded a high status and the cosmic function of the whole society, in terms of performing the sacrifice, seems to fall on him. His stage of life (*āśrama*) is accorded a higher status than the other three stages and is claimed to be their origin and support. Such is the view of the *GDhs*: "The householder is the source of the other three stages of life, because the others do not produce offspring."[24] Of the four stages of life, it is only the man living as a householder who produces offspring and thereby ensures the continuity of his lineage and the increase of society. Without him there would be

---

23 Biardeau, 1972, p.51.

24 *GDhs*. 3, 3; *Ms*. 3, 77-8; *MBh*. 14, 44, 16. See also Olivelle, 1993, pp.84-94 for a discussion of this claim in the *Dharmasūtras*.

no society. One text extends the supportive role of the householder far beyond the other stages of life:

> Child, the man who has accepted the householder status nourishes the entire universe, and through that he wins his desired worlds. The fathers, sages, gods, living beings and mankind, worms, insects and flying creatures, birds, cattle and demons subsist upon the householder and thereby become satisfied. And looking at his face, they wonder, 'What will he give us'?[25]

Here the householder functions as the most crucial link in a chain of relationships lying at the heart of the structured order of the triple world. It includes, and is more comprehensive than the set of relationships operative between men and gods alone.

The householder nourishes living beings by performing obligatory sacrifices, directions for which are given in the Gṛhyasūtras and the Purāṇas. Normally the eldest active male is acknowledged to be head of the household and is therefore the householder. He is responsible for performing the household ritual centred on the five daily sacrifices (*pañcayajña*). These consist of the sacrifice to Brahman (i.e. the Vedas) in the form of teaching and studying; offerings of water and food to the deceased fathers (*pitṛs*); a burnt oblation to be offered to the gods; a *bali* offering of grain, rice or other foods to living beings (*bhūtas*-or ghosts?) in general; and hospitality to guests.[26] The various groups of beings to whom the householder sacrifices in the *pañcayajña* comprise the limits of his world.

Study of the Vedas is vital for the householder because it is the principal (but not the only) source of *dharma*. The gods in their totality (*viśvadeva*) receive their sacrificial oblations as nourishment. In return they supply rainfall to guarantee the Earth's fertility. Traditionally the deceased fathers are supposed to derive their nourishment from an oblation offered by the eldest son of

---

25 *MkP*. 29, 3-5; *Ms*. 3, 75-8; *ŚB*. 2, 4, 1, 14. *Ms*. 3, 92 goes so far as to enjoin the householder to feed dog-eaters and dogs, both despised creatures in Indian literature and continually abused.

26 *Ms*. 3, 70; *MkP*. 29, 14; *Kp*. 2, 15, 15.

the lineage. By eating those oblations the deceased father enjoys a kind of immortality, especially since the sacrifice is supposed to be performed by the eldest son in perpetuity. If the oblations are not given the father wastes away. Kane says that the motive for the sacrifice to living beings in general and to guests is kindness.[27] Yet if the householder is believed to nourish the entire triple world, it follows that there should be a separate sacrifice for those groups not accounted for in the other sacrifices.

In summary, the world-view designated by the term *pravṛttidharma* visualizes a universe of three connected worlds each containing distinct groups of beings performing distinct and known roles. The organization of this triple world is based on functional interdependence, hence the term 'triple world', a term indicating this interdependence so well. This functional interdependence is also duplicated at the level of society. In both society and the triple world each group has its own role (*svadharma*) to perform, and if this role is not performed or another one performed, the stability of the whole is threatened. The possibility of either of these situations is a fear continually expressed in the mythology of the epics and Purāṇas, and has given rise to the abhorrence felt whenever there is a confusion of *varṇas* (*varṇasaṃkāra*). This interdependent triple world rests firmly on the pivot of the ritual (*karma*), from which there are two implications. Firstly, the ritual links together the various groups who live in this interdependent cosmos. Secondly, just as performance of the ritual is characterized by unerring regularity (laid down in handbooks filled with copious lists of regulations), so are the specific roles of the various groups in the triple world regulated by unchangeable injunctions which in their totality constitute *dharma*. Equally, just as the ritual is performed again and again, so too are the actions of the householder in society, in the sense of the forward movement implied by the prefix *pra* in the word *pravṛtti*.

---

27 HDS. 2/2, p.753. Cf. p.698.

Nivṛttidharma

The set of values designated by this term is in most ways the opposite of *pravṛttidharma*. Those who adhere to *nivṛttidharma* are renouncers who recognize no *real* spatial or temporal limits, except for those which are self-imposed. Once free of social obligations they move neither forward nor backwards. Their aim is to realize *mokṣa* (or *nirvāṇa*), a 'state' in which temporal and spatial limitations, karmic movement as it were, are completely without relevance. Once *mokṣa* is attained rebirth is over. This idea receives expression in mythology when at the time of cosmic dissolution (*pralaya*), the ascetics (*tapasvins*) who are near to *mokṣa* move to one of the other worlds located beyond the triple world. Unlike the latter, none of these worlds are destroyed in the dissolution. The ascetics remain there for the duration of the dissolution and are then liberated in *mokṣa*. For the inhabitants of the triple world, there is only destruction in the dissolution, followed by rebirth in the next *kalpa* in a life situation determined by their previous actions (*karma*).

The ascetic who renounces the social world also rejects the spatial limitations of the householder, whose point of reference is the social world, a world the ascetic depends on for his subsistence. The renouncer moves into the jungle or forest, beyond the area of the village which was the spatial location of the group. In Indian literature the forest was generally regarded as a place of 'chaos', danger and absence of order.[28] The ascetic in the forest lives in a kind of self-imposed 'chaos', away from the rigorously defined predictability of orthoprax society. The forest is an unbounded area characterized by immeasurability and lack of limits. It is symbolic of the pre-creation state, usually described in terms of darkness and indefinability.[29] In one sense it is also symbolic of the *mokṣa* that the ascetic can expect to attain, because Brahman and the *ātman* are without limits and defy definition. The person

28 Falk, 1975, pp.1-15.

29 See also below p.136.

who lives in society and sees himself as possessing an ego (*ahamkāra*), which sets him apart from others, imposes limits on his own psychological personhood. This involves the fundamental misunderstanding that he is different from others, when the truth is that the *real* part of him–the *ātman*–is also the real part of all other living beings; from this perspective difference is non-existent. Thus the ascetic's outlook is one that explicitly involves abandonment of the delimitations associated with the failure to comprehend the *real*.

In renouncing society and the obligations incumbent upon being a member of society, the ascetic is turning his back on the network of symbiotic relationships constituting society and the triple world. By renouncing this network of relationships he is renouncing *dharma*, because it is just this network which is circumscribed by *dharma*.[30] Informing the rejection of these relationships and the bondage that goes with them are the actions and views of Alarka, a king who has become an ascetic:

> After he had consecrated his eldest son as the king and completely abandoned all attachments, Alarka went to the forest for his own perfection. Then, after a long time, indifferent to duality, free of possessions, he attained the unsurpassed perfection produced by *yoga* and reached the highest *nirvāṇa*. Seeing all this universe with its gods, demons and men, bound and being constantly bound in fetters composed of the *guṇas*, this universe being dragged along by activities resulting from having sons, brother's sons, one's own and another's property and so on, burdened with pain, of fragmented appearance, and standing completely within the mire of ignorance without being raised up, the insightful man realized that his own self had passed beyond and so he uttered this *gāthā*, "Oh, alas that in the past I had occupied the kingship. At last I know there is no higher happiness than yoga."[31]

---

30 If there is a *dharma* for renouncers, it is, as Olivelle, 1976, p.80, points out, a *dharma* which "consists in the denial of the *dharma* of society."

31 *MkP*. 44, 28-33.

This rejection of family and social obligations is also a rejection of the interdependence on which all these are based. As such it finds expression in all the ascetic world-views, whether Hindu, Buddhist or Jain. Nāgārjuna, for example, extends his rejection of interdependence to more than the social organization. He argues that all matter, all phenomena, are dependent upon one another and should not in any way be relied upon as a means of fostering liberation.

Since the renouncer on the path of *nivṛtti* goes beyond society and the obligatory actions incumbent upon one living in it, he might be said to be antisocial.[32] Paradoxically, however, the renouncer is dependent upon the society he rejects, for to obtain food he must beg from householders. Without their support it would be difficult, if not impossible, for renouncers to exist. Yet despite their reliance on orthoprax society the values of renouncers are ultramundane.

The ascetic's rejection of the triple world means he assumes a kind of individuality, one contrary to his former life-style situation where his identity was solely determined by membership of a

---

32 In contemporary India the ascetic is sometimes regarded with contempt by his fellow vil!agers as one who has shirked his social responsibilities. According to Beals, 1962, p. 50, "An ascetic is required to abandon his family, to live on fruits and milk, and to wander from place to place. Nowdays, 'There are a few persons known as ascetics. They are filled to the brim with bad habits. They say bad things, they carry on family life, and they eat rice. They are all fake ascetics.' People can understand how an old man or some other person who is free of responsibilities towards others might legitimately become an ascetic. They have nothing but contempt for a man who leaves his family and jettisons his responsibilities in order to save himself. In a sense, it is considered far more virtuous to do whatever needs to be done to guarantee the support of one's wife and children, than to lead a life free of sin or desire. The role of ascetic is a coward's role. The head of a family, even though he must lie, cheat, or steal, provides for his dependents and gives them the opportunity for favourable future rebirth." Cf. Sinclair Stevenson, 1920, p.421.

group-*varṇa* and *jāti*. In society one's occupation, marriage partner and social relationships are determined by *jāti* membership. Even in the wider context of heaven and hell, the identity of the gods and demons is determined by membership of distinct groups. Only in a metaphysical sense is individuality a possibility for the inhabitant of the triple world (who is not a renouncer) and this is false individuality caused by the *ahaṃkāra*. This 'mental organ' causes a person or divine being to attribute reality to his mind and body, in place of the *ātman*, and to draw a distinction between himself and others on the level of ultimate reality. From the perspective of the renouncer, there is no *real* individuality, because the mind and body are transient and the *ātman* does not know of any distinction at all. Nevertheless, though the renouncer is aware of the *unreal* status of the *ahaṃkāra*, his act of renouncing caste affiliation means empirically, at least, he becomes an individual. Though he wants to deny this kind of individuality in the face of the universality of the *ātman*, as a renouncer he can make individual choices because he is not restricted by the sanctions of the group.

An important aspect of the renouncer's worldview and praxis is the suppression of all desire and sensuality. The strongest expression of this is celibacy. This stands in direct opposition to *pravṛtti* values. In caste society the position of the householder is strongly associated with progenation and sexuality, partly driven in response to the obligation to maintain the family lineage, both living and dead. It is essential a son or sons be produced, because only males could perform the five daily sacrifices. If these are not performed the deceased ancestors in the *piṭṛloka* are not fed, nor the other groups of beings dependent on these sacrifices for their nourishment.

Because of his celibacy and anti-sexual attitude the renouncer cannot produce sons who will perform the requisite sacrifices. Nor can he perform external sacrifices because to do so would be to engage in action motivated by desire. The rejection of the sacrifice is another expression of his refusal to take seriously the interdependence underlying the organization of the triple world.

As I have already stressed, the refusal of any group to perform its dharmically ordained duty is enough to jeopardize the tenuous coherence of the whole organization. Thus the renouncers were sometimes perceived as a threat to the whole system because they had abandoned their roles necessary for its maintenance. Perceptions of this threat and a reaction to those who are believed responsible for it are expressed in a passage of the *ViP*:

> Maitreya, those people who have followed the right path[33] become naked when they frivolously gave up the covering of the three Vedas. The religious student, the householder, the forest dweller and the wanderer as the fourth, comprise the *āśramas*. No fifth occurs. But after having completely given up the householder stage, a man who becomes neither a forest dweller nor even a wanderer, Maitreya, is called naked. He does evil.
>
> Brahmin, one who neglects the obligatory rituals for one day and night, not performing the prescribed rituals when he is able, sinks low for one day as a result of that. Maitreya, the man who is not in a state of distress yet actively abandons the obligatory rites for a fortnight, obtains purity only after a long expiation.
>
> For gazing at a man who has neglected the rite for a year, good men must constantly look at the sun. In case such a one is touched by him, a bath whilst fully clothed is the mode of purification, magnanimous man. It is said that of the evil-doer himself there is no purification. There is no greater evil-doer in the world than him in whose house the gods, sages, fathers and spirits sigh and leave without being worshipped. One should not mingle with him– either with his retinue, whether seated with him or in his house,–whose house and body has been struck by the sigh of the gods and others. Also, the man who sits with him, converses or asks after that man, becomes the same as him for a year, brahmin, because of that. Moreover, whoever eats in his house, or sits on his seat, or even sleeps on the same bed, will become like him instantaneously. Similarly, whoever eats, before having worshipped the gods, fathers, spirits and guests, experiences hell. What kind of expiation is there for him?
>
> The brahmins and the other *varṇas* who turn their faces away

33 Read *sanmārgavartino* for *tanmārgavartino*…

> from their own duty, become known as 'naked men' and are placed amongst those who have given up ritual actions.[34]

This attack is probably directed against the Jains who often wandered naked, especially if they were members of the Digambara sect. However, it could probably be taken as an attack on all ascetics who rejected the *āśramas* as a way of ordering their life.

The Reconciliation of Pravṛtti and Nivṛtti values

Many expository passages in the epics and Purāṇas which reflect one or other of these two sets of values are bitingly polemical, just like the passage cited above. The myths too engage in polemic, but the sharpness of their polemic is superficially disguised by the multitude of narrative and thematic components which go to make up their content. Just as there was polemic, so was there attempt at reconciliation. The development of the *āśrama* theory was one such attempt. It made it a matter of course that a man's life would at different times be underlain either by *pravṛtti* or *nivṛtti* values. The *brahmacarya* and *saṃnyāsin* stages are consistent with the latter, whereas the householder stage unequivocally corresponds to the former. The reconciliation is attempted in the *vānaprastha* stage, where the *vānaprastha* is a '*saṃnyāsin*' who lives with his wife in a forest hermitage and continues to perform sacrifices. Through an analysis of certain Śaivite myths O'Flaherty has shown this was an inadequate compromise.[35]

Another attempt at reconciliation involved a reinterpretation of the traditional 'aims of life' (*puruṣārthas*), each demarcating a particular area of human activity. In some passages a fourth aim, *mokṣa*, is added to the traditional three-*kāma*, 'sensuality', *artha*, 'economic utility' and *dharma*, 'lawful conduct'. The latter three fall within the realm of *pravṛtti*, whereas *mokṣa* can only be understood in terms of *nivṛtti*. Yet, at the most, this was only a theoretical resolution, probably having very little influence in

---

34 *ViP*. 3, 18, 36-48.

35 O'Flaherty, 1973, pp.79-83.

real terms. Even in the few passages where the possibility of a *caturvarga* is raised, the incompatibility of linking *mokṣa* with the other three *arthas* is immediately brought up. Typical is a passage from the *MBh*: "This class was called the '*trivarga*' by Svayambhū. Indeed, there is a fourth class called '*mokṣa*' which is a different class and has a different aim."[36] Judging from the few occasions when the compound *caturvarga* appears in the texts, it was never taken seriously as a reconciliation of *pravṛtti* and *nivṛtti* values.

A much more influential and ultimately successful reconciliation is found in the *Bhg*, the chief purpose of which seems to have been to bring renunciation and its associated set of values back into orthoprax Hindu society. In the *Bhg*. the dichotomy between *karmayoga*, 'the discipline of action', and *jñānayoga*, 'the discipline of knowledge', is laid down very forcibly.[37] *Karmayoga* is a modified version of *pravṛttidharma*. The modification was effected by the development of the idea of *karmaphalatyāga* or 'giving up of the fruits of action'. Accordingly, the motivation for the performance of actions was not the fulfillment of desire, but rather the completion of duties required by one's *svadharma*. Desire was negated, and negation of desire was one of the cardinal doctrines of all the ascetic traditions and wholly consistent with *nivṛtti* values.

The idea of *karmaphalatyāga* developed in the *Bhg*. has implications wider than those arising exclusively from its association with *nivṛtti* values. When brought into conjunction with the doctrine of *bhakti*, it was simultaneously able to express ritualist and ascetic values. The concept of 'abandonment, renunciation, giving up', designated by derivatives of the root *tyaj*, was a central part of the sacrifice. As Biardeau has observed:

It is the case, that to give-in a general way, and to give to a brāhmaṇa,

---

36 *MBh*. 12, 59, 30. Similar in intent are *ŚP*. 5, 41, 4 and *MkP*. 44, 20. Cf. *NāradaP*. 1, 106, 23; *ViP*. 1, 18, 21-25; *BdP*. 1, 7, 188. It seems to be more common in the Purāṇas than elsewhere.

37 See *Bhg*. 3, 3. Cf. Zaehner, 1966, pp.161-162.

> who alone is entitled to receive-is part of the sacrifice; that already the sacrifice is conceived of as the abandonment of something. Whilst giving the victim to be sacrificed, the sacrificer pronounces the word *tyajāmi*, 'I abandon, I give'.[38]

It is not clear whether words deriving from *tyaj* are used in the *Bhg.* to refer to the offering up of the body to God.[39] Usually such words are employed specifically to designate renunciation of the fruits of actions or renunciation of attachment to the fruits of actions. It is, however, quite possible that the ritual sense of the word may be intended even where the situation in which it occurs indicates that it means 'to renounce'.

Frequently in the *Bhg.* it is stated that the fruits of action that have been renounced can be regarded as an offering to God. It prescribes that having renounced (*tyaktvā*) attachment and having given actions to Brahman (i.e. God), one will attain *mokṣa*.[40] This is certainly consistent with the ritualistic sense of *tyaj*. What is renounced is sacrificed. Renunciation and sacrifice are identical.

This identification can be made possible only if renunciation and sacrifice are seen to serve a common goal. In the *Bhg.* this goal is Kṛṣṇa. He demands devotion (*bhakti*) from his devotees, and in return allows them to participate in his being, which is *mokṣa*. Renunciation and sacrifice become expressions of devotion. As such they can retain their individuality as separate paths of devotion leading to God, each being considered in its own way a form of *bhakti*. Or, they could be identified in the manner suggested above and still be considered as *bhakti*. Alternatively, along with *bhaktiyoga* they can be considered as three separate but overlapping paths to God. This last alternative is succinctly expressed in the following verse:

Let your mind be on Me (*madmanā*)! Be devoted to me (*madbhakta*)!

Be a sacrificer for me (*madyajī*)! Make obesiance to me! Be

---

38 Biardeau and Malamoud, 1976, p.48.

39 Two possible exceptions are *Bhg.* 4, 9; 8, 13.

40 *Bhg.* 5, 10-12; 12, 6; 4, 20,

> wholly intent upon Me! Thus, having harnessed your self, you will certainly come to me.[41]

In this *śloka* the values of *nivṛtti* are summed up in the term *madmanā*, those of *pravṛtti* in the term *madyājī*. They are brought together under the values of *bhakti* (*madbhakta*). The reconciliation is successful because each path retains its individuality, whilst still leading to *mokṣa*. understood as participation in God's being.

---

41 *Bhg.* 9, 34; 18, 65.

madmanā bhava madbhakto madyājī māṃ namaskuru /
mām evaiṣyasi yuktvaivam ātmānaṃ matparāyaṇaḥ //

Chapter 3

Brahmā's Functional Antecedents in the Vedas

Except for a few references in the Upaniṣads and the late Brāhmaṇas, Brahmā is virtually absent from Vedic literature. There are however, several gods in Vedic mythology who perform functions identical to those performed by Brahmā in epic and Purāṇic mythology. A study of these functional similarities will obviously be of help in understanding his own role in mythology, a role pre-eminently directed towards the creation and preservation of the triple world.

Tvaṣṭṛ

Tvaṣṭṛ has no hymns exclusively addressed to him in the *ṚV*, but appears frequently in the Vedic *saṃhitās* and the Brāhmaṇas. He is often portrayed as the creator and creates the world in a variety of ways, and also has strong connections with male and female fertility.

He is the first being to appear before the creation begins. This is indicated by his epithets 'belonging to the beginning' (*agrajā*) and 'going before' (*puryovān*).[1] His cosmogonic role implied by such epithets is described in only a few Vedic hymns but it emerges from these quite distinctly. In one passage he is said to have 'produced (*jajāna*) the entire universe', whilst in another he

1 *ṚV*. 9, 5, 9; 1, 13, 10; *AV*. 11, 6, 3; *MS*. 2, 7, 13.

both produced and nourished creatures.[2] He created Heaven and Earth by adorning or clothing them with forms.[3]

His role as creator cannot be separated from his status as a father figure. Two epithets-'father' (*pitṛ*) and 'progenitor' (*janitṛ*)-testify to this.[4] Kinship terms like these are widely used in the Vedas and later literature to organize the gods into the framework of a loose family structure.[5] Since Tvaṣṭṛ created Heaven and Earth he can be considered as their father. In their own turn they are the parents of the gods and the remainder of creation.[6] Thus in line of descent, their father Tvaṣṭṛ, is the grandfather of the gods whom they create.

The idea that he might be a grandfather is also supported by a famous passage in the *ṚV*. telling of the disappearance of Tvaṣṭṛ's daughter Saraṇyū:

> Tvaṣṭṛ is giving a wedding for his daughter–hearing this, the whole world assembles. The mother of Yama, the wedded wife of the great Vivasvat, disappeared. They concealed the immortal woman from mortals. Making an identical woman, they gave her to Vivasvat. Saraṇyū bore the two Aśvins, and then she abandoned the two twins.[7]

In studying this passage some scholars have sought to discover the meaning of Saraṇyū's disappearance; others see it as also pertaining to an understanding of Tvaṣṭṛ. Oldenberg thought Tvaṣṭṛ was held to be a forefather of the human race because his daughter was the mother of the first man.[8] Yet it is not clear what it means to say that Yama was the first man. At least one scholar is inclined to see him and his sister, Yamī, as representing the origin

---

2 *Vājasaneyī Saṃhitā*. 29, 9; *ṚV*. 3, 55, 19.

3 *ṚV*. 10, 110, 9; 1, 160, 2. Cf. 4, 56, 3.

4 For *pitṛ* see *ṚV.* 10, 64, 10; *mahaḥ pitur* at 3, 48, 2, and *janitṛ* at 10, 10, 5; *AV.* 9, 4, 6.

5 See Karve, 1938/9, p.72.

6 *ṚV*. 1, 159, 1; 1, 185, 4; 4, 56, 2.

7 *ṚV*. 10, 17, 1-2. Trans O'Flaherty, 1975, p.61.

8 Oldenberg, 1894, p.235; Keith, 1927, Vol. 1, p.203.

of the human race.[9] Another suggestion is that he and Manu are the protagonists in a creation myth of Indo-European antiquity.[10] This myth tells how Manu sacrificed his brother Yama and from his body the universe was created. Yama and Manu were the first king and first priest respectively. Whichever of these two views is correct it can be said with certainty that Yama is the first mortal.[11] Because of his mortality he symbolically represents mankind. As before, Tvaṣṭṛ appears here as the 'grand-father' of a figure important in Vedic cosmogony.

The passage just cited from the *ṚV.* is not a cosmogonic myth, yet all the gods mentioned in it do have some importance in Vedic schemes of cosmogony. Saraṇyū, as Yama's mother, is the mother of the first mortal being, the one who symbolically represents mankind. Her husband, Vivasvat, is sometimes attributed with the creation of offspring (*prajā*), possibly also of the gods.[12] If this group is viewed as a lineage, Tvaṣṭṛ is father of Saraṇyū and father-in-law of her husband Vivasvat. Yama is their son and, as the third generation descending from Tvaṣṭṛ, is that god's grandson. This lineage exactly parallels the other one where the family group is represented by Tvaṣṭṛ, Heaven and Earth, and their children who constitute the rest of creation. In short, there are two separate but similar traditions which envisage Tvaṣṭṛ as the first being to appear at the time of creation. He progenates Heaven and Earth in one tradition, Saraṇyū and Vivasvat in the other. From them the rest of creation proceeds. Using kinship terminology, Tvaṣṭṛ is the 'grandfather' of created beings.

The texts offer other evidence that Tvaṣṭṛ was regarded as the first being to appear at the time of creation, and that by extension, he was "the first active, or dynamic force in the universe,"[13] inasmuch as he represents the principle of life conceived of in a

---

9 Gonda, 1960, Vol. 1, p.139.

10 Lincoln, 1975, p.139.

11 *AV.* 18, 3, 13. Cf. MacDonell, 1974, p.172.

12 *ṚV.* 10, 63, 1; *TS.* 6, 5, 6; *ŚB.* 3, 1, 3, 4.

13 Brown, 1942, p.87.

sexual sense. This idea receives expression in a variety of ways. Besides his epithet 'progenitor', he is frequently envisaged as a virile male. In the *Black Yājurveda* he is invoked for human offspring and called *vṛṣabho vṛṣā*, 'virile bull'.[14] Both words carry connotations of virility and the spilling of semen. Another text says of the victim offered to Tvaṣṭṛ, that it is an animal with testicles, for such a one is a begetter (*prajanayitā*).[15] As for female fertility, he is once depicted androgynously as a pregnant male full of milk.[16]

Several times in Aprī hymns he is invoked to place within the womb a substance called *turīpa*, for it was believed this would bring the family prosperity, wealth and sons.[17] Although of uncertain etymology, the word *turīpa* may mean semen.[18] Brown thought it might mean 'element of life'; certainly it is connected with ideas of prosperity and growth.[19] Occasionally the word is qualified by the adjective *adbhutam* or 'wondrous' or according to Geldner–'*geheimnisvollen*'.[20] It is possible this adjective gives the word a connotation different from the more usual Vedic words for semen such as *retas* and *payas*, intending *turīpa* to designate a more general 'element of life', one extending beyond the confines of male or female fertility.

In an invocation to various gods to uplift the *aśvamedha*, Tvaṣṭṛ is invoked in the following way:

> 'Hail to Tvaṣṭṛ! Hail to Tvaṣṭṛ! The seminal (*turīpa*)! Hail to Tvaṣṭṛ the multiformed!' Truly, Tvaṣṭṛ is the maker of forms for the pairs of animals. With forms he uplifts it.[21]

14 *TS*. 2, 4, 5; Cf. 1, 2, 5; 3, 1, 11.

15 *ŚB*. 3, 7, 2, 8.

16 *AV*. 9, 4, 3-6.

17 *ṚV*. 1, 142, 10; 3, 4, 9; 7, 2, 9.

18 Mayrhofer, 1953-75, Vol. 1, p.515.

19 Brown, 1942, p.87.

20 Geldner, 1951, Vol. 1, p.200.

21 *ŚB*. 13, 1, 8, 7; *Vājasaneyī Saṃhitā*. 22, 20; *TS*. 7, 3, 15; *MS*. 3, 12,

He is only one of several gods and goddesses invoked, each named along with his or her specific characteristic. It is with Tvaṣṭṛ alone that *turīpa* is identified, and elsewhere the word only ever occurs in connection with him. Since he represents both male and female fertility, and is *turīpa*, it is likely he was the principle of life and growth to the Vedic poets. In line with this reasoning Tvaṣṭṛ could have been seen as the first element of a cosmogony requiring the principle of life to be present before the creative process could unfold.

This analysis of Tvaṣṭṛ's cosmogonic functions has now reached a point where similarities with Brahmā can be shown. The one fundamental similarity is that like Tvaṣṭṛ, Brahmā is a grandfather (*pitāmaha*) who is portrayed commencing the process of creation and leaving its completion to somebody else, usually his sons. In the cosmogonic myths where Brahmā is the grandfather, it is usual for him to emit from himself mind-born sons (*mānasaputra*) who are called 'Lords of creation' (*prajāpatis*). From them creatures are born and the rest of creation is produced. In a cosmogony from the *Mbh.* the creation begins after Brahmā is born from an egg:

> From it was born the Grandfather, the sole Lord Prajāpati, who is known as Brahmā, as the Preceptor of the Gods, as Sthānu, Manu, Ka and Parameṣṭhin. From him sprang Dakṣa, son of Pracetas, and thence the seven sons of Dakṣa, and from them came the twenty-one Lords of Creation. And the person, immeasurable Soul, the One whom the seers know as the universe; and the Viśve devas, and the Adityas as well as the Vasus and the two Aśvins. Yakṣas, Sādhyas, Piśācas, Guhyakas, and the Ancestors were born from it, and the wise and impeccable seers. So also the many royal seers endowed with every virtue–Water, Heaven, Earth, Wind, Atmosphere and Space, the seasons, the months, the fortnights, the days and nights in turn, and whatever else has all come forth as witnessed by the world. Whatever is found to

---

5; *TB*. 3, 8, 11, 2.

exist moving and unmoving, it is all again thrown together, all this world, when the destruction of the Eon has struck.[22]

The narrative goes on to emphasise the perpetuity of the cycle of creation and destruction. Within this cycle the progressive unfolding of creation is emphasized. Brahmā is the first to be born, followed then by Dakṣa and his sons, after whom the rest of creation unfolds.

Another version of this cosmogony adds many new elements not present in the version just cited. It still retains Brahmā as the first to be born, followed by his mind-born sons, but instead of departing the scene he continues to create:

Then a gold coloured egg appeared, lying on the waters. 'Brahmā himself, the Self-born was born in that' so we have heard. The illustrious god born in the golden womb dwelt there for one year and divided the egg into two, Sky and Earth. After that the mighty Lord placed the atmosphere amidst these two pieces, and placed the Earth, floating on the waters, and the ten-fold regions. Then he emitted time, mind, speech, desire, anger and pleasure.

Wishing to emit that form of creation called *prajāpati*, he of great splendour emitted the seven mind-born sons. These were called Marīci, Atri, Aṅgiras, Pulastya, Pulaha, Kratu and Vasiṣṭha. Of these seven who were born from Brahmā, yet were really constituted of Nārāyaṇa, it is definitely held in the Purāṇa that they were 'the seven born of Brahmā'. After that, Brahmā again emitted Rudra from his own anger, then the sage Sanatkumāra, first born of the ancients. These seven and Rudra propagate creatures, Bhārata, but Skanda and Sanatkumāra abstained, restraining their fiery energy. Seven great divine lineages attended by groups of gods and adorned with great sages came from them. These were actively propagating.[23]

After this Brahmā goes on creating various meteorological phenomena, the Vedas and other miscellaneous beings.

---

22 *MBh*. 1, 1, 30-6. Trans van Buitenen, 1973, pp.20-1.

23 *H*. I, 25-33. Cf. *ŚP*. 5, 29, 2-28; *AP*. 17, 6cd-16. Very similar is *Ms*. I, 1-50; *ChU*. 3, 19, 1-4.

In this version of the myth Brahmā does most of the work of creation, his sons remaining content to people the earth through propagation. Yet in another version of the myth Brahmā ceases to be involved in the creation after his sons are born, leaving to them the task of creating thunder, lightning and the other elements as well as animals and the people of the earth.[24]

In spite of some divergence in specific detail between Brahmā's cosmogonic role and that of Tvaṣṭṛ, the functional similarity remains. The appearance of both gods is the basic requirement for the creation to commence. This makes sense in Tvaṣṭṛ's case because he is *turīpa*, the 'principle of life'. Similarly, Brahmā is the *ahaṃkāra*, that stage of creation where the undifferentiated 'matter' that gives rise to the ordered creation becomes individualized. This is not to say there is necessarily a conceptual continuity between the notions of *turīpa* and *ahaṃkāra*, merely a functional similarity. Once on the scene, both gods create 'demiurges' and it is they who actively complete the process of creation. In the Vedic cosmogonies it is Sky and Earth who take the active role. But in the cosmogonies of the epics and Purāṇas they are completely passive and their role is performed by the *prajāpatis*.

Prajāpati

Of all the gods prominent in Vedic literature, it is this god who has the greatest number of functional similarities with Brahmā. Prajāpati is the protagonist in most of the cosmogonic myths found in the Brāhmaṇas and embodies the ritualistic values underlying the world-view implicit in this body of literature. He rarely appears as an independent god in the epics and Purāṇas, where his name is one of Brahmā's most frequent epithets.

---

24 *Ms*. 1, 34-41. This progression does not only occur in those cosmogonic myths where the motif of the cosmic egg is utilized. Cf. the cosmogony described in *MBh*. 12, 160, 11-21, where Brahmā is the first to appear, possibly coming from the primeval waters.

Cosmogony

In the cosmogonies of the Brāhmaṇas Prajāpati creates through progenation, just like the sacrifice with which he is often identified. The sacrifice itself is a womb giving 'rebirth' to the individual and the cosmos.[25] Prajāpati's association with progenation is a recurrent feature in the texts. In the *ṚV*. he is invoked to bring children in a hymn celebrating the marriage of Sūrya and Sūryā.[26] He is often referred to as 'progenitor' (*prajayanitṛ*) and frequently portrayed as a bull and a virile stallion.[27] The cosmic dimension of his progenative powers is indicated by his epithet 'progenitor of the earth' (*janitā pṛthivyai*) and from the number of times he is said to have created the physical features of the universe through copulation with Earth, sky, Vāc, etc.[28] This emphasis on creation by progenation is equally a result of his being father of creatures and of his representation of the fecundating powers of the sacrifice.

His progenative capacity is the basis of a cosmogony in a version of the incest myth that occurs in the *AB*. Prajāpati had changed into a stag in order to have intercourse with his daughter Uṣas, who had taken the form of a doe. The gods caught hold of him before he had performed intercourse and told Rudra to shoot him with an arrow. Rudra did this but Prajāpati had already spilt his semen which turned into a lake. The gods sacrificed it:

> They surrounded it with Agni, the Maruts blew upon it, but Agni did not cause it to flow. They surrounded it with Agni Vaiśvānara; the Maruts blew upon it and Agni Vaiśvānara caused it to flow. The first part of the seed that was ignited became Āditya; the second became Bhṛgu, whom Varuṇa took, and so Bhṛgu was adopted by Varuṇa. The third part, which was brilliant (*adīdet*), became the Ādityas. The coals (*aṅgārā*) became the Aṅgirases; and when the coals blazed forth again after they had been quenched, Bṛhaspati was born. The completely charred coals

25 See Kaelber, 1976, pp.343-386.

26 *ṚV*. 10, 85, 43.

27 *ŚB*. 8, 4, 3, 20; 5, 2, 5, 17; 8, 4, 2, 1.

28 *ŚB*. 7, 3, 1, 20; 6, 1, 2, 1-11.

became the black cattle; the reddened earth became tawny cattle. The ash spread in various forms–the buffalo, the ox, the antelope, the camel, the ass, and the tawny cattle.[29]

The impregnation of the 'womb', that is, of the sacrifice, by Prajāpati's semen, causes the birth of men, gods and animals here.

A version of this myth occurs in the *Mbh*, but here it is Brahmā's semen which is thrown on the sacrificial fire. Śiva was holding a sacrifice, which was attended by all the gods, the personified instruments used in the sacrifice, as well as the Vedas and Vedāṅgas. Also present were the wives, daughters, and mothers of the gods. Brahmā appeared and was sexually aroused by the mere sight of these women:

After the Self-born [Brahmā] had seen them, his semen fell to the ground. Because it was so still, Puṣan picked up in his hands the dust on which the semen lay on the groud and threw it into the fire. When the sacrificial fire began to blaze, Brahmā appeared there, offering oblations. As soon as the semen was emitted he had caught it in a ladle, and then sacrificed it with the recitation of mantras and the pouring of clarified butter.

Then he vigorously produced elementary matter (*bhūtagrāma*). From that came fiery energy (*tejas*), from which brilliance in beings was born. Beings, having darkness (*tamas*), were born from darkness. However, both groups of beings were pervaded with light (*sattva*), just as air, although in darkness, is always furnished with fiery energy. So the three–light, fiery energy and darkness–manifested in all beings when the semen was offered on the fire, mighty Lord. As did men who had handsome bodies and the three characteristics (*guṇa*) born from procreation. Bhṛgu arose from the crackling sound of the flames (*bhṛg*), the first to be born. Aṅgiras was born from the charcoal (*aṅgārā*), and in consequence of the charcoal he is called the 'wise man' who has no superior. From the shining specks of flame (*marīci*) arose Marīci, and he was Mārīca Kaśyapa. Good man, Aṅgiras arose from the charcoal and the Vālakhilyas from the pile of rocks. Lord, they say that *atra* means 'here' and he was called Atri when born. From the removal of the ashes arose the

29 *AB*. 3, 33-5. Trans. O'Flaherty, 1975, p.30.

> Vaikhānasas, resembling a group of Brahmarṣis, desirous of acquiring ascetic heat (*tapas*) and Vedic learning.
>
> The twin Aśvins were born and resembled in shape that which was not heard at the sacrifice. The remaining lords of creation were born from the stream of the sacrifice, sages from the pores of the skin and impure desires from sweat.[30]

The narrative goes on to relate how the periods of time were derived from various parts of the sacrifice. Finally, over the prior claims of Agni, Rudra and Varuṇa, Brahmā claimed the offspring as his own, since it was his semen that was sacrificed on the fire.

This version parallels the other one in several respects. Although Brahmā does not actually commit incest, the act of spilling his semen at the sight of women forbidden to him is an act of similar gravity. The use of etymology to account for the origin of certain sages is also common to both versions, as is the combination of sacrifice and semen working to set the creation in process. But the *Mbh.* version introduces material lacking in the other version. Most noticeable is the introduction of a crude *guṇa* theory, the import of which seems to be that all created beings contain within themselves different concentrations of the psychological qualities the *guṇas* represent. The list of beings born from the sacrifice also varies between the two versions, the *Mbh.* version adding other groups of sages, the lords of creation and men (*puruṣa*) as symbols of the entire human race. The inclusion of the lords of creation and the *guṇa* theory suggests this version incorporates cosmogonic material not current at the time of composition of the *AB*.

Another cosmogonic myth in the *ŚB.* attributes the creation of the various periods of time, and of good and evil to Prajāpati.[31] This myth narrates Prajāpati's birth from a golden egg floating in the primeval waters. He created the earth, atmosphere and sky by uttering their names. After he had created the seasons in the same way, he created the gods and demons:

---

30 *MBh.* 13, 85, 8-19.

31 *ŚB.* 11, 1, 6, 1ff.

> Desiring offspring he [Prajāpati] sang and performed austerities. With his mouth he emitted the gods. These gods (*deva*) were emitted on reaching the sky (*diva*), because the divinity of the gods is that they were emitted on reaching the sky. This became the sky for him who had emitted them. Thus, that which is the divinity of the gods, was for him who had emitted them, the daylight (*diva*).
>
> Then with his downward breath he emitted the demons (*asura*). These were emitted on reaching the earth. For him who had created them, this became darkness.
>
> He knew, 'Indeed, I have emitted evil. Having emitted them, this has come to be what is darkness for me' ... When he had emitted the gods for himself the day (*div*) was made into the light (*ahar*). Due to having emitted the demons there was darkness. This was made into night. These two are day and night.[32]

The narrative ends with the creation of the year and various gods. Among other things this cosmogony attempts to account for the origin of good and evil. The triad of gods, light and goodness is opposed to demons, evil and darkness, an opposition recurring continually in the epics and Purāṇas.

The substance of this myth is found in many versions of the Purāṇic cosmogony. Where it does occur it forms part of the detailed enumeration of groups of beings created during the 're-creation' (*pratisarga*). The version given here begins with the creation of the gods:

> Brahmin, created beings have developed due to the good and evil from their past *karman*. According to this view, although destroyed in the cosmic dissolution, they are not liberated. Brahmin, whilst Brahmā was engaging in the creation there was born from his mind four kinds of creatures–beginning with the gods and ending with immoveable things.
>
> Whilst Prajāpati, wanting to create, concentrated himself, an excessive quantity of darkness was manifested. First there came demons from his thighs. But he abandoned them and the body which had an excess of darkness (*tamas*) and with the body

32 *ŚB*. 11, 1, 6, 7-11.

> rejected night was immediately born. Wishing to create, he took up another body and became pleased. Then the gods having a preponderance of light (*sattva*) were born from his mouth. The mighty lord of beings abandoned that body too, and when it was rejected, the day, consisting mainly of light, was born. Then he took possession of another body containing a certain measure of light and the fathers (*pitaras*) were born from him as he considered himself as being like a father. When the mighty lord had created the fathers he abandoned that body as well and when abandoned it became the twilight standing between night and day. The Lord then assumed another body consisting of a certain measure of impetuous desire (*rajas*). Then humans were born, sprung up from the measure of impetuous desire. When he had created humans, the Lord then abandoned that body, which became the morning twilight, ending the night and beginning the day.
>
> Thus these bodies of the wise God of gods are known as night and day, evening and morning twilight, brahmin. The three, morning and evening twilight, and day, are composed mainly of light. The night consists of a measure of darkness, hence it is called 'keeping the three others in check' (*triyāmikā*). Therefore, the gods possess strength by day, demons in the night, the humans at the coming of the morning twilight and the fathers in the evening twilight.[33]

Good and evil are not so sharply contrasted here as they are in the other version of the myth. The theory of the *guṇas* asserts that all matter consists of a combination of three basic qualities, so demands the introduction of a third group of beings. This is achieved by the equation of *rajas* with humans, but it was not the intention of the myth-maker to depict humans as half-divine and half-demonic, standing midway between gods and demons, *sattva* and *tamas*. Whatever the case may be, the appearance in this version of a third group, and a fourth group, the fathers, means the contrast between good and evil is much less striking than when there are only two groups.

Sexual imagery is present in the Purāṇic version of the myth,

33 *MkP*. 48, 2-15; *KP*. 1, 7, 38-45; *ViP*. 1, 5, 26-38.

but not in the version from the *ŚB*. In the former version, the word for body (*tanu*) is always in the feminine, and Brahmā, who takes on a different body each time a new creation is required is of course masculine. The appearance of each group of beings and the corresponding time period is described as a birth (*jan*). They are the offspring of the union of Brahmā with the particular body he has entered. The nature of the four kinds of beings procreated by Brahmā is determined entirely by the kind of body he enters just prior to the birth. He assumes the nature of the body as soon as he enters it. His offspring are born 'in his own image' as it were. The view of progenation and birth here is one according to which the husband is believed to be reborn again in his son.[34] The mother's womb is just an incubator for the father's seed according to this view, and his seed becomes the embryo and later, at birth, an image of himself.

The cosmogonies of the Brāhmaṇas, epics and Purāṇas include the creation of the physical universe and its organization and of the beings who live in it. The organizational structure laid down is one conforming to the ritualistic model of organization outlined in the last chapter. Such occurs in a passage where Prajāpati determines the roles of some groups of beings:

> Living beings (*bhūtāni*) respectfully approached Prajāpati. Living beings are offspring (*prajā*). They said to him, "Direct (*vi/dhā*) us, so that we will be able to live." Then the gods, wearing the sacrificial thread and having the right knee bent, approached him. He said to them, "Your food is the sacrifice, yours is the vigour, immortality is yours and your light is the sun." The fathers, wearing the sacred thread over the right shoulder and with the right knee bent, then approached him. He said to them, "Your food will come month by month, yours is the funeral offering, swiftness like thought is yours, and your light is the moon."
>
> After having bowed, men who were dressed approached him. He said to them, "Your food shall be taken at evening and

34 Some textual references can be found at *Ms*. 9, 8; 9, 35; *MBh*. 1, 68, 36; 1, 69, 29.

daybreak, progeny will be yours and death also. Your light is fire." The animals approached him. He made them a choice, saying, "You will eat whenever you receive food, whether at the correct or incorrect time."

... Then, the demons immediately approached him", they said. To them he gave darkness and deceit. Just as this deceit of the demons conquered the offspring, so Prajāpati directed them so that they would be able to survive.[35]

These are normative roles, even the evil and deceitfulness assigned to the demons. The ritualistic basis is implicit in the instructions given to the first three groups, as the gods and fathers both derive their sustenance from the sacrificial offerings, and humans take their morning and evening meals only after having first performed the household rituals. Animals and demons are included after the first three groups because they play no active role in the ritual. Animals are the sacrificial victims and demons are given the blood of this victim when it is being dismembered before being cooked.

In the Purāṇic cosmogonies Brahmā establishes the conduct of certain groups of beings. This is done in response to a situation of conflict between the Earth and humans, a situation prompting the Earth to withdraw her fertility, presenting humans with the prospect of starvation. Brahmā resolves the conflict by milking the Earth for her fertility and apportioning duties to humans in accord with their *svadharma*:

The divine Brahmā laid down (*vi/dhā*) duties and rules (*dharmān*) for them, but when the basic form of the four *varṇas* was completely established, these creatures, through ignorance, did not follow any of these rules. Because they did not live by the rules of *varṇa* they obstructed each other. Mighty Brahmā who truly understood the goal, then assigned (*ā/diś*) a livelihood for the *kṣatriyas*–force, punishment and battle. Sacrifice, study, and thirdly, the receipt of gifts, were the duties the Lord then assigned to *brāhmaṇas*. For the *vaiśyas* he assigned protection of animals, trade and agriculture. The Lord then laid down that

---

35 *ŚB*. 2, 4, 2, 1-5. Cf. 9, 5, 1, 35.

the *śūdras* were to be craftsman and carriers. Furthermore, for the *brāhmaṇas*, *kṣatriyas* and *vaiśyas* some common duties were laid down. Sacrifice, study and the giving of gifts were common to them.

When the Lord had granted them their respective professions, he gave them positions in the next world in accordance with their skills. The Prajāpati world was for *brāhmaṇas* who perform the correct ceremonies; Indra's world for *kṣatriyas* who do not flee from battle; the world of the Maruts for *vaiśyas* who live in accordance with their own duty; and the Gandharvas' world was for the *śūdra* caste who perform services. He himself had arranged these worlds for those who performed their *varṇa* conduct correctly, and when the *varṇas* had been established he instituted the stages of life (*āśrama*).[36]

Brahmā's activity here is directed only towards the organization of society, not to the cosmos as was Prajāpati's role. Yet the similarity is clear. In both passages the groups of living beings are differentiated by functions deriving their significance from the part they play in relation to the sacrifice. Also, the creator is confronted with the problem of evil in both cases. Prajāpati creates evil when he gives deceit and darkness to the demons, Brahmā has to resolve the conflict between Earth and humans which has arisen as a result of the abusive way humans have acted in regard to the Earth.[37] Just as Prajāpati includes evil in his normative grouping of beings, so Brahmā tries to lessen it by organizing humans in such a way that conflict between themselves and between themselves as a group and the Earth will be minimized.

Another of the creator's functions is the creation of the Vedas, which as a body of knowledge is supposed to constitute the theoretical basis of social and cosmic order. The functions of the *varṇas* and the roles of gods, demons, men and animals are laid down in, and sanctioned, by the Vedas. Prajāpati creates them and uses them to further his own creation.

---

36 *VāP*. 8, 159-68.

37 *VāP*. 8, 156-158. For more on this see below pp.216-35.

In the beginning nothing existed (*asat*). Indra kindled seven bodies (*puruṣas*) from the vital airs and these combined into one and became Prajāpati. He wished to propagate himself and so performed *tapas*. As a result of this he created Brahma which was the triple knowledge [the three Vedas]. Using this as a foundation (*pratiṣṭhā*) he performed more *tapas*. Then he created the waters from *vāc*. Wishing to be reproduced from the waters, he entered them with the triple knowledge. An egg arose in the waters and when Prajāpati touched it, Brahma, the triple knowledge, appeared from it. Then in succession Agni, a horse, an ass, a goat and the Earth were born from the parts of the egg.[38]

Functionally, the Vedas and the *Vāc* are identical. *Vāc* is the ritual formula, so important in performance of the sacrifice. The source of such formulae is the Vedas. Prajāpati himself is the sacrifice. Thus the cosmogony contained in this passage is based on the assumption of the creative power inherent in the union of ritual formulae and the sacrifice. Sexual symbolism seems to be present, because *vāc*, *trayī vidyā* and *pratiṣṭhā* are all feminine words in opposition to Prajāpati, who is masculine in the strongest possible sense.

Sometimes the sexuality is much more explicit than this. Some passages portray Prajāpati copulating with *vāc* in order to complete the creation he has already begun by himself.

Prajāpati was this universe. *Vāc* was his second. He copulated with her and she became pregnant. She went away from him, emitted these creatures and re-entered Prajāpati.[39]

In the Purāṇic *pratisarga* Brahmā achieves the creation with the support of the Vedas and the sacrifice. At the beginning of the *kalpa* he wakes from the state of sleep he was in during the period of dissolution:

On reflection, having awoken and discerned by inference that the

---

38 Summary of *ŚB*. 6, 1, 1, 1-11.

39 *Kāṭhaka Saṃhitā*. 12, 5; 27, 1. Other examples are given by Lévi, 1898, p. 22.

> Earth had gone within the ocean, he resolved to act on extricating the Earth. Just as in the past at the beginning of the *kalpas* he had assumed other bodies such as that of the fish, tortoise etc., he took on the form of a boar. The Lord [Brahmā], he who goes everywhere, the origin of everything, is composed of the Vedas and the sacrifice, assumed a divine shape consisting of the Vedas and the sacrifice and then entered the waters The Lord of the universe having raised up the Earth from the lower hell, released it in the waters, being contemplated upon by those who are perfected who were assembled in Janaloka. Like a great boat the Earth stayed on that quantity of water, but did not sink because of the extension (*vitatatva*) of its body.[40]

Sexual symbolism is totally absent. Creation is the result of the creative power of the Vedas and sacrifice alone.

Boar symbolism is also associated with Prajāpati, and in a cosmogonic context where the influence of the sacrifice is quite evident:

> This universe was formerly waters, fluid. On it, Prajāpati, becoming wind, moved. He saw this [Earth]. Becoming a boar, he took her up. Becoming Viśvakarman, he wiped [the moisture] from her. She extended. She became the extended one.[41]

The idea of the earth extending herself relates directly to the sacrifice, because continuity of the ritual in the sacrifice is said to be 'extension'. As Biardeau says, "the boar of *the Brāhmaṇa* [*ŚB*. 14, I, 2, 11] extends the earth in order to fertilize it just as the sacrifice does."[42] The extending function of the sacrifice is implied

---

40 *MkP*. 47, 6-10; *ViP*. l, 4, 7-ll; *KP*. 1, 6, 7-24.

41 *TS*. 7, l, 5. Trans. Muir, 1872, Vol. 1, pp. 52-3. For other versions see Vol. 4. p. 28.

42 Biardeau, 1969, p.76. She goes on to say, "Hence we learn that the vitality of the *pratisarga* is guaranteed, not by an act of *yoga*, but by the Vedic sacrifice." However, I think that in the *MkP*. version of the myth the statement, "...being contemplated (*cintyamāno*) upon by those who are perfected," can be interpreted as referring to an act of *yoga*. If this is so the creation is supported both by the sacrifice and *yoga*.

in the Purāṇic cosmogony by use of the word *vitatatva*, describing the Earth floating on the waters of the ocean.

Maintenance of Cosmic Order

Creator gods like Prajāpati and Brahmā organize the triple world in accordance with *dharma*, or *ṛta* as it was termed in the Vedas. Often however, dharmic organization is thrown out of balance, and in mythology the inadvertent upset or the deliberate reversal of *ṛta* or *dharma* is frequently portrayed. The act of righting *dharma* in such cases has in the epics and Purāṇas been incorporated into the framework of the *avatāra* myth. Yet there are many examples in the literature of Prajāpati and Brahmā righting *dharma* when it has been overturned, but not using the guise of an *avatāra*.

Both gods are depicted as being committed to the preservation of *ṛta* and *dharma* because they have organized the triple world in terms of these behavioural categories, an organization guaranteeing harmony for all concerned. In truth both gods are in some sense the embodiment of the norm they have created. Prajāpati himself has the epithet 'firstborn of *ṛta*' used of him.[43] This has been understood to mean that the god was the first and most important embodiment of what *ṛta* represents and as such was considered to embody everything which was considered right and true in human behaviour, the affairs of the worlds and in the functioning of the rite.[44]

The implications of his embodiment, and defence, of *ṛta* are best expressed in myths where the motif of conflict between gods and demons is deployed. In the Brāhmaṇas this is not so much a conflict between good and evil, as between support for a cosmic organization based on *ṛta* or one based on its opposite–*anṛta*. The gods represent the forces of *ṛta* and demons the forces of *anṛta*. Prajāpati often intervenes in the conflict, always on the side of *ṛta*. Though he is father of both gods and demons and hence obliged

---

43 *TB*. 2, 8, 1, 3; *AV*. 4, 35, 1; 12, 1, 61. Bloomfield, 1964, p. 636. For more references see Gonda, 1989, pp.18-19.

44 Gonda, 1965, p. 282; 1960 Vol. 1.p. 78.

to treat them equally, he errs purposely on the side of the former because this is the side of *ṛta*.[45]

In the Brāhmaṇas victory in the conflict between gods and demons is guaranteed to the side in possession of the knowledge for the correct performance of the ritual. Prajāpati has this knowledge, so the gods (and sometimes the demons) continually seek to obtain it from him. A passage from the *PB*. illustrates this:

> The gods and demons competed for these worlds. The gods ran up to Prajāpati, who gave them this *sāman*, saying, "With this, you will drive them away." With that they drove them from these worlds ...[46]

In another passage the demons are shown to be defeated by a combination of their own arrogance and a failure to gain assistance from Prajāpati:

> The gods and the demons, both of whom were descended from Prajāpati, competed [with each other]. Arrogantly, the demons thought, "In whom should we sacrifice?" They continued sacrificing into their own mouths, and because of their arrogance they were ruined. Therefore, one should not think too highly [of oneself] because arrogance is the beginning of ruin.
>
> The gods continued performing sacrifices to one another. Prajāpati gave himself to them. Theirs is the sacrifice, for the sacrifice is the food of the gods. [47]

By sacrificing only to themselves and refusing to give portions to other groups, the demons refuse to acknowledge the interdependent nature of organization of the triple world. Refusal to participate in the interdependent relationship is reflected in their arrogance, symptomatic of their feeling of independence from other beings.

Their arrogance and non-participation threatens the ruin of

---

45 The name *prājāpatya*, 'derived from Prajāpati', is often used as a name for the gods and demons. See *ŚB*. 1, 5, 3, 2; 5, 1, 1, 1; Lévi, 1898, p. 27, n.5.

46 *Pañcaviṃśa Brāhmaṇa*. 8, 3, 1.

47 *ŚB*. 5, 1, 1, 1-2. Cf. Lévi, 1898, p. 55, citing *TS*. 1, 6, 10, 2.

the triple world, not only of themselves. So Prajāpati helps the gods who acknowledge the interdependent relationship between beings by sacrificing to each other. The latter is a sign of the reciprocity which goes hand in hand with brāhmaṇical functional interdependence, and is wholly consistent with *ṛta*.

The motif of conflict between gods and demons remains a pervasive feature of the mythology of the epics and Purāṇas. However, an important new element-*tapas*-has been introduced into the conflict. In the *śrauta* sacrifices of the Brāhmaṇas, *tapas* in the sense of austerity is performed primarily to render the performer pure enough to participate in the central parts of the sacrifice. By the time of the epics and Purāṇas *tapas* as ascetic heat derived from *tapas* as austerity has come to be regarded as an important source of power in itself. Śiva, for example, can burn up the triple world at the time of dissolution because of his accumulated *tapas*. Consequently, instead of the gods trying to defeat the gods with sacrifice, they try and defeat them with *tapas*.

The usual scenario begins with a certain demon who aspires to rule over the triple world, performing austerities in order to accumulate *tapas*.[48] Brahmā appears before him and offers him a boon in reward for his austerities. The demon typically requests immortality, but this is almost invariably refused. Instead, Brahmā grants him physical protection, virtually equivalent to invulnerability. On gaining the boon, the demon is able to defeat the gods in battle, usurp Indra's position as king of the gods and establish himself as sovereign of the triple world. When this happens the defeated gods go to Brahmā, tell him about the situation and he proposes a solution to rectify it. This usually entails the summoning of Viṣṇu or Śiva, who intervene in the conflict themselves or as an *avatāra*. Inevitably the demon is defeated.

In the Brāhmaṇas Prajāpati assists the gods in positive ways, by revealing the knowledge necessary for correct performance of the ritual. Brahmā's role in the conflict is a reversal of this. He

---

48 This subject is dealt with at length in Ch.9.

only helps the gods in a negative sense. When he grants a boon to a demon he effectively stops that demon from accumulating any more *tapas*.[49] For as soon as the demon accepts the boon he discontinues his *tapas*, thus opening the way for his defeat in combat with Viṣṇu or Śiva. So Brahmā's assistance to the gods is to limit the power of demons.

Like Prajāpati, Brahmā's motivation for helping the gods is his commitment to preservation of *dharma*. His association with *dharma* is clearly indicated by his epithet 'composed of *dharma*' (*dharmamaya*), though it is not entirely clear what this might mean, and the description of him as '*dharma* embodied'.[50] Similarly, as with Prajāpati, he too is father of gods and demons and is supposed to be impartial towards them and all other beings. But sometimes his impartiality is qualified as when he has to deal with the demon Tāraka:

> [Brahmā speaking] "I am impartial towards all beings, but I cannot approve of lawlessness being in the world. Tāraka who is harassing the groups of gods and sages must be killed immediately or the Vedas and rules of conduct (*dharma*) could go to ruin, best of gods."[51]

He can be impartial in his actions because he embodies *dharma*. It therefore becomes an absolute norm of behaviour for him, though not necessarily for Viṣṇu and Śiva who stand within the sphere of *nivṛtti* as much as *pravṛtti*.

His commitment to *dharma* is never more in evidence than in his refusal to grant demons immortality as a boon. If the demon were to be granted immortality his status would be that of a god, because demons are mortal by nature, gods immortal, and this situation is dharmically sanctioned. This is also one of the reasons why in the Brāhmaṇas the gods are successful with the sacrifice,

---

49 See *MBh*. 3, 259, 21-22, where Brahmā insists that Rāvaṇa and his three brothers must stop performing *tapas* before he will offer them a boon.

50 *MBh*. 12, 175, 34; *ŚP*. 2, 3, 43, 31. *Nārada P*. 1, 42, 37.

51 *Mbh*. 13, 84, 3-4ab; 8, 24, 34.

whereas demons are not. The sacrifice gave to the sacrificer a kind of immortality in the sense that it broke the continuum of repeated death. If demons had been granted this it would have belied their true status of mortality, a status consistent with *ṛta*.

It is not only adharmic demons who are a threat to *ṛta* or *dharma*. If a god or goddess does not perform his or her dharmically ordained function, the triple world is just as threatened as if a demon is on the rampage. The myth of Agni's disappearance is illustrative:

> ... Agni went away from the gods; he entered the water. The gods said to Prajāpati, "You search for him, for he shall appear to you, his own father." He became a white horse and looked for him. He found him on a lotus leaf after he had crept out of the water. He looked closely at him and Agni burnt him… .[52]

The gods are fearful of Agni's disappearance because he is the messenger between them and humans. As the sacrificial fire he consumes and brings to them the sacrificial offerings which are their food. Without Agni, that is to say, without fire, the sacrifice cannot be performed, and the whole basis of reciprocity between groups of living beings is undermined.

What is only implicit in this version becomes explicit in a later version of the myth found in the *MBh*:

> The sage Bhṛgu left his pregnant wife Pulomā to go and attend a royal consecration. A demon named Puloman saw her, became mad with love and wanted to abduct her. He saw Fire (*agni*) in the fire hall and placed an oath on him to speak the truth. He then asked if Pulomā was the woman who had once been bespoken to himself and then given to Bhṛgu in breach of the agreement. He repeatedly questioned Fire, who became afraid and whispered, "I am as frightened of speaking untruth (*anṛta*) as of Bhrgu's curse."
>
> The demon took this as assent to his question and fled with Pulomā. In their haste she aborted and her child who fell on to

---

52 *ŚB*. 7, 3, 2, 14; 6, 2, 1, 1-9. For other versions see O'Flaherty, 1975, pp. 97-104.

> the ground was called Cyavana. He burnt the demon to ashes with a glance. Brahmā comforted Pulomā and then Bhṛgu returned and asked her what had happened. She accused Fire of betraying her and Bhṛgu cursed him to become omnivorous.
>
> After he was cursed Fire said, "I am always striving after the Law and speak in accordance with the truth ... I could curse you [Bhṛgu] but I must respect brahmins... I am the mouth of the gods and ancestors through which the gods are given offerings on the full moon day and the ancestors on new moon day. How can I become omnivorous?"
>
> Then Fire withdrew himself from all sacrifices, the creatures became miserable and the three worlds lost their way. The gods and seers went to Brahmā and told him what had happened. Brahmā then went to see Agni and said, "... You are the maker of all these worlds and their end (*anta*). You are the upholder of the three worlds and the stimulator of rites ... You will not become omnivorous in the whole of your body. Flame-crested, these flames of yours will devour all that is acceptable. Just as everything touched by the sun's rays is considered to be pure, so everything that will be burnt up by your flame will be pure ... Through your own fiery energy make that sage's curse come true! Accept your own share and those of the gods which are offered into your mouth."
>
> Fire agreed to this and went back into the sacrifices. Everything returned to normal.[53]

Agni is cursed by Bhṛgu for telling the truth. According to his own testimony he had no choice but to tell the truth because he continually strives after the Law and was also held to an act of truth. It is paradoxical therefore, that his adherence to the correct behaviour (in refusing to lie about Pulomā) should lead to a situation where the Law understood as the normative and symbiotic relationship governing the conduct of beings in the triple world should be put in jeopardy. Nevertheless, this is the situation that prevails after Agni withdraws his flame due to Bhṛgu's curse. Without fire the sacrifice is ineffective, and without the sacrifice

53 Summary of *MBh*. 1, 5, 10-1, 7, 26.

gods, ancestors and humans cannot relate to each other in a way prospering them all.

At first sight there is some doubt about the meaning of Agni's omnivorous condition. Van Buitenen gives it an historicist interpretation when he says:

> It seems clear that the Fire's protest at becoming omnivorous repudiates a use of fire for certain purposes. One remembers that the Iranian cousins of the–Vedic Aryans could not use the equally sacred fire, e.g., to cremate their dead, lest its purity be impaired. The story points to some such innovation in the use of fire) ascribed as are other novelties in the fire cult to the innovative Bhṛgus.[54]

This explanation is rather vague and though the innovativeness of the Bhṛgus is well known, van Buitenen does not say what the innovation in the use of fire might have been. The myth itself suggests an alternative interpretation. If Agni became omnivorous it would mean he would consume all the sacrificial offerings placed in the fire. The implication is that polluted offerings would be consumed and all offerings in the sacrifice are supposed to be pure.[55] This surely is the import of Brahmā's advice to Agni to take everything that is acceptable in terms of purity.

If Agni is omnivorous it would have exactly the same effect as complete withdrawal of his flame. In one case the gods and ancestors would have received food unfit for them, and in the other case no food at all. Thus like Prajāpati, Brahmā has to use any means to rectify a situation which threatens the Law, any means except what is in opposition to the Law. This explains why Brahmā's solution to Agni's problem allows for the fulfilment of Bhṛgu's curse. In Indian mythology curses and boons always have to run their course. To prevent this would undermine something as basic as the continuity of the Law itself.

---

54 Van Buitenen, 1973, p.441.

55 Van Buitenen, 1973, p.441.

Bṛhaspati

The view that Bṛhaspati is the fore-runner, or at least a prototype of Brahmā has been advanced several times.[56] The consensus seems to be that Bṛhaspati is an apotheosis of the brahmin priest and as such is Brahmā's prototype. This in turn implies that Brahmā himself is the brahmin in apotheosis. Though to some extent valid, it is a view in need of qualification because, as I hope to show, it is more consistent with post-Vedic mythology to see him as a representative (or embodiment) of ritualist values, of which part is also expressed in the image of the brahmin. To be sure, Bṛhaspati has influenced those aspects of Brahmā's role that are identical with some of the functions of the brahmin. But in the past the extent of this god's influence on his mythology has tended to be overstressed, that of Prajāpati and other gods understressed.

In early Vedic literature Bṛhaspati is often associated with concepts tracing their origin back to the root *bṛh*. In the *ṚV.* and the Brāhmaṇas the epithet brahmā is often used of him.[57] He is also often said to be the *brahman,* a word which in the Brāhmaṇas can often be rendered as 'prayer' or 'hymn', but seems to denote the brahmin priest when used of Bṛhaspati.[58] If the *brāhmaṇa* is the one who possesses the brahman, then Bṛhaspati through his identity with this is the apotheosis of the power of the brahmins, and by extension of the whole class. His knowledge and control of the brahman is indicated by his alternative name Brahmaṇaspati as well as by epithets such as 'progenitor of all prayers' and 'supreme king of prayers'.[59] Emphasising his wisdom the *ṚV.* calls him 'poet of poets' (*kaviḥ kavīnām*), 'inspired' (*vipra*) and 'sage'

---

56 MacDonell, 1974, p.104; Bergaigne, 1878-83, Vol. 1, p.304; Gonda, 1960, p. 73; Joshi, 1972, pp. 106-7.

57 *ṚV.* 4, 50, 8; 10, 141, 3; *AV.* 3, 20, 4; *ŚB.* 5, 1, 4, 14; 5, 1, 5, 1; *GB.* 2. 1, 1; 2, 1, 4; *AB.* 1, 19.

58 *ŚB.* 5, 1, 1, 11. Cf. *ṚV.* 2, 23, 2.

59 *ṚV.* 2, 23,1-2.

(*ṛṣi*).[60] His lordship over prayer, his control of the brahman and his wisdom are stressed in the *ṚV*, where prayer as invocation is one of the most important ways to gain the favour of the gods. Each of these is also a characteristic of the *brahmā* priest and Bṛhaspati is the *brahmā* of the gods.[61]

In post-Vedic literature there are scattered references suggestive of Brahmā's identification with the brahmin and many more in which he is closely related to the brahmin class.[62] Some of the former are worth citing. A Buddhist text, the *Mahāvastu*, sees in the learned Mahāgovinda when he walks into a village, a king of a kingdom, a Brahmā to the brahmins.[63] In the *ŚP*, at a time when he is being attacked by Gaṇeśa, Brahmā appeals to his assailant to make peace because he is fighting with one who is a brahmin:

> Peace! Peace! 0 God! I have not come for battle. I am a brahmin who causes tranquillity and is not belligerent. I should be treated with favour.[64]

Finally, in Gandharan art and Pāli texts Brahmā and Indra are paired functionally as brahmin and *kṣatriya* respectively.[65]

Some passages in the epics and Purāṇas depict Brahmā performing some of the priestly functions attributed to Bṛhaspati in the Vedas, even though that god persists as a minor deity in post-Vedic literature. In a didactic passage Brahmā is shown advising the gods about a sacrificial site:

> Wishing to sacrifice, the gods came together to Brahmā in order

---

60 For references and comment see Schmidt, 1968, p. 29.

61 *ṚV*. 2, 23, 2; 23, 7; 25, 1. Though this may not be as clear cut as it seems. See the detailed references given in Gonda, 1989, pp.12-14.

62 Bailey, 1979, p.159, n.27.

63 *Mhv*, Trans. Jones, 1956, Vol. 3, p. 218.

64 *ŚP*. 2, 4, 15, 30.

65 Lamotte, 1958, p. 764; Joshi and Sharma, 1969, pp. 17 and 21. See also figs 3, 6a, 13. Cf. *KP*. 2, 26, 39.

to obtain a piece of ground. King, they asked for a pure spot, saying, "We would like to sacrifice." The gods said, "You are the lord of the entire Earth and the three heavens. With your authorization we would like to perform a sacrifice, illustrious god, for the fruit of sacrifice is not gained on unauthorised ground. You are the Lord of the entire world, moving and unmoving, therefore, please authorize us to perform it."

Then Brahmā said, "Bulls of gods, I will give you a piece of the earth. On that spot, sons of Kaśyapa, you will perform your sacrifice."[66]

His knowledge of sacrificial ritual is also brought up in another passage from a late Purāṇa. ln the context of the *liṅgodbhava* myth Śiva admonishes Brahmā for lying and then grants him a few boons:

I will give you another boon. You will be the honoured *guru* in regard to all sacrifices, both domestic and public. A sacrifice, although containing the correct rites and presents, will be fruitless without you.[67]

Also, like Brhaspati, he sometimes takes the role of the brahmā priest in the sacrifice.[68]

If these brahmin-like characteristics of Brahmā are rather general and relate as much to Prajāpati as to Bṛhaspati, there is another more specific aspect of Bṛhaspati's role reflected in some of Brahmā's activities. From the *ṚV.* onwards he is known in Indian literature as Indra's *purohita.* The *purohita* is a brahmin who is required to advise the king on political and religious matters, as well as to perform sacrifices on his behalf and ride into battle with him whilst protecting him with magic charms. The *ṚV.* in particular gives ample testimony to Bṛhaspati's performance of this role. He is Indra's ally and chariot driver when that god frees the waters which had been enclosed in darkness by Vṛtra.[69] In his

66 *MBh.* 13, 65, 17-20.

67 *ŚP.* 1, 8, 13-14.

68 *ŚP.* 2, 2, 27, 13. Cf. 2, 2, 20, 32.

69 *ṚV.* 2, 23, 18; 2, 24, 2; 10, 103, 4. Other details can be found in

own right he performs a number of warlike acts including fighting Vala and freeing the cows hidden in the mountains.[70]

In post-Vedic literature Bṛhaspati retains his position as Indra's *purohita*, but Brahmā's relationship with Indra also seems to some extent to be modelled on that of *purohita* and king. Brahmā performs some of the traditional roles of the *purohita*, such as consecrating Indra into the kingship of the gods and advising him when he is in trouble.[71] There are a number of occasions when Brahmā gives advice of a religious nature to Indra in order to help him out of troublesome situations. One of these arose when Indra broke an agreement with the demon Namuci:

> [Indra speaking] "I swear to you truly O friend, foremost of demons, that I will not kill you in the wet or the dry, nor during the day or at night." Having made the agreement the Lord discharged mist. Vāsava then cut off Namuci's head with some froth of water, king.
>
> But the amputated head followed behind Śakra, saying in his presence, "Hey! Evil god, killer of a friend!" Being repeatedly incited by the head and feeling tormented, he communicated the matter to the Grandfather. The World-teacher said to him, "Indra of the gods, when you have sacrificed and bathed in the Aruṇā river, the evil of killing a brahmin will be removed."
>
> When he was told this and having sacrificed correctly at the arbour on the Sarasvatī river, the killer of Vala bathed in the Aruṇā. Then, freed from the evil act of killing a brahmin, the Lord of the thirty went happily to the third heaven.[72]

A similar pattern of events occurs in some versions of the Indra/Vṛtra myth in the *Mbh*. In the *Śāntiparvan* version Indra kills Vṛtra who is a brahmin and a devotee (*bhakta*) of Viṣṇu.[73] Both Viṣṇu and Śiva also participate in the killing: Viṣṇu by entering

---

Schmidt, 1968, p.100ff; MacDonell, 1974, p.103.

70 *ṚV*. 4, 50, 5; 10, 68, 4-9.

71 *MBh*.1, 204, 24; 13, 103,30-34.

72 *MBh*. 9, 42, 30-36.

73 *Mbh*. 12, 272, 27-273, 60. In other epic and Purāṇic versions of

Indra's *vajra* and Śiva by becoming a fever and entering Vṛtra. But in the final analysis it is Indra who strikes the killing blow, and it is he who has to carry the personified sin of killing a brahmin (*brahmahatyā*) on his neck. When this happens his immediate reaction is to hide in a lotus stalk, but then he approaches Brahmā for help, and he says to the *brahmahatyā*.'This Indra of the thirty should be freed! Do this as a favour to me, passionate woman !'[74]

She gives her assent to this and Brahmā divides her into four parts giving a quarter share to each of Agni, the plants, the apsaras and the waters. Finally, Indra obtains Brahmā's permission to perform a horse sacrifice which will purify him to the extent where he can re-establish his kingship.

Despite Indra's killing of two different demons-Namuci and Vṛtra-the account of their killing and the subsequent events represent two different versions of the same myth. Both contain motifs prominent in epic-Purāṇic mythology. The *bhakti* motif is found in the second version. Vṛtra is Viṣṇu's *bhakta* and Brahmā's words cited above, persuading the *brahmahatyā* to leave Indra, hint that she is Brahmā's *bhakta*.[75] The *brahmahatyā* motif is found elsewhere in the Purāṇas and the *Rām*; the most prominent other expressions of it being Rāvaṇa's death at the hands of Rāma and Śiva's killing of Brahmā. A third motif, Brahmā's distribution of the personified *brahmahatyā*, has a parallel in an *MkP*. myth where Brahmā establishes evil actions and evil places by instructing the demon Duḥsaha to reside in such places or with people who perform such actions.[76] Both motifs function etiologically to account for the existence of evil in the triple world.

---

the myth Brahmā is largely absent. See *BhavP*. 6, 9-13; *Rām*. (C) 7, 75-7; *MkP*. 5.

74 *MBh*. 12, 273, 22a-b.

75 *MBh*. 12, 273, 22 *mucyatāṃ tridaśendro 'yaṃ matpriyaṃ kuru bhamīni. Cf. Bhg*. 12, 14-20, where Kṛṣṇa is speaking and, in several verses, ends each of his statements with the words '*sa* [*bhaktaḥ*] *me priyaḥ*.'

76 *MkP*. 50, 42ff.

In both versions of the myth Indra's position contrasts radically with what it was in the myths where he and Bṛhaspati together kill Indra. None of the motifs mentioned above are present in the Vedic tellings of the myth, nor does Indra require the help of a Viṣṇu or Śiva to kill Vṛtra. The truth of the matter is that the Indra of post-Vedic literature is different from the Indra of the Vedas, especially of the *RV*. In post-Vedic literature he has become a seducer of wives whose husbands are away and a warrior who gains victory by deceit.[77] Yet as in the Vedas he still has a brahmin to give him advice. Because of Indra's transformed status, this brahmin, who is usually Brahmā, helps him out of humiliating defeats, not to celebrate triumphant victories.[78]

In the *Mbh.* versions of the Vṛtra and Namuci myths the killing of a demon who has brahmin status is a more serious crime than permitting the existence of a demon whose very intention is directed against that *dharma* which protests so heavily against the killing of a brahmin. Clearly there is a clash of *dharma* here. When Indra kills Vṛtra and Namuci, the demons, he is acting in accord with his *kṣatriya svadharma.* However, in killing two brahmins he refuses to acknowledge the status of a higher class and abrogates the co-operative relationship between *kṣatriya* and brahmin which, according to the classical texts, was so essential for maintenance of stability in the kingdom and the larger triple world.

In both cases another brahmin has to extract him from a situation which essentially arises from his failure to recognize his *varṇa* obligations. The intervention of a brahmin is necessary for two reasons. Firstly, because Indra has committed a 'first-function' crime according to Dumézil's tri-functional scheme and this must be expiated by someone who represents that

---

77 See Hopkins, 1974, pp.129ff. for examples.

78 Though Indra's *purohita* throughout the *MBh*. Bṛhaspati plays no role in the Namuci myth. In the Vṛtra myth be tells Indra to kill the demon and requests aid on Indra's behalf from Śiva (*MBh*. 12, 272, 29 and 32).

function.[79] Secondly, to re-establish the relationship between brahmin and *kṣatriya* temporarily broken after Indra's killing of the two demons. In regard to the latter, the conflict between Indra and the *brahmahatyā* revives the tension between brahmin and *kṣatriya*, so much a feature of post-Vedic literature, and expressed explicitly in the relationships Brahmā has with Indra and Pṛthu. This tension is certainly present in this version of the Indra/Vṛtra myth and is made very explicit when at the end of the telling of the myth, Bhīṣma warns Yudhiṣṭhira to act kindly towards brahmins in every way because they are gods on Earth.[80]

Brahmā's function in both versions of the myth is to advise Indra how to rid himself finally of the *brahmahatyā*, a problem requiring religious expertise. In the Namuci version it is the purgative power of a sacred place like the river Sarasvatī that rids Indra of the *brahmahatyā*. As for the Vṛtra version, it is Brahmā's request to the *brahmahatyā* to leave Indra and his insistence that the god perform a sacred act, the horse sacrifice, to purify himself completely. Despite Indra's relative decline since the *RV*, the relationship between a king and his brahmin adviser remains intact and it is this which circumscribes the relationship between Indra and Brahmā.

In all the passages cited parallels between Bṛhaspati and Brahmā are present, but they are less striking than those which occur between Prajāpati and Brahmā. It is significant however, that like Prajāpati, Bṛhaspati is a god who embodies all that is central in the Brāhmaṇical tradition of ritual and sacrifice. N. J. Shende summarizes:

> ... Bṛhaspati is associated with the *brahman* in all its implications in different periods of the Vedic literature. In the Ṛg *Veda* he is lord of the *brahman* (the *ṛcs*). In the *Atharva Veda* he is the master of the magic (the *brahman*). In the *Brāhmaṇas*, he is the *yajña* (the *brahman*).Thus though the significance of the word

79 Dumezil, 1970, Dubuisson, 1979, pp.466-71.

80 *MBh*. 12, 273, 59.

brahman changed in the different periods, Bṛhaspati remained-
its master or lord.[81]

He is therefore a symbol of orthodoxy in all its manifestations, a fitting precursor of Brahmā in the epics and Purāṇas.

81 Shende, 1946-7, p.243, n.43.

PART THREE

Brahmā in the Cosmogonic Myths

Chapter 4

Prākṛtasarga and Pratisarga

In most of the cosmogonic myths in the *Mbh.* and the Purāṇas Brahmā is acknowledged as the creator god.[1] Behind the apparent divergence in the content of many of these myths, two basic views of cosmogony stand out. The first encompasses the notion of *prākṛtasarga*, 'primary creation' and *pratisarga*, 'secondary creation', the dominant conception of cosmogony in the Purāṇas. It is developed partially in terms of the cosmogony of the *Sāṃkhyakārikās* and partially in terms of 'evolutionary' cosmogonies associated with theism found in the twelfth book of the *Mbh.*

The second view of cosmogony is presented in a series of myths in the Purāṇas which at the level of narrative are about conflict between Brahmā, Viṣṇu and Śiva. But in terms of the motifs found in them, they are just as much concerned with progenation as a means of creation, with renunciation, *bhakti* and the problem of death. The two views of cosmogony are not exclusive of one another, but for reasons of clarity I have decided to treat them separately.

Little understanding of Brahmā's distinctive roles in these two kinds of cosmogony would be gained merely by drawing up a list of all his creative activities or by exhaustively describing the

1 It is no doubt significant that the *Rām.* contains virtually no creation myths.

cosmogonic imagery relating to him.[2] It is preferable to focus on those aspects of his creative role exclusive to him and to bring out their significance in the greater context of the cosmogonies in which he plays this role.

Prākṛtasarga–Brahmā as *Ahaṃkāra*

The *prākṛtasarga*, the creation of the entire universe (as opposed to the creation of the triple world which forms the subject of *pratisarga*) takes place every one hundred *kalpas* and lasts the duration of Brahmā's life.[3] The beginning of the creation process in the *prākṛtasarga* is impelled by an act of *yoga* performed by the supreme being, usually Viṣṇu or Śiva. This creation process takes the form of an 'evolutionary' development beginning from the *pradhāna* or 'primary matter', and ends with the appearance of an egg and Brahmā, the contents of the former described with these words:

> In the beginning Brahmā appeared as the original creator of beings. All this, the triple world with its moving and non-moving things was encompassed within that egg. Mt Meru was born from it and the mountains were the afterbirth. The oceans were the foetal fluid of the Great Self's [Brahmā] egg. In that egg was all this universe with its gods, demons, men, continents and other lands, oceans and the collection of luminous worlds.[4]

The appearance of the egg is the final stage of the 'evolutionary' development, and it is essentially mechanistic except for the initial impulse resulting from the action of a god.

Implicit in the description of the egg and the final stages of the *prākṛtasarga* following the egg's appearance is the stipulation that Brahmā's emergence as the *first individual* is the

---

2 This has already been done for the two epics by Hopkins, 1974, pp.198-201.

3 Biardeau, 1968, 1969, has studied the *prākṛtasarga* and *pratisarga* in great detail.

4 *MkP*. 45, 64cd-67ab; *KP*. 1, 4, 40-41; *ViP*. 1, 2, 56; *GP*. 4, 9cd.

necessary precondition for the egg's contents to be manifested in individualized form. One text makes this view explicit:

> Rudra, the gold coloured egg appeared, for that itself is the end product from him alone.[5] Firstly, the Lord assumed a bodily form (*śarīragrahaṇa*) for the purpose of creation. After he had become the four-faced Brahmā, who always has an over-abundance of *rajas* and had assumed a bodily form, he emitted this creation, both moving and non-moving.[6]

Brahmā's distinctive role in the *prākṛtasarga* is to be the individualizing agent (*kartā*) that allows for manifestation of the egg's contents.

In the *SK*. and many cosmogonies of the *Mbh*. and the Purāṇas, the individualizing agent is called *ahaṃkāra*. From its earliest literary appearance in the middle Upanisads and the *Mbh*. this word has been used to convey two related notions.[7] Firstly, it refers to the idea of the 'erroneous self-projection of the spirit' (*puruṣa*) into an individual form such as a body.[8] Secondly, it refers to that specific state in the cosmogonic process when undifferentiated consciousness (*mahat*) becomes individualized into name and form (*nāmarūpa*), which is a synonym for the empirical world in Sanskrit literature. It is best translated literally as 'I- maker' because it causes the *puruṣa* (at the micro-cosmic level) and the *mahat* (at the macro-cosmic level) to become embodied in the sense of assuming an empirical individuality.[9] Van Buitenen rightly finds the origin of the *ahaṃkāra* notion in the cosmogonies of the Brāhmaṇas where "...at the beginning of creation a primordial being becomes conscious of himself, formulates himself, creates

---

5 This could mean that the egg is the end result of an evolutionary sequence beginning from Viṣṇu (*GP*. 1, 4, 6-8).

6 *GP*. 1, 4, 8-9.

7 For references and comment see Biardeau, 1965, pp. 62-84.

8 For this and other definitions see van Buitenen, 1957, p. 16.

9 I am not suggesting here that the *puruṣa* is the micro-cosmic equivalent of *mahat*, only that the *ahaṃkāra* modifies both in the same way.

himself... consciousness-formulation-creation is actually one single process."[10] The vital act in these cosmogonies is the act of self-recognition, the recognition by the creator that he is an individual, an 'I' (*aham*), as opposed to a universal, an *ātman*.

In one *Mbh.* passage *ahaṃkāra* is defined in a way evoking both its philosophical and mythological aspects:

> The Great which originated first is called the ego, and when it has become the thought 'I am' it is called the second creation. And the ego is traditionally called the origin of the elements and that which is itself modified.[11] It is Prajāpati, the creation of beings, consciousness of energy and the primary element. It is the god who is the origin of the gods and the mind, the maker of the three worlds. By thinking 'I am' he is said to relate everything to himself. Of those sages who thirst after knowledge of the higher self, who have cultivated the self and who are accomplished in sacrifice and study of Vedic texts, it is the eternal world. For that man who enjoys the qualities through the ego, it is the origin of beings and so creates, hence it is the maker of the elements. As the power of modification it sets all this in motion and with its own energy it enlivens the universe."[12]

This passage is one of about a dozen in the *Mbh.* where Brahmā is identified with *ahaṃkāra*. It underscores their functional identity by bringing together synonyms and epithets common to both. In the cosmogonies of the Purāṇas and the *SK. ahaṃkāra* is divested of any of the theological affiliations of the kind present here.

Some of the epithets in this passage emphasize *ahaṃkāra's* cosmogonic role, besides which it is also attributed with influencing the formulation of the triple world. That it is said to

10 van Buitenen, 1957, p. 19.

11 The critically edited text reads *tejasaścetana* here. However, the critical apparatus records a variant reading *taijasa*, that is contained in seven manuscripts, both northern and southern, and Vādirāja's commentary. In my view *taijasa* fits the context of the passage better than *tejasa*, because the *śloka* is clearly describing the three divisions of the *ahaṃkāra bhūtādi*, *taijasa* and *vaikārika*.

12 *MBh.* 14, 41, 1-5.

stimulate the world signifies its function in causing the world to be a place of action. In itself this relates as much to the *ahaṃkāra's* micro-cosmic, as to its macro-cosmic, function. It defines the person as an agent of action as well as marking the triple world as the place where actions take place.

The micro-cosmic role of *ahaṃkāra* is fully developed in another definition given in the KP:

> "The *ahaṃkāra* is traditionally said to be presumption, the doer of acts, the thinker, the individual self and the material living body," from which come all 'activities' (*pravṛttayaḥ*). The five elements and the subtle elements were born from the *ahaṃkāra*, as were the senses and the gods. The whole world is its offspring.[13]

Each of the listed synonyms refers to the embodied individual. Even the inclusion of the *ātman* is probably meant to convey the idea of the self as it resides in the body, not yet independent of it. A similar list occurs in the *PU.* and there a clear distinction is implied between these aspects (*kartā*, *ahaṃkāra* and so forth) of the person (*puruṣa*) and the supreme self (*parātman*).[14]

Two synonyms of *ahaṃkāra* included in this list occur as epithets of Brahmā. The epithet *kartā* (Pāli-*kattā*) is used of him frequently in both Sanskrit and Pāli texts, sometimes just as *kartā*, at other times as part of a compound like *sarvakartā*, 'maker of everything', the cosmogonic significance of which is obvious.[15] *Kartā* can be rendered as 'maker, doer, agent of an act'. Even when used of Brahmā in a cosmogonic sense its other meaning 'agent of an act' is still implied. It is in this latter sense that the

---

13 *KP*. 1, 4, 19-20. This list seems to be unique to this Purāṇa.

ahaṃkāro 'bimānaśca kartā mantā ca sa smṛtaḥ /
ātmā ca pudgalo jīvo yataḥ sarvāḥ pravṛttayaḥ //
pañcabhūtāny ahaṅkārāt tanmātrāṇi ca jajñire /
indriyāṇi tathā devāḥ sarvaṃ tasyātmajaṃ jagat //

14 *PU*. 4, 9.

15 *MU*. 1, 1, 1, *MBh*. 8, 24, 101; 12, 121, 55; *ŚP*. 2, 2, 10, 30; 2, 5, 1, 28; *DN*. 1, 18; 1, 222; *MN*. 1, 327; It. p. 15.

word is used in the Upaniṣads.[16] In the *MaitrīU.* the *kartā* is the 'elemental self (*bhūtātman*) a synonym of the embodied *ātman*, that is, the *ātman* existing in a form binding it to further rebirth.[17] The *Bhg.* gives clarity to this view of *kartā* when it declares the *ātman* not to be the agent of an act (*akartā*) because 'Acts are always performed by the *guṇas* of *prakṛti*. He who is perplexed because of the *ahaṃkāra* thinks, 'I am the doer' (*kartā*).[18]

The recognition that one is exclusively *kartā* involves an ontological error: considering the impermanant mind/body to be the permanent (*nitya*) *ātman*. From the perspective of *nivṛttidharma* this is one of the fundamental characteristics of one who adheres to *pravṛttidharma*. Ultimately, *kartā* and *ahaṃkāra* stand in metaphysical opposition to *ātman*, thus reflecting the *pravṛtti/nivṛtti* dichotomy.

The other synonym of *ahaṃkāra* used adjectivally of Brahmā is *abhimāna*, a word which translates as 'presumption', but connotes the idea of 'thinking of one's self only' and implies the existence of an ego. The word is used adjectivally of Brahmā in the Purāṇic cosmogony. At the time of the *pratisarga*, after he has lifted the earth out of the ocean, he creates various kinds of beings through meditation. The first creation is characterized by extreme ignorance:

> This ignorance consisting of five components originated from the great one whilst he, with a capacity to focus on himself, was meditating, and so a creation arrayed as five-fold arose.[19]

Brahmā rejects this creation as being ineffective for attaining liberation and goes on to create three more creations. *Abhimāna* is

---

16 *BhU.* 4, 3, 10; *ChU.* 7, 8, l; *KU.* 4, 19; *PU.* 4, 9; *MU.* 3, l, 3.

17 *MaitrīU.* 3, 3.

18 *Bhg.* 3, 27.

19 *BḍP.* l, 5, 32; *LP.* 70,141; *ViP.* I, 5, 5-6; *KP.* 1, 7, 3. See also *MBh.* 12, 335, 18, where Brahmā is described as rising out of a lotus growing on Aniruddha's navel just prior to the creation of the worlds. A commentator, Vādirāja, glosses Aniruddha wirh *mahat* and Brahmā with *abhimāna*.

not conducive to liberation because it gives rise to the five forms of ignorance, the same ignorance conflating the *kartā* and the *ātman* together to be the unique *ātman*, thus placing a veil over the real, inactive and non-egoist *ātman*.

A full understanding of Brahmā's functional identity with *ahaṃkāra* is best obtained by looking at the various passages where they are actually identified. All deal with cosmogony. The first is a description of the creation given by Bhṛgu to Bharadvāja:

> There was a god named Mānasa who was known of old by the great sages. He had no beginning and was without end, being indivisible and subject neither to old age nor death. He was known as 'the unmanifest' and was eternal, unalterable and imperishable. From him created beings are born and die. He who is the mighty god who supports all beings, emitted first that which was named 'Great' (*mahat*), also known as 'atmosphere'. Water arose from the atmosphere, and fire and wind from water; then the Earth arose by the combination of fire and wind.
>
> Thereafter a celestial lotus composed of fiery energy was emitted by the Self-born, and from that lotus arose Brahmā, containing the Vedas and called Nidhi. He is the maker of the being who is the self of all beings and is known as the *ahaṃkāra*. Indeed, Brahmā, who possesses much fiery energy (*sumahātejas*), is these five primeval elements. The mountains were called his bones, his fat and flesh were the Earth, just as his blood was the sea, his belly the atmosphere. Moreover his expiration was the wind, his fiery energy fire, and the rivers were his blood vessels. Agni, Soma, and the sun and the moon were known to be his eyes, and his head was the upper atmosphere, the earth his feet, the regions his arms. Doubtless, he is hardly conceivable, even for the sages, since he is endless. Known as the 'divine Viṣṇu who is without end', he exists in the being who is the self of all beings and those who are not perfected in themselves have difficulty comprehending him. Truly, to effect the production of all beings he is the creator of the *ahaṃkāra*, from which the universe arose.[20]

In this passage appear two separate cosmogonic schemes

---

20 *MBh*. 12, 175, 11-21c.

linked by a kind of elemental theory. The first unfolds in a vertical evolution and can be conceptualized in the following way: *avyakta* → *mahat* = atmosphere → water → fire and wind → earth. The *avyakta* is the unformed absolute (Brahman), the ultimate source of all creation.[21] However, the exact nature of *mahat* in this cosmogony is not clear. In the cosmogonies of the Purāṇas and the *SK. mahat* is the first manifest but not yet individuated stage of consciousness beyond the *avyakta*. There individuality arises with the appearance of the *ahaṃkāra*, which is the state of creation following the *mahat*. The cosmogony under discussion differs from this in that the *mahat* seems to be performing the function of the *ahaṃkāra*. Its appearance produces individuality in the form of the four elements. The attribution of this function to the *mahat* is not unprecedented in the *Mbh*, because it presents another cosmogony where *buddhi* (= *mahat*) evolves into mind, senses and elements, a scheme where the *ahaṃkāra* is not present.[22]

The second cosmogony begins with Brahmā's birth from a lotus on Viṣṇu's navel. In vertical evolutionary terms the following sequence results; Viṣṇu (Svayambhū) → lotus → Brahmā = (elements). Unlike the first cosmogony, which is a sequential vertical evolution, this one is vertical for three steps and then a horizontal development ensues. The motif of Brahmā's birth from Viṣṇu's navel is suggestive of the initial stage of the *pratisarga*, but the cosmogony itself closely parallels the *prākṛtasarga*. In the latter scheme the *avyakta* emits the *mahat*, which in turn emits the *ahaṃkāra*. This consists of three distinct strands corresponding to the *guṇas*. From the *guṇas* the five sets of elements and senses are produced. These are the basic constituents of the contents of the egg in which Brahmā resides. This cosmogony can be presented in the following sequence: *avyakta* → *mahat* → *ahaṃkāra* (= the three *guṇas*) → elements and senses (= the material from which the egg is made) → Brahmā. Here there is a doubling in the sequence because functionally *ahaṃkāra* appears twice. In the

21 For details see Larson, 1969, pp.197-201.

22 See van Buitenen, 1957, p.22.

first place it appears in its normal position in the *prākṛtasarga*, directly after *mahat*. Secondly, Brahmā is *ahaṃkāra* when he is born from the egg, the act (or event?) enabling its contents to appear in individualized form.

How are these two cosmogonies, so resembling the *prākṛtasarga*, related to each other? The answer is suggested further on when Bhṛgu talks to Bharadvāja about the infinity of the universe and Mānasa. In the space of a few verses he gives a third cosmogony:

> The first to be emitted from the lotus was the mighty Lord, Brahmā, who is omniscient, embodied and contains *dharma*. He is the unsurpassed Prajāpati. Bharadvāja said, 'If Brahmā is produced from the lotus, then the lotus must be the first [to be born]. But you said that Brahmā is the first born. I am confused about this.' Bhṛgu said, 'It is said that the earth is the lotus, and it exists here as a seat for that form of Mānasa which is Brahmā.'[23]

Mānasa is Viṣṇu and he is the avyakta who becomes manifest in order to create. The lotus represents *mahat* and Brahmā is the *ahaṃkāra*, suggested by the description of him as being 'embodied' (*mūrtimān*). Embodiment or possession of an embodied form is fundamental to the notion of *ahaṃkāra*, because individuality is chiefly characterized by name and form (*nāmarūpa*) and it implies embodiment.[24] Following Bhṛgu's explanation it can be concluded that the inclusion of *ahaṃkāra* distinguishes the second view of cosmogony from the first. Down to the stage of *mahat* they are identical.[25]

---

23 *MBh*. 12, 175, 34-6. See also *GB*. 1, 1, 16 where it is said "Brahman created Brahmā on the lotus."

24 On this van Buitenen, 1957, p.19 says, 'The *ahaṃkāra* is the *ahaṃnāman*, the NAME I, by which the creator formulates himself, and to which automatically corresponds a FORM in which the I is embodied.'

25 There is one important discrepancy between Bhṛgu's explanation and the other two versions of cosmogony. Bhṛgu says the lotus is the Earth and I have suggested that it represents *mahat*. However, in neither of the cosmogonies is Earth identified with *mahat*,

As soon as individuality is introduced creation can proceed in any number of ways. In the first cosmogony the *mahat* gives rise to an evolutionary chain consisting of the elements. The second cosmogony differs from this in that Brahmā's body, which consists of the elements, breaks up and from its various parts the physical features of the universe are formed in a manner resembling the dismemberment of Puruṣa described in *RV*. 10, 90.

Another cosmogony where Brahmā and *ahaṃkāra* are identified is recounted by Vasiṣṭha to King Janaka:

> You should hear how this world passes away, protector of the Earth, and also about what does not pass away and will endure for as long as time. Know that a *kalpa* consists of twelve thousand fourfold *yugas*. It is said that a day of Brahmā elapses after one thousand *kalpas*, and that his night is just as long, king. At the end of which night, [Viṣṇu] the unembodied self (*amūrtātmā*), Śambhu, the self-born, who is the tiniest, the lightest, who can obtain everything, the unfading light, creates that great being, born first, whose actions are without end, who is embodied, the universe. He has hands and feet everywhere, eyes, mouths, faces and ears on every side. He exists in the world, encompassing all.
>
> He is traditionally called Hiraṇyagarbha, the illustrious Lord, and *buddhi*. In addition, amongst the yogins he is called *mahat* and also Viriñci. When the learned treatise on Sāṃkhyā is recited he is invoked with various names. He is traditionally called "he who has various forms, the self of all, the one, imperishable." This triple world of manifold nature is completely encompassed by his Self. Because he is many-formed he is traditionally called Viśvarūpa.
>
> Having effected a modification (*vikriyā*) of himself, he who has great fiery energy (*mahātejas*), emitted through his self the self,

---

rather it appears in the cosmogonic process several stages after *mahat*. Perhaps Bhṛgu identified the Earth and the lotus in this context because in Hindu mythology they are both important fertility symbols. For details see Gonda, 1969, p. 104, n. 52. Cf. Biardeau, 1969, p. 66, " ... it is tempting to see in the lotus where Brahmā is installed, the symbolic equivalent of the cosmic egg inhabited by the embryo of god."

> which is the *ahaṃkāra*, Prajāpati, made by the I (*ahaṃkṛtam*). From the unmanifest arose the manifest. They declare it and *mahat* to be the creation of knowledge, and that of the *ahaṃkāra* to be the creation of ignorance. Similarly, what is not an ordinance and what is an ordinance originated from that one, as well as what is regarded as knowledge and ignorance by those who contemplate the meaning of the Vedic texts and the learned treatises.
>
> Know, king, that the third creation comes from the *ahaṃkāra* and is called elemental. The fourth creation, the modified, occurs when all the elements of the *ahaṃkāra* have arisen. These are wind, light, atmosphere, water and earth. Also, there is sound, touch, form, taste and smell. There is no doubt that this collection of ten arose simultaneously. Indra of kings, know truly that the fifth creation is elemental.[26]

The elements of the fifth creation consist of the bodily organs and the mind. Altogether the number of elements in each of the groups totals twenty-four and in total they constitute all matter in the universe.

This cosmogony is another version of those already discussed, differing from them in the greater number of 'evolutionary' sequences and elements which constitute the creation. Viṣṇu retains his position as the *avyakta*, the ultimate source of creation. Brahmā is both *mahat* and *ahaṃkāra*. This is inconsistent with the other cosmogonies, but it is consistent with the view that creation occurs when a primordial unembodied being becomes embodied, hence individualized. *Mahat* becomes modified as *ahaṃkāra*. As such the *mahat* represents Brahmā in his unembodied state as Hiraṇyagarbha, whereas in his embodied state as Prajāpati he is *ahaṃkāra*.[27]

---

26 *MBh*. 12, 291, 13-25.

27 In this respect it is probably significant that in this cosmogony Brahmā is called Hiraṇyagarbha, 'he of the golden womb', when he is *mahat*. This name designates Brahmā when he is still within the golden womb, which corresponds functionally to the world egg. When he is born he is the *ahaṃkāra*.

Besides this there are several other instances where Brahmā is identified with *mahat*. In the narration of the *prakṛtasarga* his name is listed as synonymous with *mahat*:

mahān ātmā matir brahmā prabuddhiḥ khyātir īśvaraḥ /
prajñā dhṛtiḥ smṛtiḥ saṃvid etasmād iti tat smṛtam // [28]

This explanation, focussing in part on Brahmā's large size (exemplified in descriptions of him as the cosmic *puruṣa*) to clarify his similarity with *mahat*, is consistent with the meaning of this word as 'great' and 'large'. However, the second part of the explanation, emphasizing *mahat's* capacity to make things solid, is inconsistent with the function of *mahat* in the cosmogonies of the *MBh.* and the Purāṇa.[29] In these cosmogonies *mahat* is manifest consciousness which is not 'individualized'; it is the *ahaṃkāra* which brings about the individualization of the manifest creation.

Brahmā is connected with *mahat* in two other ways. In the Purāṇic cosmogony there is a listing of nine stages of creation recapitulating the most important stages of the *prākṛtasarga* and the *pratisarga*. The list begins: "The first creation was that of *mahat*. It is also regarded as the creation of Brahmā."[30]

Similarly, both *mahat* and Brahmā are attributed with performing the act of creation because they are impelled by a desire to create (*sisṛkṣur*).[31] This desire to create is such a

28 *KP*. 1, 4, 17; LP. 70, 12.

29 In the Upaniṣads the 'great self' (*mahān ātmā*), the precursor of the *mahat* of the *MBh.* and Purāṇas, performed the role of the *mahat* and the *ahaṃkāra*. About its cosmogonic role van Buitenen, 1964, p. 108, says 'The large *ātman* is the original creator who or which, has as it were embodied himself in creation.' This role originally performed by the 'great *ātman*' might explain why in the *BḍP*. *mahat* and Brahmā are regarded as synonyms.

30 *KP*. 1, 7, 13 ab; *MkP*. 47, 31 ab; *ViP*. l, 5, 19cd.

31 For *mahat* see *BḍP*. I, 3, 16cd; *LP*. 70, 11; and for Brahmā see *MkP*. 48, 4 cd; *ViP*. 1, 6, 3 cd; *KP*. 1, 7, 38. The motif of a 'desire to create' continues on from the theme of Prajāpati's wish to multiply himself (*prajāpatir akāmayata prajāyeyeti*) just prior to

pronounced feature of Brahmā in the Purāṇic cosmogony that it might exemplify a broader notion of desire to act, the hallmark of *pravṛtti* values. Such an interpretation is made credible by the fact that some of the *prajāpatis* (Brahmā's sons), whose role is to create through progenation, reject the desire to create and become ascetics.[32] They renounce all desire and action–excommunication being the hallmark of *nivṛtti* values.

In summary, identification of Brahmā with *mahat* reflects a functional identity.[33] This is especially so when Brahmā is in his Hiraṇyagarbha state which is the equivalent of unmanifested consciousness. The *ahaṃkāra* is a modification of *mahat*, albeit a radical modification. It is not fundamentally different from it; both are *prakṛti*. In the cosmogony just cited this modification occurs in the figure of Brahmā when he changes from his Hiraṇyagarbha to his Prajāpati state.

The next instance of an identification of Brahmā with *ahaṃkāra* is in a cosmogony narrated by Yajñavalkya in order to illustrate the number of *kalpas* of various *tattvas*:

> Best of men, listen to me about the duration of the unmanifest god (*avyakta*). His day is said to be ten thousand *kalpas*, and his night is just as long. When he awakes, overlord of men, he firstly emits plants for the sustenance of all living creatures. Then he emitted Brahmā who was produced from the golden egg. 'He is the material form of all beings' (*sa mūrtiḥ sarvabhūtānām*), so we have heard. When he had lived in the egg for a year, Prajāpati, the great sage (*muṇi*), left it and brought together one

---

beginning the creation. See *TB*. 2, 1, 2, 7; *ŚB*. 6, 1, 1, 8; *AB*. 10, 3.

32 *H*. 1, 32; *ŚP*. 5, 29, 19; *MkP*. 50, 7-8; *PaP*. 5, 3,162.

33 It is unlikely, as Hacker, 1960, p.350, has said, that the identification of the two stages is an attempt to retain theistic elements in a form of cosmogony becoming increasingly mechanistic. This view seems to assume the superfluity of the gods in the Purāṇic cosmogony. That this is not so is demonstrated by the Purāṇas' fundamentally theistic outlook, and because of the gods' importance as bearers of specific social values in mythology.

> half as the entire Earth and the other half as the sky. It is said about Dyaus and Pṛthivī in the Vedas, king, that amidst these two pieces the mighty Lord placed the atmosphere. It is said by the knowers of the Vedas and Vedāṅgas that the duration of his day is ten thousand *kalpas* less one quarter. Those who reflect on the supreme soul say that his night is just as much.
>
> Then the sage (*ṛṣi*), emitted the *ahaṃkāra*, that element possessing divinity, and the great sage (*mahān ṛṣiḥ*) initially emitted four further sons from his body. Best of kings, it was heard that the fathers came from these fathers. We have heard, best of men, that these worlds, both moving and stationary, were inhabited by gods; gods who were the children of the fathers.
>
> Then the *ahaṃkāra*, Parameṣṭhin, emitted the five-fold elements: earth, air, atmosphere, water and light, as the fifth. When he was completing the third creation, they said his night was five thousand *kalpas*, and the day is just as long, it is said. These characteristics (*viśeṣa*), namely–sound, touch, form, taste and smell as the fifth–are in the five great elements, Lord of kings. Prince, each day, living beings are possessed by them.[34]

The cosmogony finishes with an explanation of the number of *kalpas* which correspond to the duration of the elements.

It differs from the others discussed through the insertion of the motif of the cosmic egg into the 'evolutionary' development, a motif deriving from a tradition different from these Sāṃkhyan type cosmogonies of the *Moksadharmaparvan*. In the eyes of the epic redactors however, these two traditions must have been reconcilable, even though the ideas underlying them probably came from two different sources.

In this cosmogony each sequential stage is designated by a technical Sāṃkhyan term and by the name of the deity thought to correspond functionally to that sequence. Brahmā is the sage who creates the *ahaṃkāra*, hence he is the *mahat*. He is called *mahāmuṇi* (vs.4) after his birth from the egg and this has a correspondence in *mahān ṛṣiḥ* (vs.7) who creates the *ahaṃkāra*. *Mahān* is the nominative masculine of the neuter word *mahat*. Though as

34 *MBh*. 12, 299, 1-11.

mahat Brahmā creates the *ahaṃkāra*, he is still identified with what he creates. Perhaps significantly his own name is not given to the *ahaṃkāra*. Instead it is called Parameṣṭhin, one of his most common epithets. The use of an epithet may have been a deliberate device to stress the distinction between his *mahat* form and his individualized form as the *ahaṃkāra*.[35] As in the cosmogonies already discussed, implicit here is the notion of a formless creator who creates by formulating himself as an individual.

A slight problem in this cosmogony is the interpretation of the term '*sa mūrtiḥ sarvabhūtānām*' to describe Brahmā as he is after being born from the egg. The word *mūrti*, which I have translated as 'material form', can also be translated as 'body'. It has the etymological sense of 'thicken', 'congeal' or 'embody' and implies solidity.[36] In itself this suggests the possibility of limits, and by extension, of individuality as well. Even if *mūrti* has been correctly translated, the precise meaning of the whole phrase remains unclear. Does it mean Brahmā is the first of all beings to be embodied and as such is the 'prototype' of all other embodied beings? Or does it mean that he contains all beings within his body? Both are possibilities. The first alternative really amounts to saying that Brahmā is *ahaṃkāra*, since embodiment is a by-product of it. Twice in the cosmogonies already cited where Brahmā is identified with *ahaṃkāra* he is described as 'embodied' (*mūrtimān*).[37] A similar idea is present in the *prākṛtasarga* clothed in different terms from that in the *MBh*. The last stage of creation in this scheme of cosmogony is the appearance of the golden egg filled with the components of the universe.[38] Brahmā is born from

---

35 Cf. Arjunamiśra's commentary on 12, 299, 7: *sṛjaty ahaṃkāram iti sa brahmākhyo mahān ahaṃkāraṃ parameṣṭhyākhyaṃ sṛjati.*

36 Mayrhofer, 1953-1975, Vol. 2, p. 665.

37 *MBh*. 12, 175, 34; 291, 15. It is certainly significant that in the second of these passages Viṣṇu, who is the *avyakta*, the ultimate source of creation, is described as 'unembodied' (*amūrta*) in contrast to Brahmā who is embodied.

38 See above n.4.

it and at the time of his birth: "Brahmā existed in the beginning. Indeed, he was the first corporeal being, and was called the man (*puruṣa*), the first maker of all beings."[39]

It is individuality in the guise of embodiment that is the factor allowing the contents of the egg to be manifested in individual form. Certainly this correlates well with Brahmā's *ahaṃkāra* role in the cosmogonies already studied.

The second alternative is equally tenable. One common verbal root used to designate the act of creation is *sṛj*, a root often translated as 'to create' but which should really be rendered as 'to emit' or 'to discharge'. Creation can therefore be understood as an act of discharge from the body of the creator. In the cosmogony under discussion Brahmā emits (*sṛjati*) the *ahaṃkāra* from himself and his own sons from his body (*dehāt*).[40] Similarly, in the *prākṛtasarga* he emits the series of animals from various parts of his body.[41]

Which of these alternative interpretations best accounts for the meaning of the term? All the evidence from the *prākṛtasarga* suggests the first interpretation is the correct one. It is emphasized in this cosmogony that Brahmā's embodiment is the necessary precondition for the contents of the egg to be manifested, and this is precisely the role of the *ahaṃkāra*. In view of this the term '*sa mūrtiḥ sarvabhūtānām*' is just another way of describing Brahmā as the *ahaṃkāra*.

The two are also identified in an account of the dissolution of the cosmos. Dissolution is depicted as a process whereby Rudra-

---

39 *KP*. I, 4, 38; *MkP*. 45, 64; *BḍP*.1, 3, 24; *ŚP*. 7, 1, 10, 22.

sa vai śarīrī prathamaḥ sa vai puruṣa ucyate /
ādikartā sa bhūtānāṃ brahmāgre samāvartata //

40 *MBh*. 12, 299, 7.

41 *KP*. 1, 7, 51-60. The idea that the contents of the universe should be emitted from the creator's body may also underlie the visions experienced by Arjuna and Mārkaṇḍeya, who see the worlds and their inhabitants inside the bodies of Kṛṣṇa and Viṣṇu respectively. See *Bhg*. 11, 9ff.; *MBh*. 3, 186, 92-115.

Śiva destroys the Earth and then in successive order the *tattvas* swallow each other.[42] In the list of *tattvas* Prajāpati (Brahmā) is given as a synonym of *ahaṃkāra.*

The next instance of identification occurs in a Sāṃkhyan type cosmogony showing elements of Pañcarātra Vaiṣṇavism:

> From the darkness arose Brahmā, whose foundation is darkness, who embodies truth. He in whom the consciousness of all beings has its end, resides in the body of *puruṣa*. He who is called Aniruddha is considered to be the foundation (*pradhāna*). That which should be known as the unmanifest (*avyakta*) possesses the three cosmic qualities, best of kings. He is the mighty Hari Viṣvaksena who has knowledge for a companion. He made himself a bed on the waters and entered a yogic sleep, meditating on the creation of a world which would have variety, developing with many characteristics. Whilst meditating on creation his self (*ātman*) is traditionally called 'Great' (*mahān*). Thereafter Brahmā was born, he who is the *ahaṃkāra* and has four splendid faces, Hiraṇyagarbha, the illustrious Grandfather of all worlds. [43]

Here Viṣṇu as Aniruddha and Hari corresponds to the first two stages in the cosmogonic process–*avyakta* and *mahat*. Brahmā, the *ahaṃkāra*, is perhaps portrayed as the first individualized being to be born. The root *jan*, used here to signify his birth, is commonly used to designate child birth and the fact that he is born might be another way of saying he is the *prathama śarīra.*

Outside of the *Mokṣadharmaparvan* the most important passage where Brahmā and *ahaṃkāra* are identified occurs in the *Anuśāsanaparvan*. Vāyu is telling Arjuna about the high status of brahmins and of the great potency of their curses and favours. In the course of his speech he declares that Brahmā is the best of brahmins and attempts to justify this:

> Is not the best of *brāhmaṇas* a protector of beings and the maker of living beings? Knowing this, why are you confused? Accordingly, Prajāpati, Brahmā, is the unmanifest (*avyakta*)

---

42 *MBh*. 12, 300, 1-17, esp. vs. 12.

43 *MBh*. 12, 335, 15-19. Cf. 12, 327, 26.

and the origin and end (*prabhavāpyaya*) of all; through him the entire moving and unmoving universe is produced.

But there are some unlearned people who think Brahmā was born from an egg, and that from the split egg came the mountains and regions, water, the earth and the heavens. Yet this birth could not have been since there was a great darkness then. However, the egg is traditionally called 'the atmosphere' (*ākāśa*), and the Grandfather was born from that.

You might say, 'Where would he rest?' for at that time there would be nothing there. But it is said that the Lord exists in a state completely of fiery energy which is the *ahaṃkāra*. There is no egg, king. However, Brahmā is the creator of the world.[44]

Vāyu alludes here to two different conceptions of cosmogony, which in the *Mbh.* are considered separate, but are combined in the *prākṛtasarga*. In utilizing terms such as *avyakta* and *ahaṃkāra*, the first corresponds to those Sāṃkhyan cosmogonies already discussed.[45] It would be superfluous to discuss it further here. The second cosmogony is associated with the motif of the world egg. Vāyu alludes to this motif whilst considering the objection that Brahmā might not be the ultimate creator because he does not exist prior to the egg, an objection he counters in two ways. Firstly, due to the darkness at the time of creation, no one would have been able to see whether he was born from an egg or not. Secondly, the egg is really a concrete image of *ākāśa*, the unformed state of precreation. This is Brahmā's real birthplace, a claim possibly reflecting a tradition expressed in the *Rām.* that the *ākāśa* is his birthplace.[46] But even this view is opposed, for if

44 *MBh.* 13, 138, 14-19.

45 Besides these two, another term *prabhavāpyaya*, 'the origin and end', is used to describe Brahmā. In the Purāṇic cosmogonies this term designates the god who exists during the intervals between the *mahākalpas*, the one from whom the new creation proceeds and who destroys it at the end of the *kalpa*. It is a term often used of the supreme god and so bolsters Vāyu's argument about Brahmā's supremacy. For details see Biardeau, 1968, p.26.

46 See *Rām.* (V) 2, 110, 3-6. Is it going too far to see the *ākāśa* as

there is nothing other than the *ākāśa*, where could Brahmā stand (*tiṣṭhati*, or exist?). Vāyu's answer implies the irrelevancy of the question. For Brahmā does not need to stand anywhere because he exists in a state of fiery energy which is the *ahaṃkāra*.[47] Since he exists in this form he can be considered as the ultimate creator, not just as a demiurge.

In this passage *sarvatejogata* occurs as a synonym of *ahaṃkāra*. Though not normally found with *ahaṃkāra*, terms like *sumahātejas*, *mahātejas* and *sarvatejomaya* are often used of Brahmā in cosmogonic contexts.[48] In non-cosmogonic passages the lustrous, glowing appearance of his body is usually described by compounds whose final word is not *tejas*.[49] *Tejas* can be rendered as 'lustre' but a more comprehensive view would make it "the brilliant principle of supra normal might and dignity' which resides in kings, gods and brahmins and ascetics, whose bodies shine brightly as a consequence."[50] It can also signify 'fiery energy', 'vital power' and other related things. It is etymologically related to *taijasa*, the word denoting one third of the tripartite *ahaṃkāra* of the *prākṛtasarga*. The role of *taijasa* in the *ahaṃkāra* is functionally identical to that of *rajas*: to set in motion the other two parts of the *ahaṃkāra*, namely, *vaikārika* and the *bhūtādi*. Together they are the sources of the senses and elements, the

---

an equivalent of *avyakta*? In the Upaniṣads it is a synonym of Brahman (the unmanifest) who is often the source of creation.

47 *MBh*. 13, 138, 18. Perhaps a better reading than *sarvatejogataḥ* is *sarvatejomayaḥ* which occurs in one Northern manuscript. See critical apparatus on *śl*. 18.

48 *Sumahātejas* is used of him at *MBh*. 12, 175, 16; *sarvatejomaya* at 12, 327, 26; *mahātejas* at 12, 248, 13; 12, 250, 17; *H*. 1, 29. In non-cosmogonic contexts *sumahātejas* is used of him at *Rām*. (V) 1, 63, 2; *mahātejas* at *MBh*. 1 App.1, p. 884 line 12; *Rām* (V) 1, 2, 23; 1, 57, 6.

49 Some examples are *mahādyuti* at *MBh*. 3, 83, 47; *KP*. 1, 25, 71; *samadyuti* at *MBh*. 3, 185, 2; *brājamāṇa* and *amitaprabha* at *KP*. 1, 25, 69-70.

50 Gonda, 1969, p. 35.

components of the universe. Thus the function of *taijasa* in the *prākṛtasarga* corresponds to that of *ahaṃkāra* in its entirety in the *Mbh.*[51] In light of the correspondence between *taijasa*, *ahaṃkāra*, *rajas* and *Brahmā*, and the affinity of *tejas* with *taijasa*, it is likely that epithets ending with the word *tejas* are used of Brahmā as another way of indicating that he is the *ahaṃkāra*.

Having looked at those cosmogonies which use Sāṃkhyan terminology and conceive of creation as an 'evolutionary' process, it is now necessary to see if Brahmā is either identified with or is functionally equivalent to *ahaṃkāra* in cosmogonies other than these Sāṃkhyan ones. There are no instances of the former, but there are a few cases of the latter. In one *Mbh.* passage Bhīsma is called upon to explain the origin of the sword. He begins with a cosmogony:

> In the beginning, good man, all this was just one watery ocean, unmoving, without atmosphere and with the earth's surface indefinable. It was enveloped in darkness, intangible, apparently without bottom, without sound and immeasurable. The Grandfather was born in it.
>
> He who possessed vigour (*vīryavat*), emitted air and fire, as well as the sun, the atmosphere, the earth above and Nirṛta underworld below. Then the sky with the moon and stars, the planets and other heavenly bodies. Then came the years, days and nights, the seasons and lesser divisions of time.
>
> After this the divine Grandfather, having placed himself in a worldly body (*śarīraṃ lokastham*), produced some very splendid sons called Marīci, Ṛṣi, Atri, Pulastya, Pulaha, Kratu, Aṅgiras and Vasiṣṭha, as well as the mighty lord, Rudra. Likewise, Dakṣa Pracetas produced sixty daughters. Indeed, all these daughters and *brahmarṣis* came on earth in order to produce offspring. From them came all beings, gods, the groups of ancestors, Gandharvas, Apsaras and Rākṣasas of various kinds. Also, birds, deer, fish, monkeys, great serpents and others of various shapes and strength, wandering on the earth and in

51 In most, but not all, of the *MBh.* cosmogonies the *ahaṃkāra* is unitary. In the Purāṇic cosmogonies it is always tripartite.

the waters. And he begot plants, small insects, those born from eggs, and those born from wombs, and, good man, this entire world of moveable and immoveable things.

When he had completed the creation of beings, the Grandfather of all beings again arranged the eternal *dharma* according to how it is taught in the Vedas.[52]

Here the cosmogony ends. The remainder of the myth is taken up with the creation of the sword and its correct use. The primeval waters are described here with adjectives such as *aprameyam* and *anirdeśyamahītalam*, both portraying a pre-creation state characterized by an absence of definable limits. This is the same as saying that individuality did not exist. As soon as Brahmā is formed individuality is present, the main signs being that he is been born (*jan*) and the adjective *vīryavan*, 'vigour', used of him. Certainly, the use of this word in the masculine suggests there must be an embodied being who possesses this virility, though it might also refer to the sexual potency characteristic of many Indian creator gods. In addition, the assumption by Brahmā of a worldly body (*lokastham śarīram*) after creating the physical parts of the universe may parallel the notions of *prathamaḥ śarīrī* and *mūrtimān* in the Sāṃkhyan cosmogonies already studied.

Another non-Sāṃkhyan cosmogony where Brahmā's functional identity with *ahaṃkāra* is strongly implied occurs in some Pāli texts. The cosmogony in question should strictly speaking be called pseudo-cosmogony because its real purpose is to polemicize against certain orthodox views current in the Buddha's day. I have alluded to this passage earlier, but its importance justifies a lengthy consideration here:

There is indeed a time friends, when sooner or later after a long period has passed, this world dissolves. When, as happens, this world is dissolved, there are some beings who are reborn in the Ābhassara world. These remain there for a long time, consisting of mind, feeding on joy, radiating light from themselves, moving in the atmosphere and existing in splendour.

52 *MBh.* 12, 160, 11-21.

> A time comes friends, when sooner or later after a long period has passed, this world recommences. When this world has recommenced, the palace of Brahmā appears-empty. Then, some being who has fallen from the Ābhassara world because his life has passed or because his merit has decayed is reborn in the empty palace of Brahmā. He remains there for a long time, consisting of mind, feeding on joy, radiating light from himself, moving in the atmosphere and existing in splendour.
>
> Now because he dwelt there for a long time alone, there arose in him a dissatisfaction, an anxiety, and his mind became disconcerted, thinking, "Oh, if only other beings would come here!" And then, some other beings who have fallen from the Ābhassara world because their life has passed or because their merit has decayed, are reborn in the empty palace of Brahmā, as companions of that being. They remain there for a long time…
>
> Then friends, that being who arose first, thinks thus, "I am Brahmā, Great Brahmā, Conqueror, Unconquered, seeing the goals of others, Disposer, Lord, Maker, Creator, Chief, Assigner, Master of himself, Father of beings past and future. By me, these beings were created. Why is that? Because formerly I thought, 'Oh, if only other beings would come here!' Such was the resolve of my mind, and so these beings came here."
>
> Those beings who had arisen after him think this, "This honourable one is Brahmā… We were created by that honourable Brahmā. Why is that? Because we saw that he had arisen first, and we arose after him."[53]

This pseudo-cosmogony explains the origin of certain false views about the origin of the universe, and has a general therapeutic intention of warning people from speculating about origins to the detriment of awareness of their own *saṃsāric* situation.

Notwithstanding its purpose it does have parallels with a cosmogony found in the *BhU*. In an article on Buddhist cosmogony H. Günther has suggested several Upaniṣadic passages that might

53 *DN*. 3, pp.29-30; DN.1 pp.18-19, with slight variations. See the translation of Bodhi, 2007, pp. 66-67

have influenced this pseudo-cosmogony.[54] Of the two passages cited by him-*BhU.* 1, 4, 3 ff. and *ChU.* 6, 2, 3-the first certainly seems to have exerted an influence, but hardly the second.[55] The first passage asserts that the creator desired to create because of his intense loneliness:

> In the beginning this world was Soul (*ātman*) alone in the form of a Person. Looking around, he saw nothing else than himself. He said first: 'I am' (*aham asmi*). Thence arose the name 'I' ... He was afraid. Therefore one who is alone is afraid. This one then thought to himself: 'Since there is nothing else than myself, of what am I afraid'? ... Verily, he had no delight. Therefore one alone has no delight. He desired a second. He was, indeed, as large as a woman and a man closely embraced. He caused that self to fall into two pieces… He copulated with her. Therefrom human beings were produced.[56]

In the Buddhist pseudo-cosmogony living beings appear only after Brahmā has realized his loneliness (and by implication his individuality) and yearned for companions. When they appeared, he mistakenly believes them to be his creations.

In the cosmogony of the *BhU.* the *ātman*, having split himself in two thinks: "'I, indeed, am this creation, for I emitted it all from myself". Thence arose this creation ..."[57] By formulating

54 Günther, 1944, p.75.

55 The cosmogony of *ChU.* 6, 2, 1-4 says that in the beginning Being (*sat*) alone existed, without a second. Being (and subsequently water) desired to create, thinking, 'I should become many, I should progenate.' The only similarity it has with the Buddhist pseudo-cosmogony is that both conceive of the creator being alone at the time of creation. The Buddhist version emphasizes that the creator's loneliness is the inspiration for the desire to create. In the *ChU.* passage the desire to create is purely a spontaneous feeling, so often expressed by Prajāpati in the cosmogonies of the Brāhmaṇas.

56 *BhU.* 1, 4, 3 (summarized). Trans. Hume 1968, p. 81. I have added the Sanskrit.

57 *BhU.* 1, 4, 5. Trans. Hume 1968, p. 81.

himself (as in 1, 4, 1– '*aham asmi*') as the creation (*vāva sṛṣṭir asmy aham*) the creator has realized his individuality, and thereby initiated the creation process. Günther thinks the idea of self-formulation is present in the Buddhist version of the cosmogony. He writes, "Likewise, the realization that he is the creation because he was the first there and because he is the Great Brahmā is expressed by the god Brahmā in the Buddhist version. It is reminiscent of the statement of *BhU.* 1, 4, 10... especially of 1, 4, 5."[58] This supposition, however, does not accord with the text of the Buddhist version, since nowhere does Brahmā claim he is the creation, only the creator.

Despite Günther's overstatement, he is right to find the model for the pseudo-cosmogony of the *DN.* in the cosmogony of *BhU.* 1, 4, 1-5. This does not mean they are similar in every respect. The Buddhist version lacks certain essential features of the Upaniṣadic myth. In the former Brahmā became aware of his own individuality because he felt lonely, not explicitly because he formulated himself as an 'I', although an awareness of his own 'I-ness' is probably implied in his act of reciting his own names, beginning '*aham asmi brahmā ...*'[59] The androgynous *ātman* is not present in the Buddhist version, nor is recognition by the creator that he is the creation. The Buddhists, in their turn, attempting to make a polemic of this cosmogony, have introduced the doctrine of *karma*. In doing this they have demonstrated the falseness of the belief in an eternal creator god and of the eternality of any living being.

The sense of individuality associated with Mahābrahmā–seemingly important in the Buddhist texts–which becomes apparent in Brahmā's identification with the *ahaṃkāra* principle in the *MBh.* and beyond, may earlier be implied in all of those passages where Prajāpati expresses a desire to create, where the appropriate verb is a first person optative. However, the only close

58 Günther, 1944, pp.75-76.

59 See especially *BhU.* 1, 4, 1 and 1, 4, 10– *brahma vā idam agra āsīt tadā ātmānam evāvet / ahaṃ brahmāsmi /*

parallel I can find is in a passage from the *MaitrīU*, where Prajāpati is shown to be motivated by *abhimāna*, a word designating a mental function that works to establish a presumption of individuality in a person:

> That subtle, ungraspable, invisible one called the person returns here without previous consciousness, with a part of himself, just like one who wakes up from deep sleep without previous consciousness. That part of him is that element of intelligence in each person, the knower of the field, with the characteristics of will, determination and conceit (*saṃkalpādhyavasāyābhimānaliṅgaḥ*), Prajāpati with all his eyes. He, as intelligence, set up the body with intelligence, and he is the instigator of it.[60]

The parallel here may be with that being born in *DN*. 3, 29-30 who remembers his previous birth, but not those before them, but also the original Brahmā who shows no awareness of why he entered the empty palace of Brahmā in the first place. But this very passage goes on to describe the actual process of creation in a manner provoking another parallel with the depiction of Mahābrahmā:

> In the beginning Prajāpati stood alone. Being alone he had no enjoyment. He pondered on himself and then emitted many creatures. He saw that they lacked consciousness like a stone, that they were without vitality, standing like a pillar. He experienced no enjoyment. He thought, "I must enter into them so as to make them conscious. He made himself like the wind and entered in."[61]

Like Prajāpati, Mahābrahmā also experiences no enjoyment:[62]

---

60 Trans. in Roebuck, 2003, p.354.

61 *MaitrīU*. 6, also 5, 2. Here too there are parallels with *BhU*. 1, 4, 1-3.

62 See also J. Gonda, 1982, p.147. "In many other cases, however, an author gives us an account of details. For instance, Prajapati is described as being motivated, as desirous of offspring or propagation (TS 3.1.1.1; KB 6.1; PB 6.5.1, 7.5.1). When the reference to this state of mind is followed by particulars-for

"Alone for a long time, he experiences unease, he finds no enjoyment, ... (*tassa tattha ekakassa dīgharattaṃ nibbusitattā anabhirati*)." That there is an occurrence of the word *eka* and the verb *ram* in both passages seems a serious coincidence. And the description of Brahmā as *pathamaṃ* in the Pāli Canon versions brings out the emotion felt by the being who falls into the empty Brahmā palace. In both cases individuality is the precondition for creation to occur, but individuality makes sense only in relation to multiplicity.

There seems to be an early tradition in the Brāhmaṇas of Prajāpati being the first to appear and then wishing to create, and this is accompanied by a rather negative mental state he experiences before he creates: "Prajāpati desired, 'May I be many, May I procreate.' He grieved (*aśocat*). Whilst he was grieving he created the sun from his head."[63] I note the use of the optative here as in the case of the Buddhist accounts of Brahmā's creation where he wishes that creatures would come (*āgaccheyyun*). And another possible instance of this comes from the late *Gopatha Brāhmaṇa* 1, 1, 16a-c, where it concerns Brahmā rather than Prajāpati:

> Brahman emitted Brahmā on to a lotus. Brahmā certainly became anxious, thinking "With which letter will I experience all desires, all worlds, all the gods, all the Vedas, all the sacrifices, all words, all the dawns, and all beings moving and stationary?"[64]

As such, on the basis of this and other text passages, there is

---

example, "he was sad and unhappy" (PB 7.5.1), or "he was sorrowful and out of his head the sun came into existence" (6.5.1), or "he developed this world from his expiration" (PB 6.10 [6.4.2]), or "the domestic animals, as soon as he had created them left him" (PB 7.10.13, 17.10.2)-the conclusion seems inevitable that the author or his predecessors had reflected upon the problems or consequences of creation, the difficulties in which a creator might be involved, and so on."

63 *PB*. 6.5.1 (Cf.7, 5, 1).

64 *Brahmā ha vai brahmāṇaṃ puṣkare sasṛje / sa khalu brahmā sṛṣṭaś cintām āpede / kenāham ekenākṣareṇa sarvāṃś ca kāmān sarvāṃś ca lokān sarvāṃś ca devāṇ sarvāṃś ca vedān sarvāṃś ca*

transmitted the distinct idea that the creator, Prajāpati or Brahmā, experienced some degree of anxiety when he existed by himself and the first desire he had was not to be alone. This may be telling us that individuality occurs only in the presence of others, that oneness is different from individuality, and that individuality becomes the foundational characteristic of creation in the *MBh*. In this manner it becomes an important theme of continuity between Prajāpati and Brahmā, and it is arguably also replicated in the seven descriptions of Brahmā as Mahābrahmā in the Buddhist texts.

The passage above taken from the *MaitrīU*. continues traditions in the Upaniṣads and earlier texts relating to the uneasiness of the first being who appears–he is not himself created, and his belief that he effected the creation from his mind, in association with the idea that he was the first–*prathamam*. But we do not find anywhere this list of epithets, or anything like it in literature of a comparable time to the passages in the Pāli texts. This causes us to ask where they came from and whether they were combined like this, a) in order to heighten the extent of the fallacy of what the first being thought about himself, or b) were borrowed from a tradition about Brahmā that was known in the area of eastern India where Buddhism first emerged.

The only early reminiscence of the Buddhist collection of epithets, and it is extremely truncated, I can find is in a well known passage from the *MU*, constituting one of the earliest summaries of Brahmā's role:

> Brahmā arose as the first of the gods, the maker of everything, the protector of the world. To his eldest son Atharvan he proclaimed the knowledge of Brahmā, the foundation of all knowledge." [65]

---

yajñānt sarvāṃś ca śabdān sarvāś ca vyuṣṭīḥ sarvāṇi ca bhūtāni sthāvarajaṅgamāny anubhaveyam iti /

65 *MU*. 1,1,1. *brahmā devānāṃ prathamaḥ saṃbabhūva viśvasya kartā bhuvanasya goptā /*
sa brahmavidyāṃ sarvavidyāpratiṣṭhām atharvāya jyeṣṭhaputrāya prāha //

This is an extremely prescient summary of his later roles in mythology: creation, preservation and dissemination of knowledge. And, perhaps significantly, the first chapter of this Upaniṣad goes on to outline–what later become–the differences between *pravṛttidharma* and *nivṛttidharma* without using these technical terms or any equivalents. But these epithets are not found used elsewhere of him in the Upaniṣads, though Prajāpati in earlier texts is called is called *bhuvanasya gopā*.[66] There are also some passages where Prajāpati is addressed as 'first of the gods.'[67] Even so, this passage from the *MU*. is an important and significant statement, and I am drawn to it because it may be one source from where the Buddhist creation satires were drawn. I am struck by the occurrence of *prathamaḥ saṃbabhūva* and *viśvasya kartā*, though the question of parallels would be much stronger if there were more epithets in use in this same *MU*. passage. But the idea of Brahmā as the first–though does this mean chronologically first as in the Buddhist passages?–and the creator represent a broad parallel.

Pratisarga

Brahmā's role as *ahaṃkāra* is most pronounced in the *prākṛtasarga* and similar cosmogonies of the *Mbh*. It is not so prominent in the *pratisarga* where he creates using a variety of methods, but it is still present. The *prākṛtasarga* is different from the *pratisarga* in a number of ways, not the least of these differences being the logical and temporal rupture between the two schemes of creation. Yet in spite of these differences the values underlying them are the same.

The *prākṛtasarga* occurs at the beginning of a lifetime of Brahmā and lasts the length of his life, which is one hundred divine years. At the end of this period it gives way to the great dissolution, also lasting for one hundred years. Each *pratisarga* is a lesser creation restricted only to the triple world, occurring within the temporal framework of the *prākrtasarga*. Since each

66 See Gonda, 1986, p.21.

67 *AB*. 7.16, 3; *Śāṅkhāyana-Śrautasūtra*. 15, 22.

pratisarga lasts for one of Brahmā's days, there are thirty-six thousand of them in one of his lives. A minor dissolution (*pralaya*) occurs at the end of every *pratisarga* and lasts for a period corresponding to Brahmā's night, during which he sleeps. Though both creations differ in their respective durations, they are both organized temporarily in terms of the length of Brahmā's life.

Since Biardeau has made an extensive study of the *pratisarga*, only a summary *is* needed here:[68] Viṣṇu is sleeping on the coils of the serpent Śeṣa who floats on the primeval sea for the whole period of dissolution, one *kalpa*. At the end of this *kalpa* a lotus grows from Viṣṇu's navel and Brahmā is born from it. Gazing around himself, he sees nothing but ocean and realizes by intuition that the earth is beneath the sea. He takes the form of a boar, dives under the water and raises the Earth on his tusk up to the surface of the ocean whereon it floats. He then shapes mountains on the Earth's surface. Having established the Earth as a habitable place he begins creating beings. From his meditation four kinds of beings are created: plants, animals, gods and men. Each group derives its essential characteristics from the *guṇa* or combination of *guṇas* which pervade Brahmā at the time of his meditation. The account of the *pratisarga* is ended by a nine-stage recapitulation of both schemes of creation.[69]

As the first embodied being to make an appearance in this creation, Brahmā is playing out his *ahaṃkāra* role. The lotus from which he is born probably represents the *mahat* and Viṣṇu lying on the ocean is the *avyakta* and *pradhāna*, the ultimate foundation of creation. Even though these terms are not used, evidence from cosmogonies in the *MBh.* which employ the motif of the lotus birth suggests this conclusion.[70] Though the *ahaṃkāra* has already

68 Biardeau, 1969.

69 For the whole *pratisarga* see *MkP*. 47, 1-36; *ViP*. 1, 4, 1-5, 65; *KP*. I, 6, 1-7, 66.

70 See above p. 125 and n. 24-25 for cosmogonies employing the lotus birth motif seemingly conforming to the scheme I have suggested. This interpretation does not exclude the sexual

appeared twice in the *prākṛtasarga* it is not inconsistent that it should appear again, since the *pratisarga* covers only the creation of the triple world, the precise realm of *ahaṃkāra* and *pravṛtti* values.

The boar form that Brahmā adopts to bring the Earth up is one of Viṣṇu's most celebrated *avatāras* and Brahmā's assumption of this form not only concerns the creation process in the *pratisarga*, but also prefigures his relationship with the Earth which in many respects is circumscribed by the *avatāra* model. This boar is said to be a 'boar of sacrifice' (*yajñavarāha*) because its body consists of the Vedas and the sacrifice. As such this creation is impelled by an act of sacrifice like so many of the cosmogonies in the Brāhmaṇas.[71] If raising the earth is the first act of creation in the *pratisarga*, then the second act of creation concerns production of the four-fold group of living beings. Unlike the other, this creation is impelled by an act of meditation.

In the second act of creation the *guṇas* are attributed an important role because they determine whether each of the four groups–plants, animals, gods and men–is capable of attaining *mokṣa*. It is this standard by which each group is classified. Plants are totally dominated by *tamas*, meaning they are enclosed by the five forms of ignorance. Animals too are pervaded by *tamas* and are totally closed into their own ego (*ahaṃmāna*). Gods on the contrary are pervaded by *sattva* and so enjoy happiness and affection. It is only humans who are capable of 'realizing' (*sādhaka*) themselves and this because they are pervaded with a mixture of *rajas* and *tamas*. Only they are capable of attaining *mokṣa*. Animals and plants are dominated by ignorance and the gods are too preoccupied with their own bliss to see the need for ultimate release.

Humans are *sādhaka* because they experience pain: and they had an abundance of brightness (*prakāśa*), abounded in darkness

---

interpretation Biardeau has given to this aspect of the *pratisarga*. See Biardeau, 1969, p.66.

71 Cf. above pp. 90-91.

(*tamas*) and were excessive in impetuosity (*rajas*). Hence these humans experience much that is painful (*duḥkha*) and they are efficient [in the attainment of liberation].[72]

The high potentiality human beings have to attain *mokṣa* is not merely on account of their painful life, but also because they are pervaded and influenced by all three *guṇas*. This means they possess the characteristics–ignorance and light–of the other three groups of living beings, but also the rājasic motivation to escape from their situation. Brightness (*prakāśa*) is synonymous with *sattva*, itself sometimes given as a synonym of *mokṣa*.[73] However, brightness by itself is not enough, as is shown by the gods who possess so much *sattva* that they exist in a kind of spiritual limbo, never seeking *mokṣa*.

It is above all the existence of brightness in conjunction with *rajas* and *tamas* that makes humans *sādhaka*. The two latter *guṇas* give rise to a sense of dissatisfaction and ceaseless activity, both characteristics of *pravṛttidharma*, especially when considered from the perspective of *nivṛtti*. Awareness of the unsatisfactory nature of existence is a stimulus to seek *mokṣa*, existing latently in every human as *sattva*.

Like the other sections of the Purāṇic cosmogony, *pravṛtti* and *nivṛtti* values are prominent in the account of the *pratisarga*. The spatial realm of creation is the triple world and the beings created are those who will participate in the symbiotic relationship based on the sacrifice. Brahmā plays the central role in the *pratisarga* and his own life cycle, based as it is on divine days and nights, is paradigmatic of the transmigrating individual kept in rebirth through *karma*. Yet in spite of this manifestation of *pravṛtti* values, the creation as a whole is classified from the standpoint of *nivṛtti* values. This at least seems to be the import of rating each group in terms of its capacity to attain *mokṣa*.

---

72 *MkP*. 47, 26-7.

73 See *MBh*. 12, 336, 64-6.

Chapter 5

Creation by Progenation and Meditation

Following the *pratisarga* the 'systematic' Purāṇic cosmogony continues with narratives about the cosmology of the triple world and the creation of its inhabitants.[1] The spatial focus for these narratives remains the triple world, so their perspective is still that of the *pratisarga*. To some extent their contents parallel those of the *pratisarga* and there is considerable duplication between the narratives themselves, but each account of the creation of living beings seems to have its own specific purpose. In all there are three separate narratives, usually self-contained and often corresponding to individual chapters in Purāṇas.[2] Judging by their framing with specific introductions and conclusions they could easily be considered individual units combined together.

Progenation and Meditation

In Ch. 48 of the *MkP*. Brahmā is depicted creating the inhabitants of the triple world, meteorological features, various divisions of time, the Vedas and instruments for performance of the sacrifice.

---

1 I use the word 'systematic' because the Purāṇic cosmogony appears to have been developed from pre-Purāṇic material that has been organized into a specific sequence showing little variation from Purāṇa to Purāṇa.

2 For convenience I have followed the cosmogony of the *MkP*. as it contains the complete Purāṇic cosmogony with very little trace of the narrative expansions so characteristic of the Purāṇas. See Chs. 48-50.

This creation begins when he conceives mentally of creating gods, men, fathers and demons. Then, desiring to create (*sisṛkṣur*) he concentrated on himself (*svam ātmānam ayuyujat*) and darkness (*tamas*) arose.[3] As a result of this demons were born. Brahmā abandoned this body from which the demons came and in turn it became the night. The same process occured for each of the gods, *pitṛs* and men, each group being born from bodies containing *sattva*, or a mixture of *sattva* and *rajas* respectively. This series of creation is rounded off with some aetiologies concerning the respective powers of demons and men.[4]

These are followed by another series of creations of various kinds of divine beings ranging from demons to gandharvas. For the most part they sprout off various parts of Brahmā's body and are given their distinctive nature depending on his mood at the time they appear. Etymologies are also used to explain their nature. For example, it is said that during the night Brahmā felt hunger and thirst (*kṣuttṛḍanvitaḥ*) and so misshapen (*virūpa*) beings emaciated by hunger (*kṣutkṣāmāṇ*) were born.[5] Other creations reflect his mood, such as when angry flesh-eating monsters appear due to his anger (*krodhātman*).[6] Brahmā is hardly satisfied with this creation, and it causes him further anger and dissatisfaction. But anger only gives rise to more anger and more unsatisfactory creations.

He then creates various kinds of animals–both domestic and wild–from parts of his body, and also plants and trees. Then he performs a sacrifice, after which the narrative recapitulates some of the previous creations. This is followed by creation of the Vedas and various kinds of meters and hymns from Brahmā's four mouths. Then comes creation of meteorological phenomena and

---

3 *MkP*. 48, 4; *ViP*. l, 5, 30; *KP*. 1, 7, 38.

4 See above pp. 146-47 for a more detailed analysis of this mode of creation.

5 *MkP*. 48, 18-19; *ViP*. l, 5, 42; *KP*. 1, 7, 50.

6 *MkP*. 48, 22; *ViP*. I, 5, 45.

the periods of time. The narrative is concluded by a recapitulation of all that has gone before in the chapter.

The entire series of creations narrated in this chapter are framed between verses explaining the effect of *karma* on the life situation of created beings. At the beginning it is said that: "Brahmin, created beings have developed due to the good and evil from their past *karman*. According to this view, although destroyed in the cosmic dissolution, they are not liberated."[7] And at the end of the narrative there is a section detailing the influence of *karma* and Brahmā's role in determining the stations and occupations of people in accordance with their own *karma*. The first verse of this section is almost a restatement of the above: "Whatever actions they were endowed with from their first creation; it is with these alone that they are endowed when repeatedly being created."[8] The effect of these verses is twofold. In the first place they establish that unfolding creation is not just due to the whim of the creator. Secondly, they sustain the belief that although the cycle of birth and death continues unabated, it is ultimately subservient to *karma*, the cause of it all.

In this chapter a variety of different methods of creation are used, a variety manifested in the number of verbal roots used to express the creative act. Roots such as *sṛj*, 'to emit', *sam/bhū*, 'to arise', *jan*, 'to be born', *vini/mā*, 'to measure out' and *ut/sṛj*, 'to abandon', are all attested. Though each root has its own specific rendering, all have the general sense of 'to create'. Even *ut/sṛj* must be included because it designates Brahmā's act of abandonment of a particular body which thereafter becomes the day, night, morning or evening twilight.

Beneath this variety of verbal roots two fundamental methods of creation are suggested: Brahmā creates either by meditation or progenation. The first method is nowhere clearer than in the reference to him focussing (*yuj*) himself (*ātman*) in order to make manifest his desire to create. As such the creation of living beings

---

7 *MkP*. 48, 2; *ViP*. I, 5, 28.

8 *MkP*. 48, 39; *ViP*. 1, 5, 60; *KP*. I, 7, 61.

is impelled by an act of yoga. Progenation, the second method, is also present, for when he assumes a body (in creating demons, gods, *pitṛs* and men) it is as though he impregnates his own body. Brahmā himself is masculine and the word for body–*tanu–is* feminine. These two methods of creation are compatible in the context of this myth. Both result in the production of a successful creation. The few instances where the creation is unsuccessful, causing Brahmā's anger, indicate a possible explanation for the origin of evil, rather than an unsuccessful attempt to create.

The next chapter of the *MkP.* is presented as another self-contained unit framed by an introduction and conclusion.[9] It recounts the origin of four classes of humans, their conduct in the *kṛta* and *tretāyugas*, and their eventual transformation into the four *varṇas*. The narrative tells of the four classes of people living in harmony with the Earth in the *kṛtayuga*. Over time the standard of their conduct declined until in reaction to their abuse of her, the Earth withdrew her fertility some time near the beginning of the *tretāyuga*. In response Brahmā milked her so as to restore her fertility which was essential for the sustenance of the people. After the milking he transformed the four groups into *varṇas*, established the *āśramas* and heavens appropriate to the *varṇas*, and finally, determined the duties associated with the latter. The myth narrated in this chapter functions aetiologically in respect of the origin of the *varṇas* and also explores the normative relationship between Earth and her inhabitants. I deal with this myth in a later chapter, partially because it is not a standard feature of the Purāṇic cosmogony, partially because it is more appropriate to treat it together with other accounts of the creation of the *varṇas* and *āśramas*.

The following chapter (50) of the *MkP.* is standard in the Purāṇic cosmogony. It contains the genealogy of beings born from Brahmā's mind-born sons, a genealogy ultimately traceable back

---

9 *MkP.* 49; *VāP.* 8,1-180; *BḍP.* I, 7, 34 ff; *KP.* 1, 27, 16-48; *LP.* 1, 39, 4-70. For a detailed analysis see below pp. 216-235.

to the god himself. Brahmā initiates this creation, but not without difficulty:

Whilst he was meditating, living creatures were born from his mind, together with obligatory actions and the means of acting which were produced from his body. The knowers of the field (*kṣetrajña*) came into being from the limbs of that wise god. All of those who came into being were described by me earlier, and they, beginning with gods and ending with stationary objects, are traditionally said to be in the realm of the three *guṇas*. Such are created beings, both moving and stationary.

When all of those creatures of that wise god did not increase, he then emitted some other mind-born sons whose appearance was similar to his: Bhṛgu, Pulastya, Pulaha, Kratu, Aṅgiras, Marīci, Dakṣa, Atri and Vasiṣṭha, all mind-born. In the Purāṇas these have been definitively called the nine sons of Brahmā.

Then once more Brahmā emitted Rudra, born from his anger, and Saṃkalpa and Dharma, first born even of the ancients. These, Sananda and the rest, were emitted first by the Self-born. They were wholly focussed and showed disregard towards, and had no attachment for, the world. All of them possessed knowledge arisen spontaneously (*anāgatajñāna*), they were free from passion (*vītarāga*) and unselfish.

Since they disregarded the creation of living beings, Brahmā, the great self, became very angry. From him came forth a man (*puruṣa*) who resembled the sun and had a very large body with an appearance that was half man and half woman. Brahmā said, "Divide yourself!" and disappeared. This having been said, he separated the male and female aspects and divided the male aspect into ten parts, he being the eleventh. And the mighty Lord, the god, divided the male and female aspects into many parts, including tranquil, gentle and violent, and black and white people.

Next, Brahmā appointed the first Svāyaṃbhū Manu, who was born from him and looked like him, to be the protector of creatures, brahmin.[10] The Lord Svāyaṃbhū Manu, the god,

10 The readings *prajāpālye* for *prajāpālo* and *dvija* for *dvijaḥ* render this sentence much more meaningful.

> took for his wife Śatarūpā, the woman whose blemishes were removed by austerity. By that male [Manu], Śatarūpā gave birth to two sons, Priyavrata and Uttānapāda, who were famed through their actions. Also, two daughters were born, Ṛddhi and Prasūti, and their father gave Prasūti to Dakṣa and Ṛddhi to Ruci.[11]

Between themselves, Dakṣa and Ruci father various progeny ranging from humans, animals and gods, to certain intellectual concepts, evil and Death.[12]

Creation by meditation and progenation are very much in opposition here. Brahmā creates beings with his mind (*jajñire mānasīḥ*), but they are incapable of reproducing themselves and so his creation must be deemed unsuccessful. His own lack of success in effecting creation through meditation is highlighted by two other events narrated in this myth. The first is the refusal of his ascetic sons to engage in creation. They engage in meditation but only for the attainment of *jñāna*. In the Purāṇic cosmogonies meditation should not be considered as having a neutral value; in general it can be taken as an expression of the wider set of values associated with asceticism. A strong component of the Indian ascetic tradition is the emphasis placed on chastity. Progenation is something to be shunned. Therefore, in refusing to engage in progenation Brahmā's sons are being consistent with their ascetic values. However, Brahmā is bound to remain frustrated while attempting to produce by meditation a creation that by its nature can only be increased through progenation. For what is being attempted in this myth is a presentation of the creation of all the inhabitants of the triple world in the form of an extended family whose ancestor is Brahmā. Creation viewed from this perspective can only prosper through progenation, not by meditation alone, no matter what the intention of the creator.

The second event is the appearance of the androgynous

---

11 *MkP*. 50, 1-16; *PaP*. 5, 3, 155-201; *ViP*. 1, 7, 1-33; *GP*, 1, 5, 21cd-30.

12 Summarized translation of *MkP*. 50, 17-97.

puruṣa, a product of Brahmā's frustration and anger. The bisexual nature of the normally male *puruṣa* is a clear statement that the creation countenanced in this myth will be viable only through progenation. Conditions for creation by copulation are set up with the splitting of the male and female parts of the androgyne into many other males and females. These conditions are then actualized with the appearance of Manu Svāyaṃbhū, the Manu of the first *manvantara*, and his wife Śatarūpā. Manu Svāyaṃbhū is that Manu directly descended[13] from Svāyaṃbhū (Brahmā).

This and his similar appearance (*ātmanaḥ sadṛśam*) to Brahmā strongly suggest he is a multiform of the god. So Brahmā is born again as Manu and copulates with Śatarūpā. Together they form the primordial pair from whom the creation of lineages unfolds. Versions of the myth where Brahmā's ascetic sons refuse to create by progenation (or any other method) are common in the Purāṇas. One version found in the *KP*. includes this motif along with other motifs and develops the underlying conflict between Brahmā and Śiva which is only implied in the *MkP*. when Rudra is named as one of the ascetic sons:

> Once, in the beginning, Brahmā, Prajāpati, emitted some mind-born sons who were the equal (*sama*) of himself. Named Sanaka, Sanātana, Ṛbhu, Sanandana and Sanatkumāra, these five were learned yogins who lived whilst displaying the greatest disaffection towards worldly activities. Their minds were attached to the Lord and they did not set their mind onto creation.
>
> When they showed a disregard for the creation of beings, Prajāpati instantly became deluded (*mumoha*) from the deception (*māyā*) of the deceptive (*māyin*) Parameṣṭhin. Then Nārāyaṇa, the great yogin, great sage, who creates illusion in the world, the one who gladdens the heart of yogins, aroused him, his son. Aroused by him, Brahmā, the universal self, performed the highest austerities. Though the illustrious one was performing austerities nothing was accomplished. Then, after a long time, anger was born from suffering and from his

13 That is to say *ātmasaṃbhava*.

> eyes, when he was filled with anger, tear-drops fell. From the bent, contracted brow of his forehead, the highest Lord, the great god, the refuge, Nīlalohita arose. He is indeed the illustrious Lord, eternal, a mass of fiery energy. The wise behold that highest Lord abiding in their own self.
>
> After he had fully recollected the 'Om' and bowed, Brahmā hollowed his palms together and said to him, "You must create the various types of creatures." Having heard that speech, the illustrious Śiva, Śaṅkara, the carrier of *dharma*, created with his mind the Rudras who were similar in appearance to himself–having braided and knotted hair, three-eyed, free from fear and of colour, dark blue and red.
>
> The illustrious Brahmā said to him, "You must create creatures who are subject to birth and death.' The Lord said, 'I will not create creatures who are subject to death and old age. Lord of the universe, you must emit creatures who are bad (*aśubha*)."
>
> And having stopped Rudra, Brahmā, whose origin is the lotus, emitted all who lay claim to a place on the earth… .[14]

Brahmā goes on to create various kinds of beings including the group of mind-born sons who are willing to progenate. From them come all the lineages of living beings.

As in the *MkP*. version ascetic power (*tapas*) is ineffective for creation. Brahmā's ascetic sons refuse to countenance any form of worldly activity including sexual creation and his own attempts to create by *tapas* are a failure. The gravity of the ascetic sons' refusal is heightened by the implication of the statement that they are the same (*sama*) as him. This sameness should mean they are well disposed towards the achievement of a successful creation. Nor is Brahmā's resultant anger merely a product of their intransigent attitude, but is due just as much to his frustration at his own fruitless *tapas*. Nevertheless, the refusal of sons to obey their father's command is a direct attack on his authority over them. In the Indian extended family the father's power was absolute and his commands were mandatory for all who were beneath him. Thus Brahmā's anger arises not just because his sons refuse to create,

14 *KP*. 1, 7, 19-30a-c; *ŚP*. 7, 1, 12, 19-51.

but also because they disobey him. A passage from the *BhP*. is instructive here.

> The Self-born Brahmā said to his sons, "Sons, you must create creatures." However, they had no desire for that because they were devotees of Vāsudeva and supporters of liberation (*mokṣadharmāṇaḥ*). Disregarded by his sons who had rejected his commands) he tried to keep down the unbearable anger which arose in him.[15]

The sons' disobedience is a threat to the father's authority and in Brahmā's case, to the possibility of a flourishing creation as well.

In both versions of the myth, conflict productive of anger is of crucial importance for the effectiveness of creation.[16] Far from being entirely negative, both versions testify to its positive effects. In the *MkP*. the androgynous *puruṣa* is born from Brahmā's anger and when he divides into male and female the conditions for creation through progenation are established. Similarly, Rudra and his eleven sons are born as a result of Brahmā's anger as narrated in the *KP*. version. Rudra's appearance is followed by Brahmā's production of a successful creation.

If the conflict which produces Brahmā's anger ultimately produces a successful creation through the medium of Rudra, it also results in widening the initial conflict. This conflict between the non-ascetic Brahmā and his ascetic sons is expressed in the opposition of non-action and chastity, versus action and sexuality. The appearance of Rudra exacerbates the conflict but it is expressed differently from Brahmā's conflict with the ascetic sons. As soon as Brahmā sees Rudra, he orders him to create living beings, so Rudra responds by creating *rudras* similar to himself, therefore, presumably immortal like him. Brahmā immediately objects to

---

15 *BhP.* 3, 12, 5-6.

16 However, Brahmā's anger does not always lead to positive results. In one version of the myth, prompted by the refusal of his sons to procreate, his anger is transformed into fire which burns up the three worlds. (*PaP.* 5, 3, 163-5).

the creation of immortal beings because a triple world created in conformity with *dharma* demands the presence of death.[17] In the Indian context immortality is mainly the preserve of ascetics, since one who attains *mokṣa* also attains immortality. As such, Rudra's creation of immortal beings subject to death. This is consistent with his status as a god who transmigrates from birth to birth (*kalpa* to *kalpa*), and finally dies at the end of a hundred divine years (only to be reborn for another hundred divine years). From the perspective of *nivṛttidharma* death and rebirth are characteristics of *pravṛtti*, epitomized in Brahmā's wish to create death.

The *KP*. version of the myth contains details not present in the *MkP*. Brahmā's ascetic sons are no longer just portrayed as ascetics who have an aversion for the world; they have now become devotees of Nārāyaṇa. In addition, Brahmā is said to have become deluded by Nārāyaṇa's *māyā* after the ascetic sons indicated their attitude towards the creation. Brahmā's delusion by *māyā* produces, and is itself a product, of conflict, but one eventually resolved by the intervention of the god who is the object of the devotees' concern.

Myths in which this kind of conflict is manifested between gods of the *trimūrti* occur in many versions and most contain cosmogonic motifs. Here is one from the *KP*. given in summarized form:

> During the time of dissolution Viṣṇu lay on Śeṣa coiled up on the primeval ocean. A lotus grew from his navel and after a while Brahmā came up to look at it. He was deluded by Viṣṇu's *māyā* (*mohitaḥ ... māyayā*) and asked him who he was and what he was doing on the ocean. Viṣṇu described himself in strongly eulogistic terms and then said, "You should see in me the Grandfather of the worlds [i.e. Brahmā] and the entire world covered by mountains, great islands and the seven seas."
>
> He then asked Brahmā about himself and that god said, "I

17 For some insightful remarks on this subject see O'Flaherty, 1973, pp. 136 ff.

am the Placer, the Disposer, the Self-born and the Great-grandfather. On me everything is based. I am Brahmā with faces everywhere." After this, Viṣṇu entered Brahmā's body and saw the triple world inhabited by gods, demons and men. He was amazed at this sight and when he came out of Brahmā 's body, Brahmā in turn entered his body. There he beheld the worlds (*tan... lokān*), but after wandering about in Viṣṇu's abdomen he could see no end to it.[18]

Viṣṇu closed all doors out of his body except for his navel, out of which Brahmā emerged. As soon as he had emerged he felt important again and said to Viṣṇu, "Now, what was gained by your desire for victory over me. I alone am powerful, there is no one else who can conquer me!" Viṣṇu then pacified him by saying he had only been sporting with him. Then he told him he should be his son because of the lotus birth. Brahmā tacitly agreed to this and proceeded to eulogize Viṣṇu as the highest god. He asserted that both of them were really only one body (*mūrti*) divided into two and that there were no beings in the world superior to them.

Viṣṇu warned Brahmā against such assertions, as they could lead to his destruction because Śiva was really the highest god. Brahmā retorted angrily, accusing Viṣṇu of being ignorant about their own greatness. Viṣṇu repeated that Brahmā was deluded by *māyā*, (*mohayati… māyayā*). Then Śiva himself appeared in order to please Brahmā, but he was still deluded and did not recognize Śiva until Viṣṇu informed him who it was.

Viṣṇu saw Śiva blazing in the waters of the ocean and eulogized

---

18 The different contents in the two gods' bodies reflect the different sets of values underlying their mythology. Brahmā's body contains the triple world, the realm of rebirth and action central to *pravṛtti* values. Viṣṇu is only concerned with the three worlds during certain critical moments in their 'history' when he descends to Earth as an *avatāra*. His concern really goes beyond the triple world as is symbolized by his continued existence during the *mahāpralaya*. That there are worlds in his body, and not a fixed number of worlds, and that his body has no end, that is, no limits, implies that it is infinite, corresponding to *mokṣa* and *nivṛtti* values.

> him. Brahmā then gained the Śaiva sight (*śaivaṃ cakṣur*) from Viṣṇu and sought refuge with Śiva. After being eulogized by Brahmā, Śiva said to him, "Lord, there is no doubt you are the same as me, because you are my devotee (*bhakta*)." He then offered him a boon and Brahmā asked that Śiva should become his son. He also said he was unable to know Śiva's higher nature (*paramaṃ bhāvam*) because he was deluded by his subtle *māyā*. Finally, he requested, "Favour me, I have come for refuge and bow at your lotus feet."
>
> Śiva agreed to give Brahmā divine knowledge and commissioned him to be the creator. He offered Viṣṇu a boon and that god asked to perceive Śiva in his true self and to remain continually in devotion to him. Then Śiva directed Viṣṇu to protect the entire universe.[19]

In this and other versions of the myth Brahmā is deluded by both Viṣṇu and Śiva and is also under the influence of the *ahaṃkāra*. His subjection to *māyā* is expressed in two ways. Firstly, in his failure to perceive the true nature of Viṣṇu and Śiva because they have veiled themselves with *māyā*. Secondly, through his excessive pride epitomized in statements he makes such as, "There is no one higher than me."[20] As is said in one version of the myth, this kind of arrogant pride is prompted by the *ahaṃkāra*.[21] Viṣṇu's reaction to Brahmā's arrogance is to rebuke him. Even Viṣṇu's own understanding of his and Brahmā's real status is partially veiled by *māyā*, but he is certainly less influenced by it than Brahmā. There is even a hint suggesting Viṣṇu is a *bhakti* god, because his explanations for closing off the apertures of his body when Brahmā was inside it are said to be for *līlā* and Brahmā's own benefit (*kalyāṇa*).[22] *Līlā*, 'divine play', is an important technical term used in *bhakti* texts to serve

---

19 Paraphrased summary of *KP*. 1, 9, 5-87. Cf. *ŚP*. 1, 6, 1-8, 21.

20 See *MBh*. 3, 185, 48; *KP*. 2, 31, 6; *ŚP*. 1, 6, 6; 3, 8, 14. The pronoun I (*aham*) occurs frequently in such claims and is common in devotional texts, even Buddhist texts like the *Lalitavistara*.

21 *VāmP*. 2, 25.

22 *KP*. 1, 9, 34-5.

as the principle motive for the actions of the supreme god of the particular text. *Kalyāṇa* is what the devotee can expect from the god to which he is devoted, in return for his own worship of the god. It is an expression of the god's grace.

Śiva is the supreme god in this version of the myth. His reaction to both gods confirms his position as a *bhakti* god who extends favours to his devotees. He reveals his own true nature to Brahmā, an act instrumental in removing Brahmā's subjection to *māyā*, at the same time enlightening him about the true nature of his own self in relation to Śiva and other beings.

Although this passage is strongly influenced by *bhakti*, it does occur in a cosmogonic context and accordingly reflects certain attitudes about cosmogony. In the *KP*. myth where Brahmā's ascetic sons refuse to procreate, Brahmā was said to be deluded by Nārāyaṇa's *māyā*.[23] The implication in this myth and the one under discussion is that procreation (and any action pertaining to creation) is characteristically performed by those who are ignorant and under the influence of *māyā*. The ascetic sons who are seeking *mokṣa* are not subjected to *māyā*, hence their refusal to assist Brahmā. In itself this is consistent with their attitude in other versions of the myth which lack any mention of *māyā*. Contemplation to gain knowledge is the ascetic's aim. Action is anathema, especially action arises from desire.

Because the passage just cited is strongly influenced by *bhakti* a new twist is introduced concerning *māyā* and the pejorative attitude towards creation. After Siva has revealed his true nature to Brahmā, his *bhakta*, he instructs him to become the creator. Similarly, he commissions Viṣṇu to perform the role of protector. As devotees of Śiva both deities happily accept their stipulated tasks. Considering that Śiva has removed the *māyā* obscuring Brahmā's understanding, the willingness of the two gods to perform such '*māyā*-associated' tasks reflects their intense devotion to him. What from one point of view was formerly regarded as a pejorative act, is no longer regarded as such if the

23 See above pp.154-55.

act is performed out of an attitude of devotion. This is nothing other than *karmayoga*.

Here Śiva exhibits a positive attitude towards the creation. Similarly, in many myths where the ascetic sons refuse to create, it is Śiva who helps Brahmā effect creation through copulation. Either he assists him by making an appearance together with the Rudras and creating immortals, or in more direct ways. One of these is to create a woman for Brahmā, allowing creation to proceed by copulation. The following passage illustrates this, at the same time underlying the failure of *tapas* as an efficacious means of creation:

> When Brahmā's creation did not thrive he became anxious and distressed. A voice from the sky said, 'Create by copulation!' On hearing this he resolved to make a creation by copulation. However, at first he was unable to engage in copulation because he had not created women. He performed *tapas* in honour of Śiva who appeared before him as an androgyne combined with his *śakti*. Śiva knew Brahmā was performing *tapas* to increase the creation, so he offered him a wish.
>
> Śiva separated from his *śakti*, Śivā, and Brahmā asked that he have her as his wish for performing *tapas*. He said to her, "Śivā, in the beginning I was created by your husband, the god of gods, and was ordered by Śambhu, the supreme self, to create all creatures.[24] Śivā, everything, the gods and the rest, were repeatedly created with my mind, but they did not increase. Accordingly, having undertaken creation by the power of copulation, I want all of my creatures to increase strongly. Up till now the imperishable race of women has not come forth from you. Therefore, I do not have the power (*śakti*) to create that first race of women. All of the *śaktis* have definitely sprung up from you, so I am requesting your supreme power (*śakti*), which governs everything. Śivā, obeisance to you, give me the power to create the race of women, because you should know that Śiva is the universe both moving and non-moving, mother, beloved of Śiva."

24 Here reading *prajāḥ sarvā niyuktaḥ*.

Then he asked her to become Dakṣa's daughter, to which she agreed. She emitted another *śakti* from the centre of her brow and this *śakti* became Dakṣa's daughter. After Śivā had reentered Śiva, Brahmā became happy and the creation proceeded by copulation.[25]

From the very beginning it is made clear copulation will be the only successful method of creation. Brahmā's *tapas* again fails to increase the creation directly, but it does indirectly by causing Śiva to appear. This enables Brahmā to ask for and receive a boon, as this will give him what he could not obtain from his own *tapas*.[26] As always, the problem for Brahmā, intent upon creation by copulation, is to find a female partner or partners. The problem is resolved when Śiva's *śakti* produces another *śakti* who agrees to become Dakṣa's daughter. Dakṣa is well known in Indian mythology as the father of daughters who become wives of the gods and progenitrixes of living beings.[27] Usually Dakṣa is attributed with having fifty daughters. Though he is only given one daughter here, it is likely that in the context of this myth she represents all his daughters because her presence establishes the viability of copulation.

In this myth Śiva and Śivā do not adopt a strong ascetic line and condemn creation by copulation as they do in another series of cosmogonic myths.[28] However, whilst both support the idea of

---

25 Summary of *ŚP*. 3, 3, 2-29.

26 Brahmā's solicitation of Śiva's favour reflects the influence of *bhakti* as in the myth from the *KP*. just discussed.

27 Dakṣa is a multiform of Brahmā, sharing some of his common epithets such as *lokapitāmaha*, 'Grandfather of the worlds', and Sraṣṭṛ, 'Creator' (*MBh*. 1, 70, 4; 6, 64, 5).

28 The basic story line of these myths runs as follows: Brahmā asks Śiva to create living beings. He agrees, but before doing anything he goes off and performs *tapas*. Brahmā becomes impatient and creates another being to do Śiva's job. Having completed his *tapas*, Śiva sees the finished creation, becomes enraged and throws his *liṅgam* onto the ground, thereby castrating himself. This act of self-castration is an attack on sexuality and epitomizes

sexual creation, neither becomes directly involved with it. Śiva does not copulate with his androgynous partner, his *śakti*, as he does in other versions of the myth. His *śakti* creates a portion of herself to become Dakṣa's daughter and then re-enters Śiva. Their mild ascetic stance is still preserved even whilst assisting Brahmā to achieve a creation by copulation.

In the myths so far discussed sexuality is presented as an alternative to *tapas* as a method of creation. There is another series of myths where Brahmā's sexuality is taken to the extreme. These tell of his incestuous desire for his daughter and his subsequent punishment at the hands of Śiva, or even his own sons. Such myths which employ the incest motif often have a cosmogonic perspective, frequently occurring in a cosmogonic context with associated motifs. From the earliest appearance of this motif in Indian literature the incestuous father has always been a creator god. So there is considerable justification for understanding the incest motif in terms of sexuality as a means of creation taken to its extreme.

One version of the incest myth in the *MP*. contains several cosmogonic themes. The passage cited here begins after the description of the creation of the world and the mind-born sons:

> Brahmā put Sāvitrī into his heart in order to create people, and whilst he was chattering he split his stainless body. From one half he made a woman's body and from the other half a man's body. She is known as Śatarūpā, and is also called Sāvitrī, Gāyatrī and Brahmaṇī, great ascetic. On that basis, he considered her as being Self-born, born from his own body.
>
> On seeing her, the mighty Prajāpati, afflicted by Kāma's arrows, was immediately agitated and cried, "Oh! What beauty! What beauty!" At that, his sons, headed by Vasiṣṭha, cried out, "This is our sister!" Brahmā however, was looking so attentively at her face that he saw nothing else. He repeatedly said, "Oh! What beauty! What beauty!"

---

the anti-sexual attitude of the ascetic. See *MBh*. 10, 17, 10-26; *VāmP*. *Sarohamāhātmya*, 27, 20-34; O'Flaherty, 1973, pp. 130-6.

Again he looked towards her, as she was bowing to him. Then this beautifully complexioned woman walked in a rightwards direction around her father. Though causing shame to his sons, he gazed desirously at that beautiful woman. Then a face appeared on his southern side, with pale cheek and lip quivering in amazement. She went to his western side and there on his western side arose a fourth face, pleasant but suffering from Kāma's arrows. Another face arose, and it too was suffering from desire for her, because of his eagerness to gaze upon her body, she who had arisen suddenly. Since he had performed an extremely severe austerity for purposes of creation, it was all lost due to his desire to have sex with his own daughter. After that the wise god acquired a fifth face, a face covered with dread locks and the mighty lord concealed it.

Then Brahmā said to his sons who were born from himself, 'Emit living creatures everywhere-gods, demons and men!' This having been said, all of them emitted various creatures.

When they had left to create, Brahmā, the universal self, married that virtuous Śatarūpā who had bowed courteously to him. Wishing to be modest, the god went into the hollow of a lotus and then the mighty Lord, sick with lust, had intercourse with her. [As a result of their intercourse Svayaṃbhū Manu is born and then his sons] …

Because he had had sex with his own offspring Brahmā cursed the flower-armed Kāma saying, "Since, even my heart has been shaken by your arrows when you attacked me, before long, Rudra will burn your body to ashes."

The God of Love then propitiated the Four-faced Brahmā, saying, "Destroyer of arrogance, please do not curse me now without cause. I was created in such a form by you alone, Four-faced Brahmā, so as to cause the agitation of all bodily senses. Always and everywhere I have to vigorously excite the hearts of men and women without discrimination. You had said this formerly, Lord. Therefore I am faultless, and still, Lord, I have been cursed by you. Please, illustrious god, be favourable, and let me get my own body again."[29]

29 *MP*. 3, 30cd-43; 4, 11cd-16.

This version of the myth uses material from the Purāṇas to embellish the basic motif of incest derived from the Brāhmaṇas. Brahmā has taken Prajāpati's place and is rebuked by his own sons who represent the gods who in the earlier versions of the myth had rebuked Prajāpati. Śatarūpā is treated by Brahmā's sons as their sister, but in other similar cosmogonies where Brahmā copulates with the female aspect of himself (often called Śatarūpā), he is not rebuked for committing incest.[30] Śatarūpā's other names–Sarasvatī, Sāvitrī, Gāyatrī and Brahmaṇī-are generally held to be the names of Brahmā's wife. Despite his strongly paternalistic character and his paternal roles, there are very few passages in the epics where he is accompanied by his wife.[31] He only has intercourse with her through his multiform Svāyaṃbhū Manu.[32]

In this myth Brahmā represents the householder (*gṛhapati*), the eldest male in the household living in the stage of life where the requirements of *kāma* (understood as sexual desire), are normatively supposed to be observed. In practical terms this means he must engage in procreation for the purpose of ensuring the continuity of his lineage. His expression of *kāma* should be controlled however, and should not turn into sheer lust as in this version of the incest myth. If, as here, Brahmā craves intercourse out of lust, elsewhere his motive is a legitimate one because it is to increase creation.

The incest motif occurs in other forms, one of the most popular being Brahmā's sexual arousal at the sight of the wives or daughters of the gods. The most extreme instance, is when

---

30 See *H*. 1, 37.

31 The few epic references to Sāvitrī are at *MBh*. 13, 134, 3; 13, 151, 4; *GP*. 3, 16, 82; *KP*. 2, 37, 46; *NP*. 1, 83, 109. Gāyatrī is found at *Rām*. (G) 3, 12, 20; *AP*. 176, 2-3; *MP*. 4, 7-9. Except for Brahmaṇī each of these goddesses often appears independently of Brahmā in the epics. It is more common for him to be grouped with his wife in the Purāṇas. See *KP*. 2, 37, 46; *BvP*. 1, 8, l; *PaP*. 5, 17, 141-225; *ŚP*. 2, 2, 10, 57.

32 See above p.112.

he loses control of himself in front of Śiva's wife Satī. On one occasion Brahmā is celebrating their marriage:

> Immediately after they were married Brahmā said that although in the past he had tried to delude Śiva by conceit, he was not deluded (*moha*) himself by Śiva's divine play (*līlā*). He saw Satī's feet, immediately became filled with passion (*madana*) and was deluded by Śiva's *māyā*. Then he made the sacrificial fire smoky and, whilst all the gods were distracted, he looked at her face.
>
> When he saw her face he became helpless (*avaśa*) and his semen spilt onto the ground. He became silent and covered up the semen so that no one would know what had happened. However, by using his divine eye Śiva discovered what Brahmā had done and was very angry. He resolved to kill him because Viṣṇu had once told him he should kill anyone who glanced at Satī.
>
> Then his own sons, the gods and Viṣṇu interceded on his behalf and begged Śiva not to kill him. Viṣṇu said Brahmā had sought refuge (*śaraṇāgata*) with Śiva and this was one reason why he should not be killed. Also, if Brahmā was killed there would be nobody to create living creatures, and Brahmā was really a part of Śiva and so by killing Brahmā he would be killing a part of himself.
>
> Śiva relented and instead of killing Brahmā he cursed him to wander over the Earth with one hand stuck on his head and to perform austerities. Seeing him, people would ridicule and blame him for what he had done. His drops of semen became the clouds which cause destruction at the time of cosmic• dissolution.[33]

This myth gives fine expression to devotional values, as the three gods of the *trimūrti* act out roles paradigmatic of devotee and god. Śiva is the highest god, and, despite Brahmā's sexual excesses, the object of devotion for his two *bhaktas*, Viṣṇu and Brahmā. As always, Brahmā is the one deluded by *māyā* and this is highlighted in his arrogance in thinking Śiva to be deluded when

33 Summary of *ŚP*. 2, 2, 19.

it was he himself that was so. Through the mediation of Viṣṇu he is brought back into Śiva's favour, the god with whom he seeks refuge after having incurred his wrath.

Brahmā's uncontrollable sexuality is depicted here in the strongest possible terms. Even at a sensitive occasion such as a wedding, at which he is the officiant, he is simply unable to control his illicit lust for another god's wife. Revealing his anger Śiva says to him: "Wretch, why have you done this despicable thing? Because of your passion you have looked at my wife's face at her wedding!"[34]

The important point to note here is Brahmā's total lack of control over himself. Śiva attacks him for this as much as for his excess sexuality, for while Śiva and Indra are frequently portrayed seducing the wives of others, they do so with more discretion.[35] Brahmā blatantly pursues other women even when their husbands are there. He knows Satī is forbidden to him, and after his presumably unwished for ejaculation, he uses a ruse to distract attention from himself. Discovered by Śiva, he is ashamed, just as he was when his sons were shocked by his incestuous desire for their sister. Śiva and Indra, on the contrary are rarely ever ashamed when they are caught in the act of illicit love.

Brahmā as the Grandfather

The picture of Brahmā given in the last section is of a god deeply committed to procreation as a means of creation. In many senses he is the embodiment of *kāma*, especially when his sexuality is manifested in such extreme forms as incest. Sexuality is only one aspect of his role as father of beings, a role indicated by such of his epithets as Pitāmaha, 'Grandfather', and Pitṛ, 'father'. Like several creator gods of the Vedas who were portrayed as father figures, Brahmā is attributed with the functions of progenation, protection, and to a lesser extent of nourishment and education.

The usual meaning of the kinship term *pitāmaha* is 'paternal

---

34 *ŚP*. 2, 2, 19, 51.

35 For examples see O'Flaherty, 1973, pp.84-90; 172-204.

grandfather' and this seems to be its sense when used of Brahmā. He is also called *prapitāmaha*, a kinship term applied to the paternal and maternal great-grandfather, representing the first generation in a family of four generations. Judging from epithets such as Lokapitāmaha and Sarvalokapitāmaha, Brahmā is grandfather of living beings as a whole or of the worlds, for *loka* can mean 'living being' or 'world'.[36] Another related epithet, Sarvabhūtapitāmaha, can only mean 'grandfather of all beings'.[37]

Though *pitāmaha* and related compounds ending with this word imply a specific kin relationship within a family, no accord is paid to the correct kinship relation when Brahmā is addressed as *pitāmaha*. In general, it would be most unlikely that he would be other than a remote ancestor to the majority of the inhabitants of the triple world. Yet Karve notes that at *MBh*. 1, 6, 5, Brahmā is addressed as *pitāmaha* by Pulomā his daughter-in-law.[38] If she had used correct kinship terminology she would have called him father-in-law, or even *pitā*, rather than *pitāmaha*. Sanatkumāra, Brahmā's son is called *pitāmahasūta*, 'son of the grandfather',

36 Such references are exceptionally frequent. See *KP*. 1, 2, 5; 1, 2, 21; *MkP*. 50. 40; *MP*. 2, 36; 3, 1; 154, 156; *MBh*. 12, 59, 23; 122, 15; 160, 21; 327, 30; *ŚP*. 2, 2, 2, 16. Textual occurrences of *pitāmaha* and *prapitāmaha* are so frequent they need not be listed. On the meaning of *loka* see Gonda, 1966.

37 See *MBh*. 1, 58, 37; 9, 43, 49; 12, 200, 13; 14, 18, 24. It does not seem to occur outside of the *MBh*.

38 Karve, 1944, p. 67. One might question the validity of studying particular gods (or groups of gods) through an examination of the kinship terms used of them, since these terms presuppose some kind of social organization–perhaps one analogous to the structure of the joint family. The kinship terms for father, mother, son, daughter, etc., are used of the gods throughout Indian literature. A study should be made to determine the range of usage of such terminology and to discover whether the gods form a kind of divine joint family or some other related social structure. The Vedic terms are discussed by Karve, 1938-39, p. 72. For the epics see Karve, 1944, pp. 63-5; Hopkins, 1974, pp. 61-4.

but he is also called *brahmaputra*, 'son of Brahmā'.[39] Excluding *brahmaputra*, both examples point to *pitāmaha* being used of Brahmā in a classificatory sense, because he is a true *pitāmaha* in the sense of 'father's father' only to a few individuals and *prapitāmaha* to a few more. Similar usage of the same term is found in the case of Bhīṣma who is typically called *pitāmaha* by the Pāṇḍavas and the Kauravas.[40]

Besides the appellation *pitāmaha*, Brahmā is quite often called 'father'. The usual word for this is *pitṛ*, but at least twice he is called *tāta* and once *janaka*, the latter referring to the father's role as a begetter.[41] Often when called 'father', it is in relation to a particular divine being or group of beings such as Prahasta (a demon), the Vālakhilyas (a group of sages) or the god Dharma.[42] Sometimes *pitṛ* is used in the specific sense of 'father of all beings in the universe', for example in a stock passage from some Pāli

---

39 *MBh*. 9, 45, 85; *KP*. 1, 16, 4.

40 The sharing of the epithet *pitāmaha* is only one of several similarities between Brahmā and Bhīṣma. Just as Brahmā gives advice to the gods and demons in their perpetual conflict, so too does Bhīṣma give advice to the Pāṇḍavas (*devas*) and Kauravas (*asuras*) in the Bhārata war (cf. *MBh*. 12, 53, 24, where Bhīṣma, being approached for advice by the Pāṇḍavas, is said to be accompanied by brahmarṣis, just as Brahmā is by groups of gods). Similarly both figures are described in different contexts as being neutral. When Duryodhana is discussing ways of getting rid of the Pāṇḍavas, he says to Bhīṣma, "You are always impartial (*madhyastha*)" (*MBh*. 1, 130, 16). This very word is also used to describe Brahmā as well as other gods who stand in contrast to gods such as Indra who are fierce and partial. (See *MBh*. 12, 15, 19, and compare below Ch.9, p.298). Finally, both are great teachers of *dharma*.

41 For pitṛ see *MBh*. 12, 327, 84 vr; *EI*. 2. p. 166; *Kathasaritsāgara*, 8, 50, 19; *ŚP*. 2, 5, 35, 14; *tāta*, *MBh*. 6, 62, 1, *ŚP*. 2, 3, 49, 36; *janaka*, *ŚP*. 2, 2, 8, 33.

42 *Kathāsaritsāgara*. 8, 50, 19; *ŚP.* 2, 3, 35, 14.

texts where he is called 'Father of beings past and future' (*pitā bhūtabhavyānam*).[43]

The sense of fatherhood implicit in these epithets is certainly consistent with Brahmā's commitment to create through procreation. But they do not mean he was literally father of all beings, only that he was the sole ancestor. This at least is the conclusion to be drawn from a study of the genealogies found in the *MBh.* and the Purāṇic cosmologies.[44] These cover the same general area as the creation of living beings in the *pratisarga*, but go into considerable detail in developing the lineages of living beings, personified mental concepts and emotions.

In the *MBh.* the genealogy begins with Brahmā's mind-born sons who are called *prajāpatis*, 'Lords of creatures', whose task is to populate the triple world through progenation. This genealogy posits six mindborn sons–Marīci, Atri, Pulastya, Aṅgiras, Pulaha and Kratu.[45] Marīci had a son named Kaśyapa and it was from his marriage to the thirteen daughters of Dakṣa that various groups of lineages arose. The ādityas, for example, were born from Kaśyapa's union with Aditi, the snakes from his union with Kadrū, and dānavas from his union with Danu. With the exception of brahmins, there were no humans.

The lineages described in detail in *MBh.* I, 59 form a distinct genealogy. A second genealogy, diverging in many details from the first, is outlined in the following chapter. As in the first genealogy it begins with Brahmā's six sons.[46] After their appearance Rudra's eleven sons are listed by name and then the genealogy returns to Brahmā's sons, whose procreative capacities are hinted at by their description as virile (*vīryavat*).[47] Four of them had sages for

---

43 *DN.* I, 18; *MN.* I, 327; It. p. 15. Cf. *MBh.* 5, 45, 28, where Viṣṇu describes Brahmā as '*pitaraṃ sarvabhūtānām*'. Similarly *BhP.* 3, 13, 7.

44 *MBh.* 1, 59-60; *KP.* 1, 8; *MkP.* 50, 4-33; *ViP.* 1, 7.

45 *MBh.* 1, 59, 10–11 ab.

46 *MBh.* 1, 60, 11.

47 *MBh.* 1, 60, 4.

offspring whilst Pulasta and Pulaha produced rākṣasas, vānaras, kiṃnaras and deer, lions, tigers and kiṃpuruṣas respectively.[48] It is noticeable, that apart from sages (who may be representative of humans), humans are not included in the lists of their offspring. Next to be listed in the genealogy are Dakṣa and his wife, who were born from Brahmā's right and left thumb respectively.[49] Fifty daughters were born to them, thirteen, of whom were given as wives to Kaśyapa, ten to Dharma and twenty-seven to Soma. Dharma's wives were the embodiments of specific mental states (*mati*, *buddhi*, *lajjā*, etc), whereas those of Soma's were the stars and yoginīs. After a brief excursus on the eight *vasus* who were fathered by Prajāpati, son of Pitāmaha (Brahmā?), the genealogy returns to Dharma, He was born from Brahmā's right breast and had three sons–Śama, 'tranquillity', Kāma, 'desire', and Harṣa, 'joy.[50] After this another lineage begins, headed by Marīci whose son, Kaśyapa, produced gods and demons. Following this, the births of Bhṛgu and his sons, and of Dhātṛ and Vidhātṛ, are related. The genealogy ends with the birth of Adharma (not from Brahmā), who, with his wife Nirṛti, produced three sons–Bhaya, 'fear', Mahābhaya, 'great fear', and Mṛtyu, 'death'.[51]

These two genealogies and those in the Purāṇas which correspond to them, group the products of creation–gods, sages, demons, humans, personified mental states, *dharma* and *adharma*–into lineages ultimately traceable back to Brahmā. The Purāṇic genealogies always occur as part of the systematic Purāṇic cosmogony and their purpose might be to give expression to the products of creation in the triple world in terms of an extended family, at the head of which stands Brahmā. This would explain why they duplicate much that is narrated in other parts of the Purāṇic cosmogony. ln the *MBh.* and the Purāṇas there are several descriptions of Brahmā 's *sabhā*, 'assembly hall', and its

48 *MBh.* 1, 60, 5-7.

49 *MBh.* 1, 60, 9-10, Cf. 12, 200, 19; *ViP.* 1, 15, 79; *MP.* 3, 39.

50 *MBh.* 1, 60, 30ff.

51 *MBh.* 1, 60, 52ff.

inhabitants, who by and large correspond very closely with the lists of beings included in the genealogies.[52] It is clear from these descriptions that his *sabhā* encompasses the triple world.

The most comprehensive description of his *sabhā* occurs in the *MBh.* in conjunction with those of lndra, Yama, Varuṇa and Kubera respectively. Its inhabitants are listed as follows:

> In it sits the blessed lord, 0 king, the grandfather of the worlds who, alone, constantly creates the worlds with his divine wizardry. The Lords of the Creatures attend on the Lord. Dakṣa, Pracetas, Pulastya, Pulaha, Marīci Kaśyapa, Bhṛgu, Atri, Vasiṣṭha, Gautama, Aṅgiras; the mind, atmosphere, the sciences, wind, fire, water, earth, sound, touch, colour, taste and smell, Bhārata, source stuff (*prakṛti*) and evolute and whatever else is cause of the world. Moon with the asterisms, the sun with its rays, the winds and seasons, the ritual intention and breath. These and many others attend on the Self-existent god, and law, profit, and pleasure, joy, hatred, austerity, and self-control. The Gandharvas and Apsaras go there together, and the twenty-seven other World-Guardians, Śukra, Bṛhaspati, Budha, Angāraka, Śanaiścara, Rahu, all the Planets, Mantra, Rathaṃtara, Harimat, Vasumat, the Ādityas with their overlord, and those deities called by various double names; the Maruts, Viśvakarman, the Vasus, Bhārata, all the hosts of the Fathers, all the oblations, Ṛgveda, Sāmaveda, and Yājurveda, Pāṇḍava, the Atharvaveda and the Books, Lord of the people, epics and subordinate Vedas, all the auxiliary supplements of the Veda, the soma cups, sacrifices, Soma, all the Deities, the sāvitrī formula, Saviour from distress. The seven fold speech, wisdom, perseverance, learning, insight, understanding, fame, forbearance, the sāman chants, the lauds, the praises, the various songs, the commentaries with their arguments in an embodied form, Lord of the people. The instants, moments, hours, day, night, fortnights, months, the six seasons, Bhārata. The years, the lustrums, the four kinds of days and nights, the divine, eternal, indestructible wheel of time, Aditi, Diti, Dānu, Vinatā, Surasā, Irā, Kālakā, Devī, Surabhi, Saramā, Gautamī, the Ādityas, Vasus, Rudras, Manus and Aśvins, the Viśvadevas,

52 *MBh.* 2, 11; *VāmP. Sarohamāhātmya*. 3, 19-38.

> Sādhyas, the fathers who are fast as thought, Rākṣasas, Piśācas, Dānavas, Guhyakas, birds, snakes, and cattle wait on the Grand father.[53] There is the god Nārāyaṇa, there are the divine seers, the Vālakhilya seers, those born from wombs and those who are not. Whatever is found in the three worlds, whether moving or standing, know that I have seen it all in that hall, Lord of men. The eighty thousand ascetics who practice celibacy, the fifty thousand seers who have sons, Pāṇḍava, they and all the other dwellers in heaven come to visit as they please, bow their heads and return as they come. And to the lordly guests who come, Gods, Daityas, snakes, hermits, Yakṣas, Garuḍas, Kāleyas, Gandharvas, and Apsaras, to them the immeasurably wise Brahmā, acts as they deserve. Upon receiving their homage, the all-soul, the self-existent god of boundless lustre, bestows on them joys intended to comfort, king of men.[54]

The principal difference between this listing and that of the genealogies is in the lesser emphasis placed on *adharma* here. *Adharma* is present only in the mention of rākṣasas, daityas and piśācas, demons who are usually opposed to *dharma*.

The compass of Brahmā's *sabhā* is the triple world. In the words of the narrative itself, "Whatever is found in the three worlds ... I have seen it all in that hall", so Yudhiṣṭhira is told by Nārada.[55] Furthermore, with the exception of his *sabhā*, each of the others which are described have a definite spatial area delineated by a standard measure, the *yojana*. Śakra's, for example, is said to

---

53 After this line (*śl*.31 of the text) 23 manuscripts contain the following lines not included in the Critical Edition of the *MBh*.: "Likewise other great beings, stationary and moving; and Puraṃdara, the Indra of the gods, Varuṇa, the Giver of Wealth [Kubera] and Yama [wait upon the Grandfather]. Mahādeva with Umā comes there always, and Mahāsena, Indra of kings, waits upon the Grandfather." This addition means that all the important gods in the epic are included in Brahmā's *sabhā*, including those whose own *sabhā* is listed in the four chapters previous to this one.

54 *MBh*. 2, 11, 13-38. Following van Buitenen, 1975, pp.51-2.

55 *MBh*. 2, 11, 33.

be one hundred *yojanas* wide, one hundred and fifty long and five high.[56] Brahmā's, however, has no measure (*parimāṇa*) or shape (*saṃsthāna*).[57] This suggests it is not meant to be thought of as having spatial limits, that it should be regarded as the triple world.

The list of beings, objects and personified psychological states found in Brahmā's *sabhā* covers almost everything found in the triple world, whereas the lists of occupants in the other four *sabhās* are much more limited in extent and diversity. But what does the word *sabhā* mean? Can it be rendered as 'family house', thereby suggesting that the inhabitants of Brahmā's *sabhā* constitute his extended family? There has always been doubt as to the exact rendering of *sabhā*. On the basis of a comprehensive study of the Brāhmaṇas, Rau has suggested several different renderings: "It denoted a stall, an unboarded hall in the house of rich lords to be used for gambling and containing a fire palace and a dicing place, a social gathering, a public place, the place where eminent people gave official audience and the assembly hall in the place of a sovereign, where a committee of aristocrats, *brāhmaṇas* and himself dispensed justice."[58] Brahmā's *sabhā* corresponds best to the second-last of these, a place where eminent people give audience.

Even if his *sabhā* is not to be understood as a house containing his family, there can be no doubt it encompasses the triple world and is just another of many indicators pointing to this area as his sphere of action. However, there is much in the listing of those in his *sabhā* similar to the genealogies of the *MBh.* and the Purāṇas. Brahmā is listed first, but only under the name of *lokapitāmaha*, an epithet seemingly used to emphasize his paternality. Next to be mentioned are his sons, pointedly named the *prajāpatis*, a name with very strong overtones of procreation. After them multifarious beings are listed, not in terms of lineages, but their correspondence to the genealogies suggests it is difficult to escape the conclusion

---

56 *MBh.* 2, 7, 1-2.

57 *MBh.* 2, 11, 9.

58 Rau, 1957, p.81.

that they constitute an extended family, of which Brahmā is the head. This conclusion accounts admirably for the expression of sexuality in Brahmā's creative acts in the cosmogonies discussed in this chapter. Finally, it is totally consistent with *pravṛtti* values, of which the householder living in accord with *kāma* is such an apt symbol.

Chapter 6

Brahmā, Rajas and Pravṛtti

Considerable stress has already been laid upon Brahmā's identification with *ahaṃkāra* as one important key for understanding his cosmogonic role. In the *prākṛtasarga* the *ahaṃkāra* is tripartite, each part corresponding to one of the three *guṇas*. The one function of the *rajoguṇa* within the tripartite *ahaṃkāra* is to stimulate (or incite) the appearance of the other two *guṇas* which give rise to the physical and mental components out of which the universe is composed. Functionally then, *rajas* is identical with *ahaṃkāra* insofar as the appearance of both is necessary before the individuated creation can arise. Just as Brahmā is identical with the *ahaṃkāra*, so too is he identical with *rajas* and not just because of their function in the cosmogony. The range of meanings associated with the *rajoguṇa* corresponds directly with many of the ideas that come under the rubric of *pravṛttidharma*, the value system underlying Brahmā's mythology.

The overlapping of *rajas* and *pravṛtti* in a conceptual sense can be seen in the Puranic cosmogony. In the *prākṛtasarga* the role of the *rajoguṇa* is to stimulate the evolutionary development of the other two *guṇas*, as is shown in the following passage from the *BḍP*: "When *tamas* and *sattva* exist, *rajas* too exists as an accompaniment. *Rajas* exists as a stimulator (*pravartaka*) just like water amongst seeds."[1] Similar to this is a passage from the *MkP*. describing Brahmā: "Though born he is the source of the universe. Although he is without characteristics he takes possession of the

1 *BḍP*. 1, 4, 4; *VāP*. 5, ll-14ab.

passion characteristic (*rajoguṇa*) and becomes Brahmā when engaging (*pravartaka*) in creation."[2] The use of cognates of *pra/vṛt* is also found in cosmogonic contexts from which *rajas* is entirely absent. Such is the case when in one Purāṇa Brahmā is called the 'Stimulator of every creation' (*sarvasṛṣṭipravartaka*).[3] *Rajas* and cognates of *pra/vṛt* can be used interchangeably because both stimulate or cause the performance of activity in general, even at the cosmogonic level. It is possible to go further and say that the use of *pra/vṛt* to designate the act of creation marks this act, the first to be performed, as consonant with *pravṛtti* values.

The etymology of the word *rajas* points towards two distinct meanings. One goes back to a notion of 'space, air, heaven', whereas the second goes back to 'dust, mist, darkness'.[4] Senart has shown that in the Vedas there was a triadic cosmology of earth, atmosphere and sky, and that *rajas* designated the middle one of these, though not in a triad with *sattva* and *tamas*.[5] There is, of course, a radical shift of meaning between these oldest uses and later ones such as in the *Ms*. where the *guṇas* are defined in the following way: "*Sattva* is knowledge, *tamas* is ignorance and *rajas* is impetuosity and hate".[6] This brief statement gives emphasis to the emotive and psychological meanings of the word. A broader definition is given in *the Bhg*:

> Know that *rajas* consists of impetuosity (*rāga*) and arises from craving and attachment. Son of Kuntī, it binds the embodied self by its attachment to action. ... Covetousness, activity

2 *MkP*. 46, 13. Other passages where Brahmā and *rajas* are identified are *ViP*. 1, 4, 50; *ŚP*. 6, 15, 31; *VāmP*. 2, 22, 19; *BḍP*. 1, 4, 18; *El*. 7. p. 154.

3 *ŚP*. 2, 2, 9, 38.

4 On the etymology of *rajas* see Senart, 1915, pp. 15I-64; Pryzluski, 1930-2, pp.25-35; Burrow, 1947-8, p.649; van Buitenen, 1957, p.92.

5 Senart, 1915, p.152.

6 *Ms*. 12, 26.

(*pravṛtti*), the undertaking of actions, restlessness and desire; these originate when *rajas* is predominant, Bull of the Bhāratas.[7]

The word *pravṛtti* and cognates are frequently found in descriptions of *rajas* that occur in non-cosmogonic contexts. In one *MBh.* passage a brahmin asks a hunter to explain to him the properties of the *guṇas*. The hunter says *tamas* is characterized by delusion (*moha*), *rajas* by stimulation (*pravartaka*), and *sattva* by a great illuminating power (*prakāśabahula*).[8] He elaborates further about each of their qualities. *Tamas* is described by a string of epithets all suggesting stupidity and ignorance. The other two are described in the following way:

Governed by *rajas* is one of ready speech (*pravṛttavākya*) and good advice, friendly, argumentative, eager to learn, arrogant and proud, O brahmin seer. Governed by *sattva* is one who is illumined, steady, aloof, unprotesting, free from anger, wise and self-controlled. Enlightenment (*saṃbuddha*), the mark of *sattva*, is troubled by the ways of the world (*lokavṛtta*); when one has learned that which is to be learned, he loathes the way of the world.[9]

Here both *rajas* and *sattva* are opposed in the same way as *pravṛtti* and *nivṛtti* are so often opposed. Those governed by *rajas* are portrayed as virtual opposites of those governed by *sattva*. The attitude of loathing–or better, indifference–towards the world, listed as characteristic of *sattva*, is the attitude to be expected of renouncers. This makes *sattva* in this passage a virtual synonym of *nivṛtti*.

Another passage in the *MBh.* declares all seekers after *mokṣa*

---

7 Bhg. 14, 7 and 12.

rajo rāgātmakaṃ viddhi tṛṣṇāsaṅgasamudbhavam /
tan nibadhnāti kaunteya karmasaṅgena dehinam //
lobhaḥ pravṛttir ārambhaḥ karmaṇām aśamaḥ spṛhā |
rajasy etāni jāyante vivṛddhe bharatarṣabha ||

8 *MBh.* 3, 203, 4.

9 *MBh.* 3, 203, 6-8. Trans. van Buitenen, 1975, p.631. I have added the Sanskrit.

to be characterized by *sattva*. All others are characterized by *rajas* and *tamas*:

> Of those who are bound to bodies, the best man has a nature characterized by *sattva*, descendant of the Kurus. Tiger among men, he would be resolved upon attaining *mokṣa*. Moreover, he understands that the soul (*puruṣa*) resides in Brahma. That *mokṣa* whose chief object is Nārāyaṇa is traditionally said to be characterized by *sattva*. The one who has Nārāyaṇa for his refuge, who is devoted to one object and continually reflects upon Viṣṇu, best of men, attains his desire ...
>
> That man who is seen by Nārāyaṇa will become enlightened, but, King, the self (*ātman*) will not become enlightened through its own desire.
>
> When the characteristic influenced by *rajas* and that influenced by *tamas* are mixed together they are traditionally called the two natures (*prakṛti*). In that case, Lord of people, Hari himself does not take into consideration that person who has been born with a nature endowed with traits of activity (*pravṛtti*). Brahmā, Grandfather of the worlds, watches that human being born who is completely overwhelmed by *rajas* and *tamas*.[10]

This passage is pervaded with a strong devotional flavouring, and the type of *moksa* described is one in which the individual *puruṣa* is absorbed in Nārāyaṇa. Here too, as in the last passage, the realm of liberation is characterized by *sattva* and is quite distinct from the other realm whose general feature is activity. Brahmā is depicted as a kind of overseer who watches over humans whose dispositions are inclined towards *pravṛtti*. This is similar to another *MBh*. passage where he is presented as the overseer of the triple world, a passage just as concerned with *pravṛtti* and *nivṛtti* as this one.[11] There too, as here, he is differentiated from Nārāyaṇa. His concern is with people influenced by *rajas* and *tamas*, whereas Nārāyaṇa is concerned with those who seek *mokṣa* and are under the influence of *sattva*. The difference between the

---

10 *MBh*. 12, 336, 64-6, 70-2.

11 *MBh*. 12, 327, 1-88, esp. 84-8.

two figures is not the dfference of *pravṛtti* against *nivṛtti*, but of *bhakti* (Nārāyaṇa) as against *pravṛtti* (Brahmā).

Another much more extensive definition of *rajas* in the *MBh.* makes quite explicit its extensive correspondences with *pravṛtti*. The *Aśvamedhikaparvan* devotes three entire chapters to a description of the *guṇas*.[12] Each chapter gives a list of words, which, whilst not exactly synonymous with the *guṇa* being described, do reflect the attitudes of people under its influence. The chapter on *rajas* gives the usual psychological terms along with many others:

> Sorrow and doubt, vows and restraint, gifts motivated by desires and the continual thinking that 'This should be mine'. The performance of the *svadhā*, *namas*, *svāhā* and the *vaṣaṭ* rite, and both sacrificing and instruction, and also receiving gifts, so they say. From this quality arises the longing that 'This should be mine, this should be mine'[13] … Men whose thoughts are focused on the past, present and future of things in this world are continually obsessed with the three: 'Law, profit and desire'. They conduct themselves through desire and they rejoice due to the success of all their desires. Since their conduct is based on *rajas*, influenced by impatience (*tejas*), they are said to be on the downward stream.[14]

This list is virtually a summary of the central sociological and philosophical aspects of orthoprax society depicted in the Dharmasūtras and the *smṛti* sections of the *MBh.* and the Purāṇas. Included in the list are the duties prescribed for brahmins, names of obligatory sacrifices to be performed by householders and mention of the *trivarga*, the three aims of life guiding the twice-born in their daily lives. Of a more philosophical bent are the notions of 'I-ness' and 'mine-ness', both synonyms of *ahaṃkāra*. The idea of temporality and the strong emphasis on desire as a

---

12 *MBh.* 14, 36-8.

13 This notion of 'I-ness' and 'Mine-ness' occurs also in verse 3 of this chapter where it is called *mamatvam*.

14 *MBh.* 14, 37, 9-11ab, 14-15.

determining factor in the conduct of those influenced by *rajas*, also relates to *ahaṃkāra* and epitomizes *pravṛtti* values.

In the next chapter *sattva* is dealt with in a similar way. Many of the words used to describe it coincide with the world view of the renouncer. Words suggestive of abandoning notions of an ego (*nirmama, nirmamatva, nirahaṃkāra*), cessation of action (*śāntikarma*), freedom from desire (*nirāśi, akāmahata*), liberation (*vimocana*) and abandonment (*parityāga*) are all reminiscent of renunciation.[15] Further indication that the renouncer's view is dominant here is reflected in an attack on certain *rājasa* actions: "Giving gifts is useless, the sacrifice is useless, instruction is useless, the vow is useless and so also is receiving gifts useless. The Law is useless and austerity is useless."[16] This passage embodies the renouncer's perception of ritual practices central to the world view of the householder. The complete disavowal of their value as well as the cluster of technical terms referring to certain religious aspects of renunciation make it certain that *sattva* here represents the values and world view of *nivṛtti*.

The diverse range of correspondences given to the guṇas in the *MBh.* and the Purāṇas indicates they were used as a system for classifying phenomena in the world and also human behaviour.[17] *Pravṛtti* and *nivṛtti* could also be used as a classificatory system, one capable of having less correspondences than the guṇas. Certainly many such systems of classification occur in Indian literature.[18] Mauss and Durkheim have argued that systems of

---

15 *MBh.* 14, 38, 5, 7, 8. There are other places where *sattva* and *nirahaṃkāra* are brought together in the context of renunciation. At *MBh.* 3, 187, 16, certain ascetics (*yati*) are described by a string of epithets amongst which both of these occur.

16 *MBh.* 14, 38, 9.

17 Besides those sketched here there are other correspondences between the *guṇas* and certain phenomena. For example, *BḍP.* 1, 4, 9, equates the *guṇas* with the three worlds, the three fires and the three Vedas. *SK.* 54 also equates them with the three worlds.

18 For details of others see Held, 1935, pp. 114-26; Knipe. 1970,

classification are derived from social systems, stating that "the first logical categories were social categories, the first classes of things were classes of men, into which these things were integrated".[19] Certainly, *pravṛtti* and *nivṛtti* are based on social categories, not those of the *varṇa* groupings, which might be the first to spring to mind, but on the division between the householder and the renouncer

In his book on the *Mahābhārata* Held deals at length with classificatory systems found in that text and the Brāhmaṇas. He argues that the *guṇas* are a classificatory system, and like the other systems he discusses, he says they are an expression of a "tribal organization in its most striking feature, that of sub-division into two phratries with contrasting characteristics… ."[20] About the *guṇas* specifically he says, "The three *guṇas* together constitute *prakṛti* (nature). Now *prakṛti* is said to be to *purusha* (spirit) as man to woman [i.e. as male to feminine?], or as perishable (*ksara*) to imperishable (*aksara*); so here, too, as one phratry to the other."[21] Too little is known at present about the social structures reflected in the text, for an accurate assessment of this claim about the origin of Indian classificatory systems based on the relationship of one phratry to another. However, the social division between the householder and the renouncer is so prominent in the *MBh.* and the Purāṇas that the grouping of the *guṇas* into a two and a one could just as well reflect this division as well as, or instead of, a division into clans.

In many passages *rajas* covers the same range of meanings as *pravṛtti*, and so can be said to be identical with it inasmuch as both represent identical world views. *Sattva* stands in the same relation to *nivṛtti*. It only remains to be seen if such equivalences hold when *rajas* and *tamas* are grouped together as a unity in opposition to *sattva*.

Chs. 1-2.

19 Durkheim and Mauss, 1970, p. 82.

20 Held. 1935, p.122.

21 Held. 1935, p.123.

Such an opposition has already been cited in one *MBh.* passage where *sattva* stands for those people who have attained (or wish to attain) a *mokṣa* involving union with Nārāyaṇa.[22] Others whose nature was directed towards activity (*pravṛtti*) were said to be influenced by a mixture of *rajas* and *tamas*, and it was implied they would not attain *mokṣa*, even if they desired it. Johnson and van Buitenen have found several passages in the philosophical portions of the *MBh.* where *rajas* and *tamas* are grouped together as factors preventing liberation, and where *sattva* stands alone, being either a synonym for liberation or a stage before its attainment.[23] Passages such as the following are typical:

> Therefore *rajas* and *lamas* should be abandoned by him who is self-contained, so that his *sattva* will become spotless, free of *rajas* and *tamas*.[24] … He who will continually avoid the faults (*doṣa*) associated with *rajas* and *tamas*, and who has gone onto the *sattva* path, will see the self with the self.[25]

This kind of grouping of the *guṇas* into a two and a one definitely reflects a division between those who are still within *saṃsāra* and those who are liberated or nearly so.

Even in the late Upaniṣads a similar opposition is found. In one *rajas* and *tamas* are described, and then their effect on the self:

> With these the elemental soul (*bhūtātman*) is filled full; with these

---

22 See above p.179.

23 Johnston, 1974, p. 35; van Buitenen, 1957, pp.99-100. On p. 100 van Buitenen writes, 'Frequently one gets the impression that *rajas* and *tamas* form really *One* collective concept comprising between them all obstacles to release and so form together an antithesis to *sattva*.' Johnston, p. 35 ff. points out that *rajas* and *tamas* are grouped together in Aśvaghosa's *Buddhacarita* and also in the *akuśalamulāni* 'the roots of evil' of the *Pāli Abhidharma* literature, consisting of *rāga*, *dveṣa*, and *moha*.

24 *MBh*. 12, 205, 29.

25 *MBh*. 12, 313, 28.

it is overcome (*abhibhūta*). Therefore it undergoes different forms–indeed, it undergoes different forms.[26]

In a similar vein the same two guṇas are grouped together in another passage of this text:

For that man who practises *yoga* for six months and is constantly freed from the senses, the infinite, highest, mysterious *yoga* proceeds perfectly. For that man, who is pierced by *rajas* and *tamas* and fired up, hence attached to household, sons and wife, there is never any *yoga* at all.[27]

This is the same dichotomy occurring with such regularity in the *MBh.* and the Purāṇas. To be sure, the values represented here by *rajas* and *tamas* are those of the householder, hence of *pravṛtti*. *Sattva* is not mentioned, but in this context the word *yoga* connotes the values it would represent. Accordingly, from the brief survey of a few texts it is clear *rajas* and *tamas* are linked as a group in antithesis to *sattva*, a grouping corresponding to that when *rajas* alone is opposed to *sattva*.

On the basis of the passages so far collected it can be concluded that the *guṇas* and *pravṛtti* and *nivṛtti* understood as classificatory systems overlap at many points. The set of values commonly designated by *rajas* and *pravṛtti* provide the theoretical underlay of Brahmā's mythology. The texts continually repeat that his creative activity (*pra/vṛt*) is because he is *rajas*. Viewed from the perspective of the renouncer, the act of creation, like any other intentional action motivated by desire, is a pejorative act. It is seen as a product of delusion, itself produced by *rajas*. This is the gist of the following passage:

Then Brahmā rose up from his sleep and saw that the world was empty. And whilst deluded (*mohita*) by *rajas* he contemplated on creation.[28]

---

26 *MaitrīU*. 3, 5. Trans (slightly modified) Hume, 1968, p.420. I have added the Sanskrit.

27 *MaitrīU*. 6, 28.

28 *VāmP*. *Saromāhātmya*. 22, 19. It is usual in the texts for *moha* to be produced by the influence of *tamas*. For example, see *MaitrīU*.

The initial act in the cosmos is the act of creation. Naturally there would be no universe without this, but even the first act is held to be not conducive to knowledge (*jñāna*), hence *mokṣa*. Brahmā himself realizes this when after taking the form of a swan, a bird which is supposed to understand the distinction between ignorance and knowledge, he fails to recognize a certain form of Śiva, and justifies his mistake by saying: "How can knowledge arise in one who enjoys the activity of creation (*sṛṣṭipravṛttikāma*)? Though having the form of a swan I did not gain discriminating knowledge."[29] As the creator Brahmā is the 'actor' par excellence. Thus it is not surprising that at least once he is called *anantakarma*, "the one who acts without end".

3, 5; *MBh*. 12, 206, 1; KP. 1, 7, 2. Whether this reference points to another area of overlap between *rajas* and *tamas* is not clear from this passage. It was probably not intended to give the impression that they overlap.

29 *ŚP*. 2, 1, 15, 13.

PART FOUR

Brahmā's Role in the Avatāra Myth

Chapter 7

Dharma and Fate

In addition to his crucial role in the cosmogonic myths, Brahmā also plays an important role in the *avatāra* cycle of myths. The basic story line of the *avatāra* myth is that when *dharma* disappears from the triple world, the *avatāra* appears and restores it, at the same time banishing or rooting out *adharma*, at least temporarily. In early versions of this myth, the *avatāra* is a portion of Viṣṇu, but Brahmā himself is always present in one guise or another, not least because he embodies *dharma*. The *avatāra* myth goes far in showing the major similarities and differences between these two gods. It shows Brahmā to be locked into the *samsāric* cycle of the triple world, embodying *dharma* and deeply concerned to preserve it–as fragile as it is–but also as determining the fate of beings whilst being locked into fate himself. Viṣṇu comes out as transcending all this, whilst entering into the triple world to lessen the dharmic crises when they inevitably occur. Only in crises does a portion of him enter the triple world as an *avatāra*. Even during these periods and at most other times Viṣṇu himself remains beyond the triple world, beyond *dharma*, fate and *pravṛtti* values.

Brahmā as Dharma

The creation of *dharma* and its source–the Vedas-–receives no attention in the *prākṛtasarga* and *pratisarga*. Even in the other parts of the Purāṇic cosmogony there is only slight mention of it. In one passage Brahmā is attributed with the creation of various meters, verses from the Vedas, hymns and *ślokas*, all serving a specific purpose in the performance of the sacrifice.[1] Another group of cosmogonies repeats this, summing up the whole symbiotic relationship between humans and gods: "He [Brahmā] produced the *Ṛcs*, *Yājuses* and *Sāmans* for the success of the sacrifice. With these they worship the gods who are to be propitiated, so we have heard."[2]

Elsewhere in the Purāṇic cosmogony the Vedas are shown to be the basis on which he organizes the various groups of beings born in the triple world.

> Whatever actions they were endowed with from their first creation; it is with these that they are endowed when repeatedly created, whether it be destructiveness or harmlessness, tenderness or harshness, adherence to the law or against the law, truth or falsehood. They become what they are caused to be. Hence that is pleasing to him, the Lord, Dhātṛ [Brahmā] himself who ordained variety and occupation amongst created beings in terms of their bodies, objectives and senses. In the beginning he ordained the names and forms of living beings and the diversity of the duties of the gods and the rest, in accordance with the words of the Vedas. He gives names to the sages and to the creations amongst the gods, as well as to the others born at the end of his night. Just as the signs of the seasons appear in various forms being transformed in accord with the seasons, so too do beings at the beginning of the *yugas*.[3]

If Brahmā is attributed here with establishment of the cosmology in accordance with *dharma* (= words of the Vedas), it is also clear he can only do so within the restrictions of *karma*. This latter prescribes that living beings are born as a member of one of the groups who inhabit the triple world-gods, demons, men and animals-in accordance with actions performed in past lives. Brahmā determines the duty for each group after they are created.

Apart from these and a few other references little more is said

---

1 *MkP*. 48, 31-4; *ŚP*. 7, 1, 12, 58-60; *KP*. 1, 7, 54-8.

2 *H*.1, 35; *ŚP*. 5, 29, 21; *Ms*. 1, 23; *MkP*. 48, 31-4.

3 *MkP*. 48, 39-44. For *vs*. 44a. read *yathārtuṣv ṛtuliṅgāni* instead of *yathārttāvṛtuliṅgāni*.

in the *MBh.* and the Purāṇic cosmogonies about the creation of *dharma* and the Vedas, or their role in the creation.[4] Nevertheless, as the ordering factor in the triple world, *dharma* is implicit in most parts of the Purāṇic cosmogony except for the *prākṛtasarga*. This latter scheme of creation is not centred on the triple world, the spatio-temporal context of *dharma* and *adharma*. Outside of it these two are non-existent. Brahmā can establish the cosmology in accord with *dharma* because he is *dharma* himself. The epithet *dharmamaya*, 'he who contains *dharma*', is used of him at least once, and he is also described as being in appearance like a mass of *dharma* in bodily form (*dharmapuñja*).[5] Similarly, he is identified with the Vedas, the main source of *dharma*. This identification lies behind epithets such as *caturveda*, 'he who is the four Vedas', *vedamaya*, 'he who contains the Vedas', and perhaps also behind epithets like *vedavaktā*, 'reciter of the Vedas', and *brahmavidvān varaḥ*, 'best knower of the Vedas'.[6]

Brahmā's Ordinances

If Brahmā is *dharma*, then everything he ordains concerning the organization of the triple world must of necessity be in accord with *dharma*. This is especially so when he ordains the functions of the groups of living beings in the triple world. It is much less obvious, however, when he gives boons to demons, the boons always taking the form of an ordinance no matter what their content. Demons often utilize the ordinance (= a boon) to bring about the ascendency of *adharma*, over *dharma*, thereby setting the scene for the intervention of an *avatāra*.[7] Far from falling outside of *dharma*, this just points towards its ambiguity, because

4 But as will become clear later, there are many cosmogonic motifs in the *avatāra* myth, such that it is almost a cosmogonic myth itself.

5 *MBh.* 12, 175, 34; *ŚP.* 2, 3, 43, 31.

6 *MBh.* 3, 194, 12; 12, I75, 15; *KP.* 1, 2, 27; *ŚP.* 2, 2, 10, 30; *BhP.* 3, 8, 15; *El.* 1. p.130; 3. p.81; 4. p.228.

7 On which, see below Ch.9.

demons–who as a ‘species’ are committed to *adharma*–have their rightful place within the whole scheme of *dharma*, even though this might seem contradictory. They are created as part of the triple world, itself created in accord with *dharma*. Within the triple world *adharma*, ‘lawlessess’, or perhaps at a pinch, ‘evil’, has its rightful place.

Brahmā’s ordinances or injunctions are very often designated by derivatives of the root *vi/dhā*.[8] The verbal root *dhā* with the prefix *vi* can be rendered as ‘to ordain, lay down, direct, establish, create’ and by several other related words: the past passive participle *vihita*, ‘ordained, directed’, is the most common of these derivatives. Three nominal derivations have also been attested. There is a god Vidhātṛ known from as early as the *RV*, who is concerned primarily to lay down the organization of the cosmos at the time of creation, *vidhi*, ‘ordinance, rule, ritual’ and *vidhāna*, ‘order, rule, directing, creation’.

The name Vidhātṛ forms an apotheosization of the function designated by the verb of which it is an agent noun. The name itself appears occasionally in the Vedas, a few times as an epithet of the creator god Viśvakarman.[9] The precise function designated by the verb, hence the god, is illustrated in a passage from the *ŚB*. where Prajāpati directs organization of the cosmos:

> Here was Prajāpati. Having finished, he thought himself successful. Having set himself in the quarters he went on establishing (*dhā*) and ordaining (*vi/dhā*) everything here. Since he went on establishing and ordaining, he is called the establisher (*dhātā*). Likewise the sacrificer having set himself in the quarters establishes and ordains everything here. [10]

Organization of the parts of the cosmos is homologous with the parts of the sacrifice, itself a fundamental basis of

---

8 Whilst these are the most common, other words such as *niyoga*, *nirdiṣṭa*, *ājñā*, *vacana* and *vākyam* are also found.

9 See MacDonell, 1974, p.118.

10 *ŚB*. 9, 5, 1, 35. Cf. 2, 4, 2, 1-5. See also *AV*. 19, 9, 12 for a possible identification of Prajāpati with Vidhātṛ.

cosmic organization.[11] This is perhaps best seen initially in the cosmology of the *Puruṣasūkta*. For there, when the gods divided (*vyadadhuḥ*) the sacrificial *puruṣa*, they created the physical features of the cosmos and the four *varṇas* from the parts of his body.[12] Vidhātṛ is also a common epithet of Brahmā in post-Vedic literature, and under this name he is often attributed with the establishment of *dharma* in general.[13] In one passage of the *MBh*. Vidhātṛ's injunctions are such that they cannot be transgressed (*ativartate*).[14] This possibly represents the imposition of a notion of fate conceived in its most deterministic sense on to a function primarily of ritualistic provenance.

The noun *vidhi* designates the injunctions ordained by Brahmā, Vidhātṛ or Dhātṛ, another of Brahmā's epithets reflecting his directing function.[15] This word and its cognate *vedhas* are also quite commonly found as epithets of Brahmā.[16] The word *vidhi* has a long history, and in the Vedas it is held, at least by the Mīmāṃsā school, to be "an injunction (or exhortation) that is meaningful on account of enjoining a matter that has a (useful) purpose and it prescribes something that does not follow (or is not established) from any other authority ... The collection of vidhis in the Vedic texts forms the core of the Veda and refers to many specific rites."[17] Injunctions classified as *vidhi* are inexorable and this has led the word to become synonymous in the epics and

---

11 For details see above pp. 96-97. One also thinks of the cosmic equivalents of the five layers of the Agnicayana ritual. See Gonda, 1960. p. 192.

12 *RV*. 10, 90, 11-14.

13 *MBh*. 12, 251, 25; 13, 133, 31.

14 *MBh*. 1, 1, 187.

15 For passages where the name Dhātṛ definitely refers to Brahmā and others where it refers to a separate god see Holtzmann, 1884 p. 209. n. 6.

16 *ŚP*. 2, 2, 2, 33; 2, 2, 10, I; *KP*. 1, 6, 10; 1, 9, 18; 1, 44, 1; *ViP*. 1, 7, 9.

17 Kane, *HDS*. 5, pp. 1225-26.

Purāṇas with deterministic notions of fate. Gonda described it as "fate conceived of as regularity".[18] Despite its connections with fate, the older view of *vidhi* as an ordinance which determines the procedure of a rite is quite common in post-Vedic literature, typically in the phrase *vidhidṛṣṭena karmaṇā*, '[performed] with a rite existing in the rules.'[19]

Often when Brahmā's ordinances are judged by the gods and other beings whom they affect, they are held to be capricious and seemingly of doubtful worth. However, if viewed in retrospect in the context of a whole sequence of events such as constitutes the narrative of both epics, it becomes clear they are subordinated to a specific purpose. An excellent illustration is given in the *Rām.* where Brahmā's boons, ordinance and curses are directed towards a single purpose, the preservation of *dharma* in the face of the overpowering forces of *adharma*.

Brahmā is the instigator for much that happens in the *Rām.* because it was he who granted the boon to Rāvaṇa, enabling the demon all but invulnerability. On hearing of this boon and aware of the threat represented by Rāvaṇa, the gods are understandably puzzled as to why Brahmā should have granted it to him. When they approached him for counsel, he answered their doubts:

> ... When addressed as such by all the gods Brahmā reflected and then said, "The killer who is the means of destruction of this evil-souled demon has been determined (*vihita*). He had made this statement, 'I must not be killed (*avadhya*) by gandharvas, yakṣas, gods, dānavas or rākṣasas.' And I said, 'So be it.' Yet, contemptuously, the rakṣa did not mention humans. Therefore,

18 Gonda, 1960, p.234.

19 *MBh.* 1, 13, 37; 53, 13; 96, 52; 3, 37, 24; 76, 17; and often.

he must be killed (*vadhya*) by a man.[20] There is no other death for him".[21]

Normally it is Brahmā himself who lays down the ordinance, but because he has offered Rāvaṇa a boon, it is the demon who must announce what will happen. In effect this means he must announce his own fate. It only becomes an ordinance (or injunction) when Brahmā gives his assent to the request.

For this ordinance to be fulfilled the chain of events narrated in the *Rām*. has to take place. The first act of Rāvaṇa was to defeat his elder brother Vaiśravaṇa in battle and take his kingdom from him. This kingdom had been given to Vaiśravaṇa by his grandfather, Brahmā, who had also bestowed upon him immortality, the kingship of the rākṣasas and a son named Nalakūbara.[22] Rāvaṇa also took Vaiśravaṇa's chariot and for that the latter cursed him: "You shall never ride it! He who shall kill you in battle shall ride on it. And as you have shown me, your elder, contempt, you shall soon cease to be."[23] After this Brahmā himself took a hand in

---

20 The use of the gerundive (a precative–*bhūyāt*-in the *Rāmopākhyāna* of the *MBh*) is consistent with the Mīmāṃsaka requirement that an injunction should be announced in an optative or another similar verbal form. See Kane, *HDS*. 5. p. 1226.

21 *Rām*. (C) 1, 14, 12-14; *MBh*. 3, 260, 4-5. The *MBh*. version elaborates slightly with the addition of another ordinance. Brahmā says, "At my command (*niyoga*) the four-armed god has descended for that purpose [the killing of Rāvaṇa]. Viṣṇu that best of warriors will perform this act."

22 *MBh*. 3, 258, 15. Vaiśravaṇa was born as a rākṣasa, a demon, and demons by nature are mortal. When he is given immortality he virtually becomes a god, immortality being one of the chief characteristics of gods. This difference would probably be enough of itself to sow discord between him and Rāvaṇa, because gods and rākṣasas are usually the deadliest of enemies. That he, a god, should then be made king of the rākṣasas is quite incongruous, and even though Rāvaṇa is an usurper, his seizure of the kingship means that the rākṣasas are being ruled by one of their own kind.

23 *MBh*. 3, 259, 35. Trans. van Buitenen, 1975, p.730.

determining the subsequent course of events. As soon as he had revealed to the gods his plans for Viṣṇu's descent to the Earth, he ordered them to be reborn on Earth as monkeys and bears in order to assist Viṣṇu against Rāvaṇa and his followers.[24] Having done this he ordered a certain gandharvī named Dundubhi to be reborn on Earth as a hunch-backed woman named Mantharā 'stirrer'. The text emphasizes that all this is due to Brahmā's ordinances: "Having thus ordained (*vidhāya*) all that, the illustrious lord who prospers the world enlightened Mantharā about her tasks and the manner thereof."[25] At this stage all the tasks have been allotted to various divine beings. As for Mantharā, it was she who told Kaikeyī that Daśaratha had designs to consecrate Rāma as king. On learning of this Kaikeyī successfully plotted to have Rāma exiled to the forest and her own son Bhārata placed on the throne.

After Rāma's exile to the forest, which he attributed to fate (*daivam*, *kṛtānta*), fate takes a further hand in events.[26] Under Rāvaṇa's threat, Mārīca takes the form of a deer so as to tempt Sītā away from Rāma. What follows then is put down to fate: 'Marica showed himself to the princess of Videha in the guise of a deer, and, prompted by fate (*vidhicodita*) she sent Rāma after him.'[27] It is not clear here whether *vidhi* is meant to be fate understood as an impersonal force or whether it is Brahmā himself. Probably, it is meant to have the latter sense, because immediately this event has occurred, Brahmā, who had been watching everything with his divine eye, said, 'What had to be done has been done.'[28] Certainly, this implies that all the preceding events up to, and including, Sītā's abduction, are part of Brahmā's divine scheme to rid the triple world of Rāvaṇa. He knows Rāma will go after Sītā and that

---

24 *Rām.* (C) I, 16, 1-2; *MBh.* 3, 260, 6-8.

25 *MBh.* 3, 260, 14. Trans. van Buitenen. 1975, p. 731.

26 *Rām.* (C) 2, 19, 13-14.

27 *MBh.* 3, 262, 17. I can find no mention of any word or reference to fate in the equivalent passage in the *Rām.* (C) 3, 41, 9-21.

28 *Rām.* (C) 3, 50, 10.

inevitably he will be brought into conflict with him and will kill him.

After Sītā's abduction, fate takes a further hand in events. Rāma and Lakṣmaṇa were wandering through the forest looking for her when they came across a dānava named Kabandha, who tried to encircle them with his huge arms. Then he declared it was not by chance they had met: "Seeing me afflicted with hunger, why are you two eminent warriors standing there. You two, were mindlessly directed (*saṃdiṣṭa*) here by fate (*daiva*) for the purpose of feeding me."[29] However, the two brothers cut off his arms and to their surprise he was glad this had happened, saying that it was all due to a purposive design: "Welcome you two! Through design (*diṣṭyā*) I have met you two tigers of men, and it is through design (*diṣṭyā*) that you two cut off these two encircling arms."[30]

The dānava explained how in the past he had been of beautiful appearance, and how after having performed austerities in front of Brahmā, he was offered long life.[31] Fearing Indra's jealousy, he dared to attack him, but was struck by his thunderbolt. Instead of killing him, Indra respected the terms of Brahmā's curse and condemned the formerly beautiful being to wander about in the forest, in monstrous form, having two huge arms and a mouth in his belly, eating animals for survival. Only with the appearance of Rāma and Lakṣmaṇa, who would cut off his arms and burn his body, would he regain his former appearance.

Rāma and Lakṣmaṇa listened to his story and then proceeded to burn him. Out of the fire arose a being of beautiful countenance who told the two warriors what had become of Sītā. He then told them they should enlist the aid of the monkey Sugrīva who would help them find and bring her back. Finally, he told them the

---

29 *Rām.* (C) 3, 66, 2.

30 *Rām.* (C) 3, 66, 14.

31 *Rām.* (C) 3, 67, 1-31. The *MBh.* version (3, 263, 35-8) contains a slight variation here, where Kabandha says his horrible body was obtained as a result of Brahmā's curse stipulating birth in the womb of a rākṣasa.

monkey could be found living in a cave on a mountain constructed by Brahmā in an earlier time.[32]

As the narrative unfolds Brahmā's ordinances continue to make their presence felt. When Hanumān first arrived at the gate of Laṅkā he subjugated a rākṣasa woman who was the gate keeper. She took this as an omen marking the beginning of the end for Laṅkā. Recalling an ordinance made by Brahmā, she said:

> I am the city of Laṅkā itself, monkey, and I have been conquered by your courage, very strong hero. Now, Lord of Hari, listen to the truth which the Self-born himself said to me when he had given me the gift of a boon.
>
> 'When a certain monkey should courageously bring you under his control, then you will know terror has come to the rākṣasas.'
>
> Because of your appearance, Saumya, my arrangement with Brahmā has now ended. The Self-born's ordinance is truth, there is no avoidance of it.[33]

Nothing is left to chance, every event has been ordained to happen long before its actual occurrence. The entire framework of the epic story is guided by Brahmā's ordinances.

The inexorability of the god's ordinance is brought up in the passage just cited. The force of this motif and its great importance can be seen from its recurrence in another passage recapitulating part of the battle between the forces of Rāma and the rakṣāsas. Just after Rāvaṇa's troops have been annihilated and his own life threatened by Yama, Brahmā restrained that god with this justification:

> Huge armed Vaivasvata of unequalled valour, you must certainly not kill this night-mover with your club! Bull of the thirty, I have indeed given him a boon. You should not make it false, because I uttered this order (*vac*). He who would cause me to be false, whether he be a god or even a man, by doing that would have caused the triple world to be false. There is no doubt of that.[34]

---

32 *Rām*. (C) 3, 69, 24-32.

33 *Rām*. (V) 5, 3,46-49.

34 *Rām*. (V) 7, 22, 38-40. The equivalent passage (7, 22, 33-4) in the

The boon to which Brahmā refers is the one he gave to Rāvaṇa, stipulating that the demon could be killed only by a man. To ensure the conditions of the boon will be fulfilled to the letter, Brahmā must prevent Yama, a god, from killing Rāvaṇa. For his death requires completion of two ordinances; firstly, that Rāvaṇa be killed by a man, and secondly, that Viṣṇu be reborn as the man to do the job. Brahmā intervenes only to prevent his ordinance from being falsified.

Even in the final battles between Kumbhakarṇa and Lakṣmaṇa, Rāvaṇa and Rāma, Brahmā's presence is manifested. In the *Rāmopākhyāna*, Lakṣmaṇa defeats Kumbhakarṇa by making use of the Brahmā weapon, an arrow filled with Brahmā's power (*tejas*).[35] And when Rāma and Rāvaṇa reach a deadlock in their final battle, which has already lasted for a day and a night, Rāma is victorious only when he utilizes the Brahmā weapon.[36] Thus on both occasions when a crisis has been reached in the battle, Brahmā's intervention is timely and successfully resolves the crisis.

Brahmā's intervention does not end with Rāma's victory over Rāvaṇa. When Rāma finds Sītā he rejects her for fear she might have cohabited with Rāvaṇa whilst she was his captive. A number of gods intercede on her behalf, but only Brahmā's words finally bring about the reconciliation:

> Son, for you to act here like this is not strange in you who obey the law of the royal seers and who walk the path of good conduct, good man. Listen to these my words. You have brought down, hero, the enemy of the Gods, Gandharvas, Snakes, Yakṣas,

---

Critical Edition omits the last *śloka* about the consequences of falsifying of Brahmā's ordinance. This passage does not appear in the *Rāmopākhyāna*, the contents of which correspond to the middle five books of the *Rām*.

35 *MBh*. 3, 271, 16. The *Rām*. itself differs here, for it has Rāma killing Kumbhakarṇa with an arrow filled with the power of many gods, only one of which is Brahmā (see *Rāṃ*. (C) 6, 55, 120-1).

36 *MBh*. 3, 274, 24-30; *Rām*. (C) 6, 97, 1-14.

> Dānavas, and the great seers. Him, who had become, by my own grace, invincible to all creatures. The evil-doer was ignored for some time for some reason. Then the evil-spirited fiend abducted Sītā for his own death, and I protected her by means of Nalakūbara's curse–he had once been told that if he sought the favours of any one woman who did not love him his body was sure to burst a hundredfold as a result.[37] Have no doubt at all about this. Take her back, resplendent man. Like an Immortal yourself, you have accomplished a great feat.[38]

It should be apparent from this survey that Brahmā's ordinances have shaped much of the action in the *Rām*. and are instrumental in the development of the main plot–the banishment of Rāma and the abduction of Sītā by Rāvaṇa–and of sub-plots like the acquisition of Sugrīva's kingship. He guides the action by means of timely ordinances, curses and the giving of boons. All three are inexorable and their conditions must be worked out in the same way as karma must be worked out. They cannot be ignored or arbitrarily overturned.[39] Their influence is most apparent at times of great tension such as the seizing of Sītā, the battles of Rāma and Lakṣmaṇa with Rāvaṇa and Kumbhakarṇa respectively, the banishment of Rāma and perhaps also the battle with Kabandha. Even when the tension is at its highest–the moment when, surrounded by all the gods and famous sages, the victorious Rāma rejects Sītā–it is Brahmā who resolves his conflict by showing Rāma that she did not cohabit with Rāvaṇa. Just as Brahmā had caused her separation from her husband, at the time when prompted by fate (*vidhi* = Brahmā) she had sent him after the golden deer, it is he who finally brings her back to her husband.

From beginning to end Brahmā's influence expressed through his ordinances is felt at crucial moments. Nothing is left to chance,

---

37 Nalakūbara's curse is related at *MBh*. 3, 264, 58-9.

38 *MBh*. 3, 275, 29-34. Trans. van Buitenen, 1975, pp. 757-8.

39 There are instances in Indian literature where individuals have escaped their fate, but none of these occur in connection with Brahmā's ordinances. See Norman Brown. 1920, pp. 89-105,

no action that is of importance could be said to be the product of spontaneity. The main activities of the principal characters in the narrative are predetermined by his ordinances, a predetermination certainly marking them as fate understood as absolute determinism. To the people who were directly affected by these ordinances, the only explanation was that the hand of an impersonal fate was upon them. When Rāma learns of his banishment he speaks of the inevitability of fate, and the misfortunes suffered by Rāvaṇa. Even the latter's death is ascribed by his wives to the influence of fate.[40]

In effect, what are really ordinances directed towards the attainment of a specific objective are regarded by those whom they directly affect as fate. Rāma considers his kingdom to be lost because of fate; similarly his wife is taken from him because of fate. Much of the narrative centres on his reactions to these two events, especially to the latter. Everything he does in pursuit of his wife is predictable, except perhaps for the killing of Vālin, and this is so because everything he does accords with *dharma*. This comes as no surprise since Rāma is *dharmātman* and, as an *avatāra* of Viṣṇu, his task is to restore *dharma* when it has been overthrown. Rāvaṇa is the reversal of all this and is very much the embodiment of *adharma*. His mere existence is a threat to the order of the triple world and his abduction of Sītā, who in the *Rām*. represents the Earth, ruptures the dharmic relationship between earth and king (= Rāma) which should be one analogous to marriage.[41] Through the gift of a boon, Brahmā gives Rāvaṇa the means of obtaining all the power he desires, and to hold it temporarily at least. By allowing Rāvaṇa to choose his own boon, Brahmā enables him to choose his own fate, for the ordinance of invincibility guaranteeing Rāvaṇa's temporary success also allows for his inevitable defeat. Seen from this perspective, Rāvaṇa is trapped by fate, but a fate bearing great similarity to *karma*, whereby one's present activities determine one's future situation.

40 For references see Brockington. 1976, p. 125.

41 On Sītā's identification with the earth see Dubuisson. 1979, pp. 472-3.

Rāvaṇa determines the conditions of his own boon, conditions which trap him and from which he cannot escape. If Rāvaṇa is trapped, so too is Rāma, for he is constrained to act in terms of his 'image' as one who is *dharma* embodied. This requires him to accept Daśaratha's banishment, as a son is required implicitly to obey his father, and to reject Sītā after Rāvaṇa 's defeat.[42]

The two principal opponents in the narrative act out roles almost completely predetermined. One represents *dharma*, whilst the other represents *adharma*, polar opposites around which the gods and demons are all grouped. Rāvaṇa is plunged into a specific course of action because of his inherent adharmic inclinations and his own *karma* (Brahmā's boon). Rāma acts in a certain fixed way because of his inherent inclination to accord with *dharma* and indirectly–in reaction to Brahmā's ordinances. The tension running throughout the epic is produced by a combination of Brahmā's ordinances and the reaction against these by two characters who are fixed rigidly into certain life styles. Moreover, behind the narrative plot is the perennial opposition between *dharma* and *adharma*, an opposition prompting most of Brahmā's ordinances, all of which can be seen to have served a certain end when understood in terms of the implications of Rāvaṇa's death. When this occurs the forces of *adharma* are defeated and the ravished earth is restored to the king, but only after the mediation of Brahmā. Fate understood as Brahmā's ordinances ultimately work towards the maintenance of *dharma*. The implications of this are examined in a later section of this chapter.

Fate in Indian Thought

A variety of Sanskrit words can be translated by the word 'fate', of which the most common are these: *daivam*, 'that which comes from the gods', *vidhi*, 'ordinance', *dṛṣṭānta*, 'appointed end',

42 Cf. *MBh.* 3, 275, 12, where repudiating Sītā, Rāma says, "For how would a man like me, who knows the decision of the Law (*dharmaviniścayam*), maintain even for an instant a woman who had been in another man's hands." Trans. van Buitenen. 1975, p. 757.

adṛṣṭa, 'what is not seen', *kāla*, 'time', and *niyati*, 'the fixed order of things'.[43] Though there are subtle differences between each of them they all point towards a strongly deterministic view of the human condition. Sometimes and in addition to these, *karma*, 'actions done in a previous existence leading to inevitable results in the present existence', is considered to be an equivalent of fate.[44] Whilst *karma* itself can be placed in the mould of determinism in the sense that it must be worked out or negated by the intervention of a deity, it also raises the possibility of a very limited form of free choice. If one is aware of *karma*, as most Indians certainly are, then one can possibly determine one's actions, to be good, evil or neutral, and thus control to some extent the lot of one's future existences. In short, Indian notions of fate gravitate between the poles of absolute determinism and a limited form of free choice.

A definitive description of fate understood as absolute determinism is that given in a speech made by Draupadī to Yudhiṣṭhira when she is lamenting his forgiving attitude towards the Kauravas who have caused the Pāṇḍavas to be exiled into the forest. She says:

> It is the Lord Placer [*dhātṛ*] alone who sets down everything for the creatures, happiness and unhappiness, pleasure and sorrow, before even ejaculating the seed. These creatures, hero among men, are like wooden puppets that are manipulated; he makes body and limbs move. Pervading like ether all these creatures, Bhārata, the Lord disposes here whatever is good or evil. Man,

---

43 This list has been drawn from Gonda, 1960, p.234; *ERE*. Vol. 5. p. 790; Scheftelowitz.1930, p. 8.

44 Scheftelowitz,. 1930, pp. 6-7; Jolly, writing in *ERE*. Vol. 5. p. 791, divides the various Indian philosophical schools into two classes depending on their attitude to fate. One asserts the existence of free will [sic], moral responsibility and transmigration; whereas the other negates this. If it is considered that *karma* is ever present (until the attainment of *mokṣa*) as an influence on one's life situation, the use of the Christian term 'free-will' might be a bit too strong to be readily applied to the Indic context. See Hill, 2001, more especially for the *MBh*.

> restrained like a bird that is tied to a string, is not master of himself; remaining in the Lord's power, he is master of neither himself nor others. Like a pearl strung on a string, like a bull held by the nose rope, man follows the command of the Placer, consisting in him, entrusted to him. At no time whatever is man independent, like a tree that has fallen from the bank into the middle of a river…[45]

Draupadī's speech continues in this vein, all the while castigating the Placer for his capriciousness and unpredictability in determining the fate of creatures.

Here fate is conceived of as the design of a god, Dhātṛ, who is really Brahmā in his ordaining role.[46] Dhātṛ sets (*dadhāti*) down everything for humans, ordains (*vidadhāti*) whatever is good or evil, commands (*ādeśam*) and men obey, and impels (*prerita*) humans to act in certain ways. In his capriciousness he confuses men with his *māyā* and plays (*krīḍā*) with them as a child plays with its toys.[47] The notion of fate countenanced here is connected very much with a theistic notion of deity similar to that found in such *bhakti*-orientated texts as the *ŚvetU.* and the *Bhg*. In several passages of the *ŚvetU.* the highest god, Rudra-Śiva, is acknowledged to be the controller of the worlds, and once he is even called Dhātṛ.[48] Similarly, he is associated with *māyā* and play (*krīḍā*) in the same way as Brahmā in the *MBh*. passage. This same Upaniṣad also has much to say about fate. It asks the question of what causes the variety of conditions in which humans live and rejects such influences as *kāla*, 'time', *svabhāva*, 'inherent nature', *niyati* 'necessity' and *yadṛccha*, 'chance'.[49] Instead, it sets

45 *MBh*. 3, 31, 21-6. Trans. van Buitenen, 1975, pp. 280-1.

46 This conclusion is strengthened by the use of two of Brahmā's most common epithets–Svayaṃbhū and Prapitāmaha–for Dhātṛ (see *MBh*. 3, 31, 35).

47 *MBh*. 3, 31, 36.

48 *ŚvetU*. 3, 1; 4, 11; 6, 1; 3, 20.

49 *ŚvetU*. 1, 2; 6, 1.

up *karma* and the *māyā* produced by god as the most important direct influences on human conditions.

The effect of the fatalistic determinism and theism pervading both texts just cited (as well as the *Bhg.*) is to build up the picture of an all-powerful god who is the creator of *saṃsāra* and ordains (*vi/dhā*) the 'destiny' of humans in conformity with actions (*karma*) in a universe of *māyā*. Part of this god's power is his capacity to bring humans to enlightenment–one aspect of which is awareness of the fatalistic nature of existence in the triple world–through the exercise of his favour (*prasāda*). Inasmuch as such a god determines human destiny, it could be said he is responsible for *daivam*, 'that which comes from the gods'. *Daivam* is seen as an impersonal divine force standing in opposition to human effort (*pauruṣam*).[50] *Daivam* lies behind some of the most crucial events of the *MBh.* an example of which is evident when Duryodhana first expresses his wish to challenge Yudhiṣṭhira to a game of dice. Dhṛtarāṣṭra is initially reluctant to grant his son's wish, knowing it may well end up in battle. When he does eventually sanction the game, his own brother, Vidura, warns him that it might lead to a quarrel between the Pāṇḍavas and the Kauravas. Dhṛtarāṣṭra is unmoved and says:

> No quarrel bothers me, Steward, here. For otherwise fate (*daivam*) would run counter to dicing. This world submits to the Placer's design (*dhātrā diṣṭasya*), and thus does the world run, not by itself.[51]

There are many other examples in the *MBh.* of specific events being attributed to this impersonal divine power, and it is clearly this with which Brahmā's ordinances should be associated.

---

50 The opposition is apparent in the following statement made by Duryodhana when leaving Yudhiṣṭhira's *rājasūya*, 'I consider that which comes from the gods to be supreme, but human effort is useless.' (*daivaṃ tu paramaṃ manye pauruṣaṃ tu nirarthakam*). See *MBh.* 2. 43, 32 and 34; 8, 5, 29.

51 *MBh.* 2, 51, 25. Trans. van Buitenen, 1975, p. 124. I have added the Sanskrit. Cf. *MBh.* I, 2, 221; 34, 3; 114, 6; 2, 45, 57, etc.

Fate and Dharma

The study of Brahmā's ordinances in the *Rām*. has shown how they were directed towards the attainment of a certain end–the raising up of *dharma* in the face of *adharma*. Viewed collectively they constitute a network of commands, the effect of which is to sustain *dharma*. This notion corresponds in general to the view of *dharma* held by the Mīmāṃsakas, who believe that the

> ... vidhis properly interpreted are the main source of *dharma* ... It should be remembered that as *dharma* can only be acquired by following the injunctions of the Vedas they should all be interpreted as giving us injunctions.[52]

In its strictly ritualistic sense *dharma* encompasses a religious act (such as sacrifice) which confers the highest good such as heaven.[53] Though the word *dharma* is used in a broader sense than this in post-Vedic literature, it still refers to a system of 'ethical' acts (governed by ordinances), the observance of which leads to the highest good for the triple world and the individual. All this raises the question of the relationship between Brahmā's *vidhis* understood as fate and his *vidhis* understood as dharmic injunctions. Since Brahmā is himself *dharma*, the injunctions he announces must be in accord with *dharma*.

The acceptance that Brahmā 's ordinances are directed towards a certain end is given acknowledgement in the late seventh book of the *Rām*. Some famous sages have assembled around Rāma after he has killed Rāvaṇa, repudiated and then accepted Sītā. They say to him:

> Huge-armed scion of Raghu, we are quite well, but we consider you, without enemies as you are, to be well through design (*diṣṭyā*). For Rāvaṇa, lord of Rākṣasas, is no longer your burden, Rāma, and with your bow you will certainly be victorious over the

52 Dasgupta, 1975, Vol. 1, p.405, Kane, *HDS*, Vol.5, pp.1183-84; *Śabarabhāṣya*. 1, 2.

53 In substance this is the definition given by Biardeau, 1964, p.446. Cf. pp.69 and 90.

> three worlds. Rāma, it was through design that you killed Rāvaṇa who has sons and grandsons. Now, we see that along with your wife you are victorious, through design.
>
> Prahasta, Vikata, Virūpakṣa, Mahodara, Kampana and Durdharṣa are night walkers killed by you through design. There is no greater authority here than the authority of that. Rāma, through design you caused Kurnbhakarṇa to fall in battle. Through design you met in a duel with that Indra of rākṣasas who could not be killed by the gods. You have obtained victory. In this battle you were never once bested by Rāvaṇa. You engaged in a combat by duel and defeated Indrajit through design. Huge-armed man, though being pursued by the enemy of the gods, as if by time, you escaped and obtained victory... Hero, having given us this meritorious, auspicious present of security, through design you will prosper in victory, Kākutstha, destroyer of enemies.[54]

Similar statements are made in the *MBh.* to account for some of the factors leading up to the dice game resulting in the banishment of the Pāṇḍavas and the loss of their kingdom.[55] One passage goes so far as to say that the entire world is in the power of Dhatr's design (*dhātrā tu diṣṭasya vase kiledam sarvam jagac ceṣṭati*) and does not run of its own accord (*svatantra*).[56]

In rendering *diṣṭyā* by the words 'through design', I have followed van Buitenen who consistently employs these words for his *MBh.* translation. The word *diṣṭi* derives from the root *diś*, meaning 'to point out, produce, effect, assign, command, bestow'. In some instances it might be more appropriate to translate *diṣṭi* by the word 'command' or 'direction'. However, in the passage just cited from the *Rām.* it is clear the 'authors' of the seventh book wanted to show that much which had happened to Rāma was the result of an external force, the cumulative effect of which was to bring about the battle between himself and Rāvaṇa. The possible lateness of the first and seventh books made it possible for the

54 *Rām.* (C) 7, 1, 13-20, 22.

55 *MBh.* 2, 45, 54; 51, 25; 52, 14.

56 *MBh.* 2, 51, 25.

'authors' of these two books to give an overview of the middle five books, often considered earlier than the former. In using the word *diṣṭyā* seven times to account for Rāma's most important exploits they would seem to be trying to demonstrate the presence of a unifying force behind them all, rather than each being unique and unrelated to the other. From this perspective there is definitely a design behind all his actions, hence the rendering of *diṣṭyā* by 'design'.

Diṣṭi is not the same as *dharma*, despite Brahmā's ordinances–the equivalent of *diṣṭi*–having as their ultimate purpose the maintenance of *dharma*. The ordinances laid down by Brahmā in the *Rām*. had the effect of ensuring that Rāma and Rāvaṇa acted in full accord with their own *svadharma*. Due to his birth, Rāma is a *kṣatriya* and must act in terms of the *svadharma* of one of that status. This means he must fight to protect his kingdom and uphold *dharma* in the triple world. Rāvaṇa operates in terms of the *svadharma* of demons and this is principally to oppose the *dharma* of the triple world and replace it with *adharma* and demonic rule. Both figures are trapped within their respective status in a manner determining their roles in accordance with *dharma*. Brahmā's ordinances operate to exacerbate the tendencies towards action implied by these respective *svadharmas*, but they also hasten the inevitable clash which will result because of the opposition between demon (= *adharma*) and man (= god = *dharma*).

The belief that fate operates in connection with *dharma* is given didactic expression in the long dialogue between Draupadī and Yudhiṣṭhira in the third book of the *MBh*. where the former calls into question the motives of Brahmā as the controller of destinies.[57] Yudhiṣṭhira forcefully stresses an adherence to *dharma* at all cost and then after a range of arguments in support of the supremacy of *dharma*, he goes on to say:

> The fruition of acts, both good and bad, their origin and disappearance, are mysteries of the gods (*devaguhyāni*) my angry wife! Nobody knows them, these creatures (*prajā*) are

57 *MBh*. 3, 31-3.

> in the dark about them, they are guarded by the Gods, for the wizardry of the Gods (*devāṇāṃ gūḍḥamāyā*) is obscure ... The Law should not be doubted, nor the Gods, just because the reward is invisible; one should sacrifice, undistracted, and give without demurring; this is the eternal Law: that acts yield fruit. Brahmā told it to his son, as witnessed by Kaśyapa.[58]

Here two distinct possibilites are being put forward. Firstly, that acts have rewards, which is to say that *karma* is operative in regard to all actions. Even though tangible results are not necessarily gained, one should still act in accord with *dharma*, because *karma* ensures there will be results, even if only in a later life.[59] In the second place, it is the gods alone who comprehend the totality of actions and see order in what the agent of the act sees as a series of unconnected events determined by an impersonal fate. This makes particular sense in this context, since Draupadī, astonished at the misfortunes of the Pāṇḍavas, decries Yudhiṣṭhira for sedulously adhering to *dharma* even when the results of such a policy seem disastrous. Draupadī seems to be representing humans (= *prajā*) who are in the dark about the origin and fruition of *karma*. Over against humans are the gods who with their *gūḍhamāyā* represent *daiva*.

Having heard all this, Draupadī denies she had reviled either *dharma* or Brahmā. Then she launches into a long harangue about the need to act, in the process of which she clarifies Brahmā's role in regard to fate, *karma* and *dharma*:

> So, what a man gets from chance (*haṭha*) and divine luck (*daiva*), from nature (*svabhāva*) and plain hard work (*karma*), is the fruit of his previous acts (*pūrvakarmaṇaḥ*). The Placer himself, the Lord, ordains (*vidadhāti*) any one's acts, for whatever reason,

---

58 *MBh*. 3, 32, 33-34, 36-37. Trans. van Buitenen. 1975, p.283. I have added the Sanskrit.

59 This corresponds in essence to the view maintained in the Brāhmaṇas and amongst the Mīmāṃsakas (as the doctrine of *apūrva*) that the real result of a sacrifice is invisible, that it only occurs after death with the attainment of heaven. See Kane, *HDS*. Vol. 5. p. 1210.

> and distributes the fruits of what men have previously done. When a man does anything, whether good or bad, know that it was ordained by the Placer, arising as the fruit of acts done before. In any act this body is but the tool of this Placer, and as he moves man, so man acts, helplessly. The Great Lord, who enjoins us to this or that task, makes all creatures act, Kaunteya, whether they want it or not.[60]

So fate in the sense of Brahmā's ordinances and *karma* are two sides of the one coin. *Karma* is ultimately responsible for the situation in which a person lives, to the extent of determining the precise *varṇa* in which he/she is born, and even whether he/she will be born as a human, god, demon or animal. On the other hand, the life situation of a person is also attributed to Brahmā's ordinances, which operate to determine a person's activities once born. Brahmā seems to be attributed with exactly the same role as *karma*, but more, because he can ordain actions (independent of *karma*?) in accordance with the life situation into which a person is born. Thus he lays down ordinances to ensure that both Rāma and Rāvaṇa will act out their specific *svadharma* to the fullest possible extent.

If there is some difficulty in ascertaining the exact relationship between *karma*, *dharma* and *vidhi* (understood as Brahmā's ordinances and *daiva*) some clarity can be gained by summarizing their similarities. Each is to a certain degree deterministic in regard to those whom it affects. *Karma* is the factor determinative of the nature of the future rebirth of beings. It is totally deterministic in the sense that past *karma* must be worked out, but this determinism can be modified because a person can try to control their actions in order to influence their future rebirths. As for *dharma*, when one is born into a particular *varṇa*, as a god or a demon, one is obliged to act in accordance with the *svadharma* of that group.[61]

---

60 *MBh*. 3, 33, 18-22. Trans. van Buitenen. 1975, p.284. I have added the Sanskrit.

61 Humans are also obliged to adhere to *sādhāraṇadharma*, 'universal *dharma*', which includes non-injury, truth, purity, not-stealing, charity, etc. See O' Flaherty. 1976, p. 97.

Through scrupulous adherence to one's *svadharma*, rebirth in the heaven appropriate to one's specific group will be attained. The actual pressures to conform to svadharma must have been very strong judging from the second chapter of the *Bhg*. where Kṛṣṇa argues so persuasively that Arjuna must do his duty as a warrior.[62] Relating as it does to specific *varṇas*, *svadharma* determines rigidly how a person should act, with whom they should eat and whom they should marry. Finally, Brahmā's ordinances are absolutely deterministic insofar as once ordained they must be worked out. Their inexorability is stressed in the texts.[63]

Besides the element of determinism associated with all three concepts, each is to some extent characterized by what the Mīmāṃsakas call *apūrva* in that they produce results which only reach fruition in the future. *Karma* produces fruits which only ripen long after the initial action has been undertaken. Similarly, the conditions of a *vidhi* have to be worked out and generally only come to a head long after they have been originally laid down. Moreover, a collection of *vidhis* can produce a result such as Rāma defeating Rāvaṇa and *adharma*, where the individual *vidhi* appears to be capricious and with no particular consequence except in regard to a specific individual. This is because the interaction of them all is necessary for a result manifesting only in the future. In the same way, observance of *svadharma*, which may sometimes be difficult in the short run, as Draupadī's remonstrations illustrate well, will produce happiness in the future by virtue of rebirth in heaven.

Fate and Pravrtti

Indian views about fate gravitate between acceptance of absolute determinism epitomized by the notion of *daiva* and an acceptance of human effort (*puruṣakara*) in the context of the *karma* theory as the determinant of man's lot. These polarities can easily be

62 Cf. the arguments in support of adherence to *dharma* given by Yudhiṣṭhira in *MBh*. 3, 32.

63 *Rām*. (V) 5, 3, 48; *MBh*. I, 27, 19; 2, 53, 13; 8, 29, 38; *EI*. 8. p. 73.

categorized in terms of *pravṛtti* and *nivṛtti*. Perhaps Jolly had unwittingly hinted at a dichotomy along these lines when he wrote that: "There existed in ancient times a large number of philosophical systems, belonging to two principal classes–one asserting the existence of free will, moral responsibility, and transmigration; and the other negating the same. Both Jina and Buddha believed in transmigration, the annihilation of which was the final aim they had in view…"[64] Though 'free-will' and 'moral responsibility' are inappropriate as descriptions of *karma* and its immediate connotations, Jolly was right to associate with the Buddhist, Jains and by extension, most other groups of renouncers, the idea of *karma* being the determining factor of existence.[65] Each group recognized that *daivam* was not a contributing factor in the birth of a person into a particular situation. The real cause was the person's own actions. The cessation (*nivṛtti*) of actions, hence *karma*, was the only way to abolish future rebirth.

This conviction that *karma* is the predominant factor in human destiny is consistent with *nivṛttidharma*. The system that Jolly suggests asserted the influence of *karma* is presumably orthodox Brāhmaṇism, even though Jolly himself does not say this. One passage supporting such an interpretation is this from the *MBh*:

> Those people who understand action (*karma*) declare the predominance of human effort (*puruṣakara*); others who are priests (*vipra*) speak of' 'that which comes from the gods' (*daivam*); whereas those who reflect on the elements (*bhūtacintaka*) speak of innate disposition.[66]

The idea of reliance on human effort as expressed in this

---

64 Jolly, *ERE*, vol. 5, p. 791.

65 The sole exception being the Ajīvikas, a group of ascetics contemporaneous with Buddha who believed the total number of lives through which a person had to transmigrate was absolutely predetermined and could not be altered.

66 *MBh*. 12, 224, 50. Cf. 2, 43, 32 and 34; 3, 33, 30; 12, 137, 78-80. The term *bhūtacintaka* probably refers to a group such as the Cārvakas, who espoused a materialist philosophy.

passage is typical of traditions such as Buddhism and Jainism which at a doctrinal level so manifestly embody *nivṛtti* values. These two traditions (as well as others based on *nivṛtti* values) are essentially 'anthropological' in the sense of focussing on the individual human, who alone is responsible for his or her own enlightenment. Human effort is obviously at a premium in this situation, even though, paradoxically, the aim of the renouncer in these traditions is to subdue human effort as part of the means of preventing accumulation of *karma*. In contrast, orthodox Brāhmaṇism, represented in this passage by the *vipra* who place reliance on *daiva*, places great emphasis on the gods, collectively known as *daiva*. This reliance largely reflects the importance of the symbiotic relationship between men and gods, which lies at the heart of Brāhmaṇism and the *pravṛtti* worldview.

There is one other important reason for suggesting that deterministic notions of fate including *karma* are encompassed by the *pravṛtti* world-view. This is that Brahmā himself, an important symbol of *pravṛtti* values, is identical with fate as expressed through his epithet *vidhi*.[67] Yet another expression of this identity occurs in relation to his life span which corresponds to the temporal span of existence of the triple world. The linear-cyclical scheme of time dominant in Indian thought has sometimes been conceived as fate, as witnessed by the following statement of Geden: "The series of world cycles, therefore is independent of human will and endeavour, and so far corresponds to a conception of Fate, relentless and mechanical, with supreme and absolute control of the destinies of all, moving forwards resistlessly to a

---

67 This is the main thesis of Holtzmann's long article on Brahmā. He saw the god as *das Schicksal personificiert* and wrote, "Thus, Brahmā in the epic is above all the oracle of the gods and the knower of the future. Then, from out of this, very soon developed the idea that he would be the Lord of fate, indeed, fate itself." Holtzmann, 1884, pp.168-9. His argument rests on Brahmā's identification with *vidhi* and largely ignores the possibility that the god's life span can be seen as fate.

predetermined end."[68] These lines could equally well have been written about the Purāṇic time scheme, the basic cycles of which can be interpreted in the same way as suggested by Geden for the Buddhist notion of time.

There can be no doubt Brahmā's own life and that of the triple world are meant to be understood as being circumscribed by continual rebirth and death. This rigid continuity of rebirth and death is *saṃsāra*, in terms of which Biardeau has rightly understood Brahmā's life: "The *saṃsāra* of the individual becomes cosmic: it is Brahmā who transmigrates rather than any particular man… Thus, whereas the myth of the original creation is the recognition of the ultimate character of the renouncer's values, we can already guess that the *pratisarga* will subordinate it to the world of *dharma* of the *Veda*, in brief, to the whole body of values of caste society."[69] The analogy is an apt one. In earlier chapters I have argued for Brahmā very much as the paradigm of the person governed by *ahaṃkāra* and clouded by *māyā*, driven by desire, hence chained to *karma*. Just as the person within *saṃsāra* cannot control his future rebirths (or how long he will continue to be reborn), so too does Brahmā lack any control over his unvarying series of births and deaths. The renouncer, on the contrary, asserts such control by realizing the true nature of *karma* and by then attempting to bring it to an end.

As a transmigrating being Brahmā is necessarily a symbol of *saṃsāra* and fate. This embodiment of *saṃsāra*, a term connoting the same values as *pravṛtti*, comes to the fore in a stock formula

---

68 Geden, *ERE*. Vol. 5, p. 781.

69 Biardeau, 1968, p.45. The *prākṛtasarga* occurring at the beginning of a *mahākalpa* marks Brahmā's birth and the creation ushered in then lasts for one hundred of his years. At the end of this period he dies and the *mahāpralaya* occurs. A detailed discussion of this time scheme is given by Biardeau, 1968, pp.21-25. In view of the extent to which Brahmā's mythology expresses values similar to those implicit in the Brāhmaṇas, it is no coincidence his life span lasts for one hundred years. This was the time span allotted in the Vedas to a person who lived a full life.

found in several places. The example cited here is most fitting for its context, for a brahmin sage named Śaunaka is telling Yudhiṣṭhira what a man deluded by the senses can expect:

> At last, crazed by his sports and meals, he drowns in the maw of madness and does not know himself. Thus, in the runaround (*saṃsāra*), he falls here into womb after womb, spun around like a wheel by ignorance, *karman* and thirst. He rolls about in creatures, from Brahmā down to a blade of grass, born over and over again, in water, on land, or in the air. [70]

---

70 *MBh*. 3, 2, 67-8. Trans. van Buitenen, 1975, p.226. Virtually identical are *Ms*. 1, 50; SK. 60; *Bhg*. 8, 16; *ViP*. 3, 17, 14-34; *Devībhāgavatapurāṇa*. 6, 31, 30-1.

Chapter 8

Brahmā and Viṣṇu

In this chapter one of the most important implications of Brahmā's inseparable association with *dharma* is taken up. This association links him with the brahmin, the one who expounds the *dharma*; with the gods, who represent *dharma* over against the demons who represent *adharma*; and with *saṃsāra* as exemplified in the dharmic structure of the triple world. Each of these links is present in one way or another in the *avatāra* myth. Brahmā represents the brahmin, the conflict between the gods and demons provides the narrative framework of the myth, and it is the dharmic structure of the universe which is re-established by the *avatāra* when it has broken down following a decline in *dharma*. The *avatāra*, usually a portion of Viṣṇu, contrasts with Brahmā to the extent that he is often a *kṣatriya* or has such characteristics, and insofar as he represents an intrusion of *bhakti* values into a spatio/temporal realm dominated by *pravṛtti* values. Though Brahmā and the *avatāra* (Viṣṇu) appear sometimes to clash, their relationship is usually complementary, reflecting their roles in the *trimūrti* and the normative co-operative relationship between brahmin and *ksatriya*.

Brahmā and Pṛthu

In several versions of the Purāṇic cosmogony there is a myth justifying the origin of the *āśramas* on the grounds that they provided a means of countering the steady decline in human behaviour beginning from the commencement of the *tretāyuga*.[1] The version of the myth cited here is taken from the *MkP*:

> Once, during the time of creation, Brahmā created from his mouth a thousand pairs of humans who were characterized by goodness (*sattva*). From his breasts came another thousand. They were influenced by passion (*rajas*) and were impetuous and impatient. Another thousand came from his thighs and their status was discontentment. Being inclined towards exertion they were influenced by passion and ignorance (*tamas*). Finally, he created a thousand pairs from his feet, but they were ugly and unintelligent, abounding in ignorance.
>
> At the beginning of the *kalpa* pairs of living beings engaged in sexual intercourse prompted by love, but because women did not menstruate there were no births. However, when they died another pair was instantly born from them.
>
> This was called 'Prajāpati's first human creation'. Born from his lineage, these people respected the world and lived near rivers, streams, oceans and mountains. In the *kṛtayuga* there was very little heat or cold. The people were happy and there were no disputes amongst them. There were no demons, wicked beings, birds, animals or anything that was not of the law to hinder them. Nor were there flowers, seasons or years. Continually they were happy.
>
> With the passing of time these people attained perfection (*siddhi*). The water they drank was exquisite and all their desires were fulfilled. They enjoyed perpetual youth, suffered no afflictions and lived for four thousand years. Everywhere the Earth was with good fortune (*bhāgyena*).
>
> Eventually, however, these humans died and their prosperity disappeared with them. This happened at the beginning of the *tretāyuga*. Simultaneously, *kalpa* trees appeared and from them fruits, clothes and ornaments were produced, and on them the people lived. Passion (*rāga*) arose amongst the people and copulation occurred, followed by conception. Then the people became avaricious and egotistical. The trees died, the people

1 *MkP*. 49; *BḍP*. 1, 7, 38ff.; *KP*. 1, 27, 16-48; *LP*. 1, 39, 19-50.

> fought and experienced cold, heat and hunger. To defend themselves they began to build forts and towns.
>
> Then the *kalpa* trees disappeared and the people became confused and despondent. Then it rained and the Earth became fertile, as a result of which domestic and wild plants and fruit grew. But yet again the people were assailed by avarice and passion and tried to seize the land, trees and herbs for their own profit. Because of this the plants died before their eyes and the Earth simultaneously swallowed up the herbs.
>
> Due to the disappearance of the plants the people became completely bewildered, so, afflicted with hunger, they went to see Brahmā. He knew what the Earth had done, and accordingly, milked her, using Sumeru as the calf. After the cow was milked, corn reappeared along with seventeen types of seeds and fourteen types of plants for use in the sacrifice. These plants had to be cultivated, so Brahmā taught the people the art of cultivation as a means of livelihood. Then he established bounds of propriety (*maryādā*) in the correct manner (*yathanyāya*) and the characteristics of the people. After that, in order, he established the *varṇas*, *āśramas*, laws to protect people and the respective heavens applicable to the *varṇas* and certain classes of sages.[2]

With one important variation to be discussed later, the other versions of this myth correspond closely to this one.

The temporal setting of this narrative is the *kṛtayuga* and the beginning of the *tretāyuga*. The *kṛtayuga* is portrayed as an 'idyllic golden age.' Though the humans created by Brahmā appear to be grouped in an order analogous to that of the *varṇas*, there is no apparent hierarchy suggested in the description of their activities. Nor do the people act in accordance with any external set of 'regulations' such as *svadharma*. In fact, there is no mention of *dharma* being present in the *kṛtayuga* and so it can be assumed this was a vision of a period when the people spontaneously acted in a way guaranteeing the mutual benefit of all. Such a vision of the *kṛtayuga* does not tally with other descriptions of it found in

---

2 Summary translation of *MkP*. 49.

Indian literature.[3] In these it is described in glowing terms as an ideal time in which to live, but this is because of the predominance of *dharma* as the normative standard of conduct and the people's absolute adherence to it. As well, there is a king who is just to everyone and ensures that no mixing of caste takes place.

In this myth the decline in human conduct begins only after the commencement of the *tretāyuga*. The decline is not abrupt and is signalled by the ever-increasing hold of *rajas*, *tamas* and avarice over humans. Several signs point to the destructiveness caused by these factors; apart from the conflict between humans, the loss of the prosperity so marked in the *kṛtayuga*, the death of the *kalpa* trees and changes in climatic conditions, are all indications of this decline. Finally, and most effectively, withdrawal of fertility brings out the all-embracing nature of the decline. It is as though the Earth, which in the *kṛtayuga* had enjoyed prosperity, had decided to waste away.

As soon as the Earth reduces herself to barrenness, humans rush up to Brahmā as though he is their father. In some versions of the myth it is said they approach him seeking refuge (*śaraṇa*), a word replete with paternalistic connotations.[4] When he does actually milk the Earth it is mainly because of his altruistic attitude towards humans, but equally because this act is an essential precondition for the success of his creation. Humans cannot live without the Earth providing them sustenance, and so her fertility is necessary if Brahmā is going to establish a normative and workable form of society, one designed to prevent (or minimize)

---

3 A typical example occurs at *MBh*. 3, 191, 1-13. There the *kṛtayuga* is described in the context of the theory of *catuṣpaddharma*, according to which *dharma* is observed in its entirety in the *kṛtayuga* and metaphorically stands on four feet. In each successive *yuga* observance of it declines by one quarter, until in the *kaliyuga* it stands on only one foot. The idea that *dharma* should be absent from the *kṛtayuga* seems to be unique to the Purāṇic myth of the Earth-milker. See also the important studies of González-Reimann, 2002 and Hiltebeitel, 2011.

4 See *MBh*. 1, 58, 37; 1, 189, 4; 7, 69, 50.

human conflict and take conditions back to something like what they were in the *kṛtayuga*.

Why did the Earth withdraw her fertility, especially when in the *kṛtayuga* she had shared in the prosperity characteristic of that age? The reason must lie in the behaviour of humans towards her. In the *kṛtayuga* the world was respected (*pūjitam*) by the people who dwelt (*sevante*) near rivers, streams, oceans and mountains.[5] The verb *sev* means 'to serve, wait upon, honour, worship, and enjoy' as well as 'to resort to, inhabit', among other things. The direct implication of this is that they dwelt on the Earth in a way involving full respect for her. However, in the *tretāyuga* and prior to her withdrawal of fertility, humans had attacked and abused her. The nature of this attack is described in all versions of the myth: "These people seized (*paryagṛhṇanta*) rivers, fields, mountains, trees and herbal shrubs, after they had conquered (*prasahya*) them forcibly".[6] The verbal forms *pari/grah* and *pra/sah* both have connotations of conquering, or of violently overpowering through force. Seen in this light, her withdrawal of fertility is an act of retaliation. This suggests a relationship between the Earth and human beings, a relationship human beings have compromised. I discuss the nature of this relationship later.

As soon as Brahmā has milked the Earth he establishes 'bounds of propriety' (*maryādā*). One of the principle meanings of *maryādā* is 'limit, boundary'. By extension it can mean 'limit of behaviour', thus 'bounds of propriety', propriety corresponding in general to *dharma*.[7] In the context of the Earth-milker myth, Brahmā establishes bounds of propriety by setting up limits of behaviour. As one version of the myth states explicitly: 'Prajāpati, whose body was perfected, established bounds of propriety for their livelihood, which protected the one from the other.'[8]

---

5 *MkP*. 49, 12-13.

6 *BḍP*. 1, 7, 130; Very similar are *MkP*. 49, 62; *KP*. 1, 27, 44; *LP*. 1, 39, 43.

7 Which is not to say *dharma* should be rendered as 'propriety'.

8 *BḍP*. 1, 7, 153; *LP*. 1, 39, 46-50.

Limits of behaviour are affected by the setting up of the *varṇas* and the *āśramas*, with emphasis being put on the former. By channelling the destructive and creative abilities of humans into a hierarchical, but interdependent, structure like the system of *varṇas*, the threat of people acting as individuals, out of harmony with each other, will be avoided. For a concomitant of their independent action is abuse of the Earth,[9] causing her to withdraw her fertility. Thus in establishing the *varṇas* Brahmā is directly preventing Earth from being attacked by humans.

Another series of myths includes the motif of the milking of the Earth, but in these she is milked by the first king, Pṛthu, not by Brahmā. The Pṛthu myths have several purposes; to illustrate the ideal relationship that should exist between a king and his kingdom, and a king and the brahmins; and to emphasize that prosperity for all who exist in the cosmos results from the rule of a good king. There is much in them that can be linked with both the *avatāra* myth and the myth where Brahmā takes the role of Earthmilker. A comparison of the Pṛthu myths with the Brahmā myths is useful here, because it reveals much about how Brahmā as brahmin relates to the king (*kṣatriya*) and through the king, about how he relates to Viṣṇu, who represents kingship in so many ways.

The earliest significant appearance of Pṛthu in Sanskrit literature is in the *AV*, where he is one of many who milk Virāj for their nourishment. He milks her on behalf of mankind:

> Virāj ascended and came to men. Men called to her, ‘Come, you are full of food!’ Manu Vaivasvatin was her calf and Earth was the drinking vessel. She Virāj was milked by Pṛthu Vainya, and from her he milked grain and agriculture. These men subsisted successfully on grain and agriculture. He who would subsist successfully on agriculture is he who knows this.[10]

---

9 For example, see *MkP*. 49, 33; “Their minds pervaded by selfishness (*mamatva*), they seized these *kalpa* trees. Through their bad conduct even these trees were destroyed.”

10 *AV*. 8, 10, 24.

The genesis of the later versions of the Pṛthu myth can be seen here. But there is no indication the Earth has withdrawn her fertility, rather that Pṛthu is making a barren Earth fecund. In another Vedic text Pṛthu is depicted gathering food, yet not milking the Earth: "Now Pṛthu Vainya was consecrated first of men. He desired that he might appropriate to himself all the food here on Earth."[11]

Pṛthu's role as nourisher of his subjects is standard in all versions of the myth found in the epics and Purāṇas. One version of the myth in the *Mbh.* is similar in imagery to the myths where Brahmā is the Earth-milker. Nārada is telling Sṛñjaya the story of Pṛthu in an attempt to convince him not to mourn for those who have died honourably in battle, for even exemplary kings like Pṛthu are mortal:

> 'We have heard, Sṛñjaya, that Pṛthu Vainya died too. The great sages had consecrated him in the *rājasūya* as the universal sovereign. Because 'he would extend (*prath*) all of us', he was called Pṛthu, and '*kṣatriya*' because he would protect all of our injured. On seeing Pṛthu Vainya these delighted (*rakta*) people said, 'Hereafter he is called *rājā*'.
>
> Vainya's Earth was a cow that yielded all desires; plants ripened on uncultivated land, and all the cows gave a full pot of milk and there was honey in the hollows of trees, and there was golden *darbha* grass which was delightful and pleasant to the touch. With strips of this people covered themselves and slept in them. There were also *kalpa* trees, containing fruits, roots and honey. Since these were eaten by the people there was no hunger. Men were healthy and secure. All their wishes were gratified and they lived where they desired, in trees and houses. At that time there were no divisions in those old kingdoms and the people were joyful in following their pleasures and wishes.
>
> When Pṛthu approached the ocean its waters solidified. Mountains allowed him to pass, and his flag was not destroyed. The forest trees, hills, gods, demons, snakes, the seven sages, as well as the honest people, gandharvas, apsaras, fathers came

11 *ŚB*. 5, 3, 5, 4. Trans. Eggeling, 1882, Part III, p.81.

> to him, comfortably seated, and said, "You are a universal ruler, a *kṣatriya* and our king, protector and father. Being powerful, give us our most cherished desires, great king, for with them we shall be able to live agreeably in continuous satisfaction."
>
> Having assented, Pṛthu Vainya took Śiva's bow with its frightening and incomparable arrows, thought carefully, and said to the Earth, "Come! Come, quickly, Earth! Pour out for them the milk they want, and then I shall give you prosperity and the food which accords with your desire." The Earth said, "Hero, please consider me to be your daughter."
>
> Then Nārada said, "When she had assented, Pṛthu, the Lord, made all the arrangements and the various groups of beings milked the Earth… thus, these groups milked from Virāj the desired fluid on which they existed."
>
> The majestic Pṛthu Vainya performed various sacrifices and satiated the people with all the wishes that were dearest to their hearts…[12]

In this version of the myth the narrative divides naturally into two sections corresponding to the periods before and after Pṛthu milks the Earth. In the first period the people live much as the people in the *krtayuga* in the myth where Brahmā is the Earth-milker. Though Pṛthu is king, there is no hint of any social organization along the lines of *varṇāśramadharma*. The people and the Earth act spontaneously towards each other, not at the behest of Pṛthu. The change comes about when the various groups of beings approach Pṛthu, formally declare him to be their king and ask him to prove his worth by fulfilling their desires. He does this by subjugating the Earth with his bow. It is not all one way, however. For in demanding that the Earth give the people what they want, Pṛthu also has to guarantee to protect her, just as he is obliged to protect the people.

The Purāṇas contain many versions of the Pṛthu myth, most similar to the version just cited from the *MBh*. Usually they include an account of his birth from Vena and a description of the

---

12 *MBh*. 7. App. 1. No. 8. Lines 763-792; 815-818, pp. 1114-1118. Similar is *MBh.* 12, 29, 129-35.

horse sacrifice he performs as part of his accession to the kingship. Without exception, all stress his Earth-milking act and in a way that emphasizes it is an act of subjugation. This is particularly so in the *BhP*. where Pṛthu severely rebukes the capricious Earth for refusing to reveal her riches at his command and threatens to kill her with his bow and to support his subjects through his own yoga.[13] She relents and allows him and other groups of beings to milk her. Gonda cites yet another version where the Earth, threatened by Pṛthu, changes into a cow and seeks refuge with Brahmā.[14] He mediates between them, making Pṛthu protector of the Earth, persuading her to yield crops, and sites for building houses for gods and men. In other words he establishes the correct dharmic relationship between king and Earth.

It is also said of Pṛthu in other versions of the myth that he evens out the Earth's surface with the tip of his bow to provide room for houses and cities to be built.[15] In my view this might be interpreted as an act of aggression. However, it does have a parallel in an event which occurs in the Purāṇic cosmogony, one suggesting an alternative interpretation. In the *pratisarga* it is Brahmā who raises the Earth from the waters, levels and builds mountains on it.[16] Thus like the creator of the triple world, the king is to some extent the creator of his age.[17] He renders the Earth habitable for his subjects and if he protects her properly, she will give forth of her prosperity. If viewed in this light, Pṛthu's act of leveling the Earth is an essential part of the king's creative role in establishing (or creating) the conditions of his reign.

In spite of the differences between the figures of Brahmā and Pṛthu, it is significant that the redactors of at least one Purāṇa saw fit to integrate Pṛthu into their version of the Earth-milker myth.

---

13 *BhP*. 4, 17, 22-8. *Cf. ViP.* 1, 13, 74-75.

14 Gonda, 1969, p. 106, citing *Samarāṅgarasūtradhāra*. l, 6 ff; 6, 5 ff; 7, 7 ff.

15 *ViP*. 1, 13, 81-2. For other references see Gonda, 1969, p. 106.

16 See *KP*. 1, 6, 25.

17 Cf. *MBh*. 12, 92, 8.

The version of this myth found in the *KP*. is identical with what is found in the *MkP*. except at the point where the plants have withdrawn from the Earth's surface:

> When the people altered, these plants entered the Earth, and in accordance with the Grandfather's order Pṛthu milked the Earth. But due to the force of time all the people, who were infatuated with anger towards each other, forcibly seized each other's wives, wealth and property. Knowing that this had been done, the illustrious unborn Brahmā emitted *kṣatriyas* so that the bounds of propriety would be established and also for the benefit of brahmins. And in the *tretāyuga* the Lord set up the *varṇas* and *āśramas* and determined the procedure of sacrifices free of harm to animals.[18]

The same Purāṇa contains another version of this myth, but there, Brahmā and Indra together ask Pṛthu to milk the Earth.[19]

The redactors of this Purāṇa have judged the act of milking the Earth to be the feature common to Brahmā and Pṛthu. Yet the Purāṇic form of the Earth-milker myth has little in common with the Pṛthu myth other than the milking of the Earth and some similar imagery. Pṛthu is an anachronism here except in his capacity as Earth-milker, the only thing he does. The establishment of the *varṇas* and *āśramas* is left to Brahmā, a role wholly consistent with the other versions of the myth.

In view of the divergences between the characters of Pṛthu and Brahmā and the set of myths in which they are the protagonists, how is the act they share in common to be interpreted, and how does it relate to the roles they play in their respective sets of myths? The motive for Pṛthu's milking of the Earth is to subjugate her as a sign of his capacity for kingship. Her subjugation will demonstrate his martial powers and prove he can provide nourishment for his subjects. Brahmā's motive is one of altruism; to restore the Earth's fertility so that people can live, and to stop the abuse of her by the people living on her surface. Though there is no question of

---

18 *KP*. 1, 27, 45-8.

19 *KP*. 1, 13, 9-11.

Brahmā wishing to subjugate the Earth, the ultimate effect of her milking by the two figures is the same. Earth revives her fertility and she receives protection from the potential ravages of humans. The symbiotic relationship which should exist between humans and the Earth is thus restored.

The existence of such a relationship, one marked by mutual respect, is clearly illustrated in another version of the Pṛthu myth. In the *BhP*, after the Earth has withdrawn her fertility, Pṛthu angrily informs her that he wishes to kill her: "O Earth, I will kill you because you have disobeyed my command. She takes her share in the sacrifice yet she does not extend her wealth to us."[20] Several verses later she answers this charge:

> Of old herbs were created by Brahmā, Lord of the people. I saw them being eaten by evil people who do not adhere to vows. When the world had just become thieves, then, I swallowed the herbs for the sake of the sacrifice, as I was neither protected or respected by you, protector of the world.[21]

Here the Earth's criticism is directed against humans who have failed to offer the required oblations in the sacrifice, that is, they have not adhered to their vows to sacrifice, failing to fulfill their part in the symbiotic relationship they share with the gods and the Earth, a relationship centred on the sacrifice. If, as here, men do not sacrifice, or do not sacrifice enough, the whole cycle begins to breakdown. The Earth's reaction is to protect the plants essential for the sacrifice, but this extends the breakdown even further.

Similarly, in the set of myths where Brahmā is the Earth-milker, the Earth reacts adversely to the human's seizure of her rivers and hills. Such human abuse of her did not occur in the *kṛtayuga*. Indeed, in the *MkP.* version of the myth, the Earth is said to have enjoyed good fortune (*bhāgyena*) in this *yuga*.[22] The word *bhāgya* derives from *bhāga*, '[sacrificial] portion', a word

20 *BhP*. 4, 17, 22.

21 *BhP*. 4, 19, 6-7.

22 *MkP*. 49, 25.

found in the *BhP*. passage cited above. This may anticipate the relationship based on sacrifice which will come after Brahmā has milked the Earth and established the *varṇas* and *āśramas*. The use of the word *bhāgya* in the *MkP*. passage implies mutual respect between Earth and humans, just as the word *bhāga* in the *BhP*. passage implies that each party receives their respective share.

This interpretation is given further credence in the *MkP*. version of the myth where humans are said to have taken possession of fields, rivers, etc., 'on account of themselves' or 'for themselves' (*ātmanyāyād*).[23] This explanation of selfish behaviour corresponds to the criticism levelled in the *Bhg*. at people who claim to participate in the sacrifice, but who really cook oblations only for themselves.[24] A refusal to recognize one's obligation to participate in a reciprocal relationship underlies both situations. The selfish action of humans described in the *MkP*. amounts to a reversal (*viparyayeṇa*) of behaviour or a transgression (*doṣa*), causing the plants to disappear, swallowed up by the Earth.[25] The transgression committed almost certainly refers to their abuse of the relationship which ideally they should have with her.

In both sets of myths the activities of Brahmā and Pṛthu after they have milked the Earth, are designed to re-establish the ideal relationship between the two parties and to ensure this relationship will henceforth remain intact. Brahmā does this by establishing the *varṇas* and *āśramas* as explained above. Pṛthu is able to restore

---

23 *MkP*. 49, 62. This compound and the idea it implies contrasts with compounds such as *anyonya* and *paraṃpara*, as both imply reciprocity. The significance of the latter can be drawn from one version of the Pṛthu myth, where humans are described living in the *kṛṭayuga*. Though being without a king, they "protected each other (*parasparam*) through *dharma*." (*MBh*. 12, 59, 14). Reciprocity is the essence of the dharmically ordered organization of the triple world.

24 *Bhg*. 3, 13.

25 See respectively *KP*. 1, 27, 45; *MkP*. 49, 63; *VāP*. 8, 143; *LP*. 1, 39, 44.

and prolong the relationship merely by being a king. In ancient India it was believed the mere presence of a king was a stabilizing influence, that his presence on the Earth ensured order there.

That Pṛthu is king implies on his part an obligation to protect his subjects, one of which is the Earth. In Pṛthu's case this obligation is articulated in several distinct ways. The *ŚP*. says of him that he is "the first born of the *kṣatriyas* who has protected the Earth" and gives him the title *vasudhāpati*, 'husband (or Lord) of the Earth'.[26] There are two separate ideas here. Firstly, it is the well known obligation of the *kṣatriya* to protect the Earth as one of the king's subjects. Secondly, a husband is required to protect his wife. The word *pati* implies protection.[27] In addition, there is one further way in which his obligation to protect the Earth is brought out. Each version of the Pṛthu myth contains a passage which describes how after she has been milked, the Earth asks Pṛthu if she can become his daughter (*duhitṛtva*), enabling her to be entitled to his protection.

His obligation to protect the Earth is much stressed in these myths, and it is precisely this obligation that leads to another comparison between him and Brahmā. For in the *MBh*. the Earth is once said to be Brahmā's daughter (*sutā*), and in a passage where she is depicted seeking protection from a king:

> Of old, a king named Aṅga wished to give Earth to the brahmins as a present (*dakṣiṇā*). At that, the Earth became worried, king, and thought, "Having obtained me, the bearer of all beings, how could this eminent king want to give me, Brahmā's daughter to the twice-born. After I have abandoned my earthiness (*bhūmitva*) I will certainly go to Brahmā's abode. This king and his kingdom must cease to exist (*mā bhūd*)." Then she left.
>
> On seeing the Earth leaving, the highly focused Kaśyapa released himself from meditation, and immediately entered

26 *ŚP*. 5, 30, 21.

27 The idea of the king as the Earth's husband, the one who maintains her, has been discussed by Derrett, 1959, p. 110 ff; Hara, 1973, pp. 97 ff.

> the Earth. Possessed, the Earth became abundant everywhere with herbs and grasses. *Dharma* prevailed there and fear disappeared, King.
>
> Accordingly, for thirty thousand divine years Kaśyapa, tirelessly peforming that great duty, was the Earth, king. Then, Great king, having returned and bowed before Kaśyapa, Earth became Kaśyapī, daughter of that great man.[28]

This passage contains elements of the Earth-milker and the Pṛthu myths. The Earth is anxious because she is being abused by a king who has transgressed the limits of his relationship with her. He should protect her, not give her away. The king is allowed to grant small parts of the Earth as a *dakṣiṇā* to the brahmins, but not the entire Earth.[29]

She is to be used by all the *varṇas*, and should not be regarded as the preserve of any one *varṇa*, whether brahmin or *kṣatriya*. Her flight to Brahmā for protection and Kaśyapa's subsequent action implies she has withdrawn her fertility. Kaśyapa restores this, not by milking her, but by becoming her essence through the power of his yoga. This is a clear reversal of a motif found in the *ViP*. version of the Pṛthu myth. There, after the Earth has withdrawn her fertility, Pṛthu threatens to kill her and says, "I will support these creatures through the power of my own yoga."[30] In the Kaśyapa myth, there is yet another reversal on a motif prominent in the Pṛthu myth. Earth returns from seeing Brahmā, sees what has happened and becomes his daughter, because he has given her new life as it were. In most versions of the Pṛthu myth, the Earth becomes his daughter after she has been milked. Finally, as in the other two sets of myths discussed, *dharma* prevails after fertility has been re-established.

In this myth it is a brahmin who protects the Earth and acts in every way as though he were a *kṣatriya*. Kaśyapa is a celebrated

---

28 *MBh*. 13, 139, 1-7; *ŚB*. 13, 7, 1, 13-15.

29 Epigraphical sources show it was commonplace for kings to grant small portions of land to various groups of brahmins.

30 *ViP*. 1, 13, 75.

prajāpati, brahmin and *ṛṣi*, behind whose figure stands Brahmā himself.[31] His action exactly parallels Brahmā's in the myth of the Earth-milker. But that a brahmin should protect the Earth is an unusual reversal of norms. The implied conclusion is that when the *kṣatriya* fails, the brahmin takes over, because ultimately the brahmin is the protector of *dharma*. Nevertheless, it is the obligation of the *kṣatriya*, as the king, to protect the Earth through use of arms. This is why the redactors of the *KP*. have given the Earth-milker role to Pṛthu rather than to Brahmā in the myth where Brahmā normally performs this role.

If the roles of brahmin and *kṣatriya* are reversed in this myth, there is one version of the Pṛthu myth where Brahmā plays a prominent role and brahmin and *kṣatriya* do play their appropriate roles. This version is recited by Bhīṣma in response to a question put by Yudhiṣṭhira as to why one man and not another is made king:

> In the *Krta* age there was no king, kingdom, rod of punishment (*daṇḍa*) or enforcer of punishment, but all creatures protected each other through *dharma*. After some time the people became weary and beset with confusion, and no longer acted in accord with *dharma*. All men became covetous of the things of others, were affected by passion (*rāga*) and "they no longer took cognizance of what should be done and what not, nor of the women they should not approach for sex, nor of what should and should not be said, what should and should not be eaten, what is an is not and us not a fault…" Due to the disorder and the confusion of humans, the Vedas and *dharma* disappeared. The gods, becoming afraid, went to Brahmā and related all that had happened, saying they had become the same as mortals. Furthermore, no sacrifices were being performed, so they were not being fed. They asked Brahmā to rectify the situation so that their power would not be lost.
>
> Brahmā reassured them and composed a treatise of one hundred

31 Epithets of Kaśyapa such as *śraṣṭā lokānām and prajānāṃ patiḥ* (*VāmP. Sarohamāhātmya*. 3, 12-14) also suggest he represents Brahmā.

thousand verses dealing with the subjects of the Law, Wealth, Sensuous Desire and Liberation. In it was contained every conceivable subject concerning kingship, the duties of the *āśramas*, *varṇas*, the contents of the Vedas and the histories (*itihāsa*). Being too large for the comprehension of humans, it was given to Śiva who abridged it to a smaller size. He passed it on to another god for abridgement until finally it was passed to the great sages in a form comprehensible to mankind.

Next the gods went up to Viṣṇu and asked him to appoint a king for them. He produced a king, but for a variety of reasons he and his five descendants were unsuitable for kingship.[32] The

32 It is worthwhile digressing briefly on the reasons why the six kings before Pṛthu were deemed to be unsatisfactory. The first three, namely, Virajas, Kīrtimat and Kardama all showed ascetic tendencies with the implication that they did not wish to be kings. It is said (*MBh*. 12, 59, 95) of Virajas that he did not seek omnipresence (*vibhutva*, also 'sovereignty') on earth and that his mind was intent upon abandonment (*nyāsa*) of worldly life. His son Kīrtimat had overcome the five senses and in turn, his son Kardama performed great austerities (*atapyan mahat tapah*).

The fourth king, Anaṅga, seems to have been an ideal king. He was said to be a good protector of creatures and proficient in the science of punishment. But as his name indicates he was without a body and only an able-bodied man could be a king (see Gonda, 1969, p. 35, for several examples). Equally, Anaṅga is a common name for Kāma and this would place him in the same category as the fifth and sixth kings.

The fifth and six kings represent in varying degrees the opposite of asceticism–sensuality. Atibala who was eminent in political conduct (*nītimat*) became a great king; but was subsequently overpowered by the emotions (98). Vena, the sixth king, represented this tendency to an extreme. He was subject to passion and hate, and ruled without conformity to *dharma* (99-100).

Pṛthu is adjudged the ideal king because he does not go too far in either direction–renunciation or sensuality. Nonetheless, he does combine aspects of each of these in his personality (see 109-10, for the ascetic tendencies and 123, for the sensual tendencies).

> last of these was Vena, and he was so bad the brahmins killed him with pieces of *kuśa* grass purified with *mantras*. From his right thigh they churned a black Niṣāda [tribesman] and from his right hand they churned Pṛthu. He looked like Indra, was accomplished in the Vedas and warfare, and understood *dharma*. He asked the sages what he should do, and together with the gods, they instructed him in his duties. They told him to act resolutely and in accord with *dharma*, to protect the world utilizing *dharma* and punishment, to respect brahmins and to prevent an intermixture of *varṇas*. Having agreed to all this, Śukra became his *purohita*, the Vālakhilya sages his ministerial advisers, the Sārasvatyas his attendants, and Garga his astrologer.
>
> Pṛthu then evened out the Earth which had formerly been uneven. He was then consecrated king by Viṣṇu, Indra, Brahmā and several other gods. Straight after his consecration the Earth offered him her wealth as did the oceans, rivers, mountains and the god Kubera.
>
> Conditions of life returned to what they had been at the beginning of the *kṛtayuga* and there was no sickness, disease, lack of food, fear from serpents, thieves or from one another. Pṛthu milked the Earth of seventeen kinds of plants which provided the subsistence for, whomsoever desired it. He made all beings act in accord with *dharma*, was called *rājā* because he gladdened (*rañjita*) the people and *kṣatriya* because he protected the wounds (*kṣatatrāṇāt*) of brahmins. Viṣṇu then entered his body, saying, "No one shall surpass you, king." After that the whole world made obeisance to him.[33]

This version of the Pṛthu myth falls into two sections, one covering the decline of *dharma* in the *kṛtayuga* and Brahmā's composition of the treatise (12, 59, 22-93), and another including the myth of Pṛthu proper (12, 59, 94-141). Together they constitute

---

It is probable the two distinct groupings of kings are a reflection of the *pravṛtti/nivṛtti* dichotomy, and that the ideal king, Pṛthu, embodies in some measure both these value systems in his image.

33 Summary of *MBh*. 12, 59, 1-130. For a full translation see Fitzgerald, 2004, pp.304-311.

a version of the *avatāra* myth. This is apparent right from the beginning of the first section, because the decline in the standard of human behaviour represents a diminishment of *dharma*, this being the motive for the descent of the *avatāra* into the triple world. The nature of the decline is exemplified by the disorder arising from the confusion about the correct way to speak, act, etc, and this exactly parallels what happens in the Earth-milker myth where human disorder is transgression of the 'bounds of propriety'. The net result is disappearance of the Vedas and *dharma*, and this together with the accompanying disorder signifies that the triple world is heading towards destruction of a type reminiscent of the *pralaya*.[34]

With the disappearance of *dharma*, the gods–perceiving the triple world as going to destruction before its rightful time–run to Brahmā, whom they regard paternalistically as the symbol for the values governing the universe in which they prosper. He immediately recreates *dharma* by composing the huge treatise, the essential prerequisite for a return to an ordered creation. This act too has a parallel in the Earth-milker myth, where it corresponds to his creation of the *varṇas* and *āśramas* and a re-establishment of the relationship between humans and the milked Earth. The rationale behind all this is *dharma*.

The second section of the myth contains much found in other Purāṇic versions of the Pṛthu myth. However, there are some significant differences, which make this version identifiable as an *avatāra* myth. The first difference is the great stress placed on

---

34 This similarity to the *pralaya* is suggested in more ways than one. The disorder of human behaviour described in the initial part of the myth epitomizes the pre-creation state, for in most Indian cosmogonic speculations creation occurs only when order in the form of definable limits is established. Moreover, in the verse which describes the disappearance of *dharma*, the word *vipluta* is used to convey the idea of disorder in the world of men (*naraloka*) (12, 59, 21). This word has the literal meaning of 'to float about, swim about', suggesting the cosmic sea into which the earth sinks during the *pralaya*.

dharma. Not only does Pṛthu embody *dharma*, he also receives the *dharma* taught him by the sages who killed Vena. Functionally, they are identical with the sages who received Brahmā's abridged treatise on *dharma* and this constitutes one of the connecting links between the two parts of the myth. Also, Pṛthu is made to promise always to act in accord with *dharma* and to ensure his subjects will do the same. This obvious stress on *dharma* contrasts with other versions of the Pṛthu myth where it is barely mentioned.[35] The second difference concerns the marked presence of Viṣṇu behind the figure of Pṛthu. The latter is said to be the eighth to be born from Viṣṇu and after his consecration it is that god who enters Pṛthu, causing all the world to bow before him.[36] As a result of this the whole world is now entirely devoted to *dharma*, meaning it has been restored from its decline. This is the second main link with the first half of the myth.

To some extent this myth resolves the conflict of roles embodied in the Earth-milker and Pṛthu myths, where in the former, a brahmin performs the role of a *kṣatriya*. In this myth Brahmā and Pṛthu act out roles normative for members of these two *varṇas*. Brahmā's composition and recitation of a treatise concerned with *dharma* is consistent with the role of the brahmin enunciated in the Dharmaśāstras. Pṛthu's agreement to rule in accord with *dharma* is consistent with the *kṣatriya's* role–one who is enjoined to protect and enforce adherence to *dharma* by violence if necessary. Both the brahmin and *kṣatriya* should in all their activities be embodiments of *dharma*. As Lingat says,

> The Brahmin only performs his role successfully if he personifies *dharma* in his teachings and in his conduct. The Kṣatriya invested with the royal function is not successful in his role unless he too personifies *dharma* in his activity. At bottom there is identity of function between them; but *dharma* cannot be realized without their co-operation. The principle of the essential co-operation

35 See especially verses 105-13.

36 *MBh*. 12, 59, 130.

of the two powers is one of the fundamental elements in smṛti's theory of kingship.[37]

Besides the didactic significance of this myth (and that of the Earth-milker and Pṛthu myths)–in portraying some elements of ancient Indian political theory– it also has an important religious significance. Whilst both gods–Brahmā and Viṣṇu–represent the *varṇa* with which they are so often associated, they are also portrayed in terms of their roles as members of the *trimūrti.* Brahmā creates *dharma* in conditions somewhat suggestive of the *pratisarga* and Viṣṇu, through Pṛthu, preserves the triple world in accord with dharmic order. In addition to this, Viṣṇu comes out of the *avatāra* myth as the *bhakti* god par excellence, entering the triple world to 'save' its inhabitants from destruction, symbolic of the way the *bhakti* god breaks through the veil of *māyā* to liberate his devotee from *saṃsāra.* This pattern is repeated in other versions of the *avatāra* myth, even to the extent where the *avatāra* can liberate the *adharmic* demon who has brought about his descent. In contrast, Brahmā rarely, if ever, goes beyond the triple world and though he composes the dharmic treatise, he does function actively like Viṣṇu to rectify the situation of the triple world. Likewise, he never liberates beings from the *saṃsāra* that characterizes the triple world, because in all ways he symbolizes this *saṃsāra.* This pattern and contrast is repeated in most other versions of the *avatāra* myth as will be seen later in this chapter.

Brahmā and Vyāsa

The co-operation between Viṣṇu and Brahmā in the final version of the myth of Pṛthu analysed above is repeated in a series of myths concerned with the original recitation of the *Mahābhārata* and the *Rāmāyana.* Brahmā inspires both Vyāsa and Vālmīki to teach their respective compositions to their pupils after they have encountered problems in trying to do this orally. Similarly, when the Buddha hesitates to spread his teachings after he has become enlightened, it is Brahmā who finally persuades him to commence

37 Lingat, 1973, p.216.

teaching. All these are arguably really just versions of one mythic plot, a plot sharing many features of the *avatāra* theme, including the presence of Viṣṇu and the cosmogonic motifs so often found in the *avatāra's* role.

In a book first published in 1990 Bruce Sullivan devotes a chapter to listing and analyzing many close parallels between Brahmā and Vyāsa. He points out that "Vyāsa is the epic character having the greatest degree of correspondence with Brahmā Prajāpati, and should therefore be regarded as that deity's "transposition" in the MBh."[38] And he also focusses on their priestly role: "As a brahmin who takes the role of brahman priest, as creator and disseminator of the Veda, as the *pitāmaha* of a warring family, Vyāsa reenacts on earth much of the deity's deeds in mythology."[39] He rightly points out that both occupy the role of the *brahmā* priest, and it is their role of oversight as applying to the three worlds in Brahmā's case and to the Pāṇḍavas and Kauravas in Vyāsa's case. Equally this concern with preservation of the earth and dynasties places both within the framework of *pravṛtti* values, which they effectively disseminate through their own actions in the epic narrative and through what they teach. Arguably Bhīṣma also plays a similar role in respect of both warring parties and he too is a massive disseminator of *dharma* in the manner of both Brahmā and Vyāsa. He differs from Vyāsa by being an incarnation of Dyaus Pitar. And Sullivan insists that Vyāsa should be seen as an *aṃśa* of Brahmā rather than of Nārāyaṇa, whose *aṃśa* he is said to be only in later sections of the *MBh.*[40]

Several passages in the *Mbh.* give accounts of the epic's origin. One describes the epic first being recited in public by Vaiśampāyana during the interval between rites performed at King Janamejaya's snake sacrifice.[41] Another passage states that it was composed by Kṛṣṇa Dvaipāyana "after he had arranged the

38 Sullivan,1990, p.92.

39 Sullivan,1990, p.101.

40 Sullivan, 1990, pp.112-117

41 *MBh.* 1, 1, 18; 54, 21-2.

Eternal Veda by the powers of his austerities and continence."[42] There is yet a third explanation found in a passage not included in the Critical Edition of the *MBh.* According to this passage Dvaipāyana had some doubts about how his completed poem could be passed on to his students:

> After he had completed that best of poems, Lord Dvaipāyana worried, "In what way should I instruct my pupils in this poem now?"
>
> And even as the sage was worrying about this, the illustrious Brahmā, the world teacher himself, desiring the welfare of beings and as a favour to the great sage, remembered Dvaipāyana and came there. On seeing him, Dvaipāyana was astonished and he bowed and supplicated him with his hands. Then he arranged a seat for him who was accompanied by all the groups of gods.
>
> When he had walked around Hiraṇyagarbha sitting in that superlative seat, Vāsaveya stayed near the seat, bowing. Then delighted and very surprised, Kṛṣṇa Dvaipāyana sat near that seat after Brahmā Parameṣṭhin had authorized him to do so.
>
> He who has great splendour then said to Brahmā Parameṣṭhin, "Lord, this highly respected poem was composed by me, and, Brahmā, it contains the secrets of the Vedas, but it was named something else by me" (*yaccānyat khyāpitaṃ mayā*) ... [Then he lists the contents of the poem he has just composed]...
>
> Then Brahmā said, "Because of your excellent austerity and your making known of secret knowledge, I think you are now more excellent than Vasiṣṭha, the best of sages. Ever since your birth in Satyavatī you have been wise about the Earth and what is spoken in holy texts. And since you have called this a 'poem,' henceforth it will be a poem. The wise (*kavayaḥ*) are not competent regarding the excellence of this poem, just as the three remaining *āśramas* are not competent regarding the excellence of the householder.
>
> The world will be covered with darkness, disordered in intellect, stupid, deaf and blind, if it is not illuminated by you,

42 *MBh.* 1, 1, 52. Trans. van Buitenen. 1971, p. 22. Cf. 1, 54, 4.

> because your knowledge is like a fire. Whilst the world was enclosed in darkness due to its own actions, the opening of the eye of understanding was composed with pens containing the collyrium of knowledge, and was recited in connected sections for the purpose of elucidating *mokṣa*, *kāma*, *artha* and *dharma*. With the full-mooned ancient tales and the *śruti* which shines like a moon-lit night, you have dispelled mankind's darkness, Sun of the Bhāratas. This enlightening knowledge was composed with the lamp of history (*itihāsa*), striking at the obstructing delusion for the benefit of men who are like lotuses moist and cool. It duly makes manifest the entire sacred area of the world... [Following this the various books of the *MBh.* are compared to the trunk and branches of a large tree].
>
> The Bhāratadruma, inexhaustible to mankind as the clouds, will be to the poets that on which they live."[43]

After finishing his speech Brahmā returned to his own world and Dvaipāyana recited the epic poem to Gaṇeśa who wrote it down.

Though this passage is considered to be an interpolation, its importance for a knowledge of Brahmā's role in the dissemination of *dharma* and in the wider ambit of the *avatāra* myth is in no way diminished.[44] The myth itself is probably older than the *MBh.* passage in which it is found, because versions of it also occur in both the *Rām.* and some Pāli texts.

---

43 *MBh.* 1, App. 1. Pp.884-5, lines 1-13, 31-46, 55-6.

44 This passage is found in thirty-seven of the fifty-nine manuscripts of the *Ādiparvan* used for the Critical Edition. It is found in both Northern and Southern manuscripts, including two from Kashmir (K. 4-5). However, it is not found in the early Śāradā manuscript (K. 1), the purest of the Kashmiri versions. Nor is it found in the Nepalil Maithili and Bengali recensions. Lüders, 1929, p, 1144, reviewing the first fascicles of the Critical Edition of *the Ādiparvan*, argued that this passage and the story of Gaṇeśa which directly follows it are interpolations deriving from the South. He rests his argument on their occurrence in virtually all the Grantha, Telugu and Malayalam manuscripts, and because the Paśupata philosophy is mentioned.

Brahmā does not create or recite the text of the *MBh.* himself, but he is indirectly responsible for its communication to humans. He persuades Vyāsa to teach it to his disciples by painting a grim picture of the world if it does not have the knowledge enshrined in the text. The picture he paints is strongly reminiscent of the pre-creation state. Similes such as darkness, confusion, disordered intellect and blindness are all suggestive of this state. The dissemination of knowledge, whether of the Vedas or the *MBh.* opens the way for the introduction of an ordered universe by dispelling the darkness characteristic of the pre-creation state.

The episode recounting the origin of the *Rām.* is similar in many respects to the one I have just discussed. In the first chapter of the *Bālakāṇḍa* there is an *anukramaṇikā* listing of the contents of all seven books of the epic, and in the second chapter an account of the origin of the epic is given. There it is related how Vālmīki, deeply moved by the grief of a female bird whose lover has been shot by a hunter, recited four lines in the *śloka* meter describing the hunter's cruelty. Having done this he entered his hermitage followed by his pupil Bharadvāja, and subsequently passed into a deep meditation. Then:

> Lord Brahmā, the one of the four faces who is the maker of the worlds and has great splendour, came himself to see that excellent sage. After Vālmīki had seen him, he was surprised and speechless. Quickly he stood up and performed supplication, devoted as he was. And after he had bowed to him according to the rule and asked after his ongoing good health, he honoured the god with praises, a seat and water for his feet.
>
> When the illustrious god had seated himself on that precious chair he then assigned a chair to the great sage Vālmīki. And when the Grandfather of the worlds was seated before his eyes, Vālmīki, with his mind absent, entered into meditation, thinking, "A wretched thing was done by that evil man whose mind is seized by animosity. Who would causelessly kill a krauñca bird who had such a pleasant voice?" Directly grieving, his mind turned within, deeply affected by sorrow, he suddenly once again sang this *śloka* about the female krauñca bird.
>
> Then Brahmā laughingly spoke to that excellent sage. "You

composed this *śloka*. Without any hesitation for my pleasure alone, brahmin, this wisdom of yours has begun. Best of sages, recite all of Rāma's acts! You must relate this affair of Rāma in the world, just as you heard it from Nārada. Tell of that Rāma, whose nature is *dharma*, who is virtuous, intelligent and resolute, and of Lakṣmaṇa and of all the Rākṣasas. Tell of the women of the Videhas, whether their conduct is well known or secret. Moreover, all that is unknown–you will teach. Never will any word in your poem be false."[45]

Brahmā goes on to predict that Rāma 's story will continue to exist as long as rivers and mountains remain on the earth. Then he ascends to heaven, leaving Vālmīki to compose and recite the life of Rāma.

This episode differs in two ways from the one relating the origin of the *MBh*. Vyāsa had already composed the epic when graced with Brahmā's visit, but he was unable to transmit it to his pupils. Vālmīki, however, has not yet composed the *Rām*. when he receives Brahmā's visit. Yet the conditions necessary for its composition–the discovery of the *śloka* meter and Vālmīki's knowledge of Rāma's life as summarily recited by Nārada–were certainly present. The *Rām*. also differs in that it lacks the similes suggestive of the pre-creation state present in Brahmā's speech to Vyāsa. There is a possibility this might find a parallel in the evil of the hunter killing the male *krauñca* bird. This might be seen as a reversal of the motif of Rāvaṇa's abduction of Sītā, which, as I have already suggested, symbolizes the ravishment of the Earth by 'evil' forces.[46] Not only is this a consequence of her abduction, but also of her separation from the king (= Rāma). Clearly, a sign of diminishing *dharma*, a situation analogous to the pre-creation state.

Yet another telling of this episode occurs in Indian literature. The Pāli Canon contains several versions of it, among which there is little variation. The version cited here is taken from the

45 *Rām*.(C) 1, 2, 22-34.

46 See above pp. 200-202.

Mahāpādanasutta of the *DN*.[47] It begins just after recitation of the Buddha's attainment of enlightenment. Resting beneath a tree at Uruvelā, he thought to himself:

> Now, I have penetrated this *dhamma* which is profound, hard to perceive, hard to understand, tranquil, excellent, not to be doubted, subtle and capable of being known only by the wise. However, these are creatures devoting themselves to attachments, devoted to attachments, delighting in attachments... And, indeed, if I were to teach the *dhamma* and other men did not acknowledge it to me, that would exhaust me, that would annoy me.

Then Great Brahmā, having become aware of these thoughts, expressed considerable alarm:

> Alas! Lord! The world will perish, Alas! Lord! The world will indeed perish, because the heart of Vipassin the Exalted One, Arahant, Buddha Supreme, has no interest and does not incline towards teaching the *dhamma*.

Immediately, he appeared before the Buddha and said to him:

> Lord! May the Exalted man preach the *dhamma*! May the Well-going man preach the *dhamma*! There are beings who are hardly defiled (*apparajakhajātikā*) and they are neglected from not hearing the *dhamma*. Some of them will accept the *dhamma*.

Brahmā repeated this plea twice more until finally the Buddha became aware of his entreaty–and gazed out over the world. There he saw people of various levels of understanding, "beings sharp of sense and blunted in sense, beings of good and evil disposition".

As soon as Brahmā became aware of the Buddha's thoughts he took them to be an assent to his entreaty. He then uttered a verse praising the Buddha's decision to teach the *dhamma*. This verse contains imagery similar to that found in the verses where Brahmā

---

47 *DN*. 2, 36-40. I have slightly modified the relevant sections of the translation by Rhys Davids,1971, vol. 2. pp.29-30. Cf. *Vin*. 1, 5ff; *MN*. 1, 168ff. Bareau, 1963), vol. 1. pp. 135-43, has translated several other versions. See also *Lalitavistara*. Ch.25 for a version in Buddhist Sanskrit.

entreats Vyāsa to recite the *MBh*: "O illustrious man, you have ascended the high terrace, and so, seeing everywhere, look down without grief, upon that collection of people who are oppressed with birth and old age."[48]

This verse can aptly be compared with the words of disillusionment spoken by the Buddha when he first perceived the truth. They are packed with images which depict the people who live in the world as "consumed with passion and flaws" (*rāgodosaparatehi*) and "cloaked in the mass of ignorance" (*tamokkhandena āvutā*).[49] Such imagery compares strikingly to words used by Brahmā in the *MBh.* episode describing the situation of the world if the epic is not recited. Finally, having recited this verse, Brahmā returned to his own heaven and the Buddha went to the Deer Park to preach his first sermon.

Buddha's initial refusal to communicate his experience of enlightenment and the path leading to it seems anomalous within the general context of Buddhist ethics. Bareau has noticed this anomaly and comments:

> It does not appear to his advantage, accumulating arrogance in the appreciation of his discovery and idleness and egoism in his decision, betraying the ideal of the Bodhisattva who is always ready to sacrifice himself for the good of other beings and contravening precepts of the Buddhist teaching itself which recommends with such insistence–modesty, energy and altruism.[50]

Besides this there is more. If, as the Pāli texts claim, the Buddha is omniscient in the sense of being able potentially to know everything, but only one thing at a time, then why, when he was concentrating on the mental capacities of human beings,

---

48 *Sokāvitinṇṇam janataṃ apetasoko avekkhassu jātijarābhibhūtam* ...

49 *DN*. 2, 36.

50 Bareau, 1963, Vol. 1, p.141.

did he doubt their capacity to comprehend the *dhamma*?[51] Bareau attempts to account for this when he says:

> This apparent clumsiness seems to indicate that the original narrative was composed in a period when the Buddha was already regarded as a superhuman being to whom the most prestigious gods came to render homage and service, but whose omniscience was not yet recognised, and who therefore had need to resort to the supernatural knowledge of the divinities in question.[52]

But even within the description of the entreaty itself, the Buddha's omniscience, or at least his special insight, seems to be acknowledged. For after he has been entreated by Brahmā to teach, the Buddha looks at human beings with his special Buddha-eye and perceives they are capable of comprehending the *dhamma*. In view of this Bareau's explanation seems rather forced, and, moreover, it takes no cognizance of evidence derived from other versions of this myth, namely, those involving Vyāsa and Vālmīki.

In the Pāli texts Brahmā and gods of the Brahmā worlds are frequently portrayed encouraging the Buddha and other individuals to follow *dhamma* or to adopt the *bhikku's* life. A typical example comes from a passage in the *SN.* where it is related that after the Buddha had attained enlightenment he wondered if there was any living person whose conduct was high enough for him to follow.[53] He concluded that the only form of conduct which met his demands was *dhamma*, so he decided to follow it. On realizing the Budda's thoughts Brahmā Sahaṃpati came to him and strongly endorsed this decision. Another statement attributed to the same god also sees him justifying adherence to *dhamma*. He says: "He who is endowed with conduct and knowledge, is first amongst god and men."[54] Yet again, according to the *Janavasabhasutta*

---

51 On this idea of omniscience in Theravāda Buddhism see Jaini, 1974, p.82.

52 Bareau, 1963, Vol. 1, p.142.

53 *SN.* 1, 139.

54 *SN.* 1, 153.

this god visited Indra's assembly when Indra and the gods were seated in debate.[55] There he instructed them in the doctrine of the *brahmavihāras* and generously praised this doctrine. These few illustrations suffice to show that Brahmā's role in the entreaty was not out of character with the way the Buddhists understood him.

The best way to explain the anomaly Bareau finds in this passage is to argue that the myth is really about Brahmā and only secondarily about the Buddha. This becomes apparent when its main features are compared with those of the Vyāsa and Vālmīki myths. Such a comparison shows that the three are versions of the one basic myth.

MBh. App. 1	*Rām. 1, 2*	*DN. 2, 36-40*
The poem is completed before Brahmā arrives.	The summary of the poem has been heard and the special meter discovered before Brahmā arrives.	Englightenment and knowledge of the *paṭiccasamuppāda* is attained before Brahmā arrives.
Vyāsa expresses doubts about teaching the *MBh.* to his students.	In *Rām.* 1, 1, 1-5, Vālmīki asks if anyone in the world is *dharmātman.*	Buddha doubts the capacity of beings to understand his *dhamma.*
Brahmā appears after the doubt has been expressed.	Brahmā appears to Vālmīki after the hunter has seen the death of the Krauñca bird and invented the *śloka.*	Brahmā appears after the doubt has been expressed.
Vyāsa pays homage to Brahmā and brings him a chair.	Vālmīki pays homage to Brahmā and brings him a chair.	Brahmā bows to the Buddha

55 *DN.* 2, 212ff.

Vyāsa describes the contents of the *MBh.* to Brahmā.	Vālmīki unknowingly utters the metrical verse in Brahmā's presence.	To Brahmā, the Buddha declares his doubts about teaching the *dhamma*.
Brahmā urges Vyāsa to teach his poem to his students and predicts that by doing this he will be a lamp to an ignorant world.	Brahmā urges Vālmīki to recite the *Rām*. Using the *śloka* meter.	Brahmā urges the Buddha to teach the *dhamma*, warning that the world will perish if it does not receive the dhamma.
Brahmā departs and Vyāsa teaches the *MBh*.	Brahmā departs and Vālmīki recites the *Rāṃ*. in metrical form.	Brahmā departs after the Buddha has agreed to teach the *dhamma*.

Of the difference between the three versions, the most striking is Brahmā's homage to Buddha in the Buddhist version, whereas in the other two versions it is Brahmā himself who is an object of homage. Yet this is merely a reversal of a motif common to all three versions. This reversal of position is consistent with the status given to gods in early Buddhism. The Buddha never bows or pays homage to a god, whereas the reverse often occurs.

Each of the three tellings of the myth is concerned with dissemination of *dharma* in the triple world and the doubt of the one who bears responsibility for its dissemination. Brahmā puts their doubts to rest by painting a picture of a world without the benefit of this teaching, a picture reminiscent of the pre-creation state described in the epic and Purāṇic cosmogonies. These two conditions–the presence of one who can expound and/or embodies *dharma*, and a world enshrouded in ignorance and disorder–provide the setting for the *avatāra* myth, and the *avatāra* motif provides the best interpretative framework for these myths. This is partly because of the presence of these two conditions, but more so because of the identities and functions of the protagonists. Behind the figure of Vyāsa lies Viṣṇu and behind Vālmīki lies Brahmā. Viewed from this perspective the *MBh.* version concerns the interaction between Vyāsa/Viṣṇu and Brahmā, whereas in the *Rām.* the interaction is between Vālmīki/Brahmā and Rāma/Viṣṇu. Though it is difficult to apply this analysis to the Buddhist version, notwithstanding the fact that the Buddha became Viṣṇu's ninth *avatāra*, there are some reasons for arguing that it too fits the *avatāra* model.

It is well known that in the *MBh.* Vyāsa is an incarnation in the Viṣṇu group, specifically of Nārāyaṇa.[56] His precise role as an *avatāra* is detailed in a passage of the *Śāntiparvan.*[57] Nārāyaṇa says there that when Brahmā was born from his navel, he created beings, but the earth soon became overcrowded with humans and demons who oppressed the sages and gods. Then Nārāyaṇa announced his intention of becoming an *avatāra* to rectify this situation, a step he had taken many times in the past. Brahmā uttered the word *bhoḥ* and a sage named Apāntaratamā appeared. This sage was Vyāsa and Nārāyaṇa ordered him to divide the Vedas in each *manvantara*. He then went into specific details, telling Vyāsa that when the *kṛtayuga* comes, a family called Kuru will be born from him. There will be dissension in the family causing them to destroy one another. The temporal period of this will be the black (*kṛṣṇa* = *kali*) *yuga*, and Vyāsa... himself will be born black.[58] He will divide the Vedas in various ways and will be the

---

56 See Hiltebeitel. 1976, p. 61, for references. He cites *MBh.* 12, 334, 11 and 337, 4c, where Vyāsa is *nārāyaṇāṃśajam*. I have drawn heavily on Hiltebeitel for this treatment of Vyāsa.

57 *MBh.* 12, 337, 5ff.

58 *MBh.* 12,337, 44. Hiltebeitel, 1976, p. 62, connects the symbolism of the black Vyāsa, Kṛṣṇa and Draupadī (the so-called three Kṛṣṇas) with the darkness so characteristic of the *kaliyuga*. This view receives further support from an account of Vyāsa's insemination. When approached by Parāśara in the middle of the Yamunā, Satyavatī protests that they cannot have intercourse because they will be seen by the holy men on the banks. So

creator of knowledge (*jñānakara*) and various rules (*dharmāṇāṃ vividhānām*).[59]

Vyāsa is a sage replete with brāhmaṇical learning, a characteristic heavily stressed by the use of compounds to describe him, such as *vedamahānidhānam*, 'great receptacle of the Vedas', *bhūtabhavyabhaviṣyajnaḥ*, 'knower of the past, present and future', and *satyavādī*, 'speaker of the truth'.[60] All these are characteristic of Brahmā too, but Vyasa differs from that god because he manifests the dynamism of the *avatāra*. This dynamism is certainly meant to be conveyed in the name Apāntaratamā which 'implies one whose darkness or ignorance has been dispelled,' and the epithet *ajñātatamonudāya*, 'he who dispels the darkness of ignorance.'[61] The blackness he dispels symbolizes both the pre-creation state and the ignorance contingent upon the predominance of *adharma*.

It is important to realize here that Brahmā's role is primarily one of mediation between humans and the earth on one side, and Vyāsa/ Viṣṇu on the other side. His support for humans and the Earth is indicated clearly in the reason he gives for visiting Vyāsa, namely the welfare of beings (*lokānāṃ hitakāmyayā*).[62] His mediation here anticipates his mediatory activity in other crucial events recounted in the epic narrative.

The most important of these concerns the fundamental reason for the Bhārata war, the main subject of the *MBh*. Once, when tyrannized by demons, the Earth came to Brahmā for refuge,

---

Parāśara 'created a fog that seemed to cover the whole region with darkness (*tamobhūta*).' (*MBh*. 1, 57, 59 cd. Trans. van Buitenen. 1973, p. 133) Surely a portentous omen for Vyāsa's period of activity on earth.

59 *MBh*. 12, 337, 45.

60 12, 337, 4: 337, 38.

61 12, 337, 3.

62 See *MBh*. 1, App. 1, p. 884, 1.5. The word *loka* can be translated as 'people' or 'world', hence 'Earth'. It may have been used in this context because of its ambiguity, since in the *avatāra* myth the Earth and humans are often on the same side.

complaining that she could no longer bear the weight of beings upon her and grieving about the oppression of demons who had overrun her surface.[63] Brahmā listened carefully to her grievance and immediately ordered all the gods to be reborn on Earth where they would become the five Pāṇḍavas and the various members of their army. Viṣṇu himself would descend to the Earth as Kṛṣṇa. The Kauravas were already on Earth in the shape of the demons who were giving her so much trouble. And so with the descent of the gods and Viṣṇu, the scene is set for the Bhārata war which will lead to the eventual defeat of the Kauravas, who as demons are the visible embodiment of *adharma*. Though perhaps on a lesser scale than this, Brahmā's entreaty to Vyāsa to teach the *MBh*. will have the same effect as the Bharata war–the destruction of *adharma* and the uplifting of *dharma*.

The *Rām*. version of the myth is not as explicit in setting forth Brahmā's mediating role as is the *MBh*. version. Yet in later parts of this same text there is considerable evidence of Brahmā/ Vālmīki mediating between the Earth (= Sītā) and Rāma/Viṣṇu. Earlier I alluded to the threat the demon Rāvaṇa represented to the gods and how Brahmā ordered Viṣṇu and them as a group to be reborn on earth so as to defeat this demon and his rākṣasas.[64] In this situation he mediates between the gods who represent the triple world, and Viṣṇu, the only one who can restore dharmic order in the face of the adharmic Rāvaṇa. As the *Rām*. unfolds it becomes apparent that this adharmic situation is expressed in the abduction of Sītā (= Earth) and her ensuing separation from Rāma (= the king, who should protect her always). This situation still prevails when Rāma repudiates Sītā even after he has rescued her and killed Rāvaṇa. Into this situation Brahmā comes. Rāma had repudiated her for fear that she had co-habited with Rāvaṇa, an act that would dishonour him. Brahmā, however, is one of the strongest to speak in her defence and significantly he does this through a reminder to Rāma that he is really Viṣṇu, whose true role

63 *MBh*. 1, 58, 35-47.

64 See above p.196.

is that of *avatāra*, implying protection of the Earth from adharmic forces.[65] If he mediates so strongly between Rāma and Sītā here it is only because he wants to see the reconciliation between them that signals the return of *dharma* in the triple world. All through Sītā's abduction, Brahmā himself had been protecting (*rakṣā*) her through Nalakūbara's curse.[66]

This whole episode is repeated with slight variations in the seventh book of the *Rām*. After returning to his capital Ayodhyā Rāma became worried by rumours of Sītā having co-habited with Rāvaṇa whilst his captive. He banished her to the forest, where she dwelt in Vālmīki's *āśrama*. Some years later Rāma held a horse sacrifice to which both Vālmīki and Sītā came. Whilst there, various gods and sages tried to effect a reconciliation between Rāma and Sītā, but Rāma would only have her back if she were to take an oath on her purity.[67] Annoyed at this, Vālmīki spoke up in her favour, strongly praising her purity. Immediately after his speech Sītā made the required oath, and finished by asking the earth to open and swallow her up. This happened, causing Rāma great remorse at her loss.

The suggested functional identity between Brahmā and Vālmīki is based on their mediatory activity between Sītā and Rāma/Viṣṇu in virtually identical contexts. It also rests on another functional parallel between the two figures. Just as Brahmā protects Sītā through Nalakūbara's curse whilst she is a captive in Laṅkā, so Vālmīki vows to protect (*paripālyā*) her always, at the time when she is abandoned by Rāma and comes to his *āśrama*.[68] Furthermore, Brahmā and Vālmīki seem to be identified analogically in a *verse* about Sītā: "When Sītā was seen

---

65 *Rām*. (C) 6, 105, 11-28; *MBh*. 2,275, 29-34. A translation of the latter is given above on pp. 199-200.

66 *MBh*. 3, 275, 32.

67 *Rām*. (C) 7, 87, I4-18.

68 *Rām*. (C) 7, 48, 18.

behind Vālmīki, as though she was Śrī following Brahmā, a great acclamation of 'well done' arose."[69]

The third version of the myth, found in Pāli texts, can also be interpreted from the perspective of the *avatāra* motif, even though the doctrinal backdrop of Buddhism is much at variance with what lies behind this motif. It contains the two principal features of the *avatāra* myth and again, Brahmā plays the mediating role. He stands between the Buddha and the totality of beings (= *loka* = the Earth) whom the Buddha believes to be ignorant. In one sense too the Buddha is like the *avatāra*, for just as a portion of Viṣṇu (who remains in *samādhi* beyond the triple world) descends into the triple world, so too does the Buddha leave the repose of *nirvāṇa* and descend to the level of *saṃsāra*, there to teach the *dharma*. However, one cannot stretch the analogy too far. The Buddha is not a god and when he leaves *nirvāṇa* he does not immediately re-enter it and remain inactive after the 'crisis' has ceased which necessitated his entry into *saṃsāra*. He continues to teach for the rest of his life, unlike the *avatāra* who becomes Viṣṇu again soon after *dharma* has been re-established in the triple world.

However, in his capacity as the first creator of the Vedas, he does not create either *MBh.* or the *Rām*, giving that task to Vyāsa and Vālmīki respectively, but encouraging them both. Similar is the case of the *Manusmṛti* (1, 1-3; 1, 58) which was handed to Manu by Brahmā after he had composed it, and from him to various disciples.[70] In commenting on this and other episodes where Brahmā encourages the teaching of dharmic texts Hiltebeitel argues: "The case of the Buddha suggests that Brahmā's authorization would have to do with an implied endorsement of the Buddhist *dharma* by the god of Vedic and Brahmanical orthodoxy."[71] And he goes on to note that "Thus while Brahmā prompts Manu to transmit *dharma* in the form of Brahmā's own poetry, he also prompts

69 *Rām.* (C) 7, 87, 10. On the equation Sītā = Śrī = the Earth, see Dubuisson. 1979, p.485, n.51.

70 See also Hiltebeitel, 2011, pp.208-214.

71 Hiltebeitel, 2011, p.209.

Vālmīki to compose poetry that will be about a paragon of *dharma*, just as he comes to endorse Vyāsa's poetry about *dharma* in the *Mahābhārata*."[72] The suggestion that Brahmā represents Vedic values and leaves *dharmas* (in the plural) to be taught by other figures may be a recognition that Vedic traditions were in a state of transformation and adaptation when the *MBh*, *Rām*. and *Ms*. were being composed, a recognition also being made by the Buddha. At the same time the Vedas, and the *dharma* teachings anchored in them, were also being preserved and so Brahmā emerges as a figure embodying both the old and the new in this regard. As such, to return to Sullivan's comparison between Brahmā and Vyāsa, it might be necessary to nuance this in the sense that once again, as soon as he has engaged in his creative activity he steps back and allows somebody else to be actively engaged in completing the work at the micro-level, as it were. Vyāsa seemingly plays a much more active role in the *MBh*. than does Brahmā, whose actions are often manifested through others.

It is also noteworthy that Brahmā in the seminal *MU*. passage already cited is said to have proclaimed to his eldest son Atharvan "the knowledge of Brahma, the foundation of all knowledge." He in turn transmits it to Aṅgir, he to Bhāradvāja Satyavāha, he to Aṅgiras. Though named *brahmavidyā*, it is defined as containing the lower and the higher, the latter comprising the four Vedas, "phonetics, the ritual science, grammar, etymology, metrics and astronomy,"[73] the other simply called *akṣara*. Surely this anticipates the episodes of knowledge dissemination just discussed above and confirms Brahmā's role as establishing or finding the foundational knowledge, in this particular passage definitely marked as transitional between brahmanical ritual and the knowledge of Brahman. The latter even in this Upaniṣad implicitly critiques the sacrifice. The higher and lower knowledges are both communicated in the *MBh*, but arguably less so in the *Rāṃ* and the *Ms*, and are both critiqued in some Pāli texts.

---

72 Hiltebeitel, 2011, p.210.

73 Trans. by Olivelle, 1998, p.437.

This kind of comparison developed by Sullivan may induce us to conclude that Brahmā is given a different role in the *MBh.* than he has in the *Rām.* and the Purāṇas, though of course there are many continuities within all three. As an example, the creation myths of the Purāṇas have been much more systematized than what is found in the *MBh*, though many of their elements are found in the 12th book of the *MBh.* And in them Brahmā's role becomes substantially enframed within the general model of the *trimūrti*, though he does not receive the kind of devotional adulation associated with Viṣṇu and Śiva.

Do the detailed comparisons undertaken by Sullivan tell us much about Brahmā himself? Arguably they do reinforce how strongly he is connected to *pravṛtti* values in the *MBh*, in particular. But is this primarily because he is the creator of a world the cyclical nature of whose existence is a perfect metaphor of *saṃsāra* itself? Or is it because the brahmin as a ritualist is still locked into these values or perceived as such by the various renunciatory traditions?

Brahmā and Kingship

All the myths so far examined in this chapter have been informed by the relationship between the brahmin and the *kṣatriya*, one explored further in a series of myths where Brahmā creates or establishes kingship, or its metonym–punishment (*daṇḍa*). His concern with the creation of kingship is another facet of his identity with and support of *dharma* in the triple world. In these myths both Viṣṇu and Śiva are present, playing roles characteristic of their position in the *trimūrti*. Viṣṇu himself embodies many characteristics of the king because of the crucial part the king has in the maintenance of *dharma* in the triple world, a quality connecting him closely with the *avatāra*. The king is supposed to embody *dharma* and constantly to cause his adherents to act consistently with it.[74]

Brahmā typically creates kingship in response to a situation

74 See *MBh.* 12, 92, 8. Cf, above p.174.

of disintegration of values and behaviour similar to what occurs in the Earth-milker myth and some versions of the Pṛthu myth. An example from the *MBh.* begins with a description of the kingless society, a society without order whose central stabilizing factor–*dharma*–is no longer the criterion of behaviour.[75] When complete social disintegration had occurred, a group of people joined together, resolved to change the situation:

> So some who were very unhappy went together to the Grandfather and said, "Without lords we will perish. Divine god, assign to us a lord. Together we will honour him and he should thoroughly protect (*paripālayet*) us." He appointed Manu for them, but Manu did not acknowledge them…[76]

Manu consented to become king only after the people had agreed to supply him with corn and grain sufficient for his livelihood.

Another series of myths where Brahmā establishes kingship goes far beyond this one in its inclusion of the other two gods of the *trimūrti* and its complexity of motifs. One version narrates the creation of 'punishment' (*daṇḍa*), but since the concept of punishment in ancient India was synonymous with the figure of the king, what it says is applicable to the creation of the latter.[77] The telling of this myth occurs at the conclusion of Bhīṣma's instruction to Yudhiṣṭhira in the art of kingship:

---

75 *MBh.* 12, 67, 1 ff. This passage has been the subject of considerable scholarly attention. For other studies see Kane, *HDS*, 3. p. 34 ff; Ghoshal, 1959, pp. 201 ff.

76 *MBh.* 12, 67, 20-1. Cf. 1, 27, 18; 1, 204, 24; *MP.* 226, 1; *H.* 4, 1-16; *ViP.* 1, 22, 1-9.

77 The *MBh.* 12, 15, 1-3, gives the following definition of punishment: "Punishment (*daṇḍa*) governs all people, and punishment certainly protects. Punishment watches over those who are asleep. The wise know punishment is *dharma*. Punishment protects *dharma* as well as *artha*. Overlord of men, and punishment protects *kāma*. Punishment is said to be the *trivarga*." See also Spellman, 1963, pp.107ff. All such characteristics could be predicated on the king. See *MBh.* 12, 137, 95: '*rājā mūlaṃ trivargasya...*'

Learn, king, how the rod of force arose as the protection of the world, for the sake of guarding and disciplining creatures–it is the everlasting essence of Law. We were taught that Brahmā, the blessed Grandfather of the World, desired to perform a rite of sacrificial worship, and saw no priest who was his equal. The God then carried a fetus in his head for many many years, and after a full thousand years had gone by, that fetus popped out when the God sneezed. Thus, O tamer of enemies, the Progenitor (*prajāpati*) Kṣupa came to be, and he was then the priest at that exalted one's rite of worship. When Brahmā's solemn rite had begun, O bull among the princes of the earth, the rod of force disappeared because Brahmā was present there in a happy form. After the rod of force disappeared, people became mixed up–people did not know what they should do and what not, what they should eat and what not, what they should drink and what not, nor did they know how to assure the realization of their efforts. They did not whom they could go with and whom not, and one's own property and another's were the same. Lawlessness (*nimaryādam*) prevailed, and they harmed one another: They tore at each other like dogs fighting over a piece of meat, the strong killing the weak.

Then the Grandfather paid his respects to the everlasting blessed Viṣṇu and said to the Great God, the God who grants wishes, "You absolutely have to relieve the virtuous here. You must devise a way for there to be no confusion here." Then the Blessed One, wearing his hair in coiled braids and holding a lance meditated for a long time. Eventually that most excellent of the gods himself created his own self as the rod of force. And from that rod he created the Policy of doing Lawful Deeds, namely the Goddess Sarasvatī. She is famous in the three worlds as the Policy for the Application of Force.... [The narrative continues with Viṣṇu appointing kings over various classes of living beings and physical phenomena] ...But the lord of all the Rudras who assumes every body, who is the king of kings and the overlord of riches, is taught in Holy Learning to be "He who holds the lance." He gave that one son, the later-born Kṣupa, to Brahmā, to be the overlord of creatures and the most excellent of those that support all Laws. The Great Lord then, when this rite of sacrificial worship had begun in accordance with the prescriptions, gave the well-honoured rod of force, the protector of Law to Viṣṇu;…"[78]

Viṣṇu handed it on to Aṅgiras, who handed it down a line of sages and divine figures (including Kṣupa again) until it reached Manu, who passed it to his son.

This passage presents some problems. What is Kṣupa's precise role, for he appears at several different places in the myth? Is it Śiva, Viṣṇu or Brahmā who created the *daṇḍa*? The first question will be answered later after two more versions of the myth have been examined. As for the second, Hopkins thought it was Viṣṇu who created the *daṇḍa*, as Roy did too, but he saw a difficulty.[79] In a note to his translation of this passage he wrote, "Though *Sula* [sic] is mentioned, yet it is Vishnu and *not* Mahadeva, that is implied. Generally, the word means any weapon."[80] Yet the text itself leaves little doubt that it is really Śiva who created the *daṇḍa*, as the god attributed with its creation has braided hair. This is the sure sign of an ascetic, a favourite guise of Śiva. In addition, the god who gave the *daṇḍa* to Kṣupa is lord of the *rudras*. This can only be Śiva.

Brahmā is sometimes explicitly identified with *daṇḍa*, though in this myth the identification is implicit.[81] Prior to performance of the sacrifice he was unable to locate a suitable priest. At this time he may have been in an angry mood (though this is not made clear), a mood symbolic of *daṇḍa* which 'angrily' and vigilantly maintains order in society and punishes the transgressors of *dharma*. As soon

---

78 *MBh*. 12, 122, 14-25, 34-36ab. Trans. Fitzgerald, 2004, pp.476-478.

79 It was surely an overstatement for Hopkins, 1974, p. 198, to say about this myth that "a contest of cults results in an inextricable confusion of texts." As other versions of the myth show, it is rather an instance of Brahmā, Viṣṇu and Śiva acting out roles characteristic of them in Hindu mythology.

80 Roy, Nd. Vol.8, p.266, n.2.

81 See *MBh*. 12, 122, 50, where the *daṇḍa* is described as *pitāmahasamaḥ*.

as Brahmā's mood becomes one of happiness (*hṛṣṭarūpa*), his vigilance over the triple world relaxes with attendant catastrophic effects, depicted in the familiar imagery of the pre-creation situation (showing many parallels with the kingless state). The change of mood manifested here and its resultant effect are paralleled in another myth where Brahmā creates Death.[82] There, when he was angry, the entire world was in danger of being burnt, but as soon as he became happy the fire ceased and all returned to normal. The two myths reverse a single motif. Happiness in one case leads to cessation of destruction, whereas in the other case it leads to social destruction. There is also a reversal of Śiva's role in the two myths. His favourable side is shown in the myth of the creation of Death where he assumes the role of a *bhakti* god and intercedes on behalf of created beings, asking Brahmā (= the creator of Death) that they be spared mortality. When he emits the *daṇḍa*, really his own self (*ātman*), his destructive side is shown, though it is destruction for the benefit of the universe, just as Brahmā's creation of Death is for the ultimate good of the universe, restating the distinction between man and god, mortal and immortal.

Another version of the myth replaces *daṇḍa* with the sword, but functionally the two are the same.[83] This version is prefaced by a cosmogonic myth.[84] Brahmā created the triple world with all its inhabitants and then he created *dharma*, adhered to by all but the dānavas:

> But the lords of the Dānavas transgressed the Grandfather's commands; full of anger and greed, they caused a diminution of Law. Hiraṇyakaśipu, Hiraṇyākṣa, Virocana, Śambara, Vipracitti, Prahlāda, Namuci, and Bali. These and many other

---

82 See *MBh*. 12, 248, 13-249, 4. A partial translation is given below on pp. 309ff. The use of the capital for Death indicates the personification of the concept.

83 The sword (*asi*) and the sabre (*viśasana*) are included in a list of *daṇḍa's* synonyms. See *MBh*. 12, 121, 19.

84 *MBh*. 12, 160, 11-21. See above p.139.

> Daityas and Dānavas and their followers transgressed the bounds of Law and enjoyed themselves, committed to doing wrong. 'We are all the same kind of beings they are; as are the Gods, so are we,' they thought. Relying upon these ideas, they vied with the Gods.
>
> They showed no favor nor any compassion to beings, Bhārata. …So at this time the seers of the *brahman* approached the blessed Brahmā on a lovely peak in the Snowy Mountains– there were stars there by the trillions! Son, to bring this matter to completion for the sake of the inhabited realms, Brahmā, the most excellent of the Gods, stayed there on that best of mountain peaks that stretched for a hundred *yojanas*–… Then at the end of a thousand years, the master performed a sacrificial rite… "I have heard that a most terrifying thing happened to these seers at this rite. Something arose from the sacrificial fire, scattering its flames and sparks all about the way the moon in the clear sky night is shivered into the host of stars. Long, pinched at the abdomen, it had sharp teeth and was the colour of a blue lotus; it was very hard to look at, it was so extremely bright.
>
> Having looked at the thing that had arisen with such great disturbance, the Grandfather said this to the great seer, Gods and Gandharvas: 'This mighty thing is called a "sword," and I conceived it in my mind to protect the world and slay the enemies of the Gods.'…Brahmā then gave the blazing sword that would oppose Wrongdoing to Śitikaṇṭha Rudra, whose banner shows the bull."[85]

Rudra quickly despatched the dānavas and then handed the sword to Viṣṇu. From him it was passed along a chain until it reached Manu, lord of humans, who was instructed "to protect creatures with this sword which is redolent of *dharma*."[86] Manu gave the sword to Kṣupa, here called 'overlord of creatures,' who used it and then gave it to Ikṣvāku; finally it came to the Paṇḍavas.

The sword is produced as a result of Brahmā's sacrifice and is wielded by Śiva, who, in his destructive role destroys the *dānavas*

---

85 *MBh.* 12, 160, 26-30ab, 31-33ab, 36cd-38, 41-42, 44. Trans. Fitzgerald, 2004, pp.583-584.

86 *MBh.* 12, 160, 67.

and re-establishes *dharma*. Again, the *avatāra* motif is present even though Viṣṇu 's presence is only as a link in the chain down which the sword is passed. However, it is appropriate that the sword is first given to Śiva rather than to Viṣṇu, the one usually associated with kingship. Śiva appears here like the destroyer he is at the time of the *pralaya*. The *bhūta* itself is described with imagery suggestive of the *pralaya*:

> ... When it rose up the earth shook; the vast ocean was all astir with whirlpools and criss-crossed with waves. Shooting stars fell, there were tremendous prodigies, every quarter of the sky was troubled, an ill wind howled;...
>
> The sword then shed that form and shone, gleaming and sharp-bladed, looking like death-dealing Time poised for action.[87]

When all the dānavas have been killed and the earth is slimy with blood, Rudra abandons his terrifying (*raudra*) form and takes on his auspicious (*śiva*) form. If Śiva's role is active in both versions of the myth, then Viṣṇu's role is passive. This activity and passivity reflects their complementary roles; preservation and reconstruction for Viṣṇu, violence and destruction for Śiva, so well portrayed in the Purāṇas.[88]

In the myth of the sword's creation, Śiva assumes his

---

87 *MBh*. 12, 160, 38-40cd, 43. Trans. Fitzgerald, 2004, p. 584. The descriptions of the *daṇḍa* (See *MBh*. 12, 15) and the sword found in various parts of the *MBh*. have many similarities with each other, and with the *brahmahatyā* (12, 273, 10-12) and Death. All four are instruments of punishment used against those who commit crimes against society or who violate/abuse their position in the symbiotic relationship which structures the triple world. Symbolism drawn from the *pralaya* is present in each description, perhaps indicating what will happen if their influence is not available for the protection of society and the triple world. This symbolism combined with their horrific nature suggests the stability of the three-tiered world, constituting the realm of *pravṛtti* values, was a very fragile one indeed.

88 Hiltebeitel, 1976, Ch.4., has shown how the complementary roles of these two gods, explicit in *the* Purāṇas, are implicit in many

destructive form for the killing of demons so as to purge the earth of adharmic elements. Once this has been done the task of reconstruction can be begun. Viṣṇu is responsible for this in both versions of the myth. Firstly, both the sword and the *daṇḍa* are passed to Viṣṇu after Śiva has made use of them. Viṣṇu symbolizes the reconstruction (and stability) which will follow Śiva's destruction, so it is appropriate for Śiva to pass it to him. Secondly, after Śiva has emitted the *daṇḍa*, Viṣṇu appoints kings for various groups of living beings, an act designed to ensure the preservation of *dharma*.

This version of the myth also clarifies Kṣupa's role. He is Manu's son and accordingly is virtually a mirror image of his father. Just as Manu is a lord of humans (*mānuṣāṇāṃ ...īśvaraḥ*), so Kṣupa is overlord of creatures (*adhipaṃ prajānām*). This parallels the first version of the myth where Kṣupa is described as "the overlord of those creatures and the most excellent of those that support all Laws."[89] Significantly, in the version under discussion he is also Brahmā's younger (*anujāta*) son. Like Manu, his father, he is a king and this explains why he receives the *daṇḍa* and the sword.

Further clarification regarding Kṣupa comes from a myth about the origin of kingship, narrated to Indra by Agastya, found in a late passage of the *Rām*:

> Rāma, formerly in that *yuga* called the *kṛta* which was centred on the Vedas, there were no kings for all creatures, except for Śatakratu for the gods. These creatures rushed up to the Lord of the god of gods in order to obtain a king. They said, "God, you established Śatakratu as king of the gods. Lord of the worlds, send us a king who is a bull of a man. We whose evil acts are shaken off will go together and give him our respect." Then Brahmā, best of the gods, called together the World Protectors and the *vasus* and said to them all, "Offer portions of your fiery energy!" So then the four World Protectors gave parts of their

---

passages of the *MBh*. When Śiva is active (= destructive) Viṣṇu is usually absent or passive and vice versa.

89 *MBh*. 12, 122, 35cd. Trans. Fitzgerald, 2004, p.477.

fiery energy, whereupon Brahmā was startled, and from that a king named Kṣupa was born. Brahmā joined him together with equal parts from the World Protectors. And so, to these creatures he gave a lord, a king named Kṣupa.

Then, with Indra's portion the king commanded the earth; with Varuṇa's portion the king nourished the body (*vapuḥ*). With Kubera's portion he then gave wealth to them and that portion of Yama was the one by which he commands creatures.[90]

Here Kṣupa is definitely Brahmā's son and a king. In the second version of the myth two fathers–Brahmā and Manu–are attributed to him, but this is explicable when it is realized Manu is a multiform of Brahmā.[91] Ksupa's claim to be king is apparent in all versions of the myth, though it is not certain whether he is meant to be the first king in creation (like Pṛthu) or a prototype of the king. In addition to the instances just cited, the *MkP*. knows of a Kṣupa, son of Brahmā, who is a king, but the context where he appears bears no relation to the myth under discussion.[92]

Each version of the myth has an aetiological function regarding the particular instrument created for use by the king. Each also gives the distinct impression that in general terms the figure of the king is very much a reflection of Brahmā (= the brahmin) himself. Kṣupa is Brahmā's son and already I have alluded to the widely held Indian view of conception, according to which the father is reborn again in his son.[93] This does not mean Brahmā and the king are identical, rather that the brahmin is the source

90 *Rām*. (C) 7, App. 1. No. 12, lines 8-24.

91 This conclusion is evident from the many similarities which exist between the two figures. Manu, the *prajāpati* par excellence, is often portrayed as a creator (e.g. *MBh*. 3, 185, 49) and is connected in a positive way with the Vedas and *dharma*. The name Manu occurs at least once as an epithet of Brahmā (*MBh*. 1, 1, 30).

92 *MkP*. 119, 4.

93 See above p.95.

of the *kṣatriya*, a view countenanced in the literature from the Brāhmaṇas onwards.[94]

In addition, the necessity for the *kṣatriya* and the brahmin to embody *dharma* accounts for many of the similarities between Brahmā and the king.[95] A whole series of epithets used of Brahmā which imply protection underlie this similarity, protection of society and *dharma* being paramount functions of the king. Most of these epithets are compounds whose final member is *pati*. The following are attested: *pati*, *jagatpati*, *prajāpatipati*, *bhūtapati*, *bhūmipati*, *lokapati*, *lokādhipati* and *sarvajagatpati*.[96] None of these are used of Brahmā in any specific context, so they might be called generic names of the god.[97] The word *pati* should not be rendered as 'father'. A more precise rendering would be 'lord', 'husband' or even 'owner'. However it does have a connection with fatherhood because of its derivation from *pā*, 'to protect'. The husband (*pati*) was required to protect his wife and children, just as the king as husband of Earth was required to protect her, his wife. *Pati* represents the protective aspect of fatherhood whereas *pitṛ* represents the progenative aspect.[98]

---

94 *BhU*. 1, 4, 11 (*kṣatrasya yonir yad brahma*). *MBh*. 12, 74, 11. Cf. *PB*. 1, 3, 9; 3, 9, 2; 11, 11, 9.

95 There are a few passages in the texts where Brahmā (Prajāpati) is even called king. See *MBh*. 6, 13, 24-31; 13,138, 19vr. '*rājā*; *BḍP*. 1, 19, 141; 146.

96 See respectively *MkP*. 46, 12; 47, 1; *KP*. 1, 2, 10; *MBh*. 1, 32, 20; 58, 43; 9, 44, 43, *ViP*. 1, 22, 10; *MBh*. 2, 3, 12; 1, 64, 45; 2, 3, 14; *Rām*. (V) 6, 61, 23; *MBh*.1, 89, 17; *Ram*. (C) 3, 49, 27; *SN*. 1,181; *MBh*. 13, 84, 7. He is also called *pātā* at *ŚP*. 1, 6, 6; *prajāpāla* at *MkP*. 50, 13.

97 The epithets ending in *pati* have the same function as two other groups of epithets used of him which include the words *pitāmaha* and *guru*. All are generic names of Brahmā.

98 See Burrow, 1949, p. 50, who says about the derivation of *pati*, ... "A derivation of the root *pā*–which combines the meanings of 'to protect' and 'to govern'–is in accordance with the *pater familias* in IE patriarchal society. It is clear from the usage of

Brahmā's 'protection' of the triple world as implied in these epithets is a function of his fatherhood of the totality of living beings who comprise the population of this world. Karve's summary of the position of the father in the Indian extended family is equally applicable to Brahmā:

> Thus one who succeeded to the office of the head of the family also held all the property though it was held in order to enjoy it in common with all agnatic relations. The head of this family was the father of the family who had absolute power over all members of his family. We have thus the joint family with the joint property, the succession and inheritance from father to eldest son and the absolute rule of the father.[99]

Just as the head of the family was required to ensure the sharing of the common property, so too does Brahmā. Through balancing the diverse interests of his family, which like the extended family is organized on the basis of a hierarchical set of relationships where interests and roles often clash, he ensures the triple world and everything in it is utilized in common by all his descendants in accordance with their rightful status.

It is this knowledge, that in large part Brahmā's 'protective' role is a reflection of his paternality, which throws the most light on the functional convergences he has with the king. The king himself is often compared with the father as though the latter were in some way a model of the former. He is often enjoined to treat his subjects as a father treats his children.[100] As a father,

---

the classical IE. languages that it is this function, rather than that of progenitor, which the word primarily designates." We cannot, however, be certain whether such a strict distinction was maintained in the *MBh.*

99 Karve, 1944-45, p.125.

100 See *MBh.* 12, 137, 99-100; 4. App. 1, no. 16, line 13; *MkP.* 117, 5; *ViP.* 1, 13, 16; *BḍP.* 1, 36, 155. See also Kane, *HDS.* 3, pp. 62-3. A similar view prevails in the Pāli Canon. According to Gokhale, 1966, p. 21, 'The concept of a political society is that of a great family presided over by a morally elevated king with a father image.'

the king must prevent and eradicate harmful practices detrimental to the hierarchical ordering of society. Of particular importance is prevention of the intermixture of *varṇas*, for this will result in destruction of society and the symbiotic interdependence effectively regulating the behaviour of beings in the triple world.

The importance of the king as maintainer of order extends to the triple world in its totality. This idea underlies these lines taken from one version of the Pṛthu myth:

> The trees, mountains, gods, demons, snakes, the seven sages, as well as the honest people, gandharvas, apsaras, fathers and the oblations, came to him [Pṛthu] comfortably seated, and said, "You are a universal ruler, a *kṣatriya*, and our king, protector and father. As you are the powerful lord, give us our most valued desires, great king." [101]

In maintaining separation of the *varṇas* and ensuring each one acts consistently with its *svadharma*, the king directly upholds the symbiotic relationship in which the groups of people mentioned in this passage take part. As such he stands in the centre as controller and mediator.

The mediatory position of the king is not without parallel in the position of the brahmin priest. As an officiant in the *śrauta* sacrifice the brahmin in his capacity as performer of the sacrifice and embodiment of a specific god, mediated between humans and the gods in general. His position in the maintenance of the symbiotic relationship ranked in importance with the king's, for without the brahmin the linchpin of this relationship, namely, the sacrifice, was not operative. Even when the *śrauta* sacrifice fell into disuse and household sacrifice became the norm the brahmin as sacrificer in the household ritual retained his central position in the relationship. This very idea is expressed in the many passages which tell of the householder nourishing the universe and being

---

101 *MBh.* 7, App. 1, No. 8, lines 781-85. Cf. *Gaṇeśopapurāṇa*. 1, 2, 9. See also *MBh.* 6, 13, 24-31; *Bd.P.* 1, 1, 19, 140-7, where similar things are said about Brahmā as king of Puṣkaradvīpa.

approached by all the different groups of beings at the time of the ritual.[102]

It is this parallelism in the status and function of king and Brahmā that is implicit in the three versions of the myth under discussion. The same parallelism is also present in the figures of Brahmā and Viṣṇu and underlies their relationship in this and the *avatāra* myth. The inclusion of Śiva in the series of myths gives them a cosmogonic perspective, introducing the motif of destruction. This became a central feature of the Purāṇic cosmogony and an important element in the Indian vision of the kingless state.

Brahmā as Mediator

As mediator between gods and men, demons and gods, god and god, Brahmā himself sometimes takes on the role of *avatāra*, not in the sense of descending from a place beyond the triple world, but in action taken to uphold *dharma*. He performs this role in order to maintain the delicate balance which exists between the various forces in the triple world, forces such as the collectives of gods and demons who have conflicting and often antagonistic interests. This balance is not upset merely by the opposing forces standing for *dharma* and *adharma*; it can also be upset or severely threatened by quarrelling gods. Although the gods generally support the continuity of an order guaranteeing them the highest status in the triple world, the powers they possess render them potentially destructive. Sometimes when they quarrel amongst themselves such powers are unleashed.

Naturally the most powerful gods are potentially the most dangerous. This usually means Viṣṇu and Śiva, and on occasion they do quarrel, necessitating Brahmā's intervention. The most frequently depicted quarrel is the one found in some versions of the myth of the destruction of Dakṣa's sacrifice.[103] In the *MBh.*

102 See above p. 72, n. 26 for references.

103 *MBh.* 12, 330, 42-63; *H.* App. 1, No. 37, lines 1-28; *KP.* 1, 14, 64-9; *ŚP.* 2, 5, 41, 21-7. My intention here is not to give a full

version Viṣṇu attacked Śiva after he had been hit by the latter's arrow, the same arrow used to destroy Dakṣa's sacrifice. Arjuna asked Kṛṣṇa who won the battle that subsequently occurred between the two gods and in reply Kṛṣṇa narrated the entire story:

> Whilst these two, Rudra and Nārāyaṇa, were fighting each other hand to hand, all these worlds instantly became completely terrified. The fire did not receive the shining, well-offered oblation in sacrifices, nor did the Vedas appear to the most spiritually cultivated sages. Then, darkness and passion together took possession of the gods, the earth trembled and clouds split asunder. The fiery energies lost their lustre, Brahmā too was shaken from his seat, the ocean became dry and Himavat was shattered.
>
> After this portent had occurred, scion of Pāṇḍu, Brahmā, surrounded by groups of gods and noble souled sages, went quickly to that spot where the battle took place. After he had performed homage with his hands, the four-faced god, an expert in word derivation, made a speech to Rudra, "Lord of all, desiring what is good for the worlds, cast down your weapons so that there will be peace (*śivam*) for the world. Because, they do not consider that one who is imperishable, unmanifest, the Lord, producer of the world, standing at the top, independent of acting, to be also one who does not act (*akartā*). This is only his beneficent (*śiva*) form existing in a state of individuality.
>
> The two best gods, Nara and Nārāyaṇa, who were born as descendents of Dharma, have taken great vows and possess great *tapas*. I was born from his favour for some special reason, and you, the eternal, were born from his anger at the time of his first creation. Together with me, the gods and the great sages, let us appease the giver of boons, so there can be peace for the worlds immediately, young man."
>
> Spoken to in this way by Brahmā, Rudra abandoned his fiery anger and appeased the powerful god Nārāyaṇa. Then he went

---

analysis of this myth, but only to discuss Brahmā's position as mediator between Viṣṇu and Śiva. An analysis of the myth in its entirety is given by O'Flaherty, 1973, pp. 283-6, and for the Purāṇic versions see Mertens, 1988.

> seeking the excellent boon-giving god, Hari, for refuge. Just then, the boon-giving god, his anger subdued and his passions conquered, became pleased and met then with Rudra.[104]

As in the other myths discussed already, familiar imagery illustrates the collapse of order in the triple world. Gods and men are unable to help each other because the sacrifice is no longer operative. The Vedas are not accessible to the sages, so the main source of *dharma* has actually disappeared. Even the status of the gods is affected. Instead of being characterized by goodness (*sattva*) as they usually are, they become possessed by darkness (*tamas*) and impetuosity (*rajas*), generally held to be the principal characteristics of humans.[105] The final blow occurs when Brahmā, who embodies the values of the orthoprax society and the presence of *dharma* in the triple world, is shaken from his seat. Such is the extent of the catastrophe that in the *H.* version, the earth fears that the final dissolution has arrived.[106] By convincing Śiva that Viṣṇu is the highest god of the three of them, Brahmā successfully mediates between the two, thus allowing the worlds to return to their normal condition. As such Brahmā, like the *avatāra*, re-establishes *dharma* when it is in a state of decline.

One of the worst calamities that can befall the triple world is cessation of the sacrifice, the linchpin of the symbiotic relationship between beings in the triple world. A series of myths involves the withdrawal of Agni (= fire) from the world which illustrates the parlous state into which the triple world descends without the sacrifice. Brahmā takes on the *avatāra* role in these myths when he persuades Agni to restore his flame, allowing sacrifices to be performed again.

Many versions of this myth are available, some already

---

104 *MBh.* 12, 330, 52-62.

105 Cf. *KP.* 1, 7, 1-10; where the correspondences between the different groups of living beings–animals, men, gods, and others–and the *guṇas*, are given.

106 *H.* App. 1, No. 37, line 11.

cited.[107] One version contains different details from these but identical underlying motifs. After the marriage of Śiva and Umā the assembly of gods ask Śiva not to impregnate his wife through fear that the resulting foetus will be so full of *tapas* as to burn up the earth.[108] Śiva agrees to this request and retains his semen, but Umā, frustrated at losing her child, curses the gods with impotency. After some time the gods are assailed and scorched by a demon named Tāraka, who plunders their chariots, cities, *āśramas* and homes. In despair they run to Brahmā for refuge and he agrees to help them in fear the Vedas and *dharma* could go to ruin. The gods then tell Brahmā of their impotency, complaining that the conditions of Tāraka's boon mean he can be killed only by a human. In their condition how can they beget a child? Brahmā then explains to them that since Agni was not present during pronouncement of the curse, he is not impotent and can beget a child. Furthermore, Agni has acquired a portion of Śiva's *tejas* and if he throws this into the Ganges a son will be born. However, for some reason Agni has disappeared, so Brahmā urges the gods to find and exhort him to impregnate the Ganges with Śiva's *tejas*. After a long search they find him and he consents to their demands. Eventually Kārttikeya is born from the seed and Tāraka is killed.

Here the gods are beset by two calamities. A severe curse has been placed upon them and they are harassed by an arch enemy. Both problems represent a threat to the ordered universe; the gods are unable to reproduce themselves and the established order of the triple world, figuratively expressed as the *āśramas* and cities of the gods and sages, is being overthrown. The solution to the gods' problems again lies with Agni. This time he has escaped from the curse (previous to its utterance) by hiding in the water, unable to bear the weight of Śiva's *tejas*.[109] Like the

---

107 See above pp.104-06.

108 This is a summary of *MBh*. 13, 83, 43-84, 73. It also occurs in the *Kathāsaritsāgara*. See Penzer, 1968, Vol. 2, pp.100-103.

109 It is probable a deliberate opposition is being suggested here between fire produced by the sacrifice and fire produced by *tapas*.

other gods he fears being burnt by it, but unlike them–who ask Śiva to restrain it–he hides in the only substance able to counter fire, namely, water. His escape from Umā's curse is a reversal of a motif, for in another version of the myth (cited in an earlier chapter) he disappeared precisely when cursed by Bhṛgu. This is accompanied by yet another reversal. In this version of the myth Brahmā advises the gods as a group to find Agni, whereas in the other version he told Agni to return to the gods. Despite these changes in the narrative form, and inclusion of the motif of the demon ascetic, the underlying intention is the same; to stress the extent to which order in the triple world is dependent upon sacrifice. In the version being discussed, the threat to *dharma* is expressed in two ways. Firstly, through the explicit threat made by the appearance of the adharmic Tāraka, and secondly, implicitly, through the disappearance of Agni.

Still another version of this myth is embedded in the narrative of Agni's burning of the Khāṇḍhava forest.[110] The motive for the burning occurs in a passage found only in the northern manuscripts of the *MBh*, and this has prompted the editors of the Critical Edition to relegate the passage to an appendix.[111] Yet for the purpose of tracing the outline of the Agni myth within the context of the main narrative it is necessary to utilize the appendix along with the critically constituted text.

Here is a summary of the myth:

Agni is the sacrifice and Śiva is an ascetic, a condition stressed here by that god's willingness to retain his semen. The opposition goes further. The ascetic Śiva cannot produce a foetus. It can be produced only by the sacrifice, long regarded in ancient India as a source of fertility, human and otherwise. At a deeper level an opposition between *pravṛtti* (= the sacrifice) and *nivṛtti* (= *tapas*) suggests itself.

110 *MBh*. 1, 214-25. Trans. van Buitenen. 1973, pp.413-31.

111 *MBh*. I, App. No. 118, pp.966-69. Hiltebeitel. 1976, pp. 208-24, has made a study of this myth in which he asks whether the entire narrative makes sense without the appendix.

A king named Śvetaki sacrificed incessantly, causing his brahmin officials to become sick of performing the rituals for him. After practising severe austerities he sought a boon from Śiva, who promised to provide help in conducting the sacrifice if Śvetaki would first pour clarified butter into a fire for twelve years without stopping. Śvetaki succeeds in this test, but with the result that Agni (fire) is adversely affected. Satiated by the butter, he begins to feel depressed because he believes his *tejas* to be in a state of decline.[112] He goes to see Brahmā to complain about his condition, at the same time requesting the god's favour (*prasāda*) to allow him to return to his original condition. Brahmā tells him his malady results from Śvetaki's excessive sacrificial activity. Only by burning down the Khaṇḍava forest can he return to his original condition. Agni is also told that in the past he had reduced this forest to ashes because it had contained the gods' enemies. Subsequently, he makes some vain attempts to burn it down, only to be thwarted continually by the animals who reside there dousing his flames with water.

He returns disgruntled to Brahmā who advises him to seek the aid of Nara and Nārāyaṇa, both of whom exist on the Earth as Arjuna and Kṛṣṇa respectively. Then Agni, disguised as a brahmin, approaches them and explains his problem. He cannot burn the forest because Indra, who is friendly with a snake Takṣaka, a resident of the forest, continually douses his flames with rain. At Agni's request Arjuna and Kṛṣṇa agree to stop Indra with their weapons and to kill any animals who attempt to flee from the conflagration. Agni begins to burn the forest and the gods run to Indra for refuge, afraid the *pralaya* has set in. He attempts to douse the fire but his rain evaporates in the heat and he is driven off by Arjuna's arrows. More and more Arjuna and Kṛṣṇa dominate the action. The gods attempt to fight them but are beaten back. The two continue killing until the resultant destruction does indeed become reminiscent of the *pralaya*. Eventually the gods are assured that everything which is happening has been previously ordained, hence there is no cause for alarm. Contented, they return to their homes

---

112 *MBh*. 1, App. No. 118, line 93.

tejasā viprahīnaś ca glāniś cainaṃ samāviśat /

> and Agni continues burning until the entire forest is destroyed. At this point he is in a blissful state. This signals a return to his normal condition. The only ones to escape the fire are two snakes, Takṣaka and Aśvasena, Maya an asura, and the four Śārṅgaka birds.

All the main elements of other versions are present here considerably disguised. Agni cannot function properly because he has been abused. The agreement (cemented by *tapas*) between Śvetaki and Śiva, which puts them in opposition to Agni, corresponds to the opposition between Śiva and Agni in the version of the myth discussed previously. There the opposition was expressed in terms of chastity versus fertility, whereas here it is *kṣatriya* against brahmin. This and the brahmins' refusal to work for Śvetaki indicates that *dharma* is on the decline. The action proposed for Agni by Brahmā will allow the god to return to his normal condition, signifying the return of *dharma* as the prevalent norm in the triple world.

In his first attempt to burn the forest Agni is repulsed when animals throw water on him. This dousing by water renders his flame useless and further stresses the disappearance of his flame from the sacrifice. It corresponds to his flight to the ocean and consequent extinguishing of his flame, found in other versions of the myth.[113] Equally, in some other versions animals betray his presence to the gods because they are unable to bear his heat, just as here they douse him because of that heat. When he is finally successful, almost all the inhabitants of the forest are destroyed–including the adharmic rākṣasas, dānavas and nāgas, who are killed by Kṛṣṇa.[114] Clearly, those beings who are explicitly *adharma* must be killed before *dharma* can in any way be restored. Although the gods are at first angered by the burning, their anger changes to relief after they have been told by Brahmā that all this was previously ordained. This implies the burning of the forest is consistent with the ultimate good of the triple world, namely,

---

113 See O'Flaherty, 1973, pp.100-4 for various examples.

114 *MBh.* 1, 219, 30.

a return to *dharma*. When the entire forest has been consumed Agni becomes normal again, signifying the reestablishment of *dharma*. Another interpretation of the forest burning myth has been suggested, one emphasizing its cosmogonic significance.

Following Biardeau, Hiltebeitel says:

> ... Agni's plight is the result of a sacrifice gone wrong and instigated by Śiva, who aids king Śvetaki in his egotistical and anti-dharmic project by pushing him to an excessive sacrifice. Śiva's connection with Agni, the sacrificial fire gone awry, is thus analogous to his own role as Destroyer in the *pralaya*, where he takes on the character of the fire that exceeds its limit and burns the three worlds. Against this background a full symbolism emerges. Agni's sickness signifies the pitiful state of *dharma* and the brahmana, and the need for 'une restauration du bon ordre socio-cosmique'. Śiva's intervention indicates that the restoration can take place only through a disaster. Kṛṣṇa, with Arjuna here, thus fulfills his role as *avatāra*: restoring *dharma* and renewing the world order. Moreover, Biardeau offers an intriguing explanation of the significance of the identities of the survivors: Takṣaka, the 'Façonneur', is a 'figure du demiurge', Aśvasena (Army of Horses) is a 'nom qui semblerait designer le fonction royale'; Maya, who will soon build the Pāṇḍavas an illusion-producing palace, 'fait voir en lui la Maya' which permits the empirical world to be recreated and to subsist; and surprisingly most crucial, the four Śārṅgaka birds represent the four Vedas ... Thus the escapees, as a group, seem to symbolize the ingredients indispensable, after the *pralaya* for a new Creation.[115]

This interpretation, and it is not the only possible one, is consistent with my own. At least three important motifs are operative in the myth; that of the *avatāra*, the *pralaya* and the disappearance of Agni's flame. Only the former two are emphasized in Hiltebeitel's interpretation, but all are linked in their connection with the decline of *dharma* in the triple world. Agni, of course, does not withdraw his flame. On the contrary, it has become more powerful, even voracious. Nevertheless, the

---

115 Hiltebeitel, 1976, pp.218-19.

point remains: whether his flame is non-existent (under water) or too powerful (excess sacrificing), the effect on the triple world is the same, notably, a diminution of *dharma*.

In this final version of the myth Viṣṇu (= Kṛṣṇa) is the *avatāra* and Brahmā acts as passive adviser to Agni. Also, by explaining the purpose of the burning, he mediates between Agni and the gods who initially are horrified by the fire. Brahmā's passivity and his use of persuasion as a means of influence on Agni, leading finally to the restoration of *dharma*, reflects his affinity with the brahmin *varṇa*, for traditionally the brahmin exercises his power through his voice, in contrast to the *kṣatriya* who exercises power through physical strength.[116] Krsna and Arjuna (Nara, another incarnation of Viṣṇu) rely on physical force to assist the brahmin (Brahmā and Agni himself who appears before them disguised as a brahmin) to restore *dharma* here, repeating the pattern found in so many of the myths where Brahmā and Viṣṇu appear together.

To sum up, the myths analysed in this chapter show an underlying unity in purpose even though they contain a variety of motifs. The relationship between Brahmā and Viṣṇu epitomizes the co-operation which should exist between brahmin and *kṣatriya*. However, though the relationship is marked by co-operation, it also shows a strong tendency towards brahmin superiority. The message transmitted is clear: when the *kṣatriya* is unable or unwilling to maintain *dharma*, then the brahmin takes up the mantle in order to assume the *kṣatriya's* role. There are many examples of this; Brahmā's milking the Earth, his protection of Sītā when she is separated from Rāma, Kaśyapa's protection of the Earth, the slaying of Vena by brahmins in the Pṛthu myth, and the brahmins' and Agni's abandonment of Śvetaki's sacnfice. All point to the conclusion that not only was the brahmin the source of the *kṣatriya*, but also that his relationship with *dharma* was wider than the *kṣatriya's*.

116 Cf. *MBh.* 12, 15, 9.

Chapter 9

Brahmā and the Demon Ascetic

Further expression of Brahmā's role in the *avatāra* myth takes place within the context of conflict between gods and demons. His role in the myths illustrating this conflict differs from that in the myths discussed in the last chapter. Two important motifs, the demon ascetic himself and boon-giving–are introduced. The demon ascetic (whether asura, dānava, rākṣasa or daitya) is one who accumulates *tapas* in order to use it as a weapon to overthrow the gods' rule in the triple world.[1] Whenever this appears imminent Brahmā stops the demon from continuing with his *tapas* by buying him off with a boon. His readiness to grant boons in such circumstances has led to him being called 'Boon-giver' (*varada*).[2] He is not the only god who does this; Viṣṇu and Śiva are often found granting boons and so are certain brāhmaṇical sages such as Bhṛgu and Nārada. However, there are several distinctive features distinguishing Brahmā's boon-giving activity from that of other gods and sages. Firstly, more than any other god, he grants boons to demon ascetics. Secondly, he usually only grants boons to demon (and other) ascetics as a reward for *tapas*, in order, paradoxically,

1 Throughout this chapter the word *tapas* is used with two different meanings. Firstly, it refers to the 'substance' accumulated as a result of the performance of austerities, secondly to the austerities themselves.

2 Scholarly studies dealing exclusively with this important motif in Indian literature are relatively sparse. See Deshpande, 1966; Hara, 1975, Lalye, 2008.

to make them cease accumulating it. Finally, he alone of the gods appears to be able (and willing) to grant immortality as a boon, except for Viṣṇu and Śiva, who as recipients of devotion, grant it to their devotees as *mokṣa*.

Brahmā's role as 'Boon-giver' remains one of the least understood aspects of his mythology. One view saw Brahmā as being weak because he gives boons to demons, whom he knows intend to take over the triple world.[3] Another saw the purpose of the myth which includes the motifs of boon-giving and the demon ascetic as glorifying austerity.[4] Only one interpretation has hinted at the sacrificial nature of the demon's austerities and suggested that Brahmā gives boons to limit the destructive use of *tapas*.[5] Each of these explanations is inadequate by itself, because they concentrate on only one motif, whereas the myth of the demon ascetic contains several motifs. Moreover, no attempt is made to interpret the myth within the greater ensemble of Hindu mythology.

The Demon Ascetic

The most celebrated account of a demon ascetic who performs *tapas* for a boon is that of Rāvaṇa and his three brothers. The version of their story cited here is taken from the *MBh.* as it is richer in detail than the corresponding version in the *Rām*:

> These warriors, all knowers of the *Veda* and devoted to good conduct, dwelt happily with their father [Pulastya] on Gandhamādana mountain. At that time they saw Vaiśravaṇa– whose vehicle is men and who is possessed of great wealth–

---

3 Hopkins, 1974, p.195. Cf. Gonda, 1960. P.264.

4 Holtzmann, 1884, p.179.

5 de Gubernatis,1897, p. 29, who says, "The god Brahman [Brahmā] is always satisfied with these acts of self-sacrifice, but on the sole condition that the penance never attains to terrifying proportions. In such a case the god would be jealous of it and would not be long in seeing in the new penitent a dangerous rival, because it is not permissible for anyone, even in the absolute government of divine monarchies, to be more royalist than the king."

seated their with their father. Driven by envy they resolved firmly on austerities, and with fierce austerities they satisfied Brahmā. Ten-headed Rāvaṇa, fully concentrated, stood on one foot for one thousand years, surrounded by fire and eating air. Kumbhakarṇa lay on the ground, restrained in food and firm in vows. Wise Vibhīṣaṇa, obsessed with fasting, ate one withered leaf, and was continually engaged in muttering prayers. Very wise, he remained in a fierce austerity for some time. Khara and Śūrpaṇakha, being glad in heart, watched over and walked around those who were performing austerities.

At the end of a thousand years the invincible Daśagrīva cut off his hands and sacrificed them into the fire, by which the Lord of the universe was satisfied. Then, when Brahmā had come himself, he stopped them from performing austerities, enticing each one with the gift of a boon.

Brahmā said, "Boys, I am pleased with you, so stop. Choose your boons; just let it be whatever you wish, except for one thing, immortality. Simply by asking, any of your huge heads offered into the fire, you will regain on your body just as you wish. There shall be no deformity on your body and you will be able to assume any shape you like. Also, you will be victorious over your enemies in battle, no doubt about that."

Rāvaṇa said, "May I not be defeated by gandharvas, gods, demons, yakṣas, rākṣasas, snakes, kiṃnaras and ghosts!"

Brahma said, "Except from mankind, you will have nothing to fear from all those who were mentioned. Hail to you! I have decreed this."

Mārkaṇḍeya said, "When this had been said, Daśagrīva became satisfied for the malignant man-eater despised humans.

The Great-grandfather then spoke in the same way to Kumbhakarṇa. Having a mind affected by dullness he chose a long sleep. Brahmā said, "So be it!" and spoke to Vibhīṣaṇa, saying repeatedly, "I am pleased son, choose a boon."

Vibhīṣaṇa said, "It is my wish never to be against the Law, even if I fall into great misfortune. Also, make the Brahmā weapon, which I have not learnt, manifest to me, illustrious god."

Brahma said, "Since, tormenter of enemies, your intention is not against the Law, even though you were born into the race of rākṣasas, I will give you immortality."[6]

The narrative continues with Kubera's defeat and. subsequent banishment by Rāvaṇa. Vibhīṣana joins Kubera's forces, whilst at the same time rākṣasas and piśācas consecrate Rāvaṇa as their king. As king he goes on to oppress and harass the gods. Troubled by this, the gods led by Agni seek out Brahmā for refuge. Then having found him, Agni says:

"He who is ten-necked, Viśravas' son, is very strong and cannot be killed because of the gift of a boon made in the past by the illustrious Brahmā. He is very strong and harasses all creatures with his wicked deeds. So, illustrious god, protect us, for there is no other protector than you."

Brahmā answered, "Fire, he cannot be conquered in battle by gods or demons, but the arrangement for his subjugation was decreed in his presence. At my command the four-armed god has descended for that purpose. Viṣṇu, that best of warriors, will perform this task." [7]

Brahmā asks the other gods to be reborn on Earth and the story unfolds as in the *Rām*. proper.

The story of Rāvaṇa and his brothers is paradigmatic of the boon-giving myth. The demons know their *tapas* will attract Brahmā and this is their only reason for performing it.[8] This aim is quite explicit in the case of the sons of Tāraka: "Those three excellent sons performed *tapas* directed towards Vidhi [Brahmā]."[9] Like many other demon ascetics, they perceive *tapas* as a means of gaining a boon, not primarily as a vehicle for gaining physical or social power.

On the surface Brahmā always appears to be quite happy with demons who perform *tapas*, but his readiness to buy them

---

6 *MBh*. 3, 259, 13-31.

7 *MBh*. 3, 260, 2-5.

8 The offer of boons is only one motive for performing tapas. For other see Holck, 1969.

9 *ŚP*. 2, 5, 1, 18. Cf. 2, 5, 28, 1-5; *KP*. 1, 15, 19.

off suggests his true attitude. The other gods, namely those of the Vedic grouping of thirty-three, become very apprehensive when confronted by ascetics, demons or others. Rather than using boons to restrain a demon from performing austerities, they try to place impediments in his way, impediments of a type intended to bring about a loss of the accumulated *tapas*. An example is the god's attempts to hinder the austerities of the demons Sunda and Upasunda who wished to conquer the three worlds:

> They tempted them with gems and women, time and again, but the two of mighty vows did not break their vow. Then the gods conjured up illusions before the great-spirited pair: their sisters, mothers, wives and kinsmen were tremblingly set upon by a Rākṣasa brandishing a pike, while their ornaments and hair came loose and their clothes fell aside. All the women ran to them and shrieked "Save us!" Still the two of mighty vows did not break their vow.[10]

As soon as Brahmā comes and offers them a boon they cease their *tapas*.

Why should demons perform *tapas* and direct their efforts towards Brahmā rather than some other god? In the first place, *tapas* gives them a bargaining point from which to exact favours from the gods. Secondly, apart from Viṣṇu and Śiva, Brahmā appears to be the only god capable of granting immortality as a reward for the performance of *tapas*.

The capacity of demons and other ascetics to exact boons from deities reflects the special power of *tapas*. Referring particularly to the type of myth under study here, Holck writes: "Asceticism here is rather a much too independent and hard a currency; the rate of exchange is beyond the determination of the gods. They are free to decide but have to fulfill the ascetic's wish, provided that the necessary quantity and quality of *tapas* is produced. The gods' position is that of administrators who have to distribute according to certain standards."[11] Hara, has drawn similar conclusions. In a

---

10 *MBh.* 1, 201, 11-14. Trans. van Buitenen, 1973, p.393.

11 Holck, 1969, p.51.

study of the compound *tapodhana*, he argues that *tapas* is a kind of spiritual power analogous to currency, in that through it one's desires can be obtained.[12] Through a philological analysis of the most common verbs used with the word *tapas*, he has suggested it was 'considered as a substance which is to be gained but at the same time it is subject to decay and loss'.[13] Currency implies transactions; the cost of a boon might be described as sufficient currency– enough *tapas* accumulated.

Though there is much to be said for the interpretation of *tapas* as currency, it does not adequately account for the boons Brahmā grants to demon ascetics. Whenever he grants a boon it is not just in exchange for *tapas*. The cost of the boon is a definite undertaking by the demon that he will stop accumulating *tapas*, and Brahmā stops (*ni/vṛt* or *ni/vṛ*) them from performing *tapas* before he grants the boon. The gods too, rather than exchange a boon for *tapas*, try to thwart the ascetic's austerities, either by making him dissipate his *tapas* through intercourse with an apsaras or by inciting him to curse somebody. Only when these fail could they be said to exchange a boon for *tapas*, or rather, for a promise that *tapas* will no longer be accumulated.

Hacker has suggested that whenever Brahmā praises a demon for his austerities it is done through courtesy.[14] What really governs the relationship between ascetic and god is a magical force (*zwang*) which compels the gods to co-operate with the ascetic and grant him a boon. This, he argues, is especially so with Brahmā because the boons he grants are scarcely less than what the demon would obtain from the frightened gods. However,

---

12 Hara, 1970, pp.58-76.

13 Hara., 1970, p. 63. Comparing *tapas* and money, he writes, "The connotation of the word *ci* (accumulate) when used with *tapas* indicates that *tapas* is an entity which is earned or gained by labour, like money. The verbs *vṛdh* (increase), *hā* (be deprived of) and *naś* deny the possibility of its being no more than a static abstract concept."

14 Hacker, 1960, Vol.2, pp.111-13.

tapas is dangerous only if it is used destructively, and Brahmā gives boons in order to prevent any one ascetic from accumulating enough to use it dangerously.

Nevertheless, there is something in what Hacker says about a magical compelling force, for if the demon's *tapas* is seen as a kind of self-sacrifice to Brahmā, the latter would be forced to respond because of the reciprocity underlying the sacrifice. In the context of the myth of the demon ascetic, the difference between the demon as *bhakta*, 'devotee', and the demon as sacrificer, is an ambiguous one. As either of these the demon would be entitled to a boon. The first would be given as a gift, the second through obligation. Since Brahmā symbolizes ritualistic values it is probable that the latter applies to the demon ascetic and so the boon-giving relationship is based on the theory of sacrificial reciprocity.

In addition to this and the power associated with high levels of *tapas*, there is another reason why Brahmā is approached for boons. He is approached for favours (*prasāda*) by both gods and demons because he is their father.[15] Epithets such as *surāsuranātha*, 'lord of gods and demons', and *surāsuraguru*, 'teacher of gods and demons', certainly suggest this conclusion.[16] Both *guru* and *nātha* convey ideas of authority, venerability and deferential respect owed by inferiors. Besides this there are several passages where Brahmā refers to particular demons as his son–*putra* or *putraka*.[17] It is his paternal attitude towards the gods and demons as implied by these examples, and his professed impartiality towards all being which predisposes him to both groups.[18]

---

15 See *Rām.* (C) 1, 14, 6, where Rāvaṇa's oppression of the gods is attributed to Brahmā's *prasāda* in granting him a boon. Cf. 3, 3, 6.

16 For *surāsuranātha* see *ŚP*. 2, 5, 1, 26; *MP*. 146, 53; *surāsuraguru*– *ŚP*. 2, 5, I, 25; *Vāmp. Sarohamāhātmya*. 3, 26. Other passages where a close relationship between Brahmā and these two groups is implied are *Mbh*. 3, 213, 16; 5, 76, 7; *ŚP*. 5, 18, 67.

17 *MP*. 145, 48; *MBh*, 3, 258, 22.

18 For more on this see below pp. 296-97.

The Fear of Ascetics in Ancient India

I have suggested the most likely reason boons are granted to ascetics is to prevent the accumulation of potentially dangerous levels of *tapas*. This concern about the danger of *tapas* is not only a reflection of the gods' apprehension about the belligerent intentions of demons. It is as much an expression of their more deep-seated fear of the implications of asceticism, especially when it produces high levels of *tapas* which can subsequently be applied in physically violent ways. The intensity of the gods' efforts to thwart the acquisition of *tapas* by ascetics is an important feature in countless epic and Purāṇic myths. Such intensity plus the frequency of occurrence of the myth of the demon (or irascible) ascetic in Indian literature implies the existence of a deep apprehension held by adherents of the group religion, members of the orthoprax society, that ascetic activity with its associated set of values would undermine this religion and this orthopraxy.[19]

This apprehension is nowhere more apparent than in the series of myths narrating the conflict between Viśvāmitra and Vasiṣṭha.[20] Viśvāmitra is a king who conforms in every respect to the ideals of kingship. Once whilst travelling with his army he visits the *āśrama* of Vasiṣṭha, a brahmanical ascetic who performs sacrifices and studies the Vedas. In accordance with the rules of hospitality, Vasiṣṭha offers to feed Viśvāmitra and his entire army. He summons his magic cow, Śabalā, who instantly produces enough food for everybody. Viśvāmitra is amazed at this and asks for the cow as a present. However, Vasiṣṭha is reluctant to part with her as he depends on her for his subsistence and she also feeds his ancestors and the gods with offerings. When Viśvāmitra attempts to take her forcibly, Vasiṣṭha makes no attempt to stop him and the cow becomes dejected, but Vasiṣṭha explains that

19 Cf. above p.78.

20 The most detailed account of this conflict can be found in *Rām.* (C) 1, 50-64, which is the main source used here. See also *MBh.* 1, 65, 20-66, 10; 1, 165, 1-166, 18. *VāmP. Sarohamāhātmya*. 19, 1-30. A masterly recent study is Sathaye. 2015.

Viśvāmitra is a guest who is too strong to resist. Then Śabalā claims *brahma* power is stronger than a warrior's power and with it she is going to destroy Viśvāmitra's army.[21] The warning having been given, she and Vasiṣṭha destroy his entire army and hundred sons with *tapas*. All this is witnessed by Viśvāmitra and he loses confidence. He places his one remaining son on the throne and leaves for Himavat mountain, there to perform *tapas*. On Himavat Viśvāmitra commences *tapas* with the express intention of accumulating sufficient to destroy Vasiṣṭha. Ostensibly the subsequently unfolding conflict portrays the tensions between the brahmin (Vasiṣṭha) and *kṣatriya* (Viśvāmitra) *varṇas*.[22] At a deeper level, however, the conflict can be seen as reflecting the tension between orthopraxy and renunciation, and thus between *pravṛtti* and *nivṛtti* values at a more abstract level.

In the ensuing conflict Vasiṣṭha is portrayed as an ascetic, yet there is plenty of evidence that he is a symbol of orthopraxy. He is renowned in Hindu mythology as one of the seven sages and as a mind-born son of Brahmā.[23] Also, he is included in those lists of Brahmā's sons where special emphasis is placed on their roles as householders (*gṛhamedin*) and disseminators of *dharma*.[24] These roles and other descriptions of him in the literature suggest he epitomizes the brahmanical ascetic who has lived the stages of his life in accordance with the *āśramas*. Further corroboration is contained in an answer given by him to King Vasumanas who asks each of the seven sages which of sacrifice, *tapas* and *saṃnyāsa* is most beneficial in this world.

---

21 *Rām.* (C) 1, 53, 14

na balaṃ kṣatriyasyāhur brāhmaṇo balavattaraḥ /
brahman brahmabalaṃ divyaṃ kṣatrāc ca balavattaram //

22 Dumézil, 1968, Vol. 1. pp. 532-6, interprets this conflict along these lines.

23 For details see Hopkins, 1974, pp.181-82.

24 *KP.* 1, 7, 37; *ŚP.* 7, 1, 12, 50.

Vasiṣṭha says:

After the fully-composed man has studied the Vedas according to the rules, duly procreated children and sacrificed to the Lord of sacrifice with sacrifices, he should then go to the forest.[25]

The statements of five of the remaining six sages gravitate between an acceptance of sacrifice, *tapas* or both, as most beneficial in this world. Viśvāmitra is the odd man out and his answer to the question is very direct:

That one who is fire, pervades everything, is without end, self-born and has faces everywhere, he is Rudra and should be worshipped (*pūj*) with fierce *tapas*, but not with any other sacrifices.[26]

Though tempered by a commitment to devotional values, this is very much the renouncer's view, involving as it does a rejection of all forms of sacrifice except for *tapas*. It contrasts markedly with Vasiṣṭha's line, one much closer to orthopraxy.[27]

Whether intentional or not, Viśvāmitra's opposition to orthopraxy first appears in his decision to abandon kingship for the ascetic life. In Sanskrit literature it is stressed continually that the king should not be a renouncer as this runs contrary to the king's *svadharma*.[28] The king's pre-eminent duty was to maintain order amongst the diverse groups existing in his kingdom, and although his relationship with the forest was complex and ambivalent, the forest was generally regarded to be a place of danger and disorder.[29] The forest is the domain of the ascetic, who lives in a kind of self-imposed absence of social order, outside the rigorously defined

---

25 *KP*. 1, 19, 34. The views of the other sages are given in vss. 34-43.

26 *KP*. 1, 19, 38.

27 One might think that in his conflict with Viśvāmitra, as elsewhere, Vasiṣṭha really serves to designate ascetic values because he fights with *tapas* and lives in an ascetic's hermitage. However, in this particular conflict he is associated continually with symbols of brahmanical orthopraxy, whereas his opponent is shown continually in opposition to them.

28 See *MBh*. 1, 87, 1-12, 3, 193, 10-13; Jaini, 1970, pp. 71-2.

29 Some details of this relationship are given by Falk, 1975, 1-15.

predictability of orthoprax society. Accordingly, Viśvāmitra's decision, like that of all renouncers, is a rejection of orthopraxy and order in favour of a life eschewing all but spiritual order. As a king whose presence buttresses the structures of orthoprax society, his decision to renounce is much more radical than a similar decision made by someone whose position in society is insignificant.

The first result of Viśvāmitra's *tapas* is a visit from Śiva who wishes to know why he has become an ascetic. He subsequently offers him a boon and Viśvāmitra asks to be instructed in archery, the Upaniṣads and other Vedic texts. Having acquired this knowledge he uses it to attack Vasiṣṭha. His weapons made of fiery energy (*astratejas*) burn that sage's hermitage, causing all who live there to flee. When the hermitage is completely empty, Vasiṣṭha threatens to destroy Viśvāmitra. In warning him he again reiterates the superiority of *brahma* power over *kṣatra*; then he raises the *brahmadaṇḍa* with which to strike him. In retaliation Viśvāmitra releases some arrows filled with the power of different gods, but all of them are burnt by the *brahmadaṇḍa*. Finally, in desperation he dares to use the *brahmā* weapon, terrifying the gods, sages and making the triple world extremely frightened. Nevertheless, even when confronted with this weapon Vasiṣṭha prevails due to the strength of his *daṇḍa* and his own *tapas*, the intense heat of which causes the worlds considerable apprehension. The frightened sages praise his victory whilst begging him to release the worlds from the cause of their fear–his *tapas*. Even Vasiṣṭha, a paragon of orthopraxy in the context of this myth, is feared when he generates too much *tapas*.

Viśvāmitra bemoans his defeat by scoffing at the warrior's power:

> Damn the power which is the warrior's power! The power of fiery energy derived from *brahma* is real power! All my weapons have been destroyed by one rod of *brahma*. Once I have deliberated on this I will enter upon a great *tapas*, making placid my senses and heart, in order to become a brahmin.[30]

---

30 *Rām*. (C) 1, 55, 23-24.

This ambition is almost unprecedented in Indian literature as is his ultimate success in attaining it. It cuts across all notions of orthopraxy because it disregards the strict hierarchical division of society based on the *varṇas*. On the grounds of ritual purity alone, *kṣatriya* and brahmin were poles apart in status.

To fulfill his ambition Viśvāmitra goes to the southern region where he performs *tapas* for a thousand years, after which Brahmā comes and offers him a boon:

> Son of Kuśika, the worlds of the royal sages (*rajarṣi*) have been won by your austerity. Through that austerity we now consider you to be called a royal ṛṣi.[31]

The designation of Viśvāmitra as a *rajarṣi* is consistent with his orthoprax status as a *kṣatriya*. Yet, it marks him as Vasiṣṭha's inferior because that sage is a *brahmarṣi*, reflecting his status in society as a brahmin. This is still far short of his stated aim, so he resolves to undertake even more severe *tapas*.

At this stage another episode, almost anecdotal, is introduced into the narrative. It has the effect of further reinforcing the impression that Viśvāmitra the renouncer is completely unconcerned about orthopraxy, an attitude deeply threatening to those holding such values, merely by living in society. This episode is about a king, Triśaṅku, who wishes to undertake a sacrifice which will ensure his ascent to heaven in bodily form.[32] He asks Vasiṣṭha for aid, but the sage refuses to give it on the grounds that the sacrifice should not take place. So Triśaṅku asks the sage's sons whether they will assist him. They too decline and tell him to return to his capital, implying he should concentrate on his royal duties. When they refuse, Triśaṅku declares he will look for someone else to perform the sacrifice. Enraged at such defiance they curse him to become a *caṇḍāla*, the lowest form of humanity.

As soon as he has assumed this form all his ministerial

31 *Rām.* (C) 1, 56, 5.

32 *Rām.* (C) 1, 56, 10-59, 31.

advisers and friends flee from him. Despairing, he searches for Viśvāmitra, who hears his tale and feels compassion for him because he has lost his kingdom and friends. In this latter sense Triśaṅku is a multiform of Viśvāmitra. Both are kings who have left their kingdoms, and are despised and feared by the orthoprax members of the society they have abandoned. Also, both wish to acquire something normally forbidden to members of their *varṇa*, (or to any *varṇa*) because it means breaking certain social norms sanctioned by *dharma*.

Viśvāmitra agrees to help perform the sacrifice and sends for all the sages in other parts of the country to come and render assistance. Most agree to help, but only out of fear of Viśvāmitra's curse. The sons of Vasiṣṭha and a certain Mahodaya are the only ones who refuse to come. The former objects to the sacrifice in these terms:

> Especially considering that a *kṣatriya* is the sacrificer for a *caṇḍāla*, how will the gods and sages eat the oblations in the sacrificial enclosure when the noble-souled brahmins have already eaten food enjoyed by a *caṇḍāla*? How will they go to heaven when they are being protected by Viśvāmitra.[33]

Two arguments are being advanced against Triśaṅku's sacrifice. In the first place, the sacrifice will be polluted by impure forces. The sacrifice is supposed to be a place of absolute purity, especially if it is a *śrauta* sacrifice as this one seems to be. A *caṇḍāla*, however, was regarded as the most impure of all humans, and any food touched by him would pollute the recipients of the sacrificial portions. Secondly, a *kṣatriya* will be performing the rightful task of a brahmin. Traditionally a *kṣatriya* was supposed to provide the material goods necessary for performing the sacrifice, but he was never allowed to supervise it. For him to do this would impinge on the purity of the sacrifice and jeopardize its success.[34] Also, in that

---

33 *Rāṃ*. (C) 1, 58, 14-15.

34 The fighting and spilling of blood incumbent upon a *kṣatriya* would have been the main cause of the *kṣatriya's* impurity. It would be temporarily removed by the performance of a *dīkṣā*.

it involved a mixture of the *varṇas*, it would constitute what kings were continually imposed upon to prevent.

Because Vasiṣṭha's sons refuse to assist with the sacrifice, Viśvāmitra furiously curses them to be burnt to ashes and then to be reborn as eaters of dog flesh. The latter are almost as low as *caṇḍālas*, so the curse placed on them is identical to the one they placed on Triśaṅku. But when the sacrifice is actually performed their criticism of it is vindicated. At the correct moment Viśvāmitra invokes the gods to come but none do come. Furious at this he announces he will send Triśaṅku to heaven in bodily form by the power of his own *tapas*. Triśaṅku rises to heaven and is straight away rejected by Indra as being unworthy of entrance. He begins to fall back to earth, only to be stopped by an angry Viśvāmitra who has created an alternative heaven where Triśaṅku will be able to find a place. The gods, demons and sages hear about this and become extremely agitated. They explain that Triśaṅku is unworthy to enter heaven since he has been cursed by his *guru*. Finally, a compromise is effected. Viśvāmitra says he will make Triśaṅku a star in the new heaven he has just created. This compromise pleased both parties. Triśaṅku goes to heaven in bodily form, but not to the heaven of the gods and sages where the presence of a *caṇḍāla* would be anamolous.

An interesting reversal of the theme of the demon ascetic occurs in this myth. Not only are the gods terrified of the ascetic Viśvāmitra's threat to create a new world, both the gods and demons are terrified. In the demon ascetic myth the gods are pitted directly against a demon (or demons), because they know that on receipt of a boon the demon will replace the *dharma* of the three worlds with *adharma*. The latter means a reversal of the socio-cosmic order in terms of normative standards of conduct and of the hierarchical structure of the three worlds. Viśvāmitra's creation however, is not a reversal of what already exists but an entirely new creation. This is why the gods and demons are united in opposition here and, paradoxically, represent orthopraxy, whereas traditionally they are pitted against one another. Their conduct in the three worlds conforms to their *svadharma*, even if the one is a reversal of the other. In the context of this myth Viśvāmitra stands completely outside of orthorpraxy as is indicated by his support for a *caṇḍāla* who violates its norms and because of his preparedness to create a new world (with a new order).

After the Triśaṅku myth, yet another myth of the same type occurs embedded in the narrative. As with the latter its main motifs parallel those of the Viśvāmitra myth. It narrates how King Ambarīṣa of Ayodhyā begins a horse sacrifice which is upset when Indra steals the horse.[35] The king is told by his *purohita* that to expiate this 'mistake' it will be necessary to find another horse or human substitute, or that the king himself will die. Taking heed of this advice he leaves his kingdom and travels over forest and mountain in search of a human victim. Eventually he finds a sage, Ṛcīka, whose second son Śunaḥśepa offers himself for the sacrifice. Whilst returning to Ayodhyā they rest at Puṣkara, where Viśvāmitra is performing *tapas*. Recognizing him as his paternal uncle, Śunaḥśepa appeals to him for protection, and Viśvāmitra responds to this appeal by asking his own sons to become the sacrificial victims in place of Śunaḥśepa. When his sons accuse him of being unethical, like people who eat dog flesh, he curses them to die and be reborn as dog eaters. Then he suggests a compromise to Śunaḥśepa: when bound to the stake he should invoke Agni and chant two sacred hymns. On the stake Śunaḥśepa does this, with the result that Indra comes and grants him long life. Similarly, the king is rewarded by Indra for having successfully completed the sacrifice.

The parallels with the Triśaṅku myth and hence with Viśvāmitra are striking. Like the other two, Ambarīṣa is a king who is forced to leave his kingdom because he fails in some way to accord with orthopraxy. This is evidenced by Indra's displeasure with him culminating in the theft of the sacred horse, symbolizing loss of the king's power.[36] Also, like them, he goes to the forest to solve

---

35 *Rāṃ*. (C) 1, 60, 5-1, 61, 27.

36 On the horse as a symbol of the king's power, see Gonda, 1960, p.172.

his problem, which can only be solved by effectively completing a sacrifice, just as Triśaṅku can only attain his goal through a sacrifice. Viśvāmitra too, by performing *tapas* is engaging in a kind of internal sacrifice. His sons play the same role here as the sons of Vasiṣṭha in the Triśaṅku myth. Their refusal to take Śunaḥśepa's place as the sacrificial victim places the success of Ambarīṣa's sacrifice in jeopardy. Accordingly, the curse placed on them is identical with the curse placed on Vasiṣṭha's sons, even though this does not directly reflect the immediate status of Ambarīṣa or Śunaḥśepa, as it does of Triśaṅku. Finally, a compromise is achieved when the victim is sacrificed yet saved, because of Viśvāmitra's advice to him. The king has completed his sacrifice and orthopraxy, here represented by Indra, is adhered to.

The narrative returns again to Viśvāmitra who continues his *tapas* until he is visited by Brahmā yet again. That god declares him to be a sage (*ṛṣi*), but this is not enough for the ascetic, who continues performing *tapas* with even greater ardour. By now the gods are becoming afraid of his potential power, so they order an apsaras named Menakā to seduce him. If Viśvāmitra has intercourse with her and spills his semen, he will lose all his *tapas*. Menakā is successful and Viśvāmitra realizes he has been tricked by the gods, and so, to rebuild his *tapas* again he goes to the Kauśikī river to engage in even more severe *tapas*. Still afraid the gods resort to another ploy. They ask Brahmā to grant the ascetic a boon, one intended to induce him to cease accumulating *tapas*. He does this and declares Viśvāmitra to be a 'great sage' (*mahattvam ṛṣim*). Not content with even this status, Viśvāmitra resolves to do further *tapas*. Brahmā tells him it will be necessary for him to completely subdue his senses if he wishes to achieve his ultimate goal.

This time his *tapas* penetrates to the region of the gods who begin to feel very hot. For a third time they try to foil him, this time by sending another apsaras, Rambhā, to seduce him. Not wanting to make the same mistake twice, Viśvāmitra curses her to be turned into stone. However, in uttering the curse he again loses all his accumulated *tapas*. Despite this setback he once more begins fierce *tapas* and becomes so hot internally that smoke begins to rise from his head. This causes great fear to spread amongst the gods and demons, who tum to Brahmā, saying:

> Lord, Viśvāmitra, the great sage, has been enticed and irritated in many ways, yet he grows more and more in *tapas*. He does not appear to be at all worried. If he is not given what his heart desires, he will destroy the three worlds, moving and unmoving, with his *tapas*.
>
> All the regions are disordered and nothing is visible; the oceans are agitated and the mountains shattered to pieces. The earth is shaking and the wind blows violently. God, as long as the great sage does not place his intention on destruction, the illustrious sage who looks like a splendid fire should be appeased. Since in the past the entire three worlds was burnt by the fire of time, so if he should strive after the kingship of the gods, that wish should be granted to him.[37]

In face of their plea Brahmā goes to Viśvāmitra and declares him to be a *brahmarṣi*, that is, a *ṛṣi* who is a brahmin. To consolidate his newly won status Viśvāmitra asks that the Vedas and the syllables *om* and *vaṣaṭ* be placed within him, and also that he become the best of those who know the *kṣatra* and *brahma* knowledge.[38] Finally, as if to exact vengeance, he asks for his status as a brahmin to be publicly acknowledged by Vasiṣṭha. All these requests are granted.

The transformation of the three worlds brought on by Viśvāmitra's excessive *tapas* parallels the initial phase of the *pralaya*. This is not just a matter of the reversal of *dharma* with *adharma*, but of absolute destruction. The fear of this actually happening at the wrong time motivates the gods, who represent orthopraxy in this context, to compromise themselves so much. The radical nature of this compromise is apparent in two ways.

---

37 *Rām*. (C) 1, 64, 5-9.

38 Even when he has achieved his goal Viśvāmitra still does not consciously try and fit into the orthodox model of a brahmin. He embodies aspects of both the *kṣatriya* and brahmin.

Firstly, the very act of shifting between *varṇas* is a threat to orthopraxy because it is analogous to the confusion of *varṇas* which is to be avoided at all costs. Secondly, when viewed in relation to the myths about Triśaṅku and Śunaḥśepa, where the compromises forced upon the gods by Viśvāmitra involve them making very few concessions, the compromise they are required to make for him seems to have more depth.

The myth of Viśvāmitra illustrates well the kinds of tension that arose from the clash of orthoprax values with those of ascetics who were renouncers. Moreover, this myth is only a variant on the theme of the irascible ascetic (including the demon ascetic) whose *tapas* has to be bought off at any cost if society is to survive. The three boons Brahmā offered to Viśvāmitra were designed to buy him off before he acquired enough *tapas* to force from the gods whatever he desired. The first two boons if they had been accepted would not have represented a contradiction (or violation) of orthopraxy because they would not have resulted in Viśvāmitra changing his *varṇa*. The third one was given in desperation and in contradiction to the intention of the first two, because then the gods could see the real effects of Viśvāmitra's *tapas* manifested in its most destructive form.

The Refusal to Grant Invulnerability

Unlike Viśvāmitra who refused to accept anything less than what he had first demanded, demon ascetics are always prepared to accept a compromise. When Brahmā offers them boons they almost always ask for invulnerability, which to them is the same as immortality. It is said of the sons of Tāraka: "Together they requested from the Grandfather of all the worlds that amongst all beings they were never to be killed, king."[39] Some demons such as Indrajit and the brothers Sunda and Upasunda ask for immortality (*amaratvam*) itself.[40] Whether it is immortality or invulnerability, which in the myths of the demon ascetic are treated as identical,

39 *MBh.* 8, 24, 7; *LP.* 1, 71, 11-12; *ŚP.* 2, 5, I, 30-34.

40 *Rām.* (V) 7, 30, 7; *MBh.* 1, 201, 19.

it is refused on the following grounds: "Immortality is not for everyone, so desist from this, asuras, and ask for another boon… ."[41]

As if to compensate for the loss of immorality most demons request another boon, the conditions of which will render them practically invulnerable. Rāvaṇa actually lists the types of beings from whom he wishes to be invulnerable, omitting only men.[42] Sunda and Upasunda are granted a boon of invulnerability from all beings except one another.[43] Yet what appears to the demons as virtual invulnerability always has a loop-hole; inevitably due to their own omission they are killed, Rāvaṇa by a man, Rāma, and Sunda and Upasunda fighting each other over an apsaras, Tillottamā.

Brahmā's refuses to grant immortality because some beings are inherently immortal (gods), whereas others are inherently mortal (men, demons), and there is a balance between their numbers which should not be upset.[44] Yet when he deals with Sunda and Upasunda he gives another reason for refusing immortality:

> Excepting immortality, all that you ask shall befall you. Choose some other disposition of death that is like the immortals. Inasmuch as you have raised this great power of austerity for the sake of a purpose, therefore no immortality is ordained for you. You have undertaken it for the conquest of the universe, and for that reason, lords of the Daityas, I cannot do your wish.[45]

To grant immortality or invulnerability to the demons would not only give them the upper hand in their endless conflict with the gods, but would give them power equivalent to what they would

---

41 *MBh.* 8. 24, 8. The whole question of the necessity of death as a theme in Indian mythology has been imaginatively treated by O'Flaherty. 1976, Ch. 9.

42 See above pp. 275-76.

43 *MBh.* 1, 201, 23.

44 This is a relative kind of immortality, since demons who are killed are born again at the beginning of each new *kalpa*.

45 *MBh.* 1, 201, 20-2. Trans. van Buitenen, 1973, p. 394.

have attained had they continued their *tapas* unhindered. Since their intentions are to control the triple world Brahmā would only assist their aim by granting immortality.

There are however two occasions where he does grant immortality to demon ascetics. These are worth examining for the light they throw on his refusal of it to others. Rāvaṇa's own brother, Vibhīṣaṇa is one demon offered a boon by Brahmā on condition he cease performing *tapas*. In contrast to Rāvaṇa who asked for immortality, Vibhīṣana asked never to become against the Law (*adharma*) even when suffering great misfortune.[46] Yet Brahmā granted him immortality, because, in his own words: "Your intention is not towards lawlessness, even though you were born into the race of rākṣasas... ."[47] He is given immortality only because he denies his own birthright; instead of being a demon in his nature he becomes like a god, that is, he becomes a supporter of *dharma*. Kubera too is another who is granted immortality. There is little doubt he was originally a rākṣasa who was particularly friendly with his grandfather Brahmā, a god. As a reward for his *tapas* Brahmā made him a god (*suratvam*), and if only for this reason, it was required he be offered immortality[48]. Since immortality is a characteristic of gods, it would be anomalous if Kubera was not made immortal. Significantly, both these recipients of immortality later aid the gods in their struggle against Rāvaṇa and his army of demons.

The divine cow Surabhi is another recipient of immortality as a boon. Inspired by Aditi who was performing *tapas* in order to obtain a son, Surabhi commenced practising *tapas* of her own accord with no particular aim in view.[49] She was said to be intent upon the Law (*dharmaparāyaṇā*), so without adharmic, hence demonic tendencies. In spite of her good intentions her *tapas* heated the gods and gandharvas, who became very alarmed.

46 *MBh*. 3, 259, 30.

47 *MBh*. 3, 259, 31.

48 *MBh*. 3, 258, 15; 9, 46, 26.

49 *MBh*.13, 82, 26cd-41.

Brahmā asked her why she was performing *tapas* and offered her a boon. However, she did not ask for anything, declaring that his satisfaction with her was a boon in itself. Unbidden, he offered her immortality and said: "Goddess, because of your desire for steadiness, your *tapas* and your purity, I shall favour you with a boon. Hence I shall give you immortality."[50]

Unlike Vibhīṣana and Kubera Surabhi is already divine before she commences her *tapas*, and it is difficult to know why Brahmā should grant her immortality, apart from the need to stop her accumulating more *tapas*. Brahmā's gift of immortality to her is consistent with the other cases where he grants it, because she too like Vibhīṣana is devoted to *dharma*, adherence to which seems to be the main criterion for receipt of immortality.[51]

Immortality is only for the few, and then only for those who earn it by virtue of their adherence to *dharma* or those who are inherently immortal. If demons were given immortality or allowed to accumulate *tapas* indefinitely, they would hold an advantage over gods in the conflict, meaning the long-term predominance of *adharma* and *dharma* in the triple world.

The Aftermath of Brahmā's Boons

A demon is strengthened in two ways after receiving a boon. Firstly, as a result of the *tapas* he has accumulated before being bought off by the boon; and secondly, because having set the limits of his own vulnerability, he regards the chances of his own death to be so slight as to consider himself inviolable. Thus puffed up with pride and arrogance he leads the demons into battle in their interminable conflict against the gods.

Invariably the demons are the victors and when they have routed the gods they establish themselves as rulers of the triple

50 *MBh*. 13, 82, 34.

51 The cosmic serpent Śeṣa is another to whom immortality was given when it had not been requested. He performed *tapas* and when offered a boon, asked to be able to rejoice in *dharma*. Brahmā gave him immortality (*MBh*. 1, 32, 5-25).

world. Their regnum is generally characterized by an abrogation of dharmic order.[52] A typical illustration of this is the regnum of Sunda and Upasunda:

> The pair conquered the World of Indra ... Thereupon that pair of dread command, undertaking to conquer all of earth, summoned their soldiers and spoke these very harsh words: "The royal seers and the brahmins feed the might, strength and glory of the Gods with their great sacrifices and oblations. All these prosperous enemies of the Asuras we must attack and annihilate totally!" Having thus given all of them their orders on the eastern shore of the ocean, the two went in all directions with cruel determination. Whosoever sacrificed and whatsoever brahmins officiated at his sacrifices, the powerful pair slew them all ferociously where they found them. In the hermitages of seers who had perfected their souls the soldiers of the two took away their *agnihotras* and fearlessly threw them away. The curses sent forth by angered, great-spirited ascetics were of no avail on the pair who pridefully gloried in the boon they had received. Of no more avail were the curses than arrows loosed on a rock; and the brahmins abandoned their life rules and fled in all directions. All advanced ascetics on earth, self-controlled and given to serenity, for fear of them took flight as snakes take flight before Garuḍa, with their hermitages routed, their jars and ladles broken and scattered about. Empty was all the world, as though stuck by Time.
>
> ... Treasure-filled Earth saw sacrifice and *Veda*-study halt, kings and brahmins perish, festivals and rituals lapse, buying and selling cease, the worship of the Gods stop, and, while she cried out in fear, she was deprived of rites and marriages. And with her ploughing and cattle-tending ended, her cities and hermitages razed, Earth, bestrewn with bones and skeletons became a loathsome sight. [53]

---

52 It is not always like this. In the version of the Tripura myth contained in the *ŚP*. the three brothers are the epitome of the ideal king. Before Śiva destroys them, the gods have to corrupt and make them evil. See *ŚP*. 2, 5, 1, 60-78; 2, 5, 3, 1-7; and for analysis, O'Flahery. 1976, Ch.5.

53 *MBh*. 1,202, 9-18, 22-5. Trans., van Buitenen,1973, p. 395.

Whenever the demons bring about a reversal in *dharma*, it is most vividly manifested in the use they make of the sacrifice and in the attitude they take towards the Vedas. They may simply destroy both as in the passage just cited.[54] Sometimes they allow the sacrifice to continue, but eat the sacrificial portions themselves or prevent the gods from eating them.[55] When Hiraṇyakaśipu conquered the worlds he performed sacrifices fit for demons but not for gods.[56] This emphasis on the sacrifice harks back to the belief constantly expressed in the early Vedas that whoever controlled the sacrifice, controlled the most important means of power in the world and was able to achieve his every desire.[57] In the context of the Epics and Purāṇas the demon's manipulation or destruction of the sacrifice is principally a sign that normative relations between man and god have broken down. This is not to say 'chaos' has replaced dharmic order, merely that adharmic order is now the norm of conduct for the three worlds. In this new (or alternative) order the gods' functions are still performed, but by demons, not gods. In terms of their own adharmic scheme of conduct it is the demons who are now functioning as gods. This notion is quite explicit in the boon requested from Brahmā

54 Cf. also *ŚP*. 7, 1, 24, 28.

55 *MkP*. 104, 16; ŚP. 2, 5, 29, 20.

56 *H*. 31, 57.

57 This is well documented by Levi, 1898. It seems strange that both the gods and the demons continue in the epics and Purāṇas to see the sacrifice as the principal instrument of their struggle. In these texts *tapas* has become a source of power external to the sacrifice. One explanation for the demons' emphasis on the sacrifice, after they have gained power partially through *tapas*, might be that when they are temporarily victorious in the divine conflict they mimic the gods as closely as possible. The thirty gods (of the Vedic pantheon) still rely on the sacrifice for their nourishment; thus the demons' emphasis on the sacrifice. In addition, the majority of the population in Early Historic India would still have used the sacrifice as their principal form of socio-religious expression, not *tapas*.

by Hiraṇyakaśipu, who said: "I should be the Sun, Soma, Vāyu, the Eater of oblation, Ocean, Atmosphere, the Planets and the ten Regions."[58]

When the three worlds are reduced to this condition, indirectly because of Brahmā's boon, he himself takes no immediate action. The gods have to approach him and ask for his help to restore *dharma*. On such occasions when the gods do complain and lament about their plight, he listens seemingly unconcerned, without initially offering any support. Indeed, before announcing his support he sometimes declares his impartiality towards all beings and only after this does he lend his support to the gods, and then, only because he is opposed to the *adharma* of the demons.

His declaration of impartiality is used in the context of the boon-giving myth to re-affirm further his intrinsic support of *dharma* and his opposition to *adharma*. Such a declaration is made in one version of the Tripura myth. The three sons of Tāraka have conquered the three worlds and their cities have been filled with countless demons:

> They achieved success through their great *tapas*, increasing the gods' fear. There was no way they could be defeated in battle, king. They were ignorant and overcome by infatuation and greed. Together all of them shamelessly tore away the established order. After the demons had put the gods and their followers to flight, they rambled here, there and whenever according to their own desire, arrogant from the gift of a boon. Those evil acting demons utterly destroyed the boundaries of propriety (*maryādā*), the auspicious hermitages of the sages, sacrificial stakes, nations and all of the pleasant heavenly groves of the sky dwellers.
>
> Conqueror of foes, all the gods then came together to the Grandfather, in order to tell of the injury done by the demons. After they had told him everything as it truly was and bowed to him with their heads, they asked the illustrious Grandfather about a way of killing them. On hearing that, the illustrious god said this to the gods, "Those demons are evil minded and

58 *H*. 31, 44.

> are certainly the enemies of the gods. They are continually wronging and oppressing you.[59] There is no doubt that I am impartial (*tulya*) towards all creatures, but I will tell you how these lawless demons should be killed… ."[60]

Śiva then kills the three brothers with a single arrow, Brahmā acting as his chariot driver.

This characterization of impartiality is not just found in the context of the demon ascetic myth. It occurs elsewhere.[61] It is likely it was meant to show that his judgement in these matters was not based on arbitrary favouritism, but solely on *dharma*. Like the Indian king who is so frequently enjoined to practise a similar kind of impartiality in matters of state, Brahmā can justifiably adopt this attitude, sometimes perceived by the other gods as callousness. The normative standard by which the conduct of beings in the triple world is guided is not Brahmā's own judgement but rests on the *dharma* he lays down at the time of the creation. This is not to say that Brahmā's or the king's own judgement about something may not be identical with *dharma*, just that *dharma* is a standard absolute over the views of any individual, whether man or god.[62]

Brahmā's role in the triple world is also that of an impartial being. In a passage in the *MBh.* Brahmā, Pusan and Dhātṛ, are said to be gods who are subdued, intent upon tranquillity and

---

59 In all twenty-two manuscripts of the Northern recension of the *Karṇaparvan* this half verse is inserted here: "Whatever causes you displeasure also wrongs me."

60 *MBh.* 8, 24, 27-34. Very similar to this is *MBh.* 13, 84, 3-4.

61 *ŚP.* 2, 3, 35, 48.

62 The king's impartiality is discussed by Lingat, 1973, pp.247-8. Among other sources he cites *Yajñavalkyadharmasūtra*. 2, 1, "The king freed from anger and greed, should give justice assisted by learned Brahmins, in conformity with the (precepts of) treatises of *dharma*." Cf. *MBh.* 3, 198, 29, "Our king who uses his runners well, sees everything with the eye of the law (... *nṛpatiḥ sarvaṃ dharmeṇa paśyati*)." Trans. van Buitenen, 1975, p. 620.

neutral towards all creatures.[63] The Sanskrit word translated as 'neutral' is *madhyastha*, also meaning 'impartial' or 'indifferent', literally meaning 'one who stands in the middle.' This is a fitting description of Brahmā at least, since in so many ways he is a mediator, one who stands between the diverse groups of beings in the triple world, looking on impartially until *dharma* is upset. This is how he appears in the myth of the demon ascetic; a mediator between two groups whose conduct has serious implications for the ordered continuity of the three worlds. His impartiality refers both to his dependence upon *dharma* as a standard of judgement of conduct and his role as mediator between opposed groups.

The Defeat of the Demon Ascetic

In the myth of the demon ascetic it is almost mandatory for the assembled gods to approach Brahmā before seeking martial assistance from Viṣṇu or Śiva, the gods to whom he usually refers them.[64] It is the Vedic grouping of thirty-three gods led by Indra, who are the most affected and distressed by demonic activities and who collectively resort to Brahmā, seeking a way for the destruction of the demon. Only on rare occasions does he not act as their spokesman when confronting Viṣṇu and Śiva.[65] This time he mediates between Viṣṇu and Śiva, and the remnants of the thirty-three gods, who in the Purāṇas have become thirty.

From the time of the *Ṛgveda* onwards, Viṣṇu and Rudra were included amongst the thirty-three. In the *MBh.* and the Purāṇas they are not included amongst them and stand apart in a number of ways. Firstly, their relationship with demons is ambivalent. Certainly, both are portrayed as demon-killers, but as a consequence of the possibilities arising from devotional

---

63 *MBh.* 12, 15, 19.

64 For example, *ŚP.* 2, 5, 44, 21, says that the gods only went to see Viṣṇu about a particular demon after they had first obtained Brahma's permission (*ājñā*).

65 He is portrayed as the gods' spokesman at *MBh.* 8, 24, 36; *H.* 31, 45-52; *ŚP.* 2, 5, 3, 8-12; 2, 5, 29, 32-37.

behaviour demons are included as their devotees. In one version of the Tripura myth Śiva refuses to kill Tāraka's three sons, not just because they are ruling the three worlds in accordance with *dharma*, but equally because they are his devotees. About them he says: "Gods, these demons are my devotees (*bhaktas*). How can I kill them."[66] Prahlāda too, at one time a king of demons, is famous as a devotee of Viṣṇu.[67] Secondly, both gods have incorporated into their personalities traits associated with asceticism and orthopraxy, reflecting the *pravṛtti/nivṛtti* dichotomy. When they fight against demons in order to restore *dharma*, they reflect values associated with orthopraxy consistent with the model of the *avatāra*. Brahmā seems to be the supervisor of the whole drama, since he acts as the spokesman of the gods and instructs Viṣṇu and Śiva about their tasks.

In some passages he mediates between god and demon ascetic, in others between gods and gods. The latter occurs in one version of the Tāraka myth. Initially, when the demon is engaged in severe *tapas*, the frightened gods persuade Brahmā to buy him off with a boon. Later, after he has harassed the gods, inspired by the confidence he has received from the boon, the gods again approach Brahmā seeking some means for the demon's destruction. He then arranges for Śiva to have a son, Skanda, who will kill Tāraka. In all these situations he is not just a passive adviser, but an active mediator representing the gods whenever they wish to communicate with other beings (gods or demons) who stand outside (and perhaps opposed to) their specific circle.

As soon as he has put the gods' case to Viṣṇu and Śiva, and one of them has consented to act on their behalf, the stage is set for destruction of the demon(s). Occasionally, as in the case of Sunda and Upasunda, the demons are required to kill one another. However, most times the boon specifies that a non-demon do the job. Usually this turns out to be Viṣṇu or Śiva in some form or other. The specific form, whether animal, man or god, of the one who is

66 *ŚP*. 2, 5, 3, 6.

67 *BhP*. 7, 5-9.

to kill the demon is determined by the conditions of the boon. Yet the imagery used in describing the actual conflict suggests in most cases that it was seen as one between two ascetics using *tapas* as their weapons. The one who has accumulated the most *tapas* and who consequently is able to emit the most heat is invariably the winner.

A case in point is the imagery found in an early version of the Tripura myth. Śiva and Brahmā were waiting patiently for the three cities to become one:

> Then the triple city appeared in front of the god, the slayer of demons, whose form was indescribably fierce and whose fiery energy (*tejas*) was unbearable. The illustrious lord of the worlds, having drawn the divine bow, released that arrow–containing the essence of the triple-world–against the triple city. When it was burnt with its hosts of demons it hurled them into the western ocean. Thus the triple city and the demons, without exception, were burnt by the angry Maheśvara, who desired the well-being of the triple-world. Exclaiming loudly the three-eyed god restrained (*nivāritaḥ*) that fire born from his own anger and said to it, "You must not reduce the three worlds to ashes."[68]

Śiva's prowess in *tapas* is played up as well as the warning that even his *tapas*, presently being used to help the gods and ultimately *dharma*, must be restrained as it is a threat to the three worlds.

A later version of the same myth inserts an episode not found in the *MBh*. version.[69] Frustrated at Śiva's refusal to help them against the demons (who are his *bhaktas*), the gods turned to Viṣṇu. He agreed to assist them and sought help from the sacrifice of which he was the lord (*yajñapati*). He convinced the gods the sacrifice would help them defeat the demons and then restore the world's prosperity. After that he instructed them to make offerings to the sacrificial man (*yajñapuruṣa*=Viṣṇu?). Out of their sacrifice

---

68 *MBh*. 8, 24, 119-22.

69 *ŚP*. 2, 5, 3, 9-33; *LiP*. 1, 71, 5.

came thousands of *bhūtasaṃghas* who were armed with a variety of weapons and looked like the fire at the end of time (*kālāgni*) and the destructive form of the sun (*kālasūrya*). Viṣṇu told them to burn, break and crush the three cities, but as soon as they entered them they were burnt to ashes like moths in a fire.

The conclusion to be drawn here is that heat derived from the sacrifice is no match for that derived from *tapas*. This reflects the likelihood that in post-Vedic literature *tapas* and the sacrifice were in competition as sources of power. Here *tapas* is certainly the more efficacious of the two, for in all versions of the Tripura myth Śiva, who has gained his fiery energy through *tapas* and not from the sacrifice, finally destroys the demons.

Śiva is overtly connected with *tapas* and asceticism, but not so Viṣṇu. Nevertheless, when he is the one who kills the demon ascetic, he is depicted as shining and burning like a fire. In the guise of the man-lion he kills Hiraṇyakaśipu with his claws, not with fire. However, similes suggestive of accumulated *tapas* and destructive fire do occur in the description of his appearance as the man-lion, as in these lines:

> With his gaping tusks, the embodiment of *yoga*, resembling the burning at the end of the *yuga*, the eternal Nārāyaṇa attained his own power which produces universal destruction, and he shone like the sun at midday.[70]

In another version of this myth Viṣṇu appears incapable of matching Hiraṇyakaśipu with *tapas*.[71] As part of his boon that demon had asked specifically that angry sages should not be able to curse him using power derived from their own *tapas*. As if to underline that, Viṣṇu too is prohibited from killing this particular demon with *tapas*, Brahmā says to the gods: "Oh Thirty gods, inevitably he will obtain the result of his *tapas*. At the end of his *tapas*, the illustrious Viṣṇu will kill him."[72] Only when the power of Hiraṇyakaśipu's *tapas* has declined sufficiently will Viṣṇu be

---

70 *KP*. 1, 15, 51, *Cf.* 1, 15, 40; *ŚP*. 2, 5, 43, 26-7.

71 *H*. 31, 41-67.

72 *H*. 31, 52.

able to kill him, because he is forbidden by the conditions of the boon to use his own *tapas* and therefore must rely on animal strength.

It is appropriate for these two gods to fight demons with *tapas*, a weapon the demons themselves would use more effectively if not stopped by Brahmā's boons. Once when asked by the gods to stop Atri's wife from performing *tapas*, through which she was able to prevent the sun from rising, Brahmā enunciated a general principle: "Immortals, intense fiery energy (*tejas*) should be subdued with fiery energy, just as *tapas* should be subdued with *tapas*... ."[73]

The Necessity to control Tapas

The destructive power potentially to be derived from *tapas* was so potent it could be used as a bargaining position to attain almost anything. The danger of this situation was that ascetics who had accumulated enough *tapas* could expect to be granted demands threatening the whole fabric of orthoprax society. Perhaps the most outstanding example of this is the attempt by Viśvāmitra to elevate himself through an immobile social hierarchy. What Viśvāmitra does on the social level, the demons attempt to do on the cosmic level. Yet if either succeeds (as Viśvāmitra does), both levels are affected because of the interdependence of the three worlds.

Yet beneath this perceived threat exists a still more serious threat. Demon ascetics and other ascetics like Viśvāmitra are not exponents of *nivṛttidharma*, and do not aspire to *mokṣa* as does the total renouncer. Their goal is to gain power in the triple world and so they remain within *pravṛtti* values, even though the life style they temporarily adopt is a reversal of those values. Their real 'crime' is that they do not carry out the roles laid down for them according to *svadharma*; but nor do they become total renouncers. The demons try to be gods instead of being what they really are, demons. Their non-performance of their *svadharma*

73 *MkP*. 16, 47.

and prevention of the gods and men from performing their own *svadharma* threatens the balance of forces in the triple world. Viśvāmitra's problem is even more severe, for he causes a mixture of *varṇas*, perhaps the worst expression of *adharma* and an imminent sign of the approaching *pralaya*. Viewed from this perspective Brahmā's boon-giving activity serves as a means of social and cosmic control.

Chapter 10

The Creation of Evil

A consistent motif of the *avatāra* myth is represented by the demon who is committed to *adharma* and, therefore, creates difficulties for the gods and other groups in the triple world who adhere to *dharma*. As in the myths presented in the previous chapter, many of these demons have gained their strength through a boon given by Brahmā. If one does not accept that Brahmā is fulfilling an obligation in granting a boon for *tapas*, then one might possibly think he aids the evil designs of demons.[1] It is in any case impossible not to accept that Brahmā himself is responsible for much of the evil in the triple world, especially when it is manifested as *adharma*, because he has created the adharmic demons. Yet, as the myths show, the creation of evil, the extent of which goes far beyond the creation of demons, is essential if a complete and successful creation is to be achieved. A brief study of Brahmā's role in the creation of evil and its concomitant–death–, throws further light on his role in the *avatāra* myth as the creator of that which he eventually has to suppress. It also gives further expression to what has already been said about the god as an embodiment of *pravṛtti* values.

In Indian thought evil and good are not absolutes in their own right and are usually expressed in terms of the following sets of opposites: *adharma* and *dharma*, impurity and purity, ignorance and knowledge, death and immortality.[2] However, most of these

1 See Hopkins, 1974, p.195.

2 The definitive work on this subject is O'Flaherty, 1976, from

opposites are applicable only in the world of *pravṛtti* values, because for those whose values are *nivṛtti*, these relativities become meaningless in the face of the unitary absolute. Moreover, *pravṛtti* is predicated on the possibility of mortality, whereas *nivṛtti* is predicated on the possibility of immortality.

Brahma's Creation of Adharma

Each of the genealogies contained in the *MBh.* and the Purāṇas includes a single lineage accounting for the presence of all kinds of evil in the triple world. In the lineage contained in the *MkP.* genealogy, Adharma and Hiṃsā are the first to be mentioned, and are said to be man and wife.[3] They had six children, namely, Anṛta, 'falsehood', Nirṛti, 'destruction', Naraka, a 'hell,' Bhaya, 'fear,' Māyā, 'illusion,' and Vedanā, 'pain.' Then Bhaya married Māyā, who gave birth to Mṛtyu, 'Death,' and Naraka married Vedanā, who gave birth to Duḥkha, 'unsatisfactoriness.' The following children were produced by Mṛtyu: Vyādhi, 'sickness,' Jarā, 'old age,' Śoka, 'grief,' Tṛṣṇā, 'thirst' and Krodha, 'anger.' Mṛtyu had another wife named Alakṣmī, through whom he had fourteen sons. They are said to:

> possess men at times of perdition. Hear about them! They reside in the mind and the ten sense organs, for they attach a man and woman each onto their own object of sense. Having invaded the sense organs, they control men through passion, anger, etc., until they suffer loss through lawlessness, brahmin. And one of them is egotistical (*ahaṃkāragata*), whilst another resides in the intellect. But, addicted to delusion, these men strive after the destruction of women.[4]

This list, found in most of the Purāṇas, covers exhaustively what is placed under the rubric of evil according to most Indian views on the subject. Superficially, four related notions could be

---

which I have drawn heavily for this chapter.

3 Summary of *MkP*. 50, 29-32. Cf. *MBh*. 1, 60, 52-3; *KP*. 1, 8, 25; *ŚP*. 7, 1, 17, 16.

4 *MkP*. 50, 34-37.

posited. Firstly, there is *hiṃsā* which suggests physical violence and pain. It is related to *vyādhi*, *jarā*, *naraka*, *nirṛti* and *mṛtyu*, all connoting physical suffering, death and mortality. *Śoka* might also be included here as it refers to mental grief often caused by the.death of someone. Secondly, *duḥkha* is a blanket term encompassing all forms of frustration, anguish and physical suffering. *Tṛṣṇā* must stand alongside it because the 'thirst' for sense objects it connotes is the chief cause of action and of *duḥkha*. Thirdly, there is *māyā*, having a strong metaphysical sense and referring to that form of evil which is ignorance about the true nature of the self and the universe. Fourthly, *adharma* and *anṛta* probably should be placed together as referring to the opposite of what is regarded as normative in the universe. Despite this fourfold division, these can all be lumped together into one group, because from the perspective of the renouncer who aspires to *mokṣa* they are a catalogue of facts about the nature of *saṃsāra*. When *moksa* is achieved *māyā* has been seen through, *tṛṣṇā* is no longer operative and eventually rebirth and death will cease. *Duḥkha* has been transformed into *sukha*, 'blissful happiness' and *adharma* (and *dharma*) is no longer of importance.

This lineage is part of a genealogy headed by Brahmā, suggesting he is responsible for the creation of all these forms of evil. The kind of world created which contains this evil, is one consistent with the ideational vision of *pravṛtti* and corresponds to much that is implied by the terms *rajas* and *tamas*, two of the basic constituents of all subtle and physical matter.[5] Much of what constitutes evil is even applicable to Brahmā himself. Though he does not engage in *adharmic* acts (incest?), he dies, undergoes rebirth, experiences frustration when his creation does not prosper, and is motivated by *tṛṣṇā* when he wishes to engage in incest and desires to create. Above all he is often under the influence of *māyā* when he creates, feuds with other members of the *trimūrti* and

5 Some definitions of *rajas* are given above pp.177-79. Paradoxically without the influence of *rajas* (and *duḥkha*, with which it is almost synonymous) there would be no incentive to attain *mokṣa*.

engages in incest, for despite her name, the daughter with whom he performs incest is always the personification of *māyā*. There is nothing inconsistent in all this, for how could Brahmā create a world flawed by evil unless he contained something of that evil in himself? And how could Brahmā produce anything but a flawed creation if he is to be an effective expression of *pravṛtti* values, which from the perspective of *nivṛtti*, are expressive of all the evils listed in the lineage cited above.

The *MkP*. lineage of evil is followed by a myth about the distribution of evil in the triple world. As the myth makes clear, both Brahmā and Death are influential here:

> Another [son of Mṛtyu] is well-known as Duḥsaha and resides in mens' houses. He is emaciated by hunger, his face is downcast, he is naked, clothed in rags and has a voice like a crow. He was created by Brahmā to prey upon all living beings. Then the receptacle of austerities, grandfather of the worlds, who consists of all that is *brahma*, is pure and the eternal cause of the universe, said to him with the excessively gaping tusks, naked mouth, and exceedingly fearful, who wanted to eat him, "You must not devour the universe! Control your anger and be calm. Get rid of this dark (*tāmasī*) behaviour and discard this portion of impetuosity (*rajas*)." Duḥsaha said, "I am wasted with hunger, ruler of the universe. My strength has waned and I am thirsty. How can I become satiated and strong, ruler? And tell me, who will be my resting place and where will I attain repose?" Brahmā said, "Your resting place will be the house of men and your strength will be the lawless (*adharmika*) person. Child, you will be nourished through their neglect in the performance of the continual sacrifices."[6]

Brahmā goes on to describe in great detail what kind of offences Duḥsaha will thrive upon, ranging from rules of purity and impurity, the breaking of *varṇa* regulations and the mixing of *varṇas*, to mistakes in the household and other kinds of ritual.[7] Then he makes some positive ordinances, telling Duḥsaha to

---

6 *MkP*. 50, 38-43.

7 *MkP*. 50, 43-62.

abandon the house of all those who act with propriety and in accord with prescribed ritual (*vidhivat*).[8] These ordinances are virtually the opposite of what Brahmā had previously described to Duḥsaha as offences.

Duḥsaha's name translates as 'difficult to tolerate' and he personifies all the evil that arises when people do not perform the duties required of them through *svadharma*. Brahmā draws a clear line between good and evil actions through fear Duḥsaha will destroy the entire world. His task is to punish those who perform evil by being the embodiment of their conscience. It is not to destroy the triple world. It is paradoxical that the demon should also have to restrain his own conduct influenced by *rajas* and *tamas*, for he represents these tendencies in mankind.[9] Actions classified as evil in this context are certainly the result of tamasic attitudes dominating those who perform them, and perhaps also of rajasic attitudes.

The Creation of Death

Though death is included as an aspect of evil in the Purāṇic genealogies, it does also have a positive role. Death is necessary as a punishment for evil, to prevent overcrowding on earth, and because it is the fundamental standard of difference between mortals and immortals, humans and gods.[10] The necessity for this difference is the subject of a myth in the *MBh*. where Yama, the god of death, disappears. Once when he was engaged in performing a sacrifice in Naimiṣa forest, he neglected his *svadharma*, which is to bring death to living creatures, and creatures increased on earth very rapidly. The gods then complained to Brahmā:

And assembled, they spoke to the sovereign teacher:
"Our fear is severe from this waxing of men.

8 *MkP*. 50, 63-96.

9 Which makes him similar to the sword, the *daṇḍa*, Death and the *brahmahatyā*, for Duḥsaha consists of all those things which they must combat. See above p. 258, n. 87.

10 See O'Flaherty, 1976, Ch. 9.

And a tremble with fear, and our joys to pursue,
We have all come seeking shelter with you."

Brahmā said

"Why should you stand in fear of man, when you all are immortal? Let there never be fear in you from mortals."

The Gods said:

"Since the mortals have become immortal, there is no difference anymore.

And, upset by this equality, we have come here to seek difference!"

Brahmā said:

"The Session keeps Yama occupied,
And that is the reason that men do not die.
When he's done with the rite with his single mind,
The time of death will return for them."[11]

Here Brahmā appeases the gods' fear more or less by reminding them obliquely of the inevitability of death.

In another myth where Brahmā actually creates Death, all the reasons as to why death should be in the world are brought up. Brahmā himself is portrayed as a destroyer in this myth, before he hands that task on to Death:

When the Grandfather with his great fiery energy had created creatures at the time of creation, he could not cope with the excessively great increase of creatures again. For there was no space anywhere whatever, long-lasting king. The triple-world was crowded with beings as if it were swollen.

King, he began to think carefully about destruction, but though thinking carefully, he could not discover a cause or motive for destruction. Then, fire angrily sprang up from his apertures, great king, and with that, king, the Grandfather burned all the quarters. Then that fire which was born from the illustrious god's anger burned the earth, heaven, atmosphere and the universe of creatures both moving and unmoving.

With the Great-grandfather incensed, those creatures, both

11 *MBh*. 1,189, 4-7. Trans. van Buitenen, 1973, pp. 370-1.

> moving and still, were burnt by his great outburst of rage. Then, the god Śiva, who is the lord with the twisted locks of hair, Sthāṇu, Lord of Vedic sacrifices and killer of enemy warriors, spoke to Brahmā about refuge. Now that Sthāṇu had arrived, desirous of the welfare of all creatures, the boon-giving god who seemed to be blazing, spoke to Śiva. "In my view you deserve a boon. Now, what wish should I do for you, because I can create anything pleasant that lies in your heart, Śambhu?"
>
> Sthāṇu said, "Lord, my reason for pursuing this course of action relates to created beings. Know, Grandfather, that they were created by you. Do not be angry with them! Everywhere living creatures are being burnt due to the heat of your fiery energy, God. Having seen them I have become compassionate, so don't be angry with them, Lord of the universe."
>
> Then Prajāpati said, "I am not angry and do not wish that creatures should disappear. But to lighten the Earth destruction is needed. Oppressed by her burden, the goddess Earth is continually urging me on to their destruction. Because of her load she is sinking into the waters, Great god."[12]

Śiva persists with his plea for the preservation of creatures, but Brahmā is adamant they must be destroyed. Śiva then modifies his demand that immortality should be for everyone and asks for the lesser request that life and death be recurrent. On hearing this Brahmā becomes quiescent and suppresses his fire. When it has completely disappeared, Death personified as a woman is born. Brahmā orders her to kill living creatures, but she hesitates, fearing she will be violating *dharma*. After many requests from Brahmā she finally agrees to kill creatures, but only those who have allowed themselves to be affected by anger and desire.

Death is reluctant to kill them because she mistakenly thinks it is *adharma* for them to die. Instead she prefers to practise *tapas*, which because of its connection with renuncation, hence *mokṣa*, is associated with immortality rather than mortality. But

---

12 *MBh*. 12, 248, 13-249, 4. A complete translation of this myth is given in O'Flaherty, 1975, pp. 39-43. Cf. *MBh*. 7. App. 1. No. 8. lines 35-249.

in a cosmos ordered by *dharma* death is a necessity, death is 'dharmic'. This absolves Death of her fear. Brahmā even tells her that she is really an impartial figure, merely the mechanism of death or time.[13] Human beings are really responsible for their own death, because they transgress *dharma* when they become deluded and act under the influence of desire. So whenever Death brings about their death, she is actually purging the world of 'adharmic' elements. One aspect of this dharmic role is the distinction that must be maintained between men and gods in terms of mortality and immortality.

In this myth Brahmā initially takes the part of death, indicating all along that it is is a necessary part of creation. As in the myth where he cautions Duḥsaha against being uncontrollably voracious, and prevents this by fomulating rigid distinctions between good and evil, so too does Brahmā have to be brought under control by Śiva. He has to prevent Brahmā from destroying the whole universe with his excess fiery energy, uncontrollable as in the *pralaya*. Excess has to be avoided at all cost, for ultimately excessive performance of one's *svadharma*, even if this is killing, is adharmic because it endangers the well-defined order that is characteristic of and essential for continuity of the triple world. Moderation *is* necessary for order whereas excess complements disorder. When Brahmā does finally divest himself of the killing role and creates Death, she agrees to perform the role only if standards of good and evil are established so that she can choose 'objectively' who can be killed, and so prevent the excess that is *adharma*.

Śiva's objection to Brahmā's destructive activity is not just because it is uncontrollable. He seems to feel it is contradictory for the creator to be destroyer as well. There might also be a hint here that in the *trimūrti* it is Śiva who is the destroyer, whereas Brahmā is the creator. However, a more powerful motive for Śiva is the desire to see a creation of immortals. This is consistent with the attitude he takes in a whole series of Purāṇic myths where he

13 *MBh*. 12, 250, 34.

refuses to create death even though Brahmā virtually begs him to do so.[14] And, just as here, Brahmā himself is forced to create death.

Śiva and Brahmā are in opposition in this and other myths concerning the creation of death, because in this general context the two gods represent *nivṛtti* and *pravṛtti* values. Śiva represents immortality which falls into the sphere of *nivṛtti* in representing the negation of the triple world dominated by mortality and time. As an ascetic (in the context of this myth) Śiva opposes and rejects all the notions of evil suggested in the *MkP*. lineage because the ascetic necessarily abandons the world of relativities, outside of which dualities such as evil and good are devoid of meaning. He also necessarily shuns all the forms of evil (thirst, desire, sexuality), which, as these myths indicate, lead to death as punishment. Brahmā is always the opposite of this. Ensnared by action, motivated by desire, it would be illogical if he did not take a stance supportive of death and mortality. Also, being in a world of relativities and creating a creation which must reflect himself, he creates good and evil equally, because both are part of him.

---

14 See *KP*. 1, 7, 29; *ŚP*. 7, 1, 14, 14-21; *LP*. 1, 70, 300-24.

Chapter 11

Conclusion

From its incipient period Hinduism (as opposed to Brāhmaṇism, the prevailing religious ethos of the Vedas) has been constituted of three fundamental features; *bhakti* and its attendant theistic movements centred around gods like Viṣṇu and Śiva; many different ascetic movements all expressing a pessimistic attitude towards existence and practising renunciation of society; and a ritualist world-view which in substance is a continuity of the socio-religious values of the Vedas. Each feature is manifested as a specific set of values, a particular life style and a collective of religious practices. Together they underlie and give coherence to the many myths which form the subject of this book; Geertz beautifully sums up their connection with the myths:

> Cultural patterns have an intrinsic double aspect; they give meaning, i.e., objective conceptual form to social and psychological reality both by shaping themselves to it and by shaping it to themselves.[1]

The didactic portions of Hindu literature give a normative view of the respective value systems and their associated life styles, but they do not allow their views to be explicitly shaped much by social experience. In contrast, the myths not only present the normative but shape themselves to the real by presenting actual life styles, with all their contradictions, failures and excesses.

The myths and didactic literature reveal a fundamental conflict

1 C. Geertz. 1966, p. 8.

ideologically and socially between ritualism (i.e.*pravṛttidharma*) and asceticism (i.e.*nivṛttidharma*), a conflict resulting from their fundamentally opposed assumptions about the nature of existence. In this book I have concentrated on ritualism because the set of values associated with it provide the best interpretative–both diachronic and synchronic–framework for Brahmā's roles in mythology. The set of values called *pravṛtti* lends itself to characterization on several levels, none exclusive of the other. On the religious level it is characterized by the centrality attributed to ritual as a means of sustaining life and demarcating the relationships between living beings in the triple world. Whilst emphasis has shifted from the *śrauta* to the *gṛhya* ritual, the obligatory nature of the sacrificial contract still persists. On the sociological level it is characterized by belief in the predominance of hierarchy as a principle of organization pertinent to beings (and concepts), and of interdependence between those groups of which the hierarchy (or hierarchies) is constituted. Finally, at the metaphysical (if this can be rightly separated from the religious) level, the prevailing characteristic is a kind of particularism best expressed in the notion of *ahaṃkāra*, that which causes the mind/ body to consider itself ultimately real and different from all other things.

Each of these levels can be discerned. operating in Brahmā's mythology simultaneously, but the distinction between them is never really clear-cut. The religious level is explicit in his apotheosis of the role of the brahmin householder, in which role he disseminates *dharma* and together with Viṣṇu ensures that it remains the prevalent norm of behaviour in the three worlds. Even in doing this he is reconfirming the charter he lays down at the time of creation which establishes the respective hierarchies of living beings in the triple world. This corresponds to the sociological level of *pravṛtti*, which is also evident in his boon-giving role. Here he is motivated to preserve the harmonious order he has established, potentially endangered from the threat of anyone refusing to perform the role dictated by their *svadharma*. On the metaphysical level his identity with *ahaṃkāra* marks him as a god whose attitude towards existence in the triple world is positive, but whose desires are centred on worldly concerns, which can only hinder any chance of gaining knowledge of spiritual truth. All this makes Brahmā a total symbol of *pravṛtti* values and herein lies his distinctiveness in Indian mythology. Viṣṇu and Śiva are gods with broader capacities, and the roles they perform symbolize both *pravṛtti* and *nivṛtti* values.

The view of existence based on *pravṛtti* values is an optimistic and positive one, yet it is gained only at the expense of individual freedom. This results from acceptance of an infallible standard of behaviour–*dharma*–as governing the conduct of all beings in the triple world (except for ascetics who reject it, but even they have a *svadharma*), adherence to which will promote harmonious living and future rebirth in heaven. In accordance with this view each person has an ordained role determined by the group into which he or she is born, whether it be one of social class if a human, or a genus such as gods and demons. Outside of his group the individual has no identity, and because each group has its own specific role, it and the individual within it are dependent upon other groups for their total existence. Brahmā himself epitomizes this bondage to a role when *kalpa* after *kalpa* he is reborn into the position of creator of the universe along with all the constructive and predictable activities this implies. Again a contrast with Viṣṇu and Śiva can be made. Both gods have no difficulty in performing their *pravṛtti* roles as preserver and destroyer respectively, but then they can change roles and become *yogins*, adopting attitudes fundamentally opposed to worldly concerns.

Not all religious thinkers regarded the world as positively as is implied by an acceptance of *pravṛtti* values. Even in texts which clearly reflect these values there are some unmistakable signs of doubt about the stability of, and consolidation of living beings (*lokasaṃgraha*) in the triple world. In mythology this stability appears at the most to be a fragile one. The ease with which the triple world can be plunged into disorder of a type redolent of the pre-creation state, an ubiquitous motif in Hindu mythology, is one sign of this fragility. Creation is order and delimitation, pre-creation is a lack of any defining limits. The hierarchy of living beings and concepts in the triple world is the embodiment of a normative dharmic order laid down by Brahmā at the time of creation, but in the real world of mythology the various groups within the hierarchy jostle with one another and some even perpetrate the supreme evil of usurping the role of another. The rigid hierarchy of roles guaranteed the inevitability of conflict, a theme occuring with great consistency throughout Hindu mythology.

This fragility is symbolized also by the amount of speculation in the texts about concepts like punishment (*daṇḍa*), the sword (more than just a weapon), death, and the personification of the crime of killing a brahmin. All these are symbols of the destruction directly brought about by a violation of *dharma*, something their existence is supposed to prevent. They are quite draconian in implication. Strength, punishment and fear, which they embody, are needed to fight excess zeal and noncompliance with one's pre-ordained role, as well as anything else threatening to the divine hierarchy. Yet this fragility so clearly portrayed in mythology is surprising in a culture which has been much feted for its success in absorbing extraneous and potentially antagonistic influences throughout its history.

There were a number of consequences arising from this perceived fragility, consequences of momentous importance for the development of Indian religion and culture generally. One of these consequences was always latent within the (and any other) ritualistic world-view, and manifested itself in the tremendous importance placed on mediatory figures. In Hindu mythology the mediator is typically a figure who embodies *dharma*, a universal norm from which basis he can arbitrate or act. The king and the brahmin were supposed to embody *dharma* and I have already suggested they were important mediating figures. Indeed the king is supposed to have characteristics of both *pravṛtti* and *nivṛtti*, and according to some scholars he combines within himself the three functions reflected throughout ancient Indo-European culture.[2]

2 Dubuisson. 1978, pp.21-35.

In the first instance he is able to mediate between ascetic and non-ascetic (i.e., one who holds ritualist values) and secondly, he can mediate between the three *varṇas* which correspond with the Indo-European three functions. The brahmin is the one who performs the sacrifice and mediates between man, god, demons and whoever else takes their share of it. Some texts even speak of the brahmin as the god who is on earth, despite his true status as a human. As such he is able to stand between men and gods. As if combining within himself the position of king and brahmin Brahmā mediates between men and gods, men and Earth, men and men, gods and demons, Viṣṇu and the gods, and sometimes Śiva and the gods. This must be so because he combines in himself so many of the dualities existent in his creation, yet at the same time he is identical with its ultimate standard-*dharma*.

Another consequence of this fragility, probably the most important, were the attacks and criticisms made on the ritualist worldview by the various ascetic movements espousing *nivṛttidharma*. Though socially fragmented, they were ideologically unified. They took this fragility of the world order to its logical conclusion, adopting a wholly pessimistic view of the universe and arguing that existence in such a universe was unsatisfactory in every way, insecure and unstable. The aim of the ascetic was to find a secure foundation (*pratiṣṭhā*) beyond space, time and change, a condition wholly beyond anything in a world governed by *pravṛtti* values.[3] In terms of social organization the ascetic groups were egalitarian in outlook (if not always in practice) and the ascetic often lived a life of austerity as a recluse. However, this life style was adopted by choice, not by necessity due to birthright.

On ideological and social grounds the ritualists and ascetic movements were antagonistic towards each other and their

3 Gonda. 1975, vol. 3, pp. 340-77, has looked at the notion of the quest for a firm foundation which will take one beyond the unsatisfactoriness and transitoriness of the phenomenal world. The notion is very old in Indian thought.

antagonism has given rise to many polemical tracts in didactic literature. The teachings of the ascetic movements, especially their views about the unsatisafactory nature of existence, were so potent as to seriously threaten the viability of ritualism (on the theoretical level) in its old form. An important thrust of the ascetic teaching was the attack made on actions (*karma*) motivated by desire, for these only produced further rebirths in heaven or earth, equally unsatisfactory to the ascetics who sought a permanent release from change and suffering. This teaching hit directly at the heart of ritualism which stressed the performance of the ritual (also called *karma*) as a means of fulfilling one's desires, whether this be for sons, wealth, rebirth in heaven or all these. By the time of the earliest Upaniṣads the ascetic teaching on *karma* was widely accepted even amongst those who espoused ritualist values. In itself it constituted a threat to the performance of sacrifices, hence to the interdependent hierarchy of beings who inhabited the triple world. Not only was it a rejection of ritualism, but a real threat to it.

The worldview underlying ritualism continued (and continues) to provide the ethos for most Hindus in spite of the attacks made upon it by the ascetic movements. However, it was a new form of ritualism much modified by the transforming influence of the emergent devotional practices and theology called *bhakti*. The origins of *bhakti* are unclear but from about the beginning of the third century BCE it had a dramatic influence on the whole spectrum of Indian religious ideas.[4] Whether its popularity and influence were due to two important gods like Viṣṇu and Śiva becoming the centre of *bhakti* theistic movements, or because ideologically it was eclectic, borrowing much from *pravṛtti*– and *nivṛttidharma*, is also not easily determined. But the net effect of its prodigious growth in popularity brought with it a revitalization of the ritualist worldview. It reconciled the two opposed world views because it took seriously the criticisms which each had directed at the other. Doctrinally *bhakti* effected a re-interpretation of

4 See Bailey. 2016 for the early expressions of bhakti in Buddhism.

sacrifice and renunciation which henceforth made them identical. According to this re-interpretation, as expressed in the doctrme of *karmayoga*, *karma* is understood as ritual and the performance of one's *svadharma* is performed in the spirit of the *yogin*, i.e., the renouncer. Actions are not performed from a need to fulfill a desire, but as an act of devotion to God. No longer need a person living in society who was forced to engage in continual activity fear the constant round of rebirths arising from *karma*, because god would give liberation to whomsoever was his devotee.

The doctrine of *karmayoga* allowed *bhakti* to be doctrinally and practically very 'establishment' in the sense that it upheld and reinforced all the important institutions and concepts of the ritualist's world, except in some important areas of religion. True, it did promote a kind of egalitarianism, for although a person may have had a low social status, belonging to a low *varṇa*, all were equal in the sight of god if they were his devotees. This is the substance of the following passage from the *Bhg*:

> For, Prince, whomsoever takes refuge in me, even though they might be evil-born, woman and *vaiśyas* too, and even *śūdras*; they will tread the highest way.[5]

However, even in this attempt to foster an egalitarian attitude in the realm of religion, one perceives a slight opprobium in regard to the specific groups named who traditionally had been of low social status. This perception is confirmed overwhelmingly in the very next verse, where it is said:

> How much more, then, meritorious *brahmins* and devoted (*bhakta*) royal sages. Since you are in this world which is impermanent and without happiness, resort to me![6]

Thus at least on the social level, the ideological backdrop of *bhakti* maintained a belief in the hierarchy of beings which was such a prominent feature of ritualism. And this is not just a case of finding a few isolated passages to fit a particular viewpoint. For

---

5 *Bhg*. 9, 32. Cf. 9, 30.

6 *Bhg*. 9, 33.

throughout the *Bhg*. and the myths where *bhakti* ideology surfaces, one receives the firm impression that devotion in its most zealous form is unwavering performance of one's *svadharma*, that which most directly maintains the interdependent hierarchy of beings in the triple world. Whether it is Arjuna in the *Bhg*. or Viṣṇu and Brahmā in the many versions of the *lingodbhava* myth, the *bhakti* god is always insistent that his devotee express his loving devotion through *svadharma* performed in a spirit of utter selflessness.

Bibliography

I. Sanskrit and Pāli Texts

Agni Purāṇa, ed. Upadhyaya, B, (Varanasi, 1966); trans. Dutt, M.N. (Calcutta, 1901).

Aitareya Brāhmaṇa, ed. and trans. Haug, M, *The Aitareya Brahmanam of the Rig Veda* (2 vols., Bombay, 1863)

Anguttara Nikāya, eds. Morris, R. and Hardy, E, (6 vols. and index, Reprint 1958-76, London, 1885-1910); trans. Woodward, F.L. and Hare, E.M, *The Book of the Gradual Sayings* (5 vols., London, 1932-6)

Apastambīyadharmasūtram, ed. Buhler, G, (3rd ed., Bombay, 1932); trans. Buhler, G, *The Sacred Laws of the Aryas*, pt.1,SBE II (Oxford, 1879).

Atharva Veda, ed. Roth, R., and Whitney, W.D, (Berlin, 1855); trans. Whitney, W.D, ed. Lanman, C, Harvard Oriental Series 7-8 (2 vols., Cambridge, Mass., 1905)

Baudhāyanīyadharmasūtram, trans. Buhler, G, *The Sacred Laws of the Aryas*, pt. 2, SBE XIV (Oxford, 1882).

Bhagavadgītā. Zaehner, R. C, *The Bhagavad-Gītā. With a commentary based on the original sources*, (London, 1967).

Bhāgavata Purāṇa, ed. Acarya, N.R, (Bombay, 1950); trans. Sanyal, J., (Calcutta, 1930-4).

Bhaviṣya Purāṇa, (Bombay, 1959).

Brahmāṇḍa Purāṇa, ed. Shastri, J.L, (Delhi, 1973).

Brahmavaivarta Purāṇa, ed. Ānandāśrama Sanskrit Series, 102 (4 vols., Poona, 1935).

Bṛhatsaṃhitā of Varāha Mihira, ed., Bibliotheca Indica (Calcutta, 1865).

Devībhāgavata Purāṇa, ed. (Benares, 1960).

Dīgha Nikāya, eds. Rhys Davids, T.W. and Carpenter, J.E, (3vols., reprint 1960-67; London, 1890-1911); trans. Rhys Davids, T.W. and Rhys Davids *C.A.F, Dialogues of the Buddha* (London, 1899-1921); Walshe, M, *Thus I have heard: the long discourses of the Dīgha Nikāya (The Teachings of the Buddha)*, London 1995.

Epigraphica Indica (Calcutta and Delhi, 1892-).

Gaṇeśa Upapurāṇa, ed. (Bombay, 1892).

Garuḍa Purāṇa, ed. Bhattacharya, R, (Varanasi, 1964); trans. Dutt, M.N, (Varanasi, 1968).

Gautamīyadharmasūtram, ed., Stenzler, *A. F,* (London, !876); trans. Buhler, G, *The Sacred Laws. of the Aryas*, pt, l SBE II (Oxford, 1879).

Gayā Māhātmya, ed. and trans. Jacques, C, (Pondicherry, 1962).

Gopatha Brāhmaṇa, ed. Gaastra, D, (Leiden) 1919).

Harivarṃśa, ed. Vaidya, P.L, (2 vols., Poona, 1969-71).

Itivuttaka, ed. Windisch, E, (London 1889); trans. Woodwatd, F. L, *Minor Anthologies*, pt. 2 (London, 1935).

Jataka, ed. Fausoll, V, (6 vols. and index, reprint 1962-4; London, !887-97); trans. by various hands under the editorship of Cowell, EB, (6 vols., reprint in 3 vols., London 1957, Cambridge, 1895-1913).

Jaiminīya Brāhmaṇa, ed. and trans. Caland, W, *Das Jaiminīya Brāhmaṇa in Auswahl*, (Amsterdam, 1919).

Kathāsaritsāgara, ed. Brockhaus, H, *Die Märchensammlung des Somadeva*, Books 1-5 (Leipzig, 1839); Books 9-18, *Abhandlungen für die Kunde des Morgenlandes*, 2 (1862) and 4 (1866) (Leipzig); trans. Tawney, C.H., ed., Penzer, N.M, *The Ocean of Story* (10 vols., reprint, 1968; 2nd ed. Delhi, l927).

Kāṭhaka Saṃhitā, ed. von. Schroeder, L, (3 vols., Wiesbaden I972, Leipzig, 1900).

Kauṣītaki Brāhmaṇa, ed. Sreekrishna Sarma, E.R, (Wiesbaden, 1968); trans. Keith, A.B, *Rig Veda Brāhmaṇas: The Aitareya and Kauṣītaki Brāhmaṇas of 1he Rig Veda*, Harvard Oriental Series (Cambridge, Mass., 1920).

Kūrma Purāṇa, ed. Gupta, A.S, and trans. Bhattacharya, A, Mukherji, S, Varma, V. K, and Rai, G. S, (Varanasi, !972).

Lalita Vistara, ed. Vaidya, P. L, Darbhanga, 1958

Liṅga Purāṇa, ed. Vidyasagara, J, (Calcutta, 1895); trans. Shastri, J.L, (2 vols., Delhi, 1973).

Mahābhārata, ed. Sukthankar, V.S, et al. (19 vols., Poona, 1933-69); ed. with Nlakaṇṭḥa's commentary (6 vols., Poona, 1929-36); trans. Roy, P.C, *The Mahābhārata* (12 vols., reprint, Calcutta, n.d.); van Buitenen, J.A.B, *The Mahābhārata* (3 vols., Chicago, 1973-); Fitzgerald, J, (Chicago, 2004).

Mahāvastu Avadāna,ed. Basak, R, (3 vols., Calcutta, 1963-8); trans. Jones, J.J, *The Mahāvastu* (3 vols., London, 1949-56).

Maitrāyaṇī Saṃhitā, ed. von Schroeder, L, (4 vols. reprint, Wiesbaden, !970-72; Leipzig, 1880-81).

Majjhima Mikaya, ed. Trenckner, V, Chalmers, R, and Rhys Davids, C.A.F, (4 vols., reprint 1960-74; London, 1888-1925); trans. Horner, I.B, *Middle Length Sayings* (3 vols., London, 1954-59). Bhikkhu Ñanamoli and Bhikkhu Bodhi, *The Middle Length Discourses of the Buddha. A New Translation of the Majjhima Nikāya*, (Wisdom Publications, Boston, 1995)

Manu Smrti, ed. Acharya, N.R, (Bombay, 1946), trans. and ed. Olivelle, P, *Manu's Code of Law. A Critical Edition and Translation of the Mānava-Dharmaśāstra*, New Delhi, 2006.

Mārkaṇḍeya Purāṇa, ed., Bhattacharya, J.V, (Calcutta, 1876); trans. Pargiter, F.E. (Calcutta, 1904).

Matsya Purāṇa, ed. Bhattacharya, J.V, (Calcutta, 1876); trans. Vasu, S.C. et al. (Delhi, 1972).

Milindapañha, ed. Trenckner, V, (London, 1880); trans. Horner, I.B, *Milinda's Questions* (2 vols., London, 1963-4).

Padma Purāṇa, ed. Ānandāśrama Sanskrit Series, 131 (4 vols., Poona,1893).

Pañcaviṃśa Brāhmaṇa, ed. Chinnaswami, A, and Sastri, P, (Benares, 1935- 6); trans. Caland, *W, Pañcaviṃśa-Brāhmaṇa: The Brāhmaṇa of Twenty Five Chapters* (Calcutta,1931).

Rāmāyaṇa of Vālmīki, ed. Bhatt, G, et al. (7 vols., Baroda, 1969-76); ed. Bandhu, V, (7 vols., Lahore, 1928-47); ed. (Gorakhpur, 1963).

Ṛg Veda, ed. Aufrecht, T, *Die Hymmn des RigVedas* (2nd ed., Bonn, 1877); trans. Geldner, K, *Der Rig Veda*, Harvard Oriental Series 33-6 (4 vols., Cambridge, Mass., 1951-7).

Sāṃkhya Kārikā, ed. and trans. Larson, G.J, *Classical Sāṃkhya: An lnter pretatian of its History and Meaning* (Delhi, 1969), pp. 251-82.

Sāmavidhāna Brāhmaṇa, ed. (London, 1873).

Saṃyutta Nikāya, ed. Feer, L, (6 vols., reprint 1960-75; London, 1884- 1904); trans. Rhys Davids, C.A.F, and Woodward, F.L, *The Book of Kindred Sayings* (5 vols., London, 1929-32).

Śatapatha Brāhmaṇa, ed. Weber, A, (2nd ed. Benares 1964; Berlin, 1855). Trans. Eggeling, J, *The Śatapatha Brāhmaṇa according to the Text of the Mādhyandina Recension*, SBE XII, XXVI, XLI, XLIII, XLIV (5 vols., Oxford, 1882-99).

Śiva Purāṇa, ed. (Bombay, 1884); trans. Shastri, J. L, (4 vols., Delhi, 1970).

Taittirīya Brāhmaṇa, ed. Ānandāśrama Sanskrit Series, 37 (2nd ed., 1934-8, Poona).

Taittirīya Saṃhitā, trans. Keith, A.B, *The Veda of the Black Yajus School entitled Taittirīya Saṃhitā*, Harvard Oriental Series 18-19, Cambridge, Mass., 1914.

Upaniṣads: Eighteen Principal Upaniṣads, Vol. 1., ed. Limaye, V. P, and Vadekar, R. D, Poona, 1958; trans. Hume, R.E, *The Thirteen Principal Upanisads*, (7th imp., Madras, 1968;

London, 1921. Olivelle, P, *The Early Upaniṣads. Annotated Text and Translation*, New York, Oxford University Press, 1998; Roebuck, V, *The Upaniṣads*, London, 2003.

Vājasaneyī Saṃhitā, ed. Weber, A, (Berlin, 1852).

Vāmana Purāṇa, ed. and trans. Gupta, A.S, (Varanasi, 1%8).

Vasiṣtha Dharmasūtra, trans. Buhler, G, *The Sacred Laws of the Aryas*, pt. 2, SBE XIV, (Oxford, 1882).

Vāyu Purāṇa, ed. (Calcutta, 1880); *The Vāyumahāpurāṇam*, Nag Publishes Delhi, 1983.

Vinaya Piṭaka, ed. Oldenberg, H, and Pischel, R, (5 vols., reprint, 1929; London, 1879-83); trans. Horner, I.B, *Book of the Discipline* (6 vols., London, 1938-52).

Viṣṇu Purāṇa, ed. (Gorakhpur, 1963); trans. Wilson, H.H, (3rd ed.,Calcutta, 1961; London, 1840).

2. Books and Articles in European Languages

Alsdorf, L., 1977 'Das Bhurīdatta-Jātaka. Ein anti-brahmanischer Nāga-Roman,' WZKSA, 21 pp. 25-55.

Amner, K., 1949 'Tvaṣṭṛ: ein alt-indischer Schöpfergott,' *Die Sprache*, 1 pp. 68-77.

Bailey, G.M., 1979 'Notes on the Worship of Brahma in Ancient India', *Annali' dell Instituto Orientale di Napoli*, 30 pp. 149-70.

—, 1979, 'Trifunctional Elements in the Mythology of the Hindu *Trimūrti*', *NUMEN*, 25 pp. 152-63.

1981 'Brahmā, Pṛthu and the theme of the Earth-milker in Hindu Mythology', *IIJ*, 23 pp. 111-122.

1985 *Materials for the Study of Ancient Indian Ideologies*, Torino, Publicazioni Di Indologica Taurinensia, 19.

2005 'Contrasting Ideologies in the *Mahābhārata*', in ed. Sharma, R. K., *Dr. Satya Vrat Shastri Felicititation Volume*. New Delhi, 2005, Vol.2, pp.581-606

2016 'Devotional Elements in the *Sakkapañhasutta* of the *Dīghanikāya*', in Francis, E and Schmid, C., *The Archeology of Bhakti II. Royal Bhakti, Local Bhakti*, EFEO, Pondichery, 2016, pp.127-157.

2017 'On the Distribution, Use and Meaning of the *Dhātu Vṛt* in the *Mokṣadharmaparvan* and the *Śāntiparvan*,' *Journal of Indian Philosophy*, 45/4 pp 711–732

Forthcoming 'Preliminary Notes on Pāli *Vatt/Vaṭṭ* and Sanskrit *Vṛt* in the *Mahābhārata*'

Bailey, G. M. and Mabbett, I., 2003 *The Sociology of Early Buddhism*, Cambridge.

Banerjea, J.N., 1956 *The Development of Hindu Iconagraphy* (Calcutta, I956).

Bareau, A., 1963 *Recherches Sur La Biographie du Buddha*, 2 vols., Paris.

Basham, A.L., 1954 *The Wonder that was India*, London.

Beals, A., 1962 *Gopalpur: A South Indian Village*, New York.

Benveniste E., 1969 *Le Vocabulaire des Institutions Indo-Européenes*, 2 vols., Paris; trans. Palmer, E., *Indo-European Language and Society* , London, 1973.

Bergaigne, A., 1963 *La Religion Védique-d'après les Hymnes du RgVeda* (4 vols., reprint, Paris, 1878-83.

Bhandarkar, R.G.V., 1965 *Vaiṣṇavism, Śaivism and Minor Religious Systems* (reprint, Varanasi; Strassburg, 1913)

Bhardwaj, G.M., 1973 *Hindu Places of Pilgrimage in India*, Berkeley. Bhattacharji, S., 1970 *The Indian Theogony*, Cambridge

Bhattachacya, K., 1973 *L'Ātman-Brahman Dans Le Bouddhisme Ancien*, Paris.

Bhattacharya, T., 1969 *The Cult of Brahma* (2nd ed., 1969; Patna, 1957).

Biardeau, M., 1964 *Théorie de la Connaissance et Philosophie de la Parole dans le Brahmanisme Classique*, The Hague.

1965 '*Ahaṃkāra*, The Ego Principle in the Upaniṣads', *CIS*, 8 pp. 62-84.

—, 1968, 1969, 1971 'Études de Mythologie Hindoue:

Cosmogonies Purāṇiques 1, 2, and 3', *Bulletin de l'École Française de L'Extrême Orient*, LIV, LV, LVI, pp. 19-45; 59-!05; 19-81.

—, 1972 *Clefs pour la Pensée Hindoue*, Paris.

Biardeau, M., and Malamoud, C., 1976 *Le Sacrifice Dans L'Inde Ancienne* Paris.

Blair, C., 1961 *Heat in the Rig Veda and Atharva Veda*, New Haven.

Bloomfield, M., 1964 *A Vedic Concordance* (reprint) Delhi, Cambridge, Mass., 1906.

—, 1893 'The Marriage of Saraṇyū, Tvaṣṭṛ's Daughter', *JAOS*, 15, pp. 172-88.

Bodhi, Bhikkhu., 2007 *The All-Embracing Net of Views. The Brahmajāla Sutta And its Commentaries*, Buddhist Publication Society, Kandy

Bombay Gazetteer. 1901 27 vols., Bombay

Brereton, J., 2004 '*Brāhman* and *Brahmin*,'in Arlo Griffiths & Jan E. M. Houben, ed., *The Vedas: Texts, Language & Ritual. Proceedings of the Third International Vedic Workshop, Leiden*, 2002, Groningen, pp. 325-344

Brockington, J.L., 1976, 'Religious Attitudes in Vālmīki's Rāmāyaṇa', *Journal of the Royal Asiatic Society*, 108/2, pp. 108-29.

Brown, W.N., 1920 'Escaping One's Fate, A Hindu Paradox and its use as a Psychic Motif in Hindu Fiction', *Studies in Honour of M. Bloomfield*, New Haven, pp. 89-105.

—, 1942, 'The Creation Myth of the ṚgVeda', *JAOS*, 62, pp. 85-98.

Brückner, H., 1995 *Fürstliche Feste. Texte und Rituale der Tuḷu-Volksreligion an der Westküste Südindiens*, Wiesbaden

van Buitenen, J.A.B., 1956 'Studies in Sāṃkhya (1)', *JAOS*, 76 (1956), pp. 153-7.

—, 1957 'Studies in Sāṃkhya (11)', *JAOS*, 77 , pp. 15-25.

—, 1957 'Studies in Sāṃkhya (III)', *JAOS*, 77, pp. 88-107.

—, 1964 'The Large Ātman', *HR*, 4, pp. 103-4.

Burgess, J., 1876 *Memorandum of the Archeological Survey in Kathiawar, Dec. 1874-Jan. 1875*, London

Burrow, T., 1948 'Sanskrit *rajas*', *BSOAS*,12 3/4, pp. 645-51

—, 1949 'Shwa in Sanskrit', *Transactions of the Philological Society*, pp. 22-62.

Carpenter, J.E., 1921 *Theism in Medieval India*, London

Chakravarti, B.M., 1900 'An Inscription of the Time of Nayapāla Deva from the Kṛṣṇa-dvārikā Temple at Gayā', *Journal of the Royal Asiatic Society of Bengal*, LXIX, No.I, pp. 191 ff.

Chatterjee, A., *The Padma Purāṇa – A Study* (Calcutta, 1967).

Coomaraswamy, A., 1923 *Portfolio of Indian Art*, Boston

Cousens, H., 1906-07 'The Temple of Brahmā at Khed Brahmā,' *Archeological Survey of India: Annual Reports*, Calcutta pp.173-78.

Daniélou, A., 1964 *Hindu Polytheism*, London

Dasgupta, S. N., 1975 *A History of Indian Philosophy*, 5 Vols, Delhi, Cambridge 1922

Derrett, J. M., 1959 'Bhū-Pālana, Bhū-Bhojana. An Indian Conundrum', *BSOAS*, 22/1 pp.108-123

Deshpande, N. A., 1966 'Boons and Curses in the Rāmāyaṇa', in Neog, M. and Sharma, M. M., (eds.), *Professor Birinchi Kumar Commemorative Volume*, Gauhati pp.212-216

Deva, K., 1959 'The Temples of Khajuraho in Central India', *Ancient India* 15 pp.4-43

Dubuisson, D., 1978 'Le Roi Indo-européen et la Synthèse des Trois Fonctions', *Annales Economies*, Sociétiés, Civilizations, 33 pp.21-35

1979 'Trois Thèses sur le Rāmāyaṇa', *Annales Economies, Sociétiés, Civilizations*, 34 pp.464-489.

Dumézil, G., 1968 *Mythe et Épopée. L'idéologie des trois fonctions dans les épopées des peuples indo-européens*, Vol. 1, Paris

— 1970 *The Destiny of a Warrior*, Chicago

Dumont, L., 1962 'Kingship in Ancient India', *CIS*, 6 pp.46-67

— 1970 *Homo Hierarchicus*, London

Durkheim, E and Mauss, M., 1970 *Primitive Classification*, trans R. Needham, London, (Paris, 1903)

Falk, N. E., 1975 'Wilderness and Kingship in Ancient South Asia', *HR*, 15 pp.1-15

Geertz, C., 1966 'Religion as a Cultural System', in Banton, M., (ed) *Anthropological Approaches to the Study of Religion*, London, pp.1-46.

Ghoshal, U.N., 1959 A *History of Indian Political Ideas*, London

Gokhale, B.G., 1966 'Early Buddhist Kingship', *Journal of Asian Studies*, 26 pp. 15-22.

Goldman, R., 1969 'Mortal Man and Immortal Woman: An Interpretation of Three Ākhyāna Hymns of the Ṛg Veda', *Journal of the Oriental lnstitute, Baroda*, 18 pp. 273—303

Gombrich, R., 2001 'A Visit to Brahmā the Heron', *JIP*, 29,1/2 pp.95-108

Gonda, J., 1947 'À Propos d'un Sens Magico-Religieux de *Skt. guru', BSOAS*, 12/1 pp. 124-31

1955 'Purohita', in *Studia Indologica, Festschrift W. Kirfel*, Bonn

1969, *Ancient Indian Kingship From the Religious Point of View*, Leiden, (reprinted from *NUMEN*, 3 and 4, 1956-7).

—, 1960-63 *Die Religonen Indiens*, 2 vols., Stuttgart

1965 *The Savayajñas*, Amsterdam

1966 *Loka. World and Heaven in the Veda*, Amsterdam

—, 1969 *Aspects of Early Viṣṇuism*, 2nd ed., Delhi, 1969 (Utrecht, 1954)

—, 1975 'Pratiṣṭhā', in *Selected Studies* (5 vols., Leiden), Vol. 3, pp. 340-77

—, 1975 'The Concept of a Personal God in Ancient Indian Religious Thought', in *Selected Studies* Vol. 4, pp. l-27

1982 'The Popular Prajāpati,' *HR*, 22/2 p.147

1986 *Prajāpati's Rise To Higher Rank*, Leiden

—, 1989 *Prajāpati's relations with Brahman, Bṛhaspati and Brahmā*, Amsterdam/Oxford/New York

González-Reimann, L., 2002 *The Mahābhārata and the Yugas: India's Great Epic Poem and the Hindu System of World Ages*, New York

Günther, H.V., 1944, 'Die Buddhisrische Kosmogonie', *ZDMG*, 98 pp.44-83

de Gubernatis, A., 1897 'Brahman et Sāvitrī ou l'Origine De La Prière', *Actes du Onzième Congrés International des Orientalistes*, Paris, pp. 9-44.

Hacker, P., 1960 Prahlāda, *Werden und Wandlungen einer Idealgestalt, Beiträge zur Geschichte des Hinduismus*, 2 vols., Wiesbaden

—, 1960 'Purāṇen und Geschichte des Hinduismus', *Orientalistische Literaturzeitung*, 55 pp. 341-54

—, 1961 'The Sānkhyization of the Emanation Doctrine Shown in a Critical Analysis of Texts', *WZKSOA*, 5 pp. 75-112

—, 1964 'Zur Geschichte und Beurteilung des Hinduismus', *Orientalistische Literaturzeitung*, 59, pp. 231-45

Hara, M., 1970 'Tapodhana', *Acta Asiatica*, 19 pp. 58-75.

—, 1973 'The King as Husband of the Earth (*mahīpati*)', *AS*, 27 pp. 97 ff.

1975 'Indra and Tapas', *Brahmavidyā*, 25 pp. 29-60

Hastings, J. ed., 1974-80 *Encyclopedia of Religion and Ethics*, 15 Vols. Edinburgh, 1908-26

Hazra, R.C., 1975 *Studies in the Purāṇic Records on Hindu Rites and Customs*, Delhi, (Dacca, 1940)

—, 1958 *Studies in the Upapurāṇas: Saura and Vaiṣṇava Upapurāṇas*, Calcutta

Heesterman, J.C., 1963 'Vrātya and Sacrifice', *IIJ*, 6 pp. 1-37

1964 'Brahman, Ritual and Renouncer', *WZKSA*, 8 pp. 1-31

Held, J., 1935 The *Mahābhārata-An Ethnological Study*, Amsterdam

Hill, Peter, 2001 *Fate, predestination and human action in the Mahābhārata: a study in the history of Ideas*, New Delhi.

Hiltebeitel, 1976 'The Burning of the Forest Myth', in Smith, B.L., ed., *Hinduism: New Essays in the History of Religions* Leiden, pp. 208-24

1976 *The Ritual of Battle: Krishna in the Mahābhārata*, Ithaca and London

2011 *Dharma. Its Early History in Law, Religion and Narrative*, New York

Holck, H. F, 1969 'Some Observations on the Motives and Purposes of Asceticism in Ancient India', *AS*, XXIII pp. 45-57

Holtzmann, A., 1878 'Indra nach den Vorstellung des Mahābhārata', *ZDMG*, 33 pp. 290-341

1884 'Brahman in Mahābhārata', *ZDMG*, 38 pp. 167-234

Hopkins, E.M., 1974 *Epic Mythology* (reprint, Delhi) Strassburg, 1915

Jackson, V. ed., 1925 *Journal of Francis Buchanan-Patna and Gayā in 18ll-12*, Patna

Jaini, P.S., 1970 'Śramaṇas: Their Conflict with Brahmanical Society', in Elder, J.W.,ed., *Chapters in Indian Civilization*, 2 vols., Dubuque, vol. 1, pp. 41-81

1974 'On the Sarvjñatva (Omniscience) of Mahavīra and the Buddha', in Cousins, L., Kunst, A., and Norman, K.R., eds., *Buddhist Studies in Honour of l.B. Horner*, Dordrecht pp. 71-90

Jacob, G.A., 1891 *A Concordance ta the Principal Upanishads and the Bhagavadgītā*, Bombay

Jaiswal, S., 1967 *The Origin and Development of Vaisnavism*, Delhi

Joshi, J.R., 1972 'Prajāpati in Vedic Mythology and Ritual', *ABORI*, 53 pp. 101-25.

Joshi, N.R., and Sharma, R.C., 1969 *Gandhāra Sculptures in the State Museum, Lucknow*, Lucknow

Johnston, E.H., 1974 *Early Sāṃkhya* (reprint, Delhi) London, 1937

Kaelber, W.0., 1976 'Tapas, Birth, and Spiritual Rebirth in the Veda', *HR*, 15 pp. 343-86

Kane, P.V., 1930-1962 *History of Dharmaśāstra,* Poona, 5 vols.

Karve, I., 1938/9 'Kinship Terminology and Kinship Usages in Ṛg Veda and Atharva Veda', *ABORI*, 20 pp. 69-96; 109-44; 214-34

—, 1944 'Kinship Terminology and the Family Organization as Found in the Critical Edition of the Mahābhārata', *BDCRI*, 5 pp. 61-148

Keith, A.B., 1927 *Religion and Philosophy of the Vedas*, 2 vols., Cambridge, Mass.

Kirfel, W., 1927 *Das Purāṇa Pañcalakṣaṇa*, Bonn

Knipe, D., 1975 *In the Image of Fire*, Delhi

Kosambi, D. D., 1965 *The Culture and Civilization of Ancient India*, Bombay

Kumar, J., 1975 'Family Structure in the Hindu Society of Rural India', in Kurian, G. ed., *The Family in India-A Regional View*, The Hague

Lamotte, É., 1967 *Histoire du Bouddhisme lndien: Des Origines à l'Ère Śaka* (reprint, 1967), Louvain

Lalye, P. G., 2008 *Curses and boons in the Vālmīki Rāmāyaṇa*, Delhi

Law, B.C., 1973 *Tribes in Ancient India*, 2nd ed., Poona

Leumann, M., 1954 'Der lndo-lranische Bildnergott Twarstar', *AS*, VIII pp. 79-84

Lévi, S., 1966 *La Doctrine du Sacrifice dans Les Brāhmaṇas*, reprint, 1966; Paris,1898

Lévi-Strauss, 1972 C., *Structural Anthropology*, Harmondsworth

1969 *The Raw and the Cooked: Introductian to a Science of Mythology: I*, New York

Lincoln, B., 1975 'The lndo-European Myth of Creation', *HR*, 15 pp. 121-45

Lingat, R., 1973 *The Classical Law of India* Berkeley. Trans. by Derrett, J.D.M., of *Les Souces du Droit dans le Système Traditionnel de l'Inde* (Paris, 1965)

Lord, A.B., 1960 *The Singer of Tales*, Cambridge, Mass.

Lüders, H., 1929 Review of 'The Mahābhārata, for the first time critically edited by Viṣṇu S. Sukthankar... ', *Deutsche Literturzeitung*, 24 pp. 1138-46

Macdonell, A.A., 1974 *Vedic Mythology* (reprint, Varanasi, Strassburg, 1897)

Malamoud, C., 1976 'Village et Forêt dans l'Idéologie de l'Inde Brāhmaṇique', *Archives Européen de Sociologie*, 17 pp. 3-20

Malik, A., 1993 *Das Puṣkara-Māhātmya. Ein Religionswissenschaftlicher Beitrag zum Wallfahrtsbegriff in Indien*, Stuttgart

Malinar, A., 1996 *Rājavidyā: Das königliche Wissen um Herrschaft und Verzicht. Studien zur Bhagavadgītā*,Wiesbaden

Mani, V., 1975 *Purāṇic Encyclopedia*, Delhi, 1975

Mankad, B.I., 1949-50 'Provincial Sculptures in Gujurat under the Chalukyas and Vāgheḷas (12th-!3th c. AD): Two Images from Cambay', *Bulletin of ihe Baroda Museum and Picture Gallery*, VII pp. 49-50

Masson, J., 1942 *La Religion Populaire dans le Canon Bouddhique Pali*, Louvain

Mayrhofer, M., 1953-75 *Kurzgefasstes Etymologisches Wörterbuch des Altindischen*, 3 vols., Heidelberg

McGovern, N., 2012 'Brahmā: An Early and Ultimately Doomed Attempt at a Brahmanical Synthesis', *JIP*, 40/1 pp.1-23

Mehta, R.N., 1968 *Excavations at Nagara*, Baroda

Mertens, A., 1998 *Der Dakṣamythus in der episch-purāṇischen Literatur: Beobachtungen zur religionsgeschichtlichen*

Entwicklung des Gottes Rudra-Śiva im Hinduismus, Wiesbaden

Meyer, J.J., 1930 *Sexual Life in Ancient India*, 2 vols., New York

—, 1936 *Trilogie altindischer Mächte und Feste der Vegatation*, Zurich-Leipzig

Monier-Williams, M., 1974 *A Sanskrit-English Dictionary*, reprint, (London, 1899).

Morris-Cartairs, G., 1967 *The Twice Born*, Bloomington and London

Muir, J., 1872 *Original Sanskrit Texts*, 5 vols., London

Mus, P., 1935 'Has Brahma Four Faces?' *Journal of 1he Indian Society of Oriental Art*, 5 pp. 60-73

O'Flaherty, W.D., 1973 *Asceticism and Eroticism in the Mythology of Śiva*, London

—, 1975 *Hindu Myths*, Harmondsworth

—, 1976 *The Origins of Evil in Hindu Mythology*, Delhi

Oldenberg, H., 1894 *Die Religion des Vedas*, Berlin

—, 1916 'Zur Geschichte des Wortes *Brahman', Nachrichten von der Gesellschaft der Wissenschaften zu Göttingen*, 1916 pp. 715-44.

1919 *Vorwissenschaftliches Wissenschafi: Die Weltanschauung der Brāhmaṇa Texte*, Göttingen

Olivelle, P., 1974 'The Notion of Āśrama in the Dharmśāstra', *WZKSA*, 18 pp. 27-35

—, 1976 'A Definition of World Renunciation', *WZKSA*, 20 pp. 75-83

1993 *The Āśrama System. The History and Hermeneutics of a Religious Institution*, New York

Oppert, G., 1893 *On the Original Inhabitants of Bharatavarsha or India*, London

Przyluski, J., 1924 'Brahma Sahāmpati', *JA*, 205 pp. 155-63

Przyluski, J. and Lalou, M., 1939 'Notes De Mythologie

Bouddhique 3: Les Fils de Brahmā', *Harvard Journal of Asiatic Studies*, 4 pp. 69-76.

Radhakrishnan, S., 1962 *Indian Philosophy*, 2 vols., 7th imp., London, (London and New York, 1923)

Rajputana Gazetteer 1879-80 3 vols., Calcutta

Rau, W., 1957 *Staat und Gesellschaft im Alten lndien nach den Brāhmaṇa Texten Dargestellt*, Wiesbaden

Renou, L., 1960 'La Destin du Veda dans l'Inde', *Études Védiques et Pāninéenes*, Tome VI, Paris

Renou, L., and Silburn, L., 1949 'Sur la Notion de Brahman', *JA*, 279 pp. 7-46

1953 *Religions of Ancient India*, London

Roth, R., 1847 'Brahma und die Brahmanen', *ZDMG*, 1 pp. 66-86

Ruben, W., 1947 *Die Philosophie der Upaniṣaden*, Bern

Sankalia, H.D., 1941 *The Archaeology of Gujarat*, Bombay

Sastri, H., 1942 'Nalanda and its Epigraphic Material', *Memoirs of the Archaeological Survey in India*, Calcutta

Sathaye, A., 2015 *Crossing The Lines of Caste. Viśvāmitra and the Construction of Brahmin Power in Hindu Mythology*, New York

Scheftelowitz, J., 1930 *Die Zeit als Schicksaslgottheit in Indien und Iran*, Leipzig

Schmidt, H.P., 1968 *Bṛhaspati und Indra*, Wiesbaden

von Schroeder, L., 1887 *lndiens Literatur und Cultur*, Leipzig

Senart, E., 1915 '*Rajas* et la Théorie Indienne des Trois *Guṇas*', JA, 11th series, vol. 6 pp. 151-64

Settar, S., 1971 'The Brahmadeva Pillars', *Artibus Asiae*, 18 pp. 17-38

Silburn, L., 1955 *Instant et Cause. Le Discontinu dans la Pensée Philosophique de l'Inde*, Paris

Sompura, K.F., 1968 *The Structural Temples of Gujarat*, Ahmedabad

Stevenson, S., 1920 *The Rites of the Twice-born*, London

Sullivan, B., 1999 *Seer of the Fifth Veda. Kṛṣṇa Dvaipāyana Vyāsa in the Mahābhārata*, Motilal Banarsidass Publishers, Delhi, (Leiden, 1990)

Thapylal, K.K., 1972 *Studies in Ancient Indian Seals*, Lucknow

Thieme, P., 1960 'Brahman', *ZDMG*, 102 pp. 91-129

Thomas, P., 1958 *Epics, Myths and Legends of India*, 5th ed., Bombay

Tod, J., 1914 *Annals and Antiquities of Rajasthan*, 2 vols., reprint, London

Wagle, N.K., 1975 'A Study of Kinship Groups in the Rāmāyaṇa of Vālmīki', in Kurian, G., ed., *The Family in India-A Regional View*, The Hague, pp. 1-42.

P. Visigalli, 2016 'The Buddha's Wordplays: The Rhetorical Function and Efficacy of Puns and Etymologizing in the Pali Canon' , *JIP* 44/3, pp.809-832

Watters, T., 1904-05 *On Yuan Chwang*, 2 vols., London

Weinrich, F., 1929 'Entwicklung und Theorie Der Āśramalehre im Umriss', *Archiv far Religionswissenschaft*, 27 pp. 77-92

Zaehner, R.C., 1966 *Hinduism*, London

Zimmer, H., 1946 *Myths and Symbols in Indian Art and Civilization*, New York

Index

C

D

O

P

R

S

W

Y